Richard Laymon was born in Chicago in 1947. He grew up in California and has an BA in English Literature from Williamette University, Oregon, and an MA from Loyola University, Los Angeles. He has worked as a schoolteacher, a librarian and as a report writer for a law firm. He now works full time as a writer. Apart from his novels, he has published more than sixty short stories in magazines such as *Ellery Queen*, *Alfred Hitchcock* and *Cavalier* and in anthologies, including *Modern Masters of Horror*, *The Second Black Lizard Anthology of Crime* and *Night Visions 7*. His novel *Flesh* was named best horror of 1988 by *Science Fiction Chronicle* and also listed for the prestigious Bram Stoker Award, as was *Funland*. Richard Laymon is the author of more than twenty acclaimed novels, including *The Cellar*, *The Stake*, *Savage*, *Quake*, *Island*, *Bite*, *Body Rides*, *Fiends*, and *After Midnight*. He lives in California with his wife and daughter.

For up-to-date cyberspace news of Richard Laymon and his books, contact Richard Laymon Kills! at: http://www.crafti.com.au/~gerlach/rlaymon.htm

Savage

Richard Laymon

**From Whitechapel to the Wild West
on the track of Jack the Ripper**

First published in 1993
by HEADLINE BOOK PUBLISHING

First published in paperback in 1993
by HEADLINE BOOK PUBLISHING

A HEADLINE FEATURE paperback

11 13 15 17 19 20 18 16 14 12

ISBN 0 7472 4120 1

Phototypeset by Intype, London

Printed and bound in Great Britain by
Mackays of Chatham plc, Chatham, Kent

HEADLINE BOOK PUBLISHING
A division of Hodder Headline PLC
338 Euston Road
London NW1 3BH

THIS BOOK IS DEDICATED
TO BOB TANNER
GENTLEMAN AND SUPER AGENT.

WITH YOUR GUIDANCE AND HELP
I'VE GONE BEYOND WHERE I THOUGHT
I COULD GO.

—ON TOP OF WHICH—
YOU SUGGESTED AT LUNCH A WHILE BACK
THAT I TRY AN ENGLISH SETTING.
SO I DID.
SO THIS BOOK IS YOUR FAULT.

I love my work and want to start again. You will soon hear of me with my funny little games . . . My knife is nice and sharp. I want to get to work right away if I get a chance. Good luck.

Yours truly

Jack the Ripper

from a letter dated 25 September 1888, attributed to Jack the Ripper

God did not make men equal, Colonel Colt did.

anonymous Westerner

CONTENTS

PROLOGUE

Wherein I aim to whet Your Appetite for the Tale of my Adventures

London's East End was rather a dicey place, but that's where I found myself, a fifteen-year-old youngster with more sand than sense, on the night of 8 November 1888.

That was some twenty years back, so it's high time I put pen to my story before I commence to forget the particulars, or get snakebit.

It all started because I went off to find my Uncle William and fetch him back so he could deal with Barnes. Uncle was a police constable, you see. He was a mighty tough hombre, to boot. A few words – or licks – from him, and that rascal Barnes wasn't ever likely to lay another belt on Mother.

So I set out, round about nine, reckoning I'd be back with Uncle in less than an hour.

But it wasn't in the cards for me to find him.

The way it all played out, I never saw Uncle William again at all, and I wasn't to set eyes again on my dear Mother for many a year.

Sometimes, you wish you could start from scratch and get a chance to do things differently.

Can't be done, however.

And maybe that's for the best.

Why, I used to pine for Mother and miss my chums and wonder considerable about the life I might've known if only I hadn't gone off to Whitechapel that night. I still have my regrets along those lines, but they don't amount to much any more.

You see, it's like this.

I ended up in some terrible scrapes, and got my face rubbed in more than a few ungodly horrors, but there were fine times aplenty through it all. I found wonderful adventures and true friends. I found love. And up to now, I haven't gotten myself killed.

Had some narrow calls.

Run-ins with all manner of ruffians, with mobs and posses after my hide, with Jack the Ripper himself.

But I'm still here to tell the tale.

Which is what I aim to do right now.

With kindest regards from the Author

Trevor Wellington Bentley
Tucson, Arizona 1908

PART ONE

Off to Whitechapel and on to America

lout after he'd taken a few sips, going foul of mouth and mean of temper. However, he'd fought at my father's side in the second Afghan war. The way he told it, they'd been great chums to the bitter end. I always reckoned him a liar on that score, but Mother wasn't about to find fault with the man. From the very start, she'd treated him like a regular member of the family.

Not that she was gone over him. She had the good sense, at least, to reject his amorous advances (so far as I know). Even after declining his marriage proposal some years ago, however, she'd never turned him away from our door.

And tonight, by all appearances, she had dragged him through it.

'Where did you find him?' I asked as we fought our way up the stairs.

'He'd fallen in a heap in front of the Boar's Head.'

'Ah,' said I. The pub was just at the corner. 'He was likely waiting in ambuscade, and fell in his heap when he saw you coming along.'

'Trevor!'

With that, I concentrated on the job at hand.

Barnes grumbled and cursed all the while as we helped him into our flat. Mother responded with murmurs of 'Poor fellow' and 'You're soaked through' and 'You'll catch your death for sure' and 'What shall we do with you?'

What we did with him was remove his coat and settle him down on the sofa. It fell upon me to remove his sodden boots while Mother took off her own coat, then hurried off to make tea.

I reckon it was her mistake, leaving me alone with him.

My mistake, speaking up.

I spoke up mostly to myself. Muttering, really. I didn't expect a chap in his condition to hear me, much less comprehend.

What I said was, 'Bloody cur.'

Quick as the words left my lips, his fist met my nose and sent me reeling backwards. I dropped to the floor. In the next few moments, Barnes proved himself quite lively for a fellow far gone with drink. He bounded over to me, dropped onto my chest, and pounded me nearly senseless before Mother came running to my aid.

'Rolfe!' she shouted.

He clubbed my face once more with his huge fist. Then

he tumbled off as Mother tugged his hair. My mind all a fog, I tried to muster the strength to rise. But I could only lie there and watch while Barnes grabbed Mother's wrist and scurried up. He pulled her to him and struck her face such a blow that it rocked her head sideways and sent spittle flying from her lips. Then he flung her across the room. She fell against an armchair with such force that she rammed it into the wall. On her knees before it, she lifted her head off the cushion and tried to push herself up.

Barnes was already behind her. 'Too good for me, is it?' He swatted the back of her head. 'You 'n' your scurvy whelp!' He smacked her head again and she cowered against the chair, burying her face in her arms.

Barnes clutched the nape of her neck with one hand. With the other, he tore the back off her blouse.

'No!' Mother gasped. 'Rolfe! Please! The boy!'

She tried to raise her head, but he cuffed it again. Then he tugged her underthings down to her waist, baring her back entirely.

I was not so stunned by the several blows that I didn't flush with shame and outrage.

'Stop it!' I yelled, trying to get up.

Ignoring me, Barnes snatched the heavy belt from around his waist. He doubled the leather strap and swung it. With a crack like a gunshot, it lashed my mother's back. She let out a startled, hurt yelp. Across the creamy skin of her back was a broad, ruddy stripe.

He got in two more licks.

I had tears in my eyes as I swung the fireplace poker with all my strength. The iron rod caught him just above the ear and sent him stumbling sideways, the belt still raised overhead in readiness to strike another blow against Mother. He shouldered a wall, bounced off it, and dropped like a tree.

I pranced around for a bit, kicking him. Then I realized he was knocked out and in no condition to appreciate my efforts, so I figured to finish him off. I straddled him, got a good grip on the poker, and was all set to stove in his skull when a shout stopped me.

'Trevor! No!'

Mother, suddenly standing before me, threw out an arm to ward off the blow.

'Stand back,' I warned.

'Leave him be! See what you've done to him!' With that, she fell to her knees at the scoundrel's head and hunkered over him.

I gazed at her poor back. The thick welts were blurry through my tears. Here and there, trickles of blood made bright red threads along her skin.

'Thank the Lord, you haven't killed him.'

'I jolly well *shall*.'

She looked up at me. She said not a word. Nor was a word needed. I hurled the poker from my hand, then stepped away from the still body and wiped my eyes. I sniffed. The sore, wet feel of my nose got me to look down, and I found the front of my shirt soaked with blood. I dragged out a handkerchief to stop my nose from bleeding, then dropped into a chair. I would've liked to tip back my head, but I dared not take my eyes off Barnes.

Mother came to me. She stroked my hair. 'He hurt you awfully.'

'He *whipped* you, Mum.'

'It was the liquor, no doubt. He's not an evil man.'

'Evil enough, I should say. I do wish you'd let me spill his brains.'

'Such talk.' She ruffled my hair in a manner that seemed rather playful. 'It comes of reading, no doubt.'

'It comes of watching him whip you.'

'Novels are wonderful things, darling, but you must remember they're make-believe. It's an easy matter to dispatch a villain in a story. He isn't flesh and blood, you see, he's paper and ink. Spilling a bloke's brains can be rather a lark. But that's not life, m'dear. If you killed Rolfe, it would weigh on your soul like a cold, black hand. It would trouble you all your life, keeping you awake at night and tormenting you every day.'

Well, she spoke in such an earnest, solemn manner that I was suddenly mighty glad she'd stopped me from dispatching Barnes. Though I was sure she'd never killed a person, she knew deep in her heart about the burden of it.

Since that time, I've sent many a fellow to Hell. I've lost more than a trifle of sleep over it. But the greater burdens on my soul don't come from those I killed. They come because I didn't kill some rascals soon enough.

Anyhow, Barnes was still among the breathing. It'd be wrong to polish him off, or so we were both convinced at the time, but I got to worrying about what might befall us if he should wake up.

When her lecture ran down, I got off my chair and said, 'We've got to do something about him, you know? He's likely to be at us again.'

'I'm afraid you're right.'

We both stared at him. So far, he hadn't stirred. But he was snoring a bit.

'I know just the thing,' I said, and hurried off to my room. I returned a moment later with a pair of steel handcuffs, a Christmas gift from Uncle William who thought I'd make a fine constable one day and wished to whet my appetite for the calling.

Together, Mother and I rolled Barnes over. I brought his hands up behind his back and fastened the bracelets around his wrists.

We stood up and admired our work.

'That should do splendidly,' Mother said.

'Shall I go out and fetch a Bobby?'

Her face darkened. She frowned and shook her head slowly from side to side. 'He'd be carted off to gaol for sure.'

'That's where he *ought* to be!'

'Oh, I'd rather not have that.'

'Mum! He *whipped* you! There's no telling what mischief he'd have done if I hadn't bashed him. He must be dealt with.'

She was silent for a while. She stroked her cheek a few times. She flinched once, probably due to the sorry state of her back. Finally, she said, 'Bill would know what to do.'

I liked the sound of that.

Bill would know what to do, all right.

Give him a peek at his sister's back, and he would deal with Barnes in a most appropriate manner.

'I'll go and fetch him,' I said.

Mother glanced at the clock on the mantel. So did I. It was nearly nine. 'Best wait for morning,' she said.

'He doesn't go on duty till midnight. I've plenty of time to catch him before he sets off.'

'And there's the rain.'

'A drop of rain won't hurt me.' I tucked the bloody handkerchief back into my pocket, rushed across the floor and hefted the poker. 'You keep this at hand, and don't hesitate to use it.'

Nodding, she accepted the poker.

I hurried into my room. There, I snatched up my ivory-handled folding knife – another gift from Uncle. I thought to offer it to Mother. A good sharp blade might be better than a poker for helping Barnes to mind his manners. However, I decided she might be loath to use such a deadly weapon, so I kept it for myself.

And a good thing I did so. Later on, it was to save my life.

When I returned to the front room, Barnes was still snoozing. I got into my coat.

Mother gave me a few shillings. 'Take a hansom, darling.' Then she forced an umbrella on me.

She gave me a hasty kiss.

I said, 'Be careful now, Mum. Don't trust him an inch.'

Then I was on my way.

CHAPTER TWO

I Set Out

From the street, I gazed up at our bright, cheery windows and didn't mind the cold rain on my face. What I minded was leaving Mother with Barnes. I wished I'd bashed him better. He was bound to wake up and Mother, being so good-hearted and forgiving, would take pity on him.

She'd want to ease his distress. Given half the chance, she'd unlock the handcuffs so he could stretch his arms and get comfortable and take a sip of tea, and then he'd be at her again.

She might have a problem finding the key, however, as I had it in my trouser pocket.

I was feeling a bit pleased about that when Mother came to one of the windows. Spying me, she raised a hand and wiggled her fingers. I waved back, never guessing this would be my last glimpse of her for many a year. Then I opened the umbrella and set off at a quick, splashy pace.

It didn't take long to reach the cab rank at the corner of Baker Street and Dorset Street, where my eyes lit on the familiar, round figure of Daws. Glad to find him on duty, I hurried over to him. Daws and his horse were both spouting white clouds, the one from a briar pipe turned upside down to keep out the rain, the other from its nostrils as it snorted.

'Master Bentley,' he greeted me, the pipe bobbing in his teeth and shaking out a shower of sparks that drifted down and sprinkled the bulging front of his coat.

'Good evening, Daws. Hello, Blossom.' I gave the horse a solid pat on the neck. 'I'm off to my uncle's, 23 Guilford Street.'

''N' how's Mum?'

'We've had a spot of trouble,' I said.

'Hello. Trouble, is it?' He gave the brim of his top hat a

14

tug. 'Bill's just the chap to set it right, I'd say. Jump aboard.'

I scurried into the cab. It pitched like a skiff in a storm when Daws, at the rear, hurled his bulk into the driver's seat.

'Mind yer teeth!' he called out.

With a snap of the reins, we were off at such a lurch that I was thrown against the seatback. We raced along at an amazing clip. I should've thought Blossom incapable of such speed. Her hooves clamored like cannon shots on the pavement as Daws shouted and cracked his whip near her rump. On more than one occasion, dashing around street corners, we tipped and nearly overturned. It was a rousing ride from start to finish, and I should've enjoyed it greatly if my mind hadn't been burdened with worries about Mother.

When I found us in front of Uncle's lodging house, I leaped to the street before we had stopped.

'Watch yer step!' Daws called. Rather too late.

I wasn't in the puddle but a moment before I regained my feet. With a drippy wave to assure Daws that I hadn't ruined myself, I ran for the front door of Uncle's.

But it was Aunt Maggie who opened to my knocking.

She looked greatly surprised to see me.

'Trevor! And you out on such a night?' She darted her head about, peering into the darkness behind me. 'Where's Catherine?'

'She sent me to fetch Uncle William. We had a row with Rolfe Barnes, and she's home keeping guard on him.'

'Come in out of the wet.' Though in a haste to be off, I followed Aunt's instructions. When dealing with the female breed, I knew even then that explanations wasted a passel more time than simple obedience. They're a thick-headed lot. For stubbornness, they've got mules beat by a mile.

'You're a dreadful sight,' she said. 'You're soaking wet. You'll catch pneumonia for sure. What happened to your face? Oh, dear.' She touched my cheek, which hadn't hurt much up till she started poking at it. 'Barnes did this to you?'

'Yes, and he whipped Mum with his belt.'

Aunt's eyes widened. Her mouth fell open, then closed a bit and she pursed out her lips. 'Oh, Bill will just about kill him.'

'That's what I'm hoping for,' I admitted. And wished she would get around, someday, to calling for him. 'My cab's

15

ready to go.' I pointed it out to her. Daws answered with a cheery wave.

'Bill's not here, of course.'

Of course.

'He's not?'

'Why, no.'

'He hasn't gone on duty yet?'

'He went off *hours* ago. It's this horrid Ripper business, you know. They have him working double shifts so that the poor man's rarely home at all.'

The news didn't perk me up. *Now*, what was I to do?

'Mum wants me to fetch him,' I muttered.

'That's quite impossible, really, I should think. Would you care for some tea and a bite . . . ?'

'The cab.'

'Oh, yes. You'd best ride it on home, then.'

'I'm supposed to fetch Bill.'

Aunt Maggie frowned. 'Are you quite all right?'

'I don't much care to leave without him.'

'He isn't here, Trevor.' She said those words very slowly as if speaking to a half-wit.

'Yes. I understand. He's on duty.'

'Quite. Rest assured, however, I'll certainly tell him first thing about Barnes and he'll take the matter in hand.'

'Tomorrow.'

'First thing tomorrow. Now, you hurry on back to Catherine.'

'Yes, ma'am.'

'Yes, ma'am, is it?' With a tilt of her head, she fixed her eyes on me and squeezed them narrow. Studying me out. Though I tried real hard to look innocent, it didn't wash. She nodded to herself. 'I'll have a word with the cabman, if you please.'

I hailed Daws. He climbed down off the hansom and scurried for us nimble and quick, puffing smoke. While I waited, Aunt Maggie hot-footed it into the parlor. I heard her clinking some coins. She came back about the same time Daws showed up at the door and doffed his hat.

'I wish you to return young Trevor here straightaway to his own lodgings,' she said. 'I fear he has other intentions, but you're to mind what I tell you, as I'm paying his fare and giving you a bit of something extra.' She emptied her fist into Daws's hand. 'Ride him to 35 Marylebone High

16

Street, and nowhere else. Is that quite understood?'

'Quite, quite, yes. Not to worry. Back to his mum it is, or I'm no Daws and I am. Yes.'

She gave me a quick look as if choosing a target, then kissed the bruised part of my cheek. 'Now, off with you,' she said.

'Come along, Master Bentley.'

Polite as you please, I bid farewell to Aunt Maggie and hurried off with Daws.

'Could you take me home by way of the Leman Street police station?' I asked.

'Ah, but I couldn't do that. Daws gave his word, he did. His word's his bondage.'

'But you're my friend, aren't you?'

'I'm pleased to think so.' He gave me a swat on the back. 'Now you wouldn't ask your friend to break his word, would you?'

'I suppose not,' I muttered, and stepped aboard.

The cab shook as it did before when Daws climbed to the driver's seat, but this time it didn't bound away with a lurch. Daws clucked and Blossom snorted and we started rolling along. I sat there, having lowdown thoughts about Aunt Maggie. She always had been rather a stick in the mud, and now she'd done her best to spoil my mission.

Well, it just wasn't in me to get carted home like a prisoner.

I'd set out to fetch Uncle William, and that's what I aimed to do.

As John McSween would later say, 'You do what you reckon needs the doing, and damn them that tries to stop you.' Though I wouldn't be meeting up with John for a spell yet, that was just how I felt about matters while Daws was turning the hansom around.

I jumped out. This time, my feet cooperated. I hit the street running.

'Trevor!' Daws shouted.

'Cheerio!' I yelled. With a glance back and a wave, I raced around a corner.

I rather expected Daws to give chase, and he proved me right. Blossom came along at a trot and the cab rattled by, Daws keeping a lookout for me from his perch. Well hidden in the dark of an alleyway, I watched them pass.

Soon, they were gone. And so was Mother's umbrella,

17

which I'd left behind in the heat of my escape. The umbrella was in good hands, however. An honest fellow like Daws was bound to drop it home for me.

Feeling rather proud of my derring-do, I crept out of the alley. A four-wheeler went by, but there was no sign of any hansom, so I returned to Guilford Street and struck out, heading east.

Directly across the road was Coram Fields, and a straight shot up Guilford Street should take me to Gray's Inn Road. There, a turn to the right would lead to Holborn, which I could follow eastward to the area where a map might've proved quite useful if I'd had one at hand.

With confidence born of youth and ignorance, however, I never doubted that I'd somehow find my way to the Leman Street station and locate Uncle William.

CHAPTER THREE

Me and the Unfortunates

And so I set off at a brisk pace for Gray's Inn Road.

I kept a sharp lookout for hansoms. Daws may have given up on me, but I took no chances and ducked out of sight on the rare occasions a cab came rolling along.

Gray's Inn Road led me, sure enough, to Holborn. I scooted along at a fair clip that had me huffing and warm in spite of being soaked to the skin.

Whenever I got an urge to slow down, I pictured Mother alone with Barnes, maybe watching out the window and wondering why I hadn't shown up yet with Uncle Bill. Barnes wasn't likely to harm her, not shackled like he was. He might even snooze along till morning. But Mother would like as not have a rough night of it, anyhow, what with waiting for me. She was bound to worry. And she'd be worrying all the more if Daws should pay her a visit and tell her how I'd dodged away.

By the time Holborn started to be Newgate Street, I'd stopped dodging hansoms. I even gave some thought to hailing one and taking a ride back home. Dang my hide, though, my pride just wouldn't allow it. I'd started off to fetch Uncle Bill, and I aimed to get the job done.

Before I knew it, I was hot-footing it past the Bank of England. I cut across the road, rushed on by the pillars in front of the Royal Exchange, and got to Cornhill.

Cornhill went in the right direction, and I followed it. Pretty soon, I was in foreign territory. Leadenhall Street? I'd never been this far east. But east was where I wanted to go.

So far, there'd only been a handful of people about. But that changed. The farther I walked, the more turned up. They roamed the streets, sat in the doorways of lodging houses, stumbled out of pubs and music halls, leaned against lamp posts, lurked in dark alleys. They were a sorry looking lot.

I saw mere tykes and many youngsters no older than myself. Some just roamed about like stray dogs. Others seemed to be having a good time with their chums, chasing each other and such. Every one of them was barefoot and coatless and dressed in rags. They shouldn't have been out in the cold and rain, but I figured they must have no place better to go.

Some of the grownups wore boots and coats, but plenty didn't. A lot of the women had shawls pulled over their heads to keep the rain off. There were men in hats with brims pulled down as if they didn't want anyone to see their faces. Nobody at all had an umbrella, so it was just as well I'd lost mine.

Even without a brolly, the cut of my duds made me stand out all too much. Heads turned as I hurried by. Folks called out to me. Some came my way, but I picked up my pace and left them behind.

They're likely just curious, I kept telling myself. They don't mean to harm me.

Mother liked to call such folks 'unfortunates'. Uncle Bill, when he had me alone to regail me with Ripper stories, put it otherwise. To him, the unfortunates were 'a godless crew of cutthroats, whores, riffraff and urchins' who dwelled with vermin, carried horrible diseases, and would cheerfully slit a fellow's gullet for a ha'penny.

I figured Mother's view was tempered by the goodness of her heart, while Uncle Bill's was likely jaundiced by the nature of his work, and the real truth might fall somewhere in the middle.

The people all around me sure did look unfortunate, but they couldn't all be ruffians and whores. I'd read enough to know plenty of them worked hard at such places as slaughter-houses, docks and tailoring shops. Some were peddlers, carters and dustmen. They did the hard and dirty work, and just didn't earn much at it, that's all.

As I walked along, however, I couldn't help but get the jitters. Uncle Bill might have a tainted view of things, but that didn't mean he was altogether wrong.

I kept a sharp eye out.

As John McSween would later tell me, 'Look sharp, Willy. You wanta spot trouble before it spots you.'

And what I spotted, just about then, was a gal up against a lamp post. Her curly hair was all matted down with rain. She looked older than me, but not by much. Except for a bruised, puffy eye, she was rather pretty. She wore a long dress and had a shawl wrapped around her shoulders. As I got closer, she pushed herself away from the post and took a step toward me.

I pulled up short.

This might be one of those whores Uncle Bill'd told me about.

I got all hot and squirmy inside.

Figuring the wise move would be a quick bolt for the high ground, I glanced across the street. But over there was a legless fellow propped against a wall. He had a patch over one eye and a bottle at his mouth. He wasn't about to chase after me, but I didn't much relish getting any closer to him than I already was.

So I stayed my course.

The gal walked right up to me. I stopped and gave her a smile that made my lips hurt. Then I did a sidestep, hoping to dodge her. She sidestepped right along with me. She grinned.

'What's your awful hurry?' she asked. I reckon that's what she asked. It sounded, like 'Wot'sur ohfulurry?' Her breath fairly reeked of beer.

'I'm afraid I've lost my way. I'm trying to find . . .' There, I hesitated. It might not do, at all, to let such a person know I was looking for a police station. 'I'm on my way to Leman Street,' I told her. 'Is that far from here?'

'Leman Street, is it? Well, Sue, she'll take you right there, won't she?'

Once I'd figured out what she'd said, I felt my stomach sink. 'Oh, that's not necessary. If you'd just be good enough to *tell* me . . .'

But she stepped right in against my side, took my arm and commenced to drag me along. Mixed with her beery fumes was a flowery sweet odor of perfume that wanted to clog my nose.

'No, it's quite all right,' I protested.

'A young toff such as yourself and you'd be sure to run afoul of the likes of which would do you horrible harm and likely leave you for dead and you shouldn't want that now should you? Sue, she'll see you safely along and we'll get

21

where you're bound to be going by and by.'

'Thank you, but . . .'

'This way, this way.' She steered me around a corner.

We were on a street even narrower than the one we'd left behind. Several of the gas lamps were out, leaving big patches of blackness. On both sides were lodging houses, many with broken windows. Few had lights inside. I glimpsed people in doorways and leaning against walls and roaming about in the darkness ahead of us.

If I had to be in such a place, I was glad to have company.

'What's your name?' Sue asked.

'Trevor.'

'And Trevor, do you like me?' She pulled my arm so it met up with the swell of her bosom.

Not wanting to offend her, I let it stay.

'You're very kind,' I said.

She gave a throaty laugh. 'Kind, is it? Oh, but you're a sweet young toff and a brave one at that.' She turned her face to me and her beery breath rubbed my cheek. 'Am I a pretty one?'

Her face was only a blur in the darkness, but I easily recalled how she'd looked under the streetlamp. Besides, I would've agreed that she was a pretty one even if she'd looked like the back end of a horse. Just to keep her happy. 'You're quite pretty,' I said.

'You'd like a go at me, now wouldn't you?'

A go?

I wasn't sure what that might entail, but it scared me plenty. My mouth got dry and my heart started whamming so hard I could barely catch my breath.

'It's awfully late,' I said. 'And I really am in quite a rush. But thank you, anyway.'

'Aw, you're such a shy one you are.'

With that, she steered me into an alley.

'No, please,' I protested. 'I don't think . . .'

'Now it won't take any time at all, Trevor, and then we'll be right along on our way.'

Sue was just about my own height. She might've outweighed me some. But I was strong for my size, and quick. Could've broken away from her, if I'd tried.

Didn't try.

For one thing, I didn't relish losing my one and only guide through dangerous territory.

For another, I didn't want to hurt Sue's feelings.

And then, too, I'd never had a 'go' at anyone. Here was my chance to learn, first hand, what it was all about.

By the time I decided this was neither where I wanted to do my learning nor who I wanted to learn it from, Sue had me pushed against a brick wall.

She unbuttoned my coat and spread it open. Then she commenced to rub me through my shirt. It felt just fine. But that was nothing to when she rubbed me down below. If this was what having a 'go' was all about, I'd been missing plenty. I was all-fired embarrassed, but that didn't count near as much as the rest of the way I was feeling.

Before I knew it, she'd unwrapped her shawl and lifted my hands and planted them smack on her bosoms. There was nothing except thin wet cloth between them and me. I could feel their heat coming through. They were big and springy and soft, with parts that pushed like little fingertips against my palms.

I knew I shouldn't be touching her there. I reckoned it was a sin, for sure, and I might be risking hell.

If Uncle Bill could see me now, he'd tan my hide. Mother would likely faint dead away.

But I didn't care a whit about that.

All I cared about was how good those bosoms felt and how good Sue's hands were making me feel. Nobody'd ever touched me down there, that was for sure.

Whore or not, Sue seemed just then to be the finest human being I'd ever encountered in my whole life.

Then she fetched me up a whack.

A quick, hard punch below decks.

I felt like my guts were exploding up through my stomach. She scampered out of reach. I crumpled. My knees hit the mud. As I clutched myself, I heard her call out in a rough whisper, 'Ned! Bob!'

In a trice, the three of them were having at me. They trounced me good, but I got in a few licks. I caught Sue a good one on the chin, which pleased me greatly. All around, though, I took the worst of it.

They stripped me of my coat and shirt and shoes. But when they went for my trousers, I hauled out my knife and got the blade open right smart and split open the nearest arm. Don't know whether it belonged to Ned or Bob, but whichever, he let out a howl and scurried out of range.

23

I got to my feet and fell back against the wall and slashed at the fellows when they tried for me.

They grunted and cursed and leaped away from my blade.

'Come on, y' bloody swines!' I raved. 'I'll rip your guts out! Come 'n' get it! I'll cut y' up for bangers.'

Sue stood back, watching, hanging onto the booty.

I kept ranting and slashing.

Ned and Bob finally gave up trying for me. They backed off, huffing for breath, one of them clutching his gashed arm.

'Well, go in and get him, you fools,' Sue said. 'We ain't got nary a bob off him yet. He's got a pocketful of coins, he does, I felt them there.'

They both looked at her.

'Well, go on!'

The one I hadn't cut took her up on it.

He came rushing at me, growling. He flung out an arm to block my knife. I went in under it. He slammed me hard against the wall.

My blade punched straight into his belly.

His breath gushed out, hot and stinky in my face.

For a while, he didn't move. I felt his blood pouring over my hand, running down my belly and soaking the front of my trousers.

Then he backed away. He slid off the blade. Clutching his stomach, he took a couple of steps. He sat down hard. From the splashing sound, he must've found himself a puddle.

'Bloody hell,' he muttered. 'I've been killed.'

Sue and the other fellow bolted.

I was alone in the alley with the man I'd stabbed. He was making awful sounds. Whining and moaning and crying.

'I'm sorry,' I told him. 'But you shouldn't have come at me.'

'You gone and killed me dead is what you done.'

'I'm awful sorry,' I said. And I was.

He let out a bellow that curdled my blood. I ran. Not out into the street. That's where Sue and her confederate had gone. Instead, I dashed the other way, deeper into the black pit of the alley.

CHAPTER FOUR

The Mob

I hot-footed around the corner of a building at the end of the alley and almost ran down a woman standing there under a streetlamp. I thought, for just a blink, that she was Sue. She gave me an awful start.

But I gave her a worse start.

She screamed as I skidded to a stop in front of her.

She was much too large to be Sue.

To her, however, I must've looked just right for Jack the Ripper.

'Murder!' she shrieked, and flapped her hands in the air. 'Help! Murder! It's *him*! The Ripper!'

There I stood, bare to the waist, my trousers bloody, a knife in my hand. Can't say I blamed her much for getting riled.

'I'm not,' I gasped. 'Please.'

Still shouting and waving her arms, she stumbled backward a few steps and fell on her bum. 'Help!' she blurted. 'Murder! Bloody murder!'

Suddenly, she wasn't the only one yelling. From all up and down the street came cries of alarm and rage.

The voices had people with them.

People running toward me.

Plenty of them.

I lit out.

They were coming from both sides, so I raced straight across the street, aiming for another alley. Through all the shouts of 'Murder!' and 'The Ripper!' and 'He won't get away!' and 'He'll get a taste of steel from me!' and 'Kill him!' came the high shrill piping of police whistles.

From the sounds of things, I had three constables after me.

Where in tarnation had they been when I was getting attacked?

25

I made it into the alley well ahead of the mob and chugged along through the darkness wondering if Uncle Bill might be one of the whistle-blowers, but mostly wishing the sounds hadn't come from so far away.

The folks on my tail had blood on their minds. I reckoned I wouldn't have none left by the time the police caught up.

While I was still running through the alley, I folded my knife and dropped it back into my pocket. That was a good move. With the knife out of sight, I didn't get myself jumped by the excited folks on the next street over.

Before any of them took a notion to grab me, I gasped out, 'Which way'd he go?' I tried to sound like a neighborhood fellow. The words came out, 'Wichwydeego?'

Shoulders shrugged. Heads shook.

'Who?' asked a man with a clay pipe.

'What's going on?' asked a fat woman.

'Didn't you *see* him?' I blurted.

'Ain't seen . . .'

'The Ripper!' I cried out. Then I pointed down the dark, rainy street. 'There he is!'

Several women started yelling and screaming.

'Come on!' I shouted. 'Let's get him!'

I vamoosed without more than a few seconds to spare before the mob came pouring out of the alley. Now, I was at the head of my own little mob. It consisted of four men who were all a bother to chase down the Ripper, same as those behind us, but who didn't figure I was him.

We were fresher than the other bunch. We managed to stay ahead of them. Every now and again, I'd yell 'There!' and point and we'd rush around a corner.

This section of town had corners galore. The streets were short and narrow and twisty, chock full of alleys and doorways and courts and just more corners than you could shake a stick at.

By and by, when it looked clear behind us, I grabbed my side like I had a stitch in it and slowed down. The others looked back at me. I waved them forward. 'Go on,' I huffed. 'Don't let him get away. Went to the right up there.'

They hurried on ahead.

I ducked into the dark under an arch, and not a moment too soon. Along came the other crew. They were looking mighty haggard. One fellow flung up an arm and waved at my crowd. 'We're with you!' he called. 'Get him!'

The whole bunch hurried by. I counted eight of them. Not a constable in the bunch. Not one in uniform, at least. That made me durn glad I'd outfoxed them.

Well, I stayed where I was for a while, catching my wind and trying to figure out a safe move. Returning to the streets didn't seem to be it. Not a few folks had gotten a look at me, and even more had likely heard that the Whitechapel murderer was a fifteen-year-old chap running about shirtless.

I had to get a shirt.

Then I'd be all right.

And I wouldn't be freezing so bad, either.

What with all the action, I hadn't been bothered much by the rain and cold. But the longer I crouched there in the darkness, the worse I felt. Even though the arch kept rain from falling on me, I was already drenched. Before long, I was all a-shiver. My teeth took to chattering up a storm. I hugged my chest and rubbed my goosepimply arms, but that didn't help much.

A shirt was just what I needed.

That and a coat and shoes. And a pair of dry trousers, too.

A magic wand would've come in right handy.

Lacking that, my only recourse appeared to be thievery. I'd already handled the breasts of a whore and stabbed a man, so turning robber didn't seem like any great sin.

Besides, it was necessary for self-preservation.

When it comes down to saving my own hide, I'll do pretty much anything short of betraying a friend. That's a fact. It grieves me to think about some of what I've had to do over the years when it was touch and go with the Grim Reaper. Stealing some duds is about the least awful on my whole long list.

It seemed like a big thing at the time, though.

I'd never stolen anything, up till then. But I sure did need a shirt.

So finally I stood up and stretched out my kinks.

Turning away from the street, I crept through the narrow passageway and found myself in the courtyard of a lodging house. The arch wasn't over my head any more, and rain was falling on me again. I figured some of the rooms had to

27

be empty, though. All I had to do was find one and break in.

The nearest door, just to my right, was for room No. 13. That ain't a lucky number, so I passed it by for the moment and scouted around.

A few of the other rooms, further on, had lights glowing dim in their windows. I heard people laughing and carousing in some of them.

But the window just around a corner from No. 13 was dark. It was broken, too, and had a rag stuffed in its hole to keep the weather out. I listened for a while. No sound at all came from beyond the window. That didn't mean the room was empty, but it gave me hope.

I went back to the door and rapped it softly a few times.

Nobody spoke up, so I tried the knob. The way it gave, I could tell the door wasn't locked. But I couldn't shove it open. Figuring it must be bolted from the inside so the room wasn't deserted, after all, I nearly gave up.

Then it came to me that whoever lived there might've used a different door to leave by.

Back at the window, I pulled out the rag. I put my face to the hole in the glass and called softly, 'Hello? Is anybody here?'

No answer came.

I stuck my arm in through the hole, reached around toward the door, and the very first thing I touched was its bolt! Well, this seemed like the greatest luck ever.

Thirteen might be an unlucky number for some, I thought, but not for me.

I slid that bolt back real easy, then pulled my arm out of the window being careful not to get it cut. After that, I stuffed the rag into the hole just like it was before.

I went to the door and eased it open. It didn't get very wide before it bumped something. It was wide enough to let me in, though. I entered and stood still, keeping it open for a quick escape. Nobody let out a cry. About the only sound other than my own heartbeat came from outside. That was the rain smacking down on the stone courtyard and splashing into puddles.

If the room had been much darker, I couldn't have seen a thing. The window and open door let in a trifle of light, though. Enough to let me make out that what the door had bumped up against was a small table by a bed. Not enough to show whether anyone was stretched out on the bed.

Sure hoped not.

Creeping forward, I reached down and felt among the bedclothes.

Probably would've screamed if I'd found a foot there.

But the covers were smooth.

Beside the other end of the bed was another table. There was a chair nearby.

Everything *in* that room was nearby. It was about the smallest room I'd ever seen, and I pitied any person who had to live in such tight quarters. Why, there was hardly enough space for the bed. It was pushed up tight into a corner, and you couldn't even open the door without whacking the table by its foot.

Standing there, I felt like an intruder on someone's misery.

But at least I was out of the rain. Even though the room had a chill, it beat the weather outside.

I shut the door. I was about to slide the bolt home to make sure there wouldn't be any surprise visitors when it came to me that the place didn't seem to have any other way out. That was quite a puzzle. What did the lodger do, reach through the broken window to work the bolt every time she came and went?

It was a she, I was pretty sure of that but didn't know why at first.

Then it came to me. Along with burny smells from the dead fire and some other smells like sweat and beer and some I couldn't put my finger on, there was an odor of perfume that was so sweet it made me feel a little sick.

It smelled the same as what Sue'd had on.

This better not be Sue's digs, I thought. And I could just picture her coming in along with Bob or Ned (whichever rascal I hadn't stabbed in the alley) and the both of them cornering me.

I shut that bolt right quick.

And wondered where I'd hide if someone should show up.

No place at all but under the bed.

I hunched down and made sure there'd be enough room for a fellow my size. There seemed to be. That made me feel a little less trapped, so I tried to stop fretting about who might come along, and started scouting the room.

On the table by the head of the bed were a couple of

bottles. I uncorked one and gave it a sniff and went woozy with the stink of flowery perfume. Then I tried the other bottle. It was a lot bigger. It smelled of rum.

Well, rum could turn fellows into nasty drunken louts like Barnes, but Mother had sometimes administered a bit of it to me for medicinal purposes. Shaky as I was with the cold and wet, I was in sore need of such medication.

I took a few swallows real quick. It scorched my throat on the way down and lit up a cozy fire in my belly. The stuff chased off my chills so quick I drank some more. And then some more.

Feeling considerably better, I corked the bottle, set it down and did some more exploring.

What I found next was almost better than the rum.

On the chair was a whole heap of clothing. I picked up the items one at a time, and held them toward the dim light from the window for a better look. There were two big shirts that smelled ripe, a smaller shirt that looked like it might belong to a boy, an overcoat, a bonnet and a petticoat.

Well, this was just about the best luck in the world!

Figuring to keep one of the big shirts and the overcoat, I put everything else back on the chair. And jumped a mile when a woman laughed close by.

'Ain't you the randy one!' she blurted.

My heart stopped cold when I saw the rag get plucked out of the window hole.

Quick as I could, I dropped the shirt and coat on the chair and scurried. As the bolt clacked, I belly-crawled under the bed. The door swung open, letting in a chill and the smell of rain. Then it bumped shut. The bolt slid.

'Ah, Mary, Mary, Mary,' a man said.

This wasn't Sue, at least. But I still didn't relish the idea of getting caught. I tried to hold my breath, and hoped they couldn't hear my heart drumming.

'Now let go for a bit,' Mary said. 'You'll be wanting your coat off.'

'I'll be wanting more than that off you.'

She laughed.

There was a sound like a coat might make hitting the floor.

Then footsteps. Someone sat on the bed. A match scratched. In the orange, fluttering glow, I saw the booted feet of the man just beyond my shoulder. The woman was crouched at the fire grate. She had her back to me.

When the fire was going good, she stood up straight and turned around.

'We'll have it cheery and warm in no time at all,' she said.

'I've got to be off in a bit,' the man told her.

That was welcome news.

'We'll be quick then, won't we?'

With that, Mary started to shed her duds. While she worked at them, the man pulled off his boots. Then he swung his legs up. The bed slats moaned a bit, and I knew he must be stretching out.

From my hiding place, I couldn't see any higher than Mary's knees. She stood barefoot on top of her coat and clothes kept dropping to the floor around her. Her legs had a ruddy glow in the firelight. Scared as I was, I got an awful urge to scoot closer to the edge of the bed for a better look at her. I was curious, but mostly I was feeling excited like I'd been with Sue before that gal whacked me.

Long about the time I decided to make my move, Mary came hurrying over to the bed and climbed on.

Those old slats groaned and creaked and pressed against my back. Pretty soon, the bed was shaking and jumping. From the sounds Mary and the fellow made, you'd think they were pitching fits. They thrashed about something fearful. They huffed and grunted and gasped. They both used vile language that doesn't need repeating here. I was just commencing to believe that 'having a go' might entail a fight to the death, but then Mary started in blurting, 'Oh! Oh yes! Harder! Harder! Oh, yes! Oh, deary! Yes!' If she was being killed, she was liking it. Then she let out a squeal that sounded closer to rapture than to pain.

After that, things settled down. The bed stopped moving. There was some hard breathing as if they'd both tuckered themselves out.

Then the man swung his legs over the side. He got into his boots, stood up and stepped over to the table by the head of the bed. Coins jangled. 'A bit of something extra for you, Mary,' he said.

'And would you care to go again?'

'Gotta be off, I'm afraid.' He bent over his coat and picked it up.

'You wouldn't want me to be going back out on such a night, now would you? And with that murdering fiend about?'

31

'That's none of my concern.'

'Be a dear. Please. I'm in arrears. I'll *needs* go out again if you don't give me more.'

'Take care,' was all he said. Then the bolt slid back. A chill gust swept over me, but went away a moment later when he shut the door.

Mary let out a sigh that made my heart ache.

I thought about the shillings in my pocket. I'd fully intended to leave them behind in payment for the rum I'd consumed, for the coat and shirt I intended to take. If she had them now, she might not need to go out again.

She would be ever so grateful.

And I knew I'd feel good for doing her such a kindness.

But I was keenly aware of her lying naked on the bed above me. Though I wanted a look at her, I feared what she might have me do.

Also, how could I make myself known to Mary without giving her a terrible fright? Why, she'd likely scream. I'd already had a narrow escape from those who mistook me for the Ripper. One round of that was enough to last me.

I decided to stay put, and leave the money after she had gone.

That was a decision I'll always regret.

I should've scurried out and planted all my money in her hand and risked whatever screams or shows of gratitude she might have thrown my way.

I should've done whatever was needed to stop her from going out again.

Well, you just don't know what's going to happen in this life, or you'd do a lot of things different.

Even though I wanted to give her that money, I chose to play it safe for myself and stay hidden.

Soon, Mary climbed off the bed. She walked over to her pile of clothes. I kept my eyes on her, hoping for a peek at her good parts, but never saw more than her legs and arms, not even when she bent down to pick up her things.

It was something of a letdown, really.

Though I didn't know it just then, I would be seeing Mary sprawled out naked on her bed before the night was out. And that was a sight such as I wouldn't wish on anyone.

CHAPTER FIVE

Bloody Murder

Mary finished dressing and went out the door. I stayed hidden under the bed, figuring she'd reach in through the window hole to shut the bolt.

Well, I waited and listened and wondered what was taking her so long.

Maybe she'd decided not to bother with the bolt. But I was in no hurry to crawl out. If she'd just forgotten, she might come back in a minute or two when she remembered.

Besides, I was feeling pretty good. My fears of being caught had eased off, now that I was alone, and that left me rather weak with relief. What with the fire, the room was warm and toasty.

But I reckon it was likely the rum that kept me pinned to the floor. I'd never imbibed more than a trifle of such stuff before tonight. It had me all lazy and comfortable.

By and by, I figured Mary wouldn't be coming back to bolt her door, after all, and I'd best grab the clothes and make my getaway.

Being so cozy, though, I wasn't eager to move on.

Figured to wait a few more minutes.

Well, I drifted off. Right there under Mary's bed, the warmth and rum and my general tiredness got me.

I believe I slept longer than a few minutes. It might've been more like a few hours.

When I woke up, it was too late to skeedaddle.

I hadn't even heard them come in.

A squeal is what woke me up. It came from right above me on the bed. It wasn't at all like the squeal Mary'd let out last time. This one sounded full of shock and pain, but muffled as if her mouth were covered. It ended quick.

The bed kept shaking. I heard wet, smacking sounds.

And grunts like a man putting a lot of energy behind his work.

Blood started to drip off the edge of the bed and splash the floor beside me. It looked purple and shiny in the firelight.

For a bit there, I tried to believe I hadn't woken up at all and this was just a horrid nightmare. It was too awful to be happening for real. But I couldn't convince myself. I knew it was real.

Mary'd found a fellow and brought him back to the room while I was dozing, and now he was busy killing her.

Couldn't be anyone else but Jack the Ripper himself.

He was butchering her right on top of me.

I wanted to scream, but kept my teeth gritted tight and lay there shivering, the scaredest I'd ever been.

From all I'd heard about the Ripper, he didn't seem like a man at all. More like a creeping phantom or a raging demon out of the pits of hell.

I commenced to pray in my head that he'd finish up quick with Mary and go away.

Pretty soon, he climbed off the bed.

I figured the Lord had answered my prayers.

Wrong.

The Ripper wasn't near ready to leave yet.

What he did was stand in front of the fire. It was burning low, giving off just a murky glow and not much heat. All I could see were his shoes and the legs of his dark trousers. Then he tossed in a waistcoat and shirt. His own, I reckoned. They flamed up. He stood there for a bit as if warming himself, then walked over to the chair where those other clothes were heaped up. He returned to the fire. He added in the bonnet and petticoat. With a good blaze going, he came back to the bed. But he wasn't done adding fuel. He stepped up to the fire again and stuffed in a big blanket.

When that caught, the room fairly lit up and heat came rolling against me.

He got out of his shoes and trousers. He had to bend down to take off the pants, but didn't get low enough for me to see his face.

Or for him to see mine.

He didn't add his shoes or trousers to the fire.

He came to the bed again, and climbed aboard.

Mary was probably already dead, by then. But he wasn't done with her.

He went to work all over again.

Every now and then, he'd say something. 'Oh, yes' and 'Quite nice, really' and 'Come on out of there, you tasty morsel'. He didn't talk like the East Enders. He talked like a gent. 'I do believe I'll have *this*,' he said. And 'Off you come, my charming tidbit.'

Sometimes, he chuckled softly.

Sometimes, he seemed to get worked up and breathless.

Throughout it all, there came the most awful wet tearing sounds and lots of sloshing. I even heard him eat something. There were chewy noises, smacking lips, sighs.

It's a wonder I didn't fetch up my supper.

I tried not to listen. I tried not to think about what he was doing to Mary. I tried to keep my mind busy figuring a way to save my own hide.

The knife in my pocket was pressed between my leg and the floor. I could get to it. But even with the weapon in hand, what chance would I have against such a monster? He'd get me for sure if I tried to scamper out from under the bed.

The only thing to do was wait and pray and hope he'd leave without finding me.

I spent a lot of time staring out at the room. There wasn't much to see. If he had a hat and coat, they were somewhere out of sight. His shoes and pants were in front of the blazing fire. The wooden handle of a tea kettle on the grate was burning. Mary's clothes were hanging off the seat of the chair. Her dress draped the tops of her muddy shoes.

I was gazing out at these things, wondering about my chances of making a dash for the window and maybe taking a dive right through it to the courtyard, when a gob of flesh dropped to the floor. It hit with a sloshing splash right before my eyes. It was a dripping red mound with a nipple on top.

When I realized what it was, my head fogged up. My mouth filled with spit, the way it does if you're about ready to toss. I heard a ringing in my ears. Each time I blinked, sharp blue lights flashed around everything. So I shut my eyes, swallowed and tried to pretend I was somewhere else.

I started off pretending I was safe at home, comfortable in my chair and reading *Huckleberry Finn*. By and by, I turned into Huck himself. I was on the raft with Jim, floating along the Mississippi at night, sprawled on the deck and gazing up at a sky full of stars. It was all silent and peaceful, and I felt just grand. I wanted to drift down the river for ever and ever.

I must've been passed out cold.

But then I came to just in time to see the Ripper's feet right beside the bed. He bent down. My heart almost gave out. I figured he was onto me, and any second he'd be yanking me out from under the bed and slitting me open. But what he did was clamp a bloody hand over the breast and pick it up. He didn't have a good enough grip on it, though. It slipped out of his fingers and fell again. This time, it landed on its side and sort of caved in a bit. He used both hands to scoop it up.

He took a couple of steps to the table.

Then he went over toward the fire. He got into his trousers and shoes. When they were on, he walked off to the side where I couldn't see him because my shoulder was in the way. I heard some rustling of clothes, and hoped it meant he was putting on his coat.

There came a sound like creaking leather. It put me in mind of stories that the Ripper was thought to carry a valise like maybe a doctor's bag, that he toted his knife or scalpel in it, and used the satchel to carry off innards from his victims.

Well, he came back to the bed and stood there, near enough for me to reach out and touch his shoes. From the goppy sounds that came next, I figured he was putting something from Mary into his case.

My mouth filled up again. My ears rang. I saw those old blue flashes. But I hung on.

And finally he went to the door. It opened, letting in a breeze that chilled my bare back and made the fire blaze even brighter than before.

The door shut.

I stayed put.

It was a puzzle, what came next.

He locked the door. He didn't reach through the window and slide the bolt, he used a key from the outside. I heard that key scrape its way into the lock, heard a loud clack, and then the key pulling out.

I wondered if he'd found the key on Mary. But if she'd

had it, how come she didn't use it instead of reaching through the window for the bolt?

I wondered why I was even bothering my head with such a mystery.

The main thing was, the Ripper was gone.

He might've locked me into the room. That was fine, though. I could get out by the window.

I thought about waiting a while to make sure he wasn't coming back. But what I wanted more than anything was to get shut of this room and all that had happened here.

I scurried out from under the bed, slipping and sliding on the bloody floor. On my feet, I made the mistake of looking back.

There was Mary.

She didn't look much like a person at all, the way she was carved up. It was so awful, if I did any kind of job telling you about it here, you might get so revolted you'd quit reading my book. Besides, I'd feel guilty for putting such pictures into your head. My aim is to inform you and entertain you with the tale of my adventures, not to give you black thoughts or put you off your feed.

Let me just say, the way the Ripper left Mary, you couldn't have figured out whether she was a man or a woman. She didn't have much face, either.

I looked longer than I should've, mostly because it took me a spell to figure out what the mess on the bed really *was*. When I caught on, I gagged and looked away. But I looked away in the wrong direction, so I saw the stuff on the table. Both her breasts, and a gob of innards.

I started to keel over, but somehow stayed on my feet and stumbled to the window. I shoved it open. Tried to climb out, but fell out instead. The cold and rain cleared my head some. As I picked myself up, I recalled why I'd snuck into the room in the first place. But I wasn't raring to climb back in to fetch any shirt and coat. I saw them on the chair when I pulled the window down, and kept my eyes on them so I wouldn't catch another look at Mary.

Then I ran through the courtyard. The rain quit when I was under the arch. I stopped running, and leaned out far enough to glance up and down the street, scared the Ripper might be there. I didn't see him or anyone else. But the gas lamps didn't give off a whole lot of light, and left plenty of black spaces where someone might be lurking.

All I wanted, just then, was to find my way home without running into more trouble. The last thing I wanted was to meet up with the Ripper. But a close second was getting took for the Ripper myself.

Being shirtless and bloody in the Whitechapel area at an hour like this, I was bound to rouse suspicion in anyone who might see me. That being the case, it shouldn't matter a whit whether I tried to walk casual or raced along like the devil was on my heels.

At least if I ran, I'd be quicker about getting away to somewhere safe.

I stepped out from under the arch. The rain came down on me. While I tried to decide which way to go, I rubbed my hands together until I figured most of the blood was off. Then I rinsed my chest and belly real quick.

Being lost, it didn't matter much which direction I picked.

So I turned to the right and kicked up my heels. I went splashing through the street top speed. So much motion started my head to hurting something fierce, but I kept on chugging. At a corner, I checked both ways. My heart did a tumble when I spotted some folks off to the left. One was a constable. Nobody let out a shout, though, so maybe I wasn't seen.

Safe past the corner, I wondered if maybe I shouldn't go back and tell the Bobby everything. Just didn't have the gumption, though. First thing you know, he'd be thinking *I* was the one that done in Mary.

And I *was* the one that stabbed Ned or Bob in the alley tonight. Rain or not, there might still be blood on my knife from him. I could throw my knife away. Didn't fancy doing that, however. Aside from it being a gift I prized, it was my only weapon and I might need it.

So I figured my best plan was to keep shut of constables or anyone else.

Well, I rushed around a bend in the road and pulled up short and lost my breath. My stomach dropped down to my heels.

Not that I recognized him. Cramped under the bed that way, I hadn't seen enough: just his legs, his hands when he reached down a few times, his trousers and shoes. There was nothing particular about any such thing.

The fellow walking past the street lamp ahead of me wore

a hat and overcoat. Below the hem of the coat were trouser legs. They might've belonged to the pants I'd seen in Mary's room. Looked the same. But dark pants are dark pants. From where I stood, I couldn't see enough of the shoes to know if they were like the Ripper's.

But he carried a leather case like a doctor's bag.

That was enough for me.

I just knew, deep down, this was Jack the Ripper. In my rush to hightail, I'd chanced to take the same route as him, and caught up.

What with the distance and the rain smacking down all around us, he hadn't heard me come around the corner. Or if he did hear, he didn't look back. He kept on walking, and left the glow of the street lamp behind him.

I stood still and watched.

It'd likely take me hours to scribble out all the thoughts that went through my head then. But they boil down to this: much as I wanted to get away from the Ripper and go home to bed and pull the covers over my face, I reckoned as how it was my duty to follow him.

And that's what I did, even though it scared the tarnation out of me.

I was fifteen and wet and cold and terrified, and as I followed Jack the Ripper in those dark morning hours I reckoned I might not live to see the daylight.

But I kept after him, all the same.

Here's the thing.

He was a monster who'd done unspeakable things, not only to Mary but to a handful of other women. He deserved the worst kind of punishment for that. More important, though, there'd be more women falling under his blade if somebody didn't put a stop to him.

Maybe it was chance. Maybe it was fate or the will of God. But somehow, I'd ended up being the fellow with an opportunity to put the quits to his string of bloody murders.

It wasn't a job I could walk away from.

CHAPTER SIX

I Tail the Fiend

My plan was to follow the Ripper to his digs, wait till he'd settled in, and then fetch the police. I sure didn't aim to tangle with him. He'd had a lot more practice in the way of knives, and he was a head taller than me so he'd have me beat on reach. Besides, I was scared witless of him. I'd be doing enough if I just stayed on his trail.

He led me this way and that, picking streets that were mostly deserted. I hung back. I kept off to the side so I could duck into doorways or alleys in case he might take a notion to look over his shoulder.

He acted like he didn't have a worry. He never once checked his rear. I got a side view of his face a few times when he turned corners, but couldn't tell much. Just too dark, and his hat brim shadowed it from the street lamps. All I could see was he had a beaky nose and a weak chin.

I judged as how it might be a good thing to get a close-up look. But I didn't dare have a go at that. Knowing his face wouldn't count for much if I ended up dead for trying.

The trick was to stay alive and not lose him.

After a while, it started seeming like a fairly simple trick. He wasn't being cautious or dodgy. He walked along like a gentleman out for a stroll. I didn't have a bit of trouble keeping my eyes on him.

Though we sometimes walked by other folks, they minded their own affairs. A few gave me odd looks, but none spoke to me or raised any sort of fuss.

I got to pondering what a hero I'd be for tracking Jack the Ripper to his lair. Why, I'd be the most popular bloke in London, in the whole of England, for that matter. Her Majesty the Queen, herself, would likely honor me. Mother, she'd be just so proud . . .

That reminded me of Mother's plight, the reason I'd set

out in the first place. Well, I hadn't managed to fetch Uncle Bill, but it didn't seem very important just now. Barnes wouldn't be getting out of the handcuffs. Mother ought to be all right.

What I should do, I decided, was go and find Uncle Bill first thing after discovering the Ripper's lodging place. That way, he'd get in on the glory.

I picked up my pace when the Ripper vanished around a corner. I got him in sight again. He was strolling toward a street lamp, toward a woman who stood there holding on to the post.

She spoke to him. I couldn't make out her words.

He walked over to her.

There was nobody else on the street that I could see.

I went all soft inside and felt like my heart might explode, it was thumping so hard.

He doesn't dare! I thought.

I stood frozen while the woman took his arm and snuggled up against him and they started walking off together.

He'd done two in one night before, so this shouldn't have surprised me. But it sure did. I'd just *known* he would lead me straight to his lodgings and I'd end up a hero.

It wasn't about to happen that way, though.

Mary hadn't been enough for him. He was fixing to butcher this gal, too.

It'd be my fault, if I let it happen.

I dug the knife out of my pocket, pried open its blade and rushed after them.

My father had died in battle. If it was good enough for him, it was good enough for me. I reckoned I might be meeting up with him any second. Eager as I was for the reunion, though, I hoped it wouldn't happen for considerable more years.

I didn't want to die just yet. But I couldn't let this gal get killed, either.

I slowed down a trifle as the distance closed. Pretty soon, I was no more than a few paces behind them. The gal wore a bonnet. Her head was leaning against his shoulder, and her arm was hooked around his back. He had one arm around her. His other swung the leather case along at his side.

They hadn't heard me yet. I was holding my breath. It helped, too, having lost my shoes to the thieves.

It went against the grain to back-stab a fellow.

41

I went on and did it anyway.

Charged right up behind him and jammed my blade through his coat.

He let out a sharp cry. I tugged the blade out to get ready for another go. Before I could stick him again, he whirled around. His case clobbered the side of my face and sent me staggering. As I fell on my rump, the woman took to screaming. Then she took to her heels.

The Ripper didn't go after her.

I'd saved her.

But matters were looking dicey for me.

I scrambled to get up as the Ripper came at me. He didn't seem to be in any great hurry. He switched the case to his left hand, reached inside the front of his coat, and came out with a knife. Likely the same knife he'd used on Mary.

'You're Jack the Ripper!' I blurted as I got to my feet.

'Am I now?' he asked.

It was the same voice I'd heard on the bed above me.

I backed away into the street and slashed about with my knife to keep him at a distance.

His knife was a damn sight bigger. He didn't swing it at me. He just held it steady in front and looked like he didn't plan to fool around, just ram it through my gizzard and hoist me off my feet with it.

'Give yourself up,' I said, 'or I'll run you through.'

He laughed at that. Can't say I blamed him.

I kept backing away. He kept coming.

I kept hoping he'd topple because of the stabbing I'd given him, but my blade must've hit a place that didn't count for much.

Suddenly, he made his move.

He lunged, thrusting at my belly.

I leaped aside. His blade missed me by a hair, and I whipped mine down. I didn't have any target in mind, just hoped to slash him somewhere, hurt him the best I could. But what happened, I whacked off most of his nose. It came clean off and fell.

He squealed.

Sounded a bit like the squeal he'd torn out of Mary.

He dropped his satchel and clutched his spouting stub and *roared*. The sound of that roar made my heart quake.

I made like a jackrabbit.

It might sound cowardly, but I'd had enough. That roar

did it for me. He stopped being a wounded man and turned into the monster that had cut Mary into a faceless, gutted carcass. That had *eaten* her.

I wanted shut of him for good.

And I'll tell you, I didn't feel much like a coward as I raced off. I'd done my duty. I'd saved that woman from him and I'd marked him in a way he couldn't hide.

I figured, if I could only make my escape and live to tell my tale, Jack the Ripper would either disappear forever or end up in gaol next time he showed his noseless face.

I hadn't killed him. I hadn't captured him. But I'd stopped his reign of terror.

That's what I thought, anyhow.

Even though he was chasing after me, I figured he wouldn't catch up. After all, I was young and quick. And I wasn't hurt.

From the sounds of him dashing along behind me, I hadn't lost him yet.

I took a glance back when we were near a lamp, and saw how near he was and shriveled up inside. The knife in his right hand was pumping up and down. He'd lost his hat. His coat had come open, and was flapping behind him. His face and bare chest were black with blood.

He looked like the worst kind of nightmare spook.

I took to yelling for help. Not that I had much breath to do it with. The yelling came out feeble. And nothing seemed to come of it. After a while, I gave up and put all my energy into staying ahead of him.

I dashed down streets and alleys. I plowed around corners. Every so often, something came out of the dark and bumped me. I tripped a few times, but always got up and running again in time to keep from getting killed.

We ran past people sometimes. None was a constable. None tried to help. They all either ignored us or cowered or ran out of our way.

That eager mob must've turned in early.

Well, I'd about had as much running as I could take, but I kept at it. And so did he. He wasn't about to give up the chase. I wasn't about to let him catch me.

The race seemed to go on for hours. Couldn't have been that long, really, but it felt like it.

And then I dashed out of a space between a couple of warehouses or factories or something and straight across the

43

road from me was the river Thames.

I made for it.

The Ripper was quick on his feet, but how would he be in the water? If he wasn't much at swimming, I'd be in fine shape.

I raced out onto a dock that had some boats beside it. I glimpsed some other boats moored a ways offshore, and saw Tower Bridge off in the distance. The bridge gave me a clue as to where I'd ended up, but where I was didn't count for much. All that mattered was getting into the river ahead of the Ripper, who was clomping along the boards behind me, snorting and growling.

The tide was in, so I figured I wouldn't wind up pounding myself into the sand.

At the end of the dock, I flung my arms out straight and dived, shoving off as hard as I could. It seemed I was in the air forever. Then the river smacked my front. It wasn't much colder than the rain, and I was so hot from all the running that it almost felt good. I kicked along, staying below the surface and fighting my way through the currents. No splashes came from behind me, though I'm not sure I would've heard them anyhow.

Maybe he hadn't followed me into the water.

Or any second he might just grab one of my feet.

I changed my angle a bit to throw him off.

I needed a breath in the worst way, but I stayed under and kicked and paddled with my arms. The knife in my right hand was slowing me down. Figured I might have a call to use it, though, so I kept hold. Wasn't long before my chest felt like it might either burn up or explode, so I surfaced. My head popped out of the water. I sucked in air, and twisted around.

And saw the Ripper.

He was nothing more than a dim shape in the rain and darkness, but the way he was crouched at the edge of the dock, busy working on a task I couldn't rightly see, I figured what he must be up to.

Untying a painter that belonged to one of the dinghies floating by the dock.

He aimed to come after me in a boat!

Didn't seem fair. But I wasn't about to waste any time cursing him or my fate. I swung around and churned the river.

Next time I looked back, he was in a boat and rowing after me.

I took to diving under and changing course. Thought about doubling back on him, but knew I couldn't hold my breath long enough to pull it off. On top of that, I was getting mighty tuckered out from struggling with the currents.

Then it came to me that I might take cover behind one of the bigger boats that were moored nearby.

Even better to board one. Then I might have a chance at bashing him if he tried to climb up after me.

I swam for a sloop that was anchored off to the right. The way it floated there, all dark and quiet, it looked deserted.

That's where I'd make my stand.

The Ripper's dinghy was still a good distance off when I reached up and grabbed the anchor chain. I clamped the knife between my teeth, pirate fashion, and shinned up to the prow. It was no easy trick, but I made it. I clambered over the side and got the deck under my hands and knees. Felt so tuckered I wanted to flop and rest, but the Ripper wouldn't give me any time for that.

I stumbled to my feet and took the knife out of my teeth. As I turned to look for him, a shape came rushing at me.

I didn't have time to say hello or ask for help or duck.

The bloke laid a club across my head.

The night flashed real bright for a bit. Then the deck pounded my knees. Then I didn't feel a thing.

CHAPTER SEVEN

On the Thames in the *True D. Light*

It came as a great surprise to wake up at all. If I'd been aware enough to give the matter any thought, I would've concluded that my days of waking up were over for good.

When I opened my eyes, I met so many surprises they pretty much left me dumbfounded.

It was daytime, gray light coming through the portholes of the narrow cabin where I was stretched out.

There was a mattress under me, covers heaped on top of me.

I felt ropes around my wrists and ankles.

The way everything pitched and rocked, it didn't take much figuring to realize I was on a boat. Probably the same boat I'd boarded hoping to fight off the Ripper, the same boat where someone had brained me senseless.

So what had become of Jack the Ripper?

Though my head was aching fierce, I raised it off the pillow for a look around.

The young woman on the other bed wasn't covered. She wore a white nightdress. Her arms were lashed against her sides, her feet bound together. Her head rested on the lap of a man wearing trousers and a heavy sweater and a bandage that masked most of his face. The bulk of the bandage was where his nose used to be.

The bandage was muddy brown in its center with blood that had seeped through and dried.

This was my first good look at the Ripper. Though finding him sitting just a few feet away gave me an awful turn, he didn't appear particularly fiendish in the daylight. His black hair was neatly trimmed, parted up the middle. He had rather dainty eyebrows. His brown eyes were small and close together, while his ears stuck out like big flaps. His mouth wasn't much more than a slit, and had only a trace of lips.

What with his thin lips and sunken chin, his upper front teeth stuck out in a way that might've been comical if I hadn't known who he was.

With his right hand, he stroked the woman's hair. The knife was in his left, resting on her belly while he stared back at me for a spell. Then he raised it and gave the blade a twirl in the air.

'Greetings,' he said. He sounded like he had a stuffed up nose.

The woman was wide awake, gazing up at him with weary, scared eyes.

'I've spared your life, you miserable whelp, so I expect your everlasting gratitude.' He said that as if it were a joke.

'Bugger off,' I told him.

He laughed.

The gal darted her eyes over at me.

I sat up. The covers fell down to my waist. I was shirtless. From the feel of the bedclothes, I was trouserless as well.

The Ripper kept his eyes on me. They looked amused.

'You wouldn't like to leave your bunk,' he said. 'There *is* a lady present.'

'And you'd better not harm her, if you know what's good for you.'

She gave me a wild, pleading look as if she hoped I'd settle down and not get myself killed in her presence.

'I shouldn't risk vexing me,' the Ripper said, 'were I in your rather precarious position. I'm quite displeased with you. It would do my heart wonders to peel the hide off your body and enjoy your screams.'

'It did *my* heart wonders to lop off your nose,' I said.

His upper lip twitched. He pounded his left hand down on the gal's stomach. Her wind gushed out and she bucked, half sitting up. He yanked her hair so her head dropped down on his lap again. Her face was bright red as she gasped for air.

'I quite enjoyed that,' he said.

His message was clear. If I should do anything to displease him, he would take it out on her.

'I suppose you have a name,' he said to me.

'Trevor. Trevor Wellington Bentley.'

'What a high-sounding name for a scurvy ruffian.'

I held my tongue.

'Trevor, you *know* who I am, I daresay.'

'Jack the Ripper.'

'Bravo! A keen mind. In plain truth, however, my name is Roderick Whittle. And this dear morsel is Trudy Armitage, a Yank. Trudy has agreed to play the role of Helpless Captive for the duration of our voyage. You have the honor of being aboard her family yacht, the *True D. Light*. Rather disgustingly clever wouldn't you say?'

I chose to say nothing, and just stared at him.

He stared back.

After a bit, he said, 'You led me a merry chase, young Trevor. I was quite set to cut your heart out, you know, but all's well that ends well, as the Bard is apt to say. You rendered me a service, leading me here. Things were getting quite warm for me. I'd been considering the merits of a sea voyage, and you led me to just the proper craft for such a venture. It hasn't the necessary provisions for the trip I have in mind, but it came equipped with crew and captive.' He stroked Trudy's thick brown hair, and smiled down at her. 'They were all set to sail with the tide, Trudy and her groom fast asleep while her father busied himself with final preparations. I was forced to dispatch the father.'

When he said that, Trudy's eyes blinked and watered. Her chin trembled.

Whittle patted her head. 'There, there, no use in crying over Papa. He's with the Lord now – and the fish.'

She cried all the harder, gasping and shaking as the tears rolled down her face.

I felt mighty sorry for her. I knew how hard it was, having a father killed. But that wouldn't be nearly as hard as what Roderick Whittle likely had in mind for her.

She was a pretty thing, no older than twenty. She looked buxom and healthy, broad across the shoulders and hips, with heavy bosoms that bounced around under her nightdress because of how she shook with her crying. I caught myself watching how they moved, and looked away quick.

Not that the sight of them stirred me up. Not after the pair I'd seen in Mary's room.

I watched Whittle stroke her hair.

And feared what might be going through his head.

'Where are we going?' I asked, intending to distract him.

He looked over at me. 'Just now, we're sailing down the Thames. The original destination was to be Calais. Isn't that right, Trudy?'

She nodded and sobbed.

'However, my command of the French language is really quite poor. I'd be quite silly to take up residence where the natives don't speak my tongue. No, such a place is not for me. I rather fancy trying my luck in America, instead.'

'*America?*'

'I'm sure you must've heard of it. The Colonies?'

'That's *three thousand miles* away.'

'Quite. A trifle farther, actually.'

'We can't make a crossing this time of the year!'

'Oh, but we shall certainly have a go at it.'

The man was mad. But that goes without saying when you consider what he'd done to women. I chose not to point it out. Trying to sound calm, I asked, 'Is this boat large enough for such a voyage?'

'How do you suppose it came to our fair isles?'

'We made our crossing in the summer,' Trudy pointed out between sniffles. 'And Michael had . . . Father and I to help him. He won't . . . be able to manage it alone.'

'Which proves my foresight in sparing young Trevor. Have you ever been to sea?' he asked me.

I shook my head.

'Not to worry. You're a quick study, and we have ample cause to know you're agile and strong. We'll give you double duty as my servant and as Michael's hand. No doubt you'll perform admirably.'

I gave it some thought. Though the idea of seeing America appealed to me, going there trapped on a boat with Whittle sure didn't. I wanted more than anything to get home to Mother. By now, she was likely frantic with worry. If I let myself get shanghaied, I'd be on the seas a month and she'd figure me lost forever or dead before I might find any way to let her know otherwise.

Of course, I reckoned I'd never get a chance to let her know a thing.

Trying to cross the Atlantic in November in a boat that couldn't be more than fifty or sixty feet from stem to stern, with only me and a stranger named Michael for its whole crew, we'd probably all wind up blowing bubbles.

If somehow we got lucky enough to survive the ocean trip, Whittle was bound to butcher all three of us the moment we got in sight of land.

Just no way he'd let us go free.

It all looked mighty bleak except for one thing. He aimed to have me help out, and I couldn't do that trussed up with ropes.

I lifted my bound hands out from under the covers. 'When would you like me to start?'

He laughed at that.

'Michael might need help,' I explained. 'You wouldn't want him to run aground or anything, would you?'

'Nor would I want you to jump ship. I'm quite certain of Michael's eagerness to cooperate. He's in love with Trudy, and knows I'll rip her, so to speak, should he vex me. I trust him entirely. At least so long as I keep Trudy within reach of my blade. She means little or nothing to you, however.'

'I don't want you hurting her.'

'I shall, of course, if you cause me trouble. Nevertheless, your heart isn't bound to hers. You might choose to risk her for the sake of your own freedom.'

'I wouldn't,' I told him. To this day, I don't know whether or not I spoke the truth.

I surely was eager to get untied and up on deck where I could dive overboard and swim for shore. But if that meant cashing in Trudy's life . . . well, I just don't know.

But I was spared the need to decide.

Whittle said, 'You'll remain here in the cabin with us until we're well out to sea.'

It wouldn't do to argue. Any kind of fuss from me, and he'd give Trudy a punch, or worse.

I laid back down and worked the covers up around my neck and turned my back to the both of them. Would've been a blessing to fall asleep, but I was in too much turmoil. Besides, my head hurt from the bash Trudy's father had given it.

He'd whacked me a good one, but I'd killed him just as sure as if the knife had been in my own hand. There he'd been, fixing to set sail for France with his daughter and son-in-law, and I'd led the Ripper right to him. It weighed on me. I told myself it was his own fault for knocking me senseless. If he hadn't been so quick with his club, I could've warned him. Together, we might've handled Whittle.

Well, I'd snuck onto his yacht in the wee hours, bare to the waist and a knife in my teeth. He couldn't be blamed for getting the wrong idea. Then Whittle'd rowed up, no doubt with a story about being attacked on the streets by me, and the old man must've allowed him aboard to take me off.

If only I'd picked a different boat, Trudy and her father and Michael, they'd all be on their way to Calais.

I'd done this to them.

For a spell there, I had a mighty hard struggle not to start crying. That would've given Whittle no end of amusement and besides I didn't want Trudy to take me for a sniveling boy.

I wondered if she hated me for bringing the Ripper into her life.

Right then I vowed to save her.

CHAPTER EIGHT

Ropes

'Trevor? Trevor?'

A sweet, quiet voice woke me, so I must've fallen asleep after all. Though I knew it wasn't Mother calling to me, just for a bit I thought I was home in my own bed.

But my hands and feet were bound and the bed was bouncing up against me and rocking from side to side. That reminded me, all too quick, of where I was and how I'd gotten there.

Opening my eyes, I rolled over. It was night. The cabin was aglow with murky light from an oil lamp.

Whittle was gone.

Trudy lay under covers, only her face showing.

'Where is he?' I asked.

'He went to the galley for food.'

I could scarcely believe that he'd left us alone. With Michael manning the boat and both of us tied, however, he had no choice but to fetch food himself or starve. I rather hoped he would bring some for us. The mere thought of it was enough to set my dry mouth watering, my stomach growling.

'We've got to do something,' Trudy said.

I sat up, dragging the bedclothes to my chest. They did little to warm my backside, but this was no time to worry about the cold. Shivering a bit, I gave the cabin a study. It was narrow and just long enough for the two berths, with walls at each end. The wall near my feet had a door in it.

'Where does that go?' I asked.

'Aft,' Trudy said. She sat up, too. Her covers tumbled down to her lap. I could see she was still tied, arms pinned to her sides by ropes wrapped around her middle. 'We're in the forward cabin. The galley's aft.'

'Through that door?'

'There's the head, then the main saloon, then the galley.'

I didn't know what she meant by some of that, but figured she was trying to tell me that Whittle'd gone pretty near to the other end of the boat.

'He quizzed me about our supplies,' Trudy said. 'He wants a hot meal. So he's bound to be away for a while. Come over here and untie me.'

'Well . . .' I said.

'Quick!'

'Is there a way to get *out* of here?'

'We shan't know that until we try. Now, don't argue.'

'I'm not wearing a stitch of clothing, ma'am.'

'Do as I say.'

Some of my sympathy for Trudy leaked away. For a poor helpless damsel in distress, she seemed a trifle bossy.

But I gave it some thought and saw how this might be a chance to save ourselves. It'd be a shame to miss it on account of my modesty. So I swung myself off the bed. I stood up. Cupping my private parts, I hopped across the space between our beds. Before the jumping floor got a chance to throw me down, I dropped to my knees.

The air fairly froze me. I clenched my teeth to stop their clicking, and reached up for Trudy.

The way my hands were bound at the wrists, I had free use of my fingers. I used them to pluck at the knot in front of Trudy. It was tight against her belly. The twisted bundle of hemp felt hard as iron. My shaky fingers picked at it, slipped off, and tried again.

'Use your teeth.'

I pushed my face in against her and clamped my front teeth on the knot. She was nice and warm through her gown. I could feel her press against me when she breathed. I tried to pay her no mind and only think about the job.

The knot gave some.

I kept on tugging. It made my teeth ache, but I could feel it loosen. I pulled my head away and tore at the knot with my fingers until it came open.

Trudy pulled her arms out of the ropes. She flung her covers aside and leaned forward to work on her ankles. While she was busy with that, I gnawed on the knot at my wrists. I undid it some, and got my hands free.

Sitting on the cold wood between the beds, I struggled with the rope around my ankles.

It seemed like some kind of a race to see who'd get done first. But the race was really to get clear of the ropes before Whittle came back through the door.

Not that I had a notion what we'd do once we got ourselves untangled.

Likely as not, we'd only accomplish getting ourselves killed a little quicker than otherwise.

Trudy beat me at getting free. I was still unwrapping my ankles when she stepped down off her bed and rushed to the door. She tried its handle.

'Drat,' she said. 'He locked it.'

'He'd be a fool not to.' I kicked the rope away and got to my feet. While Trudy still had her back turned, I yanked a blanket off my bed and wrapped it around myself. 'We might be able to bash through it,' I suggested.

'He'd hear the ruckus.'

She came toward me. I retreated a few steps, and watched her stretch for something that looked like a trap door in the ceiling. She unlatched it and pushed up against it.

'Where does that go?' I asked.

'It's the hatch to the forward deck.' She shoved again, grunting.

'Let me have a go at it.'

'It's no use. It must be latched topside.'

'Shouldn't Michael be able to open it for us, then?'

She didn't answer that, but commenced to knuckle the hatch with both fists. For a gal opposed to the ruckus of breaking through a door, she was raising a mighty racket.

I doubted it would do much good, though. Even the way we were closed away below the main deck, I could hear all kinds of noise from outside: waves slapping against the hull, sails whapping, the mast creaking, wind whistling through the rigging, all manner of other groans and rattles and clanks. Unless Michael had his ear to the hatch, I didn't hold out much hope of him catching the sound of Trudy's whacks.

But Whittle wasn't likely to hear them, either.

While she kept on punching at the hatch, I knelt on her bed and checked a porthole. It wasn't big enough to squirm out through, so I didn't even try to get it open. But I pushed my face against the glass.

All I could see were rough waves, not a blink of light anywhere from a boat nor shore.

'I don't believe we're on the Thames any more,' I said.

She paused in her banging long enough to say, 'Of course not, silly. We're out in the Channel.'

I sank inside with the news of that. It wouldn't do, now, to jump ship and swim for land.

Trying to perk myself up, I thought how the *True D. Light* was bound to have a lifeboat or dinghy of sorts. That didn't accomplish much in the way of perking, though. Even if we could get outside, Whittle would surely be on us before we could lower such a craft.

I reckon Trudy hadn't thought that far ahead, for she continued thumping the hatch.

She stopped when the boat gave a sudden pitch that banged my forehead against the glass and flung her onto me. She pushed and shoved and got herself off, and stumbled backward and dropped onto the other berth.

I turned myself around.

'He's bound to come back soon,' Trudy said.

'I'm afraid so.'

She shook her head. She sighed. Then she said, 'You'd best tie me up.'

'What?'

'Tie me *up* again.'

'We just finished getting ourselves *un*tied.'

'But there's no way out. We can't let him know we tried to escape.' She flung herself back across the aisle, bent over beside me and snatched up one of the ropes. 'Get off.'

I stood up. With one hand, I kept the blanket on my shoulders. With the other, I grabbed the handle of the hatch to keep myself from being tossed off my feet.

Trudy sat on her bed and stretched out her legs. She reached the rope toward me. 'Be quick about it.'

'No.'

'What did you say?'

'No. I'm not going to tie you up.'

'You'll do as I say, boy.'

It goes against my grain to argue with women. Besides, it's generally a great waste of time. But Trudy was starting to irk me with her bossy ways. I told her, 'If you had no better scheme in mind than hoping we might slip out a door, you shouldn't have insisted that I untie you in the first place. Since we *are* untied, however, we're no longer entirely at Whittle's mercy. We'll have the element of surprise in our favor. And it'll be two against one.'

55

'Don't be a fool.'

'I say we put up a fight.'

'What do you know? You're a *child*.'

'I fought him once before and made a good showing. It was me who cut off the blighter's nose, you know.'

'And a lot of good that did. If you'd left him well enough alone . . .'

'He would've murdered a woman on the streets. I saved her from his blade.'

'And led him to our boat.'

'I know. And I'm sorry for that. I'm sorry for what he did to your father, too. But he's *Jack the Ripper!* You've no idea what a monster he is. I saw what he did to one poor woman. He must be put a stop to, or he'll do the same to you.'

'He needs me.'

'He'll butcher you.'

'Don't be silly. He doesn't dare kill me, not if he wants safe passage to America. But he'll certainly punish us for getting free of the ropes, so quit your arguing and tie me up.'

I let go the hatch handle and took the rope from her. She pressed her arms against her sides, ready to have herself trussed.

'Lie down,' I said.

'You've got to tie me first.'

'No.'

'Trevor!'

'All right, then!' Though I wasn't keen on being naked again, I needed both hands so I tossed my blanket to the other bed. Trudy turned her head away. Not before giving me a look, however.

On my knees again, I tucked one end of the rope under her arm, then wrapped her around the middle.

'Tighter,' she said. 'He can't know the difference.'

I gave the rope rather a rough tug. She winced. She deserved a little hurt for being obnoxious, but right away I felt bad about it and apologized.

'Shut up and tie the knot.'

'I'd much rather not. Let me leave it undone. I'll cover you up, and you lie down and pretend to be asleep. I'll do the same. We'll wait for just the proper moment, then jump Whittle and throttle him.'

'There'll be no jumping of Whittle.'

I sighed.

I didn't put up any more fuss. I knotted the rope, then scurried down and bound her ankles. When they were secure, I covered Trudy with the bedclothes.

I hurried over to my own berth and gathered the ropes Whittle had used on me. Feeling a bit down on Trudy, I said, 'Now, of course, I'm supposed to tie myself.'

'Do your feet first. That shouldn't present any great difficulty.'

I swung my legs onto the bed, spread them apart, and dropped one of the ropes between them. Then I drew the covers up over my lap.

'What do you think you're doing?' Trudy asked, her tone snappish.

'I may be a silly child and a fool, thank you, but I'm not a coward.'

'Tie yourself this minute!'

'I have a better use for Whittle's rope.'

The one in my hands wasn't nearly so long as the coil I could feel under the backs of my legs. After dragging the covers to my shoulders, I stretched it across my chest and wound its ends around my hands.

'What are you planning?'

'To have a go at playing Thuggee.'

'What are you talking about?'

'The Thuggee. A cult of fanatical murderers in India who employ the garrote to strangle . . .'

I went mum at the sound of a clacking latch. The door swung open. Whittle came in. He carried a bottle and a steaming pot that had a spoon in it. Clamping the bottle under one arm, he turned around to lock the door.

Secured from this side, it wasn't meant to keep us in but rather to keep Michael out. I supposed he must be keeping all the doors and hatches locked so he wouldn't need to worry about the fellow sneaking below for a try at rescuing Trudy.

He might as well have spared himself the bother. As I found out later, Michael didn't have the grit for such a venture.

After fastening the door, Whittle started to turn around. I shut my eyes before he got a look at me.

'Sit up, deary,' he said in that stuffed voice of his thanks to losing his nose. 'We shouldn't like to have you withering away, now, should we?'

I looked. He was on his knees, facing Trudy. He held the pot near her face. With his other hand, he spooned food into her mouth.

'Quite tasty, I daresay. I don't fancy myself a master of the culinary arts, but this stew is really quite exceptional.'

The odor was delightful. It set my parched mouth to watering again, my hollow belly to grumbling.

He kept shoveling, giving Trudy a few moments to chew and swallow between each spoonful. I wondered if he aimed to save any for me.

It wouldn't come to that, though.

I slipped out from under the covers, swung myself around and lowered my feet to the floor. Trudy, chewing, shook her head at me. Whittle started to look over his shoulder. I sprang. Whipped the rope down past his face. Jerked it across his throat as I rammed against his back. The blow flung a spoonful of stew into Trudy's face. Then he knocked her flat and fell across her chest.

Riding his back, I pulled at the rope for all I was worth. He made choking, gaggy noises. He twisted and bucked under me. He stabbed at my shoulder with the spoon. His other hand dumped the pot down my back. The grub was hot enough to sting, but it didn't hurt enough to make me ease off. I kept on strangling him.

If Trudy'd lent a hand, I might've killed the Ripper then and there and saved the world a heap of grief.

But she was nicely tied because she'd insisted and I'd given in to her.

So she just lay there helpless, leaving the job to me.

Whittle bashed the side of my head with the pot. The world flashed bright, but I held on and kept tugging at the rope. Then he lit into me again and again. I lost count after the fifth bong. But I didn't lose my wits entirely.

Before long, I was sprawled on the floor and Whittle was sitting on me, wheezing for air, clobbering my face with the bottom of the pot. When he got tired of that, he roped my hands in front of me. He sat quiet for a spell, just staring at me and trying to get his wind back.

'What *shall* I do with you, Trevor?' he finally asked.

I was too dazed to give an answer, but I reckon he wouldn't

have heeded my advice, anyhow.

He pulled out his knife.

He tapped the end of my nose with its blade.

'Shall I nip it off?' he asked. His other hand reached around behind him and fingered my private parts. 'Perhaps I ought to make a girl out of you. Which would you prefer, young man?'

'Cut my throat and . . . go bugger yourself.'

That got the swine laughing. 'You're too much fun to ruin,' he said. 'But you simply must be punished. Ah! I know just the thing!'

He put his knife away, climbed off, and lifted me onto my bed. As he worked on tying my feet, he said, 'This will be just the perfect torture for a stout-hearted lad such as yourself. It ought to give you second thoughts, even third and fourth, should you ever take it into your head to tangle with me again.'

He covered me to the shoulders with the bedclothes.

Then he crossed over to Trudy's berth and slapped her across the face.

'Leave her be!' I yelled.

He struck her again.

'I didn't *do* anything,' she cried out. 'It was *him*. It was all *his* idea!'

He gave her a back-handed smack that knocked her head sideways. She didn't say much after that. She didn't fight him, either. She just acted like a big, limp doll while Whittle threw off her covers, sat her up and untied her feet. When he told her to stand up, she obeyed.

He made a loop at one end of the rope, and dropped it over her head. He tightened the loop around her neck.

'Strangulation is most unpleasant,' he said. He glanced at me. 'I know that from recent experience at the hands of young Trevor.'

He passed the other end of the rope through the handle of the hatch above Trudy's head, pulled the slack out of it, then ducked down, hoisting her.

Trudy's arms were lashed fast against her sides, just as I'd left them. Her legs thrashed. Her body, wrapped in the white nightgown, twisted and swung. She let out the most awful retching sounds.

'No!' I cried out. I sat up so fast my head seemed to whirl inside.

'Stay or you'll make it worse for her!' Whittle yelled.

With that, he lowered Trudy until her feet met the floor. She stood there, weaving and choking, dancing about some in order to keep her balance as the boat rocked and bounced.

'That's enough,' I said. 'I'll be good. I promise. Please. Let her be.'

'A promise quickly forgotten once the heat of sympathy has cooled.'

'No! I promise! As God is my witness!'

'Witness this, my friend.' He let the rope fall from his hand. While Trudy staggered about, trying to stay on her feet, he stepped around to the front of her and removed the rope that bound her arms to her sides. He slipped the nightgown off her shoulders, pulled it down her body until it lay in a heap at her feet.

She just stood there, letting him.

I just sat on my bed, watching. He'd said he would make it worse for her if I interfered, and I believed him.

After stripping her naked, he tied Trudy's hands.

Then he grabbed the rope that was dangling from the hatch above her head. He slipped it between her legs, reached behind her to find it, brought it around to the front, gave it a pull that made her yelp and jump, then tied it around the top of her thigh.

'How's that, deary?' he asked her.

She answered with a whimper.

He patted her face. 'Steady as she goes,' he said. 'Should you lose your sea legs, I fear you may hang yourself. And such a pity that would be.'

He squeezed past her. He smiled over at me. 'See what you've done to Trudy?'

Well, it was just too much for me and I started to weep. 'Please,' I blubbered. 'Please, let her down.'

'By and by. Perhaps.'

He withdrew the leather belt from his trousers, doubled it, and whipped Trudy's back. She flinched and squealed. She pranced to keep from falling.

I thought of Barnes whipping Mother with *his* belt. And I wished I had finished him off with the fireplace poker, and I wished I had killed Whittle and I prayed for the Lord to strike him dead and I vowed to kill him myself if God let him get away with this.

I cried and pleaded and cursed.

It was all just a blur through my tears. It seemed to go on for hours. I wished it was me instead of her. She looked so beautiful and helpless it just twisted my heart to see the way Whittle lashed her. Each time he struck, she jumped and twitched and cried out. Even in the dim glow from the lamp, I could see red stripes all over her back and rump. A few times, she lost her footing and strangled for a moment before she got the floor under her again.

When Whittle finally lowered his arm, I thought he was done with her. But what he did was turn Trudy around. He commenced to whip her front, laying the belt across her face and arms and breasts and belly.

At last, he put his belt back on.

Trudy hung there, limp and whimpering, shaking all over, shuffling her feet so she wouldn't fall again.

When his belt was buckled, he grinned at me. He winked. 'Now for my favorite part.'

He went up close to Trudy, held on to her hips, and took to licking her.

'Nothing like the taste of blood,' he said.

He spent a long time licking her. He licked her all over, front and back. Then he fell into Trudy's bed, pulled the covers over him, and said, 'Sleep well, my friends.'

CHAPTER NINE

A Rough, Long Night

I couldn't hardly believe Whittle was just going to *leave* Trudy dangling. I figured he'd get up again, pretty soon, and let her down. But he didn't. He no sooner covered himself up with her blankets than he got to snoring.

What with the cold and the way the boat bounced around, Trudy didn't stand a chance of lasting through the night. It was a toss-up whether she'd freeze to death or hang.

Didn't Whittle care? Even though her life meant nothing to him, it seemed he'd want to keep her breathing just so he wouldn't lose his hold on Michael. Besides that, being the monster that he was, he'd be missing out on a heap of pleasure by killing her this way instead of butchering her with his knife. Didn't make any sense at all.

Well, there's no accounting for the whims of a madman.

I stayed in bed, listening to him snore and keeping my eyes on Trudy. She'd let up on her sobbing. She just stood there, her head up, her legs apart and bent just a bit, her feet shuffling as the floor tried to throw her. The way shadows hid her eyes, I couldn't tell whether she was watching me. But she must've suspected I was looking at her, for she always kept her hands low as if she was worried I might get a peek at what was between her legs.

I'd been in her fix, I would've been holding on to the rope over my head and let folks look where they pleased.

She needn't have bothered trying to cover that part, anyhow, since I got glimpses every now and again when the boat lurched and she couldn't help but jerk her hands up as she stumbled about. I didn't see nothing but a bunch of hair, and it pained me how the rope looked like it was digging up into her.

The sight sure didn't stir me up, and neither did her bosoms which jiggled and shook considerable.

There'd been times when I'd longed something awful for

a chance to spy what girls had under their clothes. Why, it used to drive me crazy wondering how it might be, and what it would feel like to touch certain places.

I reckon Sue the whore had a hand in souring my appetite for such things. But nothing like the way Mary soured it, thanks to Whittle. And now here was Trudy, bare as the day she was born and near enough to reach out and touch, and yet I was no more thrilled than if she'd been a fellow.

· It was a peculiar business to be worrying about while she stood there at the end of a rope. But the truth is, I felt cheated. Even though I knew it'd only make me feel guilty if I was taking enjoyment out of watching Trudy, I figured it would've been the natural thing.

Maybe I was just hurting too much to appreciate her. After all, my face and head purely throbbed with pain from the drubbing Whittle'd given me. Or maybe it had to do with feeling so awful about the way he'd tormented Trudy – on account of me.

I suspect all that played a part in it, but the main thing was Whittle's work on Mary. She'd been the first gal I ever saw naked, and that was a sight to turn the stomach. I got to thinking Whittle might've put me off women forever.

And I hated him for that. Not that I needed any more reason to hate the filthy swine. The extra bit of hate over how he'd ruined women for me, though, was enough to make me lose caution.

I pushed my covers down and sat up.

'What're you doing?' Trudy whispered.

'Shhhh.' Not that I figured Whittle could hear her through his own snoring.

As I swung my legs down, Trudy shook her head wildly.

'Stay where you are.'

'He'll be the death of us both if I don't kill him.'

'You *can't* kill him.'

'I'll slash his throat with his own knife before he even wakes up.'

'If you leave your berth, I'll scream.'

'What's the matter with you?'

'Look what you've already done to me with your foolishness. It wasn't *you* he strung up and whipped.'

'I wish it had been me. Honest.'

'It wasn't. If you try for him again, there's no telling what he'll do to me.'

'Nothing he won't do, anyway, if he lives.'

'Lie down and be still. I swear to the Almighty, I'll scream if you don't.'

Well, I stretched out and pulled the blankets back on top of me. 'If you hadn't made me tie you up,' I muttered, 'we would've had him. It'd all be over, now. He wouldn't have hurt you like he did do. We'd be sailing back to London this very minute.'

'Hush up and go to sleep.'

'I'll hush up.'

'And go to sleep. I've had enough of your staring at me.'

'I'm only looking out for you.'

'I know what you're doing. You're horrible and nasty. Now, stop it and turn your head away.'

'No, ma'am. I'm sorry. If you'd rather I not see your front side, you might turn around.' I don't know why *she* hadn't thought of that.

'If you must know, I need to see the lamp.' It was by the door past my feet. 'It helps me keep steady.'

'Well, then, stay the way you are. Rest assured, I'm not taking any special enjoyment from the view.'

She muttered, 'Beast,' and then went quiet.

I kept my eyes on her. She kept shifting about. She seemed to know just which way the floor'd tip next, and changed her footing ahead of time. Good as she was, though, I had my doubts she'd be able to keep it up all night – or until Whittle quit his sleeping and unhanged her.

I could see how the cold was getting to her. She'd been goosebumpy and shivering all along. As time went by, though, the shivers got worse till she was fairly shuddering. Her teeth chittered together. She shimmied from head to toe. It put me in mind of exotic Arabian harem dancers I'd read about. Then she got too out of control for any sort of dancer. The way she shook and twitched and jittered about made her look like a marionette – one that had a fellow with an attack of palsy running the strings for it.

All of a sudden, the boat nosed down and pitched Trudy off her feet. She dropped backwards till the noose stopped her. She let out a choke. Her tied hands flew up and grabbed the rope beside her face while she heeled the floor. Just when she almost got herself standing, another lurch of the boat flung her feet out from under her all over again.

Whittle kept on snoring.

A shout might've stirred him up. But I figured he might just let her swing.

I hurled myself out of bed. My bound feet landed on stew. I gave the floor a smart slam, but didn't let that stop me. In a blink, I was on my hands and knees, scooting myself toward Trudy. Tied like I was, I didn't know how to go about saving her.

What happened, though, I pushed right into her kicking legs. After giving me a few thumps, they quit thrashing and used my shoulders for braces. I scooched forward, head between them, forcing them back, and before long Trudy was standing. She coughed and gasped for a spell, but I could tell she wasn't getting strangled any more.

She stood there, shaking and panting, and mashing my head with her knees till I feared my skull might cave in.

'Let go,' I whispered.

'I'll fall.' Her voice had a whiny, scared sound.

Somebody laughed. It wasn't me. It wasn't Trudy.

'Whittle!' I cried out. 'Help us!'

'It's been a jolly fine show. I shouldn't like to spoil it now.'

Had he not been asleep, at all – the snoring a mere ruse?

'Let her down, damn your eyes!'

'Please,' Trudy sobbed.

'You're both doing splendidly without my interference. Carry on.'

I railed at him something fierce and Trudy kept on pleading. Whittle laughed as if thoroughly enjoying himself. But finally he must've grown tired of our voices, for he said, 'Quit your blithering, now, or I may lose my patience.'

'Let her down at once!' I demanded.

I heard a loud clap. Trudy yelped and flinched and near crushed my skull. Then she took to blubbering.

After that, we both kept mum.

We stayed just the way we were. What with my hands and feet tied, I was none too steady. Trudy's grip on my head helped to keep me from going over sideways, and I kept her from falling forward or backward. A peculiar arrangement, but it worked most of the time.

Every so often, we'd take a spill. Then Trudy'd commence to choke till I could get back to my hands and knees and she'd latch onto my head again.

The cold made me shake. So did the strain of fighting to

65

stay up. Every muscle in me took to jumping around under my skin. I don't know how a person can work up a sweat when he's freezing, but I sure did, and the air grabbed hold of all that sweat and made it feel like ice.

Would've felt wondrous to crawl back to my bed and get under the covers. Nothing stopped me from doing that except I knew Trudy wouldn't last five minutes if I didn't stay put.

It got so bad I started figuring it might be best to go ahead and let her hang. After all, Whittle was bound to kill her anyhow, sooner or later. If her neck got stretched tonight, it'd only save her from more misery later on.

Never quite convinced myself of that, though, I'm glad to say.

I stuck it out.

By and by, all the cold and aches seemed to go away. I fancied I was home in bed, safe and cozy. I even heard Mother, off in another room, playing sweet music on her violin.

I woke up and thought I *was* home, for I was warm under covers. But the boat was rocking me gently. I opened my eyes, saw daylight, and felt like I wanted to die. Much as I'd hoped to save Trudy, I must've lost my wits and crawled back into my bunk, leaving her to swing. I'd betrayed her. I'd killed her.

I couldn't look, didn't want to see poor Trudy slumped at the end of her rope.

Then I noticed I wasn't tied any more.

Confused by that, I went on and turned my head. Trudy wasn't hung, after all. She was stretched out on her berth, all but her face hidden under blankets. Her face was mighty pale except for bruises and a couple of red marks from Whittle's belt. Her eyes were shut. I could see her eyes sliding around under the lids, so I knew she wasn't dead.

Well, she was such a fine sight I got teary. I hadn't let her die, after all. And neither had Whittle. Sometime during the night, he must've let her down and put us both into our beds. Not that he'd taken pity on us. He had no pity in him. It simply went against his plans to have us turn up our toes when we still had the whole voyage ahead of us.

He wasn't on either bed, so I reckoned he'd left us by ourselves.

I rolled onto my side, flinching and moaning with all my

aches, and saw he was gone, all right. He'd shut the door after him. On the floor between our berths were Trudy's nightgown and a lot of stew – dried gravy and chunks of meat and potatoes and vegetables.

The sight of that food set my belly to grumbling.

I got down there. My knees hurt fierce. The air chilled me some, though it felt warmer than last night. I plucked up pieces of meat and potatoes and carrots and jammed them in. They were cold. They tasted almighty fine, though I had a rough time working up enough spit to swallow.

After a few mouthfuls, I remembered Trudy. She hadn't gotten much into her before my attack on Whittle, so I reckoned she might be near as hungry as me.

I gathered some grub in my hands and crawled over to her.

She looked so peaceful, asleep like that, I hated to disturb her. Did it anyhow, though, figuring she'd appreciate the food and might not get another chance at some for a while.

'Trudy,' I whispered, close to her face. 'Trudy, wake up.'

Her eyelids squeezed tighter as if she wanted nothing to do with waking up. Then her face scrunched. She let out a few little whimpers.

'Whittle's not here,' I told her.

She opened her eyes and blinked at me.

'You might wish to eat a bit,' I said, raising my cupped hands so she could see the food.

She looked at it, but didn't move.

'I saved it for you.'

'Where is he?' she asked, her voice all quiet and scratchy.

'I hope he's gone to the Devil, but I imagine he's only gone to another room. Are you untied?'

She nodded her head ever so slightly.

'You ought to sit up and eat, then.'

'Go away. Leave me alone.'

Here she was, giving orders again. But she didn't put much pep behind them.

I dumped one hand into the other, then pinched up a chunk of meat and put it to her lips. She kept them shut and shook her head. I rubbed the meat across her lips, greasing them up.

'Stop.'

She sounded so pitiful, I quit. But then her tongue came

67

out to clean off the mess, and she must've liked the taste. She opened her mouth. I put the meat in. She chewed and chewed on it, and made awful faces when she tried to swallow.

'If you want more,' I said, 'you'd best sit up.'

She rolled onto her side, pushed herself up on one elbow, and brought out her other arm to hold the covers against her bosom. She was in a sorry condition. Her shoulders and what I could see of her chest were just as smooth and white as cream where she hadn't been lashed. But Whittle's belt had left little that wasn't dark with purple bruises, or welted, or striped with threads of dried blood. Her neck was rubbed raw from the noose. It was shiny red and oozing. My knees had looked like that, just the summer before, after I went chasing Tipper Bixley across Marylebone High Street and took a spill and scraped them up something awful. I wound up with scabs that lasted to the start of the school term.

Trudy's wrists were bruised and raw, too, but not near as bad as her neck.

I looked her over pretty good while I stuck food into her mouth. I wasn't quite fit as a fiddle, myself, but all that damage on Trudy made my heart ache. I felt so sorry for her. But mostly I felt guilty as sin. I'd done all this to her, just as surely as if I'd strung her up, myself, and given her the whipping.

'I won't let him hurt you again,' I said.

She chewed and swallowed. She looked into my eyes. All I saw in hers were tiredness and pain. She didn't say a thing. She didn't try to boss me or scold me or nothing.

It was just awful.

Whittle hadn't killed Trudy, but he'd sure taken the starch out of her.

When the last of the old stew was gone, she turned onto her back and covered herself to the chin. She stared up at the ceiling.

'Everything will be all right,' I told her.

I knew it was a lie. So did she, more than likely. But she didn't tell me so, just lay still and gazed.

Back in my bed, I licked the stew gravy and grease off my hands. Then I spent a while licking my wrists, which were pretty much as raw as Trudy's.

I gave some thought to having another go at Whittle. But

remembered all of what he'd done to Trudy after my last try.

If I should attack him again and muck it up, she would be the one to pay.

I decided to call it quits and behave.

Reckon I'd lost near as much starch as Trudy.

CHAPTER TEN

Patrick Joins Our Crew

By and by, Whittle came in. His arms were full of clothes, and he left the door open. 'Good afternoon, my friends,' he said, sounding wonderful chipper. 'I trust you slept well.'

With that, he commenced to split up his bundle, tossing garments and shoes onto our beds.

'You'll have free reign of the ship for a while,' he explained. 'We're anchored at Plymouth, and I've sent Michael ashore for all we'll be needing.'

He stood with his back to the doorway, watching as we sat up and dressed ourselves. He'd brought heavy sweaters for both of us, trousers for me, pantaloons and a skirt for Trudy, along with stockings and shoes. The clothes were too large for me. I reckoned they belonged to Michael or to Trudy's dead father. Michael, I hoped. It didn't set well, the idea of wearing a dead chap's duds. Why Whittle hadn't returned my own trousers to me, which would've fit properly, I didn't know. I allowed I wouldn't make a nuisance of myself, however, by asking.

He watched me cinch the belt tight.

'Should you consider using that to strangle me, please remember what came of your previous mischief.'

'You needn't worry,' I said. 'I'll not attack you again.'

'It will go very hard with Trudy, should you forget yourself.' With that, he patted the handle of the knife at his hip.

Trudy'd managed to get herself dressed, but she just sat on her bunk when Whittle told her to stand. He pulled her up. She hobbled, stiff and moaning, as he ushered her past me. I followed them out of the cabin.

He let her go alone into the lavatory. He shut the door and we waited in the narrow aisle. I saw he'd changed his bandage. The new one was fresh and white, without blood and such leaking through.

'I take it you've grown rather fond of Trudy,' he said.

'I shouldn't like to see her hurt, is all.'

'Such a gallant lad. I was quite impressed with your efforts to save her from hanging, last night.'

'You could've lent a hand.'

'Oh, but I had such a merry time watching.'

'We might have perished.'

He laughed and clapped my shoulder. 'Not allowed, my boy. Nobody dies while I am captain of the *True D. Light*.'

Trudy finally came out, and I got my turn. In a mirror above the wash basin, I took a gander at my face. It was a frightful sight, all puffy, dark with bruises, stained with dried blood. I cleaned off the blood, then sat down to relieve myself. I'd had no opportunity for that since setting off for Whitechapel. Two nights ago? Three? Sitting there, I realized I had no certain knowledge of how much time I'd spent aboard the yacht. I was aware of two nights passing, but others might have been missed while I was asleep or unconscious. Though I'd had little to eat and nothing whatsoever to drink during that period, the toilet proved itself welcome.

Done, I stepped out and was surprised to see that Trudy and Whittle had wandered off. I spotted them beyond a narrow doorway at the far end of a room considerably larger than the one where we'd so far spent our captivity. This, I supposed, must be the main saloon Trudy had mentioned last night.

It had berths along both sides which were more spacious than ours. One looked as if it had been slept in. No doubt, this was where Whittle had spent the night after returning Trudy and I to our beds.

There were cabinets, seats, a table, and even a gas burner which accounted for the warmer air in this section of the boat. Through portholes, I glimpsed other crafts anchored near ours. Thoughts of escape set my heart to pounding, but I pushed them away, fearful of the outcome for Trudy if I should arouse any suspicion or anger in Whittle.

I joined them in the kitchen – or galley, as Trudy had called it. The room was as wide as the main saloon, but not so long. At the far end, a few stairs led upward to a closed door.

The galley was equipped with a stove, a sink with water pumps, counters and cabinets. Whittle sat at a small table while Trudy stood at the stove, preparing ham and eggs.

Whittle gestured for me to sit down across from him. I did so.

'I'll have a dab more tea,' he said.

I filled his cup from the pot on the table, and eyed the cup in front of me.

'Do help yourself, Trevor.'

I poured steaming tea into my cup, and sipped at it.

'Had I known we'd be embarking on this little adventure,' he said, 'I should've asked Elsworth to join us. However, I fear I'll be forced to get along without his services. A fine fellow, Elsworth. What's to become of him? I didn't even find an opportunity to provide him with a reference.'

'Shall we go back for him?'

Whittle laughed. 'I think not.'

'Are you certain you wouldn't prefer to . . . return home?'

'You've made that rather impossible for me,' he said, and lightly fingered the bandage where his nose used to be. 'Besides, I've long had my heart set on America.'

'Why?'

'Just the place for a gentleman of my tastes. Particularly the Wild West, don't you know? Why, with any luck, my various depredations will be laid at the feet of the aborigines, the redskins. They're really quite keen on a wide variety of mutilations.' Whittle put down his cup and leaned toward me, his eyes agleam. 'I understand that they not only scalp their victims, but have been known to skin them alive, dismember them – oh, they have a jolly time of it.' He patted his lips with a napkin. 'Perhaps I'll join up with a band of marauding savages and show them a few new tricks.'

'Perhaps you'll find yourself scalped.'

That set him to laughing again. 'Oh, Trevor, you're marvelous. A fellow of infinite jest.'

I didn't care much for the reference to Yorick. After all, he was dead, nothing more than a skull, when Hamlet made that remark about him. Nevertheless, I judged I ought to count myself lucky that Whittle found me so amusing. It might help to keep me alive, at least for the duration of the voyage.

Trudy brought the food over. She sat down and joined us. We ate in silence for a while. It was wonderful to wrap my teeth around the hot eggs and ham. Trudy merely picked at

72

hers. She seemed just as tired and gloomy as she'd been when I first woke her up.

'Why so downcast?' Whittle finally said to her.

She didn't answer. She just stared at her plate and pushed around a bit of egg.

Whittle smiled at her. Then he jabbed her arm with his fork.

She flinched and tears filled her eyes.

'Speak when you're spoken to.'

She nodded.

'Am I to take it you're not enjoying your voyage?'

'I . . . I'm not feeling well.'

'You *must* take better care of yourself.'

'You're going to kill me.'

'Not at all. Perish the thought. Perish it,' he said again, and tipped me a wink. 'Even should I face a sudden urge to – how shall I put this tastefully? – *slice* your sweet flesh, why, I should most certainly resist it. I've already explained how important you are to the success of our venture. I must keep Michael cooperative, don't you know? Now there's a stout fellow,' he added, turning to me. 'I doubt he's slept a wink since we set sail, and I'm sure it's been no easy task to skipper this yacht single-handed. He's made quite a fine account of himself, all in all. And, unlike some I might mention, he's given me not a moment of aggravation.'

When we were done with the meal, Whittle set us to work. I pumped a bucket full of salt water at the galley sink, and went off to scrub the stew off the floor of our quarters. While I was busy at that, Trudy washed the dishes.

The scrubbing didn't take long. Whittle carried my bucket topside, going up the stairs and out the door at the rear of the galley. Then he came down and ordered Trudy to bake some loaves of bread.

'We'll be having company this evening,' he told her.

I saw some life come into her eyes. 'Michael will be eating with us?'

'More than Michael, I daresay. He's to fetch along an able-bodied seaman.'

I rather hoped he might fetch along, instead, a troop of constables. Or perhaps a concealed revolver.

'He was all done in, actually. I realized it would be the height of folly to attempt our crossing without an extra hand.'

'It's no less the height of folly,' I said.

As usual, he laughed.

'We'll all find ourselves in Davy Jones' Locker.'

'Full fathom five, is it?'

'Make sport of me, then. You'll be whistling a different tune when we capsize in a gale or fetch up on an iceberg.'

'We should take the southern route,' Trudy said, all at once showing some more interest in matters. Maybe my talk of going down had stirred her up.

'A southern route?' Whittle asked.

'Instead of making our way west, we should sail south to the Canaries.'

'A foul idea.' He eyed me, but I gave no hint that I'd caught on to his word-play.

'This is just the best possible season for it,' Trudy went on. 'We'd have fine, sunny weather for our crossing, and ride the tradewinds and currents all the way.'

'All the way to where, might I ask?'

'To the West Indies.'

'I've no use for the West Indies. Nor for the Canaries. The Canaries! Unless my schooling has been for nought, those islands lie off the coast of *Africa!* And they're in the control of the bloody Spaniards. Isn't that correct, Trevor?'

'Lord Nelson lost his arm there,' I pointed out.

'You see? That's no place for an Englishman. I'll have none of it.'

Trudy knew better than to push him. So she hauled out the flour, after that, and got started on the bread. Whittle stayed with her.

I went into the main saloon. It had a small library. I found a collection of tales by Edgar Allan Poe, set myself down and tried to read. Couldn't manage it, though. Here I'd been a day or two on the rough seas of the channel without so much as a touch of sickness, but trying to keep my eyes on the lines of a story while the boat was rocking ever so gentle put my breakfast in jeopardy. By and by, I gave up.

I just sat there thinking and worrying. When the nice smell of baking bread came along, it made me just so lonesome for home I near cried. Later on, Trudy staggered by. She didn't give me a glance or a word, but went straight to the forward cabin and plonked down on her bed. Whittle went topside.

He was up there for a long spell before he hurried down.

He locked the door on Trudy, then said to me, 'Come along. Michael's returning.'

I followed him through the galley and up the stairs, coming out on a section of deck toward the rear of the yacht. I glimpsed the wheel and a passel of instruments. Didn't give them much of a look, though. It was the harbor that caught my eyes. Every sort of boat and ship was moored around us, plenty near enough to reach with a good, quick swim. The shore itself, with all its docks and markets and crowds, was less than a quarter mile off. The water looked gray and cold, but calm.

Well, I was sorely tempted to plunge in. I didn't have a single doubt but that I could make an escape. I'd be free of Whittle for good, I'd miss out on drowning in the Atlantic, I'd find my way home and be safe and Mother'd weep for joy at my return.

And Whittle'd likely open Trudy with his knife.

I told myself he'd do it anyhow, sooner or later.

But if he killed her on account of me . . . I just couldn't stomach the idea of that.

Besides, I judged that sooner or later, one way or another, I might somehow get to save her. Couldn't do that if I jumped ship.

That all went through my head as I went with Whittle to the stern and we stood there waiting for the skiff to reach us.

It had two men in it, so Michael'd found himself a hand for our trip. The broad-shouldered fellow had his back to me. A seam of his sweater was split. A tweed cap, tilted at a jaunty angle, topped his scraggly red hair.

The other sat at the stern, his head down. I took him for Michael, as he looked so thin and beaten-down.

The boat was fairly heaped with a seabag and all manner of bundles and kegs and boxes and sacks.

Whittle called, 'Ahoy!' That caused Michael to lift his head. He looked up at us. He was still a fair piece away, but the distance wasn't enough to stop me from seeing the dull, sorry look on his face. He said something to the oarsman.

That fellow checked over his shoulder. He seemed younger than Michael and not more than a couple years older than myself. His rosy face was rather square, with a wide nose and heavy chin.

'He's up and hired a bloody Irishman,' Whittle muttered.

'Perhaps the fellow's French,' I said.

He glared at me. 'Better that than an Irish addle-head. Blast him!'

As the skiff glided in close, we tossed out lines to Michael and his crewman. Before long, it was tied up snug alongside.

The Irishman smiled up at us and touched a finger to the small brim of his cap.

'And who have we here?' Whittle said, sounding miffed.

'Patrick Doolan, sir,' the fellow answered.

Turning his gaze to Michael, Whittle said, 'Were you unable to find a full-grown man?'

'He's an experienced sailor,' Michael explained, his voice weary. 'And he's eager to go to America.'

'If it's after a strong, hard-working seafarer you are, sir, you'll not find one in these parts the match of Doolan himself.'

Whittle groaned. But he laid off with the complaints, maybe figuring it wouldn't help any to turn Patrick against him.

Both fellows commenced to hand up the supplies, which we piled on the deck all around us. Each time I went back to the rail for another helping, I gave Michael a look. Not once did he have a pistol in his hand for blowing Whittle to kingdom come, so by and by I concluded either he'd had no luck in finding himself a weapon or he'd been too yellow to take any such risk.

I wondered what he might've told Patrick about our plight. More than likely, not a whit. Patrick went about his unloading chores as if he hadn't a care, all helpful and smiley.

Once the skiff was empty, we lowered a ladder over the side for Patrick and Michael to climb aboard. Then we towed the skiff along toward the bow. We hoisted it out of the water, turned it bottom-up and lashed it secure to the deck. Whittle had us tie it down directly on top of the forward hatch. His idea, more than likely, was to make things all the harder for Michael in case he might take a mind to open the hatch and let Trudy out.

Not that Michael had the sand for such a trick. He was shorter on gumption than any fellow I ever ran across.

Why, there wasn't a reason in the whole world he couldn't have fetched himself a pistol while he was ashore buying up supplies and looking for a crewman. If he'd done that, would've been no feat at all to put a ball of lead into Whittle. The man was a monstrous fiend, but not so powerful that a bullet wouldn't have laid him low.

Later on, when we were far out at sea and had a few minutes that the waves weren't trying to kill us, I asked Michael how come he hadn't latched onto a pistol back at Plymouth and filled Whittle with lead.

He gave me just the queerest look.

He said, 'I should've thought of that.'

He wasn't just a coward, but a numbskull to boot.

CHAPTER ELEVEN

Patrick Makes his Play

By the time we got done stowing the gear and supplies, it was night. Trudy had stayed locked inside our quarters all the while. Whittle finally went and let her out, so she could make us supper.

Michael and Patrick both looked mighty shocked to see her. It seems like Patrick hadn't known, till then, we had a woman aboard. I'd gotten used to her battered face and skinned neck, but not so her husband or the Irishman. We'd gathered in the saloon and lit the lamps, so there was plenty of light for them to see her injuries by.

Michael let out a moan and rushed to her and threw his arms around her. She petted his hair and wept.

Patrick watched, frowning and looking confused.

Whittle watched, grinning. I don't know which amused him more, how those two were carrying on or how Patrick seemed so perplexed by such matters.

At length, Whittle said, 'They're husband and wife.'

Patrick nodded. 'And what is it that's befallen the lady, and yourself and Trevor? It's only Michael here that hasn't a bit of injury to him.'

'Young Trevor befell me,' Whittle said, and touched the bandage in the middle of his face. 'I befell Trevor and Trudy.'

Then he told all. He didn't fudge on a bit of it, but explained how he was the very same Jack the Ripper as had cut his way through the East End whores, and how I'd attacked him in the street and lopped off his nose, and how we'd come aboard the *True D. Light* where he'd slit Trudy's father with his knife and taken her prisoner, and how Michael had sailed us single-handed from London to Plymouth, and how Whittle himself had overpowered me and Trudy when we'd tried to mutiny on him, beating us and causing our injuries, and how the aim of it all was to sail for America where he might journey to the Wild West and cut up women all he pleased, like an Indian.

Well, Patrick sat silent, taking it all in. He frowned and bobbed his head and stroked his chin like he was getting a lesson in mathematics, maybe, and was working hard to keep it all straight.

'Is the situation quite clear to you now?' Whittle got around to asking him.

'Is it that you're a foul Devil of a murdering poltroon?'

Whittle smiled, 'Precisely.'

'And is it that you've slain this poor lady's own father and it was your own cruel hands that thrashed her so sorely?'

'Quite.'

'And will you make *this* clear to me?' he asked, drawing a knife from the scabbard on his belt. He was seated on the berth beside me, facing Whittle across the narrow aisle. Course, I'd seen he had a knife all along. Just show me a seaman without one. Whittle hadn't tried to get it off him, either.

Seemed a bit reckless, admitting all his crimes to an armed man – even if the fellow wasn't more than seventeen, and Irish.

Well, when Patrick pulled the knife, my heart commenced to wham like thunder. Michael and Trudy laid off hugging and kissing and weeping so they could watch. Whittle, he sat calmly and didn't even go for his knife.

Patrick pointed his blade at Whittle, shook it at him as he said, 'Will you make it clear to Doolan, here, why he ought to refrain himself from sending you down this minute to the fires of Hell which are surely waiting for you?'

'It's quite simple, really. I've no intention of harming you. You seem a fine, stout lad, and I'm sure you'll be a splendid addition to our merry crew. As for my crimes, I've committed none against you or your kin. You needn't bother yourself about them, really.'

'By all the saints, you're a strange one.'

'Oh, I agree. Strange, but not mad. I'm quite sensible, actually. Quite practical. I'm well aware that, for a successful passage, I must have the cooperation of everyone on board. To insure that, I'll be keeping Trudy close at hand. So long as I'm given no trouble, however, I'll not harm her. At the conclusion of the voyage, I'll take my leave of the three of you and we shall all be free to go about our business.'

'And it's your business to shed the blood of sorry, helpless women.'

'I'm not asking friendship of you, merely your help in seeing us safely across the sea.'

'Kill him!' Trudy ripped out.

I jumped half a mile.

Maybe Patrick had already made up his mind to go for Whittle. Or maybe he'd been about ready to put his knife away. But Trudy no sooner shouted 'Kill him!' than Patrick hurled himself at the Ripper, going for his throat with the blade. Quick as lightning, Whittle blocked Patrick's slash, snatched out his own knife and jammed it into Patrick's belly so hard it hoisted the young chap off his feet and made his cap fly off. Patrick gave out an awful grunt. As he folded at the middle, Whittle sprang up and hung on to him so he wouldn't fall and kept the knife in him and jerked it around some, making Patrick twitch and yell.

I got up quick, thinking to join in, but Whittle fixed me with a look that stopped me cold. Besides, I was too late to help Patrick.

Michael and Trudy, they weren't stirring themselves. They only just stood there, looking sick.

So I sat back down.

'Good lad,' Whittle said. He kept his hold on Patrick and stuck him ten or twelve more times. When Patrick was all limp and saggy, Whittle eased him down to the floor. There was more blood than I'd seen since Mary's room. It was too much for Michael. He heaved and got some on Patrick's head. Trudy just stood there and shook.

Whittle, he picked up Patrick's knife off the cushion.

'The ignorant sod,' he said.

Then he told me to give him Patrick's belt. I crouched down beside the poor fellow. His belt was all bloody so I got my hands red, but that didn't bother me much. I felt awful sorry for him. He looked so lonesome. His eyes were open, and full of surprise and sadness.

I hadn't known him more than a couple of hours, but I'd liked him. Seemed pretty clear to me that Trudy'd got him killed. I allowed I should try not to hold it against her, though.

Well, I got the belt off him and handed it up to Whittle.

He buckled it around his waist, then shoved Patrick's knife into the leather sheath.

'I'm afraid we'll simply have to do without his services,' Whittle said. 'Trudy, I'm famished.' With his own bloody knife, he pointed to the galley.

'What about Patrick?' I asked.

'He won't be joining us.'

'Shouldn't we . . . do something with him?'

'He'll keep.'

Well, we left him and all went into the galley. I pumped out salt water and cleaned my hands, but Whittle kept his red. Trudy prepared our meal. There wasn't room for all of us at the table, so I ate on my feet. I had a rough time downing much, for I felt plain miserable about poor Patrick. I could see him sprawled out on the floor if I looked through the doorway. And Whittle wasn't much better of a sight what with his soaked sweater and how he piled food into his mouth with bloody hands.

I forced myself to clean my plate, anyhow. Michael and Trudy did the same, though they both looked a trifle green. Nobody said anything.

When we finished, it was clean-up time. Trudy had the easy job. She got to stay and wash the supper things. Seemed as how she rightly deserved to clean up the ugly mess in the saloon, her being the one that got Patrick killed. That job was given to me and Michael, though.

First off, Whittle told us to lug the body into the forward cabin.

'We'll heave it overboard,' he explained, 'once we're out to sea.'

I could see how it might be a risky business to drop Patrick in the harbor where we might get noticed, so I didn't complain but just grabbed his ankles and lifted. Michael took him by the wrists. We commenced to carry him along. My feet slid around on his blood, but I was careful not to step in any of Michael's mess.

We got him into the cabin and Whittle had us put him on the floor between the berths. This was *our* quarters, mine and Trudy's. I sure didn't relish the notion of spending the night in it, locked up with Patrick's remainders.

Turned out, it didn't come to that. Which should've been a relief to me, but wasn't much of one.

81

Michael and I, we shared a nasty time swabbing up the floor of the main saloon. Whittle manned the bucket. He took it topside now and again to dump it over the side.

When he got done, he told Michael we wouldn't sail till dawn. That way, Michael could have a good night of sleep to get set for the voyage. I was to help out on deck.

Well, it came time to turn in.

Time for me and Trudy to get locked inside that tiny cabin along with Patrick.

What Whittle did, though, he told me and Michael to sleep in the saloon. Then he took Trudy along to our usual place, closed the door after they were both in, and locked it.

They were all three shut up tight together in that one little room.

We stared at the door for quite a spell. Finally, Michael sat down at the side of a bunk and hunched over and rubbed his face.

'We'd better get some sleep,' I said.

'He's a madman,' Michael muttered. 'Completely mad. And Trudy . . . oh, poor Trudy.'

'I'm sure he won't kill her.'

'Some things are worse than death.'

'That may be so, but if we bide our time and keep our eyes open for the proper opportunity, we might kill Whittle and save her yet.'

He gave me a sour look. 'It's your fault we're in this fix.'

'I'm terribly sorry for that,' I told him. 'However, we're in it, so we'll simply have to carry on.'

After that, he crawled under the covers. I shut down the lamps, and got into the other bed. I was no sooner stretched out and comfortable than there came a quick, high 'No!' from Trudy. Then Whittle let out just as mean a laugh as I'd ever heard.

That was the start of it.

For just the longest time, all manner of horrid sounds came through the dark from behind that door. Thumps. Shuffles. Whimpers. Trudy pleading and Whittle chuckling. Not a peep came out of Michael. He stayed in bed, but I didn't reckon he was any more asleep than me.

I took a notion to get up and listen at the door. The thing is, I didn't *want* to hear what was going on in there, so I gave up on the idea.

Well, Trudy fetched up a shriek that turned the marrow

of my bones to ice. It ended with a hard clap. Next time she came out with one, the noise of it was soft and muffled, so I knew Whittle must've thrown a gag across her mouth. He'd likely done it to keep her from being heard by folks in the boats around us, or even ashore, she was that loud.

The gag quieted her down considerable, but didn't stop the yelps and squeals and howls. Every now and then, Whittle'd say something I couldn't quite make out. And he laughed and chuckled pretty often, like he was having himself a jolly time.

I lay there, trying hard not to wonder what he was doing with her. Couldn't get it out of my head, though, that whatever it was, it included Patrick.

By and by, I plugged my ears. That helped. Somehow, I got to sleep.

CHAPTER TWELVE

Overboard

Come sunup, Michael woke me. I looked at the shut door, and then at him. He had misery all over his face.

'I'm sure he didn't kill her,' I said. 'He wouldn't do that. She's his only hold over us.'

'I don't wish to discuss it,' he told me.

Well, we went up on deck. The morning was cloudy, with a stiff breeze blowing. Seagulls were squawking away, and you could hear folks talking soft on boats all around us while they got ready to haul. It seemed mighty peaceful, but peculiar too. We were on a yacht chock full with madness and death, and nobody had a clue but us.

Michael didn't talk except to give me instructions. Together, we raised anchor and set the sails. He took the helm, and we fairly scooted clear of the harbor.

Later on, he sent me below to fetch coffee and food. No sign of Whittle or Trudy. Their door was still shut. And it stayed that way while I made up a pot of coffee and threw together some bread and marmalade. I used a dull little knife that didn't even have a point on it for spreading the jelly. But it gave me ideas, so I hunted high and low for a decent knife or any other thing that might do for a weapon. I came up with nothing but forks and dull knives. Whittle'd had plenty of time on his own, and must've scoured the galley to get rid of whatever might be turned against him.

I thought to give the saloon a going over, but held off, not wanting to risk it with the door so near. Besides, Whittle wouldn't have left any sort of weapon-like items lying about in there, either.

So I gave up, for the time, and carried our coffee and bread topside. It tasted mighty fine. We were cutting through the waves at a fair clip, the sails all billowed out pale in front of us, and my only care for a while was how to drink my coffee without spilling half of it.

I sort of let on, just in my own head, that me and Michael were a couple of buccaneers setting forth on a grand adventure. We were on our way to the Far Tortugas or the Happy Isles or somesuch, where there'd be warm breezes and long white beaches aplenty and whole scads of tawny-skinned native girls with bare breasts.

But I no sooner pictured those native girls than Mary's breast plopped down on the floor in front of my face, and that led to a raft of other thoughts, just as real and terrible, till there I was again on the Death Boat thinking about what I'd heard last night in the dark.

I saw we were empty, so I went down for more coffee. The door was shut yet. Just the sight of it gave me the fantods.

I didn't linger about, but hurried right up to the deck as fast as I could.

Later on, the coffee got to me. I couldn't bring myself to go below and take care of business. What they called the head was just too near that awful door. I feared it might open up in front of me and I'd have to see what was in there. So I did it over the side.

Michael had me take the helm while he did the same. After he was done, he let me stay and gave me lessons in a tired voice about how to steer and keep the canvas full. It was bully, actually. For a time, I got to forget about the horrors.

Land was still in sight, though a considerable distance off and not much more than a long smudge way out across the water. There weren't any other boats near enough to worry about smashing into. Now and then, the sun peeked out from among the clouds and felt uncommon warm and friendly. I did a fair job of steering us along, and Michael told me so, and I judged he wasn't such a sorry bloke, after all, even if he was a coward.

The whole while, we didn't speak a single word about Trudy or Whittle. They must've been on Michael's mind, though. They were sure on mine, like a heavy black ugliness that I couldn't shake off for more than a minute or two at a time.

The longer they stayed locked away, the worse it all seemed.

They didn't come out, and they didn't. The whole morning

went by. Then the afternoon crawled along. I got hungry, but didn't mention it to Michael for fear he'd send me down to fetch food.

Near sundown, just after we'd passed Land's End, Trudy came up through the companionway. She was barefoot, so we didn't hear her. All of a sudden, she stepped out and was right there with us. We both gawped at her, but she didn't so much as look at us. She hadn't on a stitch of clothes. She was blood all over. It was mostly dried and brown. Her hair was caked with it.

She carried Patrick's head along with her, holding it against her belly by its ears.

Just as casual as you please, she walked past us real slow to the stern and dropped the head overboard. Then she stood there, feet spread and arms out to keep her balance on the pitching deck. She stood there and gazed out behind us. Like she was watching for the head to float off in our wake, though it must've sunk like a rock.

We didn't know Whittle was with us till he spoke up. 'Good day, me hearties,' he said, all full of vim and fun.

He gave us a smile. Only his teeth and eyes were white. The rest of his face and the bandage on it were stained with blood. He wore the sweater and trousers from yesterday. They looked stiff.

He just gave Trudy a glance, then swung his head about, surveying the sea. 'I trust you managed swimmingly in my absence.'

'My Lord, man,' Michael said, 'what have you *done* to her?'

Whittle smiled, nodded, and patted Michael's shoulder with a bloody hand. 'You needn't bother your . . .'

Splash!

We all jerked our heads aft. No Trudy.

Whittle muttered, 'Damnation,' Michael stood gaping like an idiot, and I went for the stern. Hanging on to the bulwark there, I studied the water behind us while I kicked off my shoes. I spotted her. Only just her head and shoulders. She was way back, and getting farther off every second. I skinned off my sweater and dove.

The cold water squeezed the breath right out of me. Coming up for air, I heard a call and glanced around. Whittle, at the rear, flung a life-ring after me. It landed short, so I had to lose some time swimming for it. While I did that, I saw Michael turning the boat so it wouldn't get away from us altogether.

With the life-ring tucked under one arm, I went for Trudy again. For a while, she was out of sight and I figured maybe she'd gone under for good. But then a wave picked me up high and I caught a peek at her.

If she'd meant to drown herself, she must've changed her mind. Otherwise, wouldn't she just have let herself sink? I wondered if she hadn't fallen overboard by accident, but then I judged she'd done it on purpose – if not to put an end to her miseries, then 'cause she simply couldn't stand all that blood on her body for even a second longer and had to either bathe it off in the ocean or die trying.

Each time a swell hoisted me, I got a look at her. The space between us shortened, but she was still a good piece off. The cold water stiffened me up something awful. She'd been in longer than me, so we didn't either of us have much time left. I figured it was all up, just about.

Well, then Trudy noticed I was coming after her. She hadn't seen me before, I reckon, on account of the rough waters. All of a sudden, she came swimming straight at me. It wasn't but a couple minutes before we joined up, and she hooked an arm through the ring.

We both hung on it, shivering and gasping for air. She didn't say a thing, not even to thank me. I didn't hold it against her, though. Neither of us was in any shape to talk, and besides, it was just her way not to appreciate a thing I ever did for her.

We clung to that ring like a couple of strangers. Now and then, our legs collided or tangled, the way we were kicking to help the floater stay up.

Each time the waves hoisted us, we got a look at the *True D. Light*. It came circling around real slow, and I didn't hold out much hope of it reaching us before we froze up and sank. But then one time we came out of a deep valley and there was Whittle rowing the skiff toward us.

And wasn't I glad to see him!

By and by, he paddled right up beside us. Trudy let go the ring. She grabbed an oar he held out to her, worked her way along it, and draped herself over the gunnel. The boat near capsized, but Whittle scurried to the other side and it was all right.

She didn't have a trace of blood on her. Not that I could

87

see, and I guess I saw every part of her, pretty near, while she struggled into the skiff and then later, after I was in. I didn't see any fresh wounds, either. She had all the bruises and marks from the whipping and hanging Whittle'd given her, but nothing fresh. So every bit of the blood must've been Patrick's. In its own way, that was almost worse to think about than if the blood had come out of her own body.

Anyhow, froze up as I was, I somehow managed to haul myself into the skiff. We got the life-ring aboard, and then Whittle commenced to row us for the yacht.

I sat in the bow, hunched over and shaking apart. Trudy, she was on the other side of Whittle, lying on the bottom, curled and hugging her knees.

'You gave us an awful scare,' he told Trudy, but he sounded more like she'd given him a jolly show. 'This is rather inclement weather for a swimming party. Did you enjoy it?'

She didn't answer.

Her rump was in easy reach of his foot. He fetched it a smart kick that made her flinch. But she still didn't say anything.

He kicked her again. Then he laughed, and laid off conversation the rest of the way to the yacht.

Michael had reefed the sails, so the *True D. Light* was only moving around because of the currents and waves and such. When we came up alongside, he lowered the boarding ladder. I tossed him the bow line. He tied us up. Whittle climbed the ladder, leaving me with Trudy in the tossing skiff.

She only just laid there.

Michael stared down, all pale and hang-jawed, like Trudy was something strange and revolting.

He was no more use than a neck ache.

'Trudy,' I said, 'you've got to get up. We've reached the yacht.'

She might as well have been deaf.

'Help her,' Whittle called down to me.

It was what I'd aimed to do, anyhow. I couldn't see a way around it. So I kept low and made my way to where she lay. I crouched by her rump. 'Trudy?' I asked. 'Please get up.'

She didn't stir, not even when I put a hand on her cold hip and gave it a shake.

So then I pried her top arm away from her knees and

hauled it toward me. She rolled. Her knees swung up and knocked me sideways. The gunnel jammed my ribs. Next thing I knew, my feet were kicking at the sky. Then I hit the ocean head-first.

I tumbled around underwater for a spell, clawed for the surface and banged my head on the underside of the skiff, and finally got to air. I reached for the skiff, but a wave snatched it away so I missed. Before my hand slapped down empty, what do you know if Trudy didn't reach out and catch my wrist.

It must've brought her senses back, knocking me overboard.

Whittle, he was up on the yacht, looking down at us and laughing like he might bust a seam.

Trudy towed me up close, till I could hook my elbows over the gunnel. Then she scooted to the other side to keep things steady. While I hung there, trying to squirm into the boat, she clutched me under the arms and hauled. She didn't let up, but kept pulling even when my head pushed into her breast. She squished me against her and helped me turn over and eased me down.

'Are you all right?' she asked.

I nodded up at her. She frowned down at me. And right then I forgave her everything and was mighty glad I'd worked so hard at saving her.

She crouched over me for a spell, then got up and climbed the ladder all by herself. I followed her up. I had one leg over the bulwark when Michael went to hug her and she slapped him across the face.

He stood there, blinking, and Whittle laughed, and Trudy went down below.

Whittle clapped me on the shoulder. 'You've done splendidly, Trevor,' he said. 'Go down, yourself, and bundle up, before you catch your death.'

He was the cause of all our troubles, but right then I near forgot how much I hated him. I hurried myself down the companionway.

I found Trudy in the saloon, squatting down to light the heater. All a-tremble, she shook out two or three matches trying. While she worked at that, I saw that the door to the forward quarters was open.

I turned away quick, though not quick enough by a long sight. Just a glimpse was too much. Not only Patrick's head was gone. He had no arms or legs, either. More was missing, but I don't aim to tell about that. And what was left of him had been split open and hollowed out considerable.

It made me plain sick to see such a thing. I dropped down onto the bunk I'd used last night, and remembered all the noises that'd kept me awake – Trudy whimpering and screaming and such. Much as I felt sorry for Patrick, I felt a lot sorrier for her. He'd been dead, and shut of the business. But poor Trudy, she'd had to watch and I didn't want to think about what Whittle must've done to her, or made her do.

She got the heater going, then took a couple of towels out of a cabinet and gave me one. I stripped off my wet trousers and socks. We both rubbed ourselves dry. We climbed under our covers, and didn't it feel fine to lay in a warm bed!

I thought to ask her what had gone on last night. Kept mum, though, figuring it wouldn't do her much good to talk about it and she more than likely wouldn't tell, anyhow.

So we just kept quiet.

By and by, Whittle came along with Michael.

'Oh, my God!' Michael blasted when he saw what was past the door. 'What did you *do* to him?'

'Why, I *ripped* him, of course.'

'Where's the *rest* of him?'

'Fish food, no doubt.'

He must've tossed the missing parts out a porthole. If he ate any, like he did with Mary, he didn't let on.

Michael came out with another, 'My God.'

'All the less for you to deal with,' Whittle told him.

'I don't see why *I* have to do it,' Michael whined.

'Would you rather I ask Trudy to clean up the leftovers?'

The way Michael didn't answer, I reckon he would've preferred it that way.

'And poor Trevor's all done in from the business of saving your bride from the ocean depths.'

'I belong at the helm,' Michael said.

'You belong where I tell you. I'm certain the boat will manage itself spendidly until you've finished.'

'Please. It's not . . .'

Whittle, he hauled off and kicked Michael's rump. That sent the fellow stumbling along. I bolted up to see better. At the doorway, Michael lost his feet altogether and, crying out, flopped down right on top of Patrick. He squealed like he'd been stuck, then took to blubbering.

I settled back down and turned my head away, not wanting to watch any more of this. Trudy, she'd pulled the covers over her face when the two first came in.

Pretty soon, Whittle said, 'You see? He's no trouble – hardly weighs more than a dog.'

Michael walked by me, gasping and sobbing.

When he and Whittle were gone, I looked and saw a trail of red drippings and other mess on the floor between our berths. I kept my eyes from wandering into the front cabin.

Pretty soon, along they both came again. This time, Michael carried a bucket and mop.

It was dark by the time he finished cleaning the place.

He never spoke a word to me or Trudy. But he sighed and sniffled considerable.

Whittle let me and Trudy stay warm in our beds till Michael was all done. Then he fetched us fresh sets of clothes. We got up and dressed ourselves. Trudy made supper. We all ate, and then he sent Michael and me topside to get us under way again.

Michael didn't say one thing about any of what had happened that day. He gave me orders and instructions, and that was it.

Once we were sailing along nicely, he turned over the helm to me. He said we'd man the boat in shifts, three hours at a turn. If I should run into any trouble, I was to fetch him quick. Then he went below.

I was glad to be rid of him. I kept my eyes on the compass and sails, and kept us heading in the proper direction, more or less, until he showed up to relieve me.

Whittle and Trudy weren't to be seen. The door to their cabin was shut. I climbed into my bunk in the saloon. Tonight, no sounds came from the other side of that door. And I knew they didn't have Patrick in there with them any more, which was a mighty relief.

CHAPTER THIRTEEN

High Seas and Low Hopes

Michael kept a ship's log. I saw plenty of it, for he scribbled on it every day. It didn't say much, mostly just gave our location in degrees of latitude and longitude, which he figured out somehow by using a sextant along with various tables and charts. He tried to figure that stuff out each day at noon if the sun was showing. That wasn't often, let me tell you. But it came out now and again, and we stayed on course.

We were making for New York Harbor, which is where Michael and Trudy and her father had set out from when they left for England, and Whittle said it suited him fine.

The trip took us thirty-six days and nights and seemed to last about ten years.

It was pretty much the same routine the whole time except when we hit storms. Michael and I took turns at the helm, though it seemed like we spent hours each day fooling with the sails, raising and lowering them because we wanted to keep as much sail flying as we could, but had to reef the mainsail whenever the wind kicked up too hard.

Trudy fixed all our meals. When she wasn't busy with that, she came topside and stood look-out. Whittle shared the look-out duties with her. We all took our turns at it, for none of us was eager to fetch up on an iceberg. We ran into a passel of those, and steered clear of them.

We all got along the best we could, pitching in to help each other, and such.

Trudy stayed cold toward Michael for a spell, holding it against him that he hadn't jumped in the ocean to save her instead of me doing it, I reckon. She never did warm up to me. When she wasn't bossing me around, she acted like I wasn't there at all. She was always civil and meek to Whittle, and didn't once give him any lip.

Michael acted like a whipped dog around Trudy and Whittle both. If he'd had a tail, it would've been drooping between his knees most of the time. He sure knew how to sail the yacht, though. He'd turn into a man again when nobody was around but me and all he had to do was navigate and steer and muck about with the sails or rigging, and give me orders. The dicier it got with the weather, the better he handled himself. Why, you never would've guessed he had a yellow streak at all if you could've seen him skippering us through a gale with waves higher than mountains. Then later on you'd see how a look from Trudy or Whittle made him wither, and you just couldn't believe it.

Whittle, he acted the whole voyage like he was having just the bulliest time ever. He paraded about like Long John Silver himself, a knife on each hip, and hardly a word ever passed his lips that wasn't an 'Aye, matey' or an 'Avast, me hearties' or a 'Shiver me timbers'.

Whereas pirate sorts generally sported an eyepatch, Whittle took to wearing one where his nose used to be. After he'd healed enough to stop bandaging himself, he fashioned a whole variety of patches that he tied onto his face. One day, he'd be sporting a disk of red silk. The next, he might have one made of white lace or leather or velvet or tweed. I don't suppose Trudy had a dress or petticoat or blouse or hat or shoe that didn't wind up with a round hole in it the size of a gold piece. She wore some of those things after Whittle'd been at them, and you could see where he'd gotten the material for this or that nosepatch.

Every so often, when he was feeling ornery or full of mischief, he'd take and pluck his patch up to his forehead and make us sick.

Taken all round, though, he behaved a sight better than I might've expected from the likes of him. He'd come near losing Trudy and me, that first day out of Plymouth. If we'd gone and drowned on him, it would've put an awful wrinkle in his plans. I figure he realized that, and chose not to push his luck. He went ahead and gave us a fair share of thumps and kicks, but he never tormented any of us much – not as I knew about, leastwise.

Each night, he took Trudy into the forward cabin and locked the door, leaving the saloon as sleeping quarters for me and Michael when we weren't taking our turns topside. I never heard much out of her, though. When she'd come out the next day, she didn't look like she'd been strung up or otherwise abused.

Her neck got better slowly. By and by, the scabs fell off and her skin was pink and shiny across her throat.

As for me, I behaved. Plenty of chances came along for me to bash Whittle or shove him overboard, but I always resisted. Whenever a chance showed itself, all I had to do was remember how he'd dealt with Patrick, or how he'd punished Trudy after I'd failed at garroting him. It was never a sure thing that a bash or push would've put an end to him, so I never dared.

When things got slow and I had time for my mind to wander, I often longed for home. But I grew curiouser, all the time, about America. I'd read a heap of books about the place. It sounded grand, and I allowed what a shame it'd be to travel so far and only just turn around, first chance, and return to home. The plan I hit on was to send off a message to Mother, letting her know I wasn't dead, after all, and then explore around a bit.

I'd no sooner get excited about all that, however, than the glooms would set in. I judged I was bound to end up killed and never reach America. If the ocean didn't swamp us, Whittle'd carve us down to torsos once he stopped needing a crew.

My odds were on the ocean, though.

It never let up. At the best of times, it shoved us up and down and jolted us and pitched us from side to side. At the worst of times, it gave up toying around and did its best to demolish us. While that was going on, you'd never see hide nor hair of Whittle or Trudy. They'd be hiding down below with the door shut tight while Michael and I worked like mad, tied to safety lines so as not to get swept overboard. One of us would wear out our arm on the bilge pump while the other manned the wheel, and sometimes one or the other of us had to climb in the rigging or go up the mast, and wasn't that just the most fun?

There were times my heart near gave out from the fright of it all, when we'd be in that tiny boat at the bottom of a gorge, the waves like cliffs looming over us, and then one would avalanche down on top of us, or almost, but more often than not we'd go sliding up a slope and hang on the crest and go shooting straight down into the next chasm, diving down so steep it seemed we might flip end over end, or strike the bottom so hard the boat would fly all to flinders.

The wind, it'd be shrieking through rigging like a banshee. Water'd be smashing against us, trying to tear us loose and throw us into the seas. By the time it'd all ease off, we'd be dripping icicles off our noses and hair, and near dead.

We'd get maybe a day or two of normal roughness, and then we'd find ourselves in just such another fix and it's a mighty wonder the *True D. Light* didn't give up and call it quits and fall apart underneath us. But she held together, and so did we somehow.

It's a plain miracle, is all I can say, that we were all still alive to look out and spot land off in the far distance on the thirty-sixth day of our voyage.

CHAPTER FOURTEEN

Our Last Night on the *True D. Light*

As Whittle wanted no truck with customs people or any other brand of officials, he decided we ought to avoid the New York harbor and pick a section of shoreline where we weren't likely to get noticed.

So we hung well off the coast till after sundown. Then Michael steered us into a place he said was Gravesend Bay. We went in behind a jut of land for shelter from the wind and rough seas. There, a couple of hundred yards from the mouth of Coney Island Creek, Whittle had us reef the sails and drop anchor.

Safely moored on the quiet waters, we went below and ate our last meal aboard the *True D. Light*. I didn't have much stomach for food. On the one hand, I was mighty glad to be shut of the ocean at last. It had done its most to kill us, but we'd gotten across alive. On the other hand, though, Whittle'd had uses for us when we were on the high seas. Now, he didn't need a crew or cook or captive. He didn't need us at all. That dampened my appetite considerable.

I could see that Michael and Trudy were worried, too. They fidgeted and picked at their food and didn't say much. Nobody asked what Whittle aimed to do. None of us had the grit, I reckon. Maybe they were like me, and figured talking about it might only serve to give him ideas. Maybe if we just let it lie, he'd forget it was about time to kill us all.

When Whittle finished eating, he patted his lips with a napkin and sighed. He wore a flimsy silk nosepatch that I reckoned had left a good pair of Trudy's bloomers with a hole in them. It kind of drooped in the middle and clung to his tiny nubs at both sides, but puffed out like a sail when he sighed.

'Taken all around, me hearties,' he said, 'it's been a marvelous voyage. You were fine shipmates and companions. I

96

daresay I'll be quite sorry to take my leave of you. However, all good things must come to an end.'

Trudy, she turned a shade of gray and caught her lower lip between her teeth.

Whittle gave her a cheery smile. 'You've nothing to fear, Trudy. Am I so ungrateful as to harm you now that we've reached safe harbor? I may indeed have some mischievous ways about me, but I am not a heartless fiend. I count you as my friend. I count you *all* as my friends,' he added, nodding and smiling at Michael and me. 'We've sailed the vast reaches of the sea together – we band of brothers. And sister,' he added, tipping Trudy a wink. 'We honored few.'

He went on spouting such rubbish for a spell. He laid it on thick as molasses about how highly he thought of us and how grateful he was and how we were his comrades and mates and chums and how he wouldn't even *think* about hurting us in any way. Well, he jabbered on about it till I lost any doubt but what he aimed to kill us all.

Finally, he yawned and said, 'I'm all done in. I suggest we retire for the night. We'll rise early, for I'm quite keen to be on my way. Just before dawn would seem the best time to set out, I should think. I'll take the skiff ashore, and you three may carry on as you fancy. Make for the city or the warm Carib or Timbuktu, it's all the same to me.'

Trudy was set to clean the supper dishes, but Whittle told her there was no need. Then he led her off.

Michael watched her go. From the look on his face, he figured he was never going to see her again. Not alive, anyhow.

As soon as Whittle shut the door, I said, 'We've got to save her. There's no time to lose.'

In a snap, his face changed. He wiped off his sorrow and hopelessness, and came up looking all superior and scornful. 'Don't be ridiculous,' he said.

'If we don't stop him, he'll butcher her. You know it as well as I do.'

'He'll do no such thing.'

I was plain astonished. Shouldn't have been, though. I'd seen enough of Michael to know he had no spine when it came to dealing with Whittle. 'We can't sit here and allow her to be killed!'

'Don't raise your voice to me, boy.'

'Do you *wish* him to murder Trudy? You saw how he

97

carved up poor Patrick Doolan.'

His face went a bit slack at the reminder of that.

'*I* saw the work he did on a London whore. Why, he just carved her up something awful. He even *ate* parts of her. I heard him do it. He'll do the same to Trudy if we don't stop him.'

'Nonsense,' he muttered.

But I could see he believed me.

'Trudy will be perfectly fine,' he said, 'so long as we do nothing to rock the boat.'

'We might have a go at burning it,' I said. 'If we set a fire . . .'

'Are you mad?'

'I've given it quite a bit of thought.' I told him. It was the truth. Thirty-six days on the Atlantic had given me plenty of time to hatch schemes, for I'd known it would come down to this if we lived through the voyage. 'Once we get the fire going, we'll cry out an alarm. Whittle, he'll come leaping out through the door all in a heat to save himself. He won't care a bit about killing Trudy. One of us will be waiting topside to bring Trudy up through the hatch.'

'The skiff's on top of the hatch,' Michael pointed out. He sounded tired and annoyed.

'Why, don't you think I know that? We move it clear before we light the fire.'

'Whittle would hear the commotion.'

'We'd need to be quite stealthy about it.'

'The hatch may be locked from below.'

'Trudy can handle that.'

'Suppose she can't? Just suppose we're unable to open the hatch, and she's trapped by the fire. And where is Whittle through all this? If he gets past the fire, he'll come topside and then we'll be in a fix.'

I had already considered that. 'We block the companion-way door. He might not be able to break through it at all before the fire gets him. And if he does, it should still delay him and give the three of us time to escape in the skiff.'

It was quite a bully scheme, actually. I'm sure Huck Finn would've been proud of me. And Tom wasn't here to ruin it with fancy trimmings. Neither of them were here, except in my head. My only audience was Michael.

While I explained how we'd keep Whittle below with the

fire and make our getaway, he simply scowled and shook his head.

'It's too risky,' he finally said.

'It's time for risks,' I told him. 'Unless you're eager to have Trudy cut into pieces, we'd better have at it.'

He only just sat there and kept on shaking his head.

'Do *you* have a plan?' I blurted out.

'The only sensible thing is to leave Whittle be. He promised he wouldn't harm Trudy. In the morning, he'll row ashore and that will be the end of it.'

'It's certain to be the end of Trudy long before that.'

'We've no choice but to trust Whittle and hope for the best.'

'I'll do it myself, then.'

With that, I hurried on over to the stove and grabbed some matches. Michael went after me into the saloon. There, I snatched a book down from the cabinet. It was an Emerson. I'd never had much use for him, anyhow. I tore out pages by the handful, crumpled them and piled them up on the floor between the berths. While I worked at that, Michael pranced around me, fuming and railing at me in a hushed voice so Whittle wouldn't hear. He said, 'Stop this nonsense,' and, 'Don't you dare,' and, 'You'll be the death of us all,' and such. But I went on with what had to be done. I was yanking a cover off one of the bunks when he jumped me from behind.

He hooked an arm across my throat and commenced to choke me. I went wild, thrashing and kicking. I tried to tear his arm clear so I could breathe, but that was no use. I went at him with my elbows, punching them backward. Got in a few good licks. He never let up, though. He kept on squeezing till I thought my eyes might pop out. I saw some dandy fireworks. They went off with crashes like cannons, which weren't cannons at all but my heart thundering.

Well, I allowed I'd had it. Seemed mighty peculiar that I'd gone and gotten myself killed by Michael instead of by Whittle, and all I'd hoped to do was save the hide of his wife.

All of a sudden, I wasn't aboard the *True D. Light* any more. I was standing in an East End alley with my back to a wall, looking at the fellow I'd stabbed. He was sitting in a puddle, hunched over. He said, 'You gone and killed me is what you done.'

I felt mighty sorry for him and wished I hadn't done it.

Then I was on my back, Michael crouched over me and pulling off my belt. All I could do was fight to suck in air. He propped me up and crossed my hands in front and wrapped the belt around me. He cinched it in tight and buckled it. Then he hoisted me onto the bunk.

I lay there, glad to be alive and figuring him for the biggest fool that ever drew a breath.

He should've helped me, not throttled me.

Well, he put what was left of Emerson back into the cabinet. Then he picked up all the paper balls and took them topside, where I guess he pitched them overboard. He didn't want any evidence left around to upset Whittle, I reckon.

When he came back, he bent over me and made sure I hadn't slipped my arms out of the belt. 'Now you lie still,' he said. 'If you give me any more trouble, I'll pound you silly.'

He got under his own covers. But he left the gaslamps burning so he could keep an eye on me.

No sounds came from the other side of the door. If Whittle'd already killed Trudy, he'd been quiet about it and done it so quick she never got a chance to let out a yelp.

Maybe he'd told the truth, though, and aimed to row away in the morning and leave us alive.

But I knew the stripe of Whittle.

Trudy was either dead by now, or soon would be.

By and by, I figured it was too late for doing her any good. Or any harm, either. I felt awful about that.

Trudy'd been bossy and annoying, and hadn't lent a hand the time I had my chance to strangle Whittle. She'd never acted friendly toward me at all unless you count the time she helped me onto the skiff after she'd knocked me overboard. Even still, I never hated her. I only felt sorry for her, mostly, and blamed myself near as much as Whittle for her miseries. I'd saved her from hanging and from drowning, and I might've saved her from Whittle's knife tonight if Michael hadn't stopped me.

Resting there on the bed I still wanted to have a go at saving her. But I didn't see how I could manage it, not with Michael set to get in my way. Besides, I figured Whittle'd already had plenty of time to cut her up.

I decided I might as well write her off and do what I could to save myself.

It didn't take much work to squeeze my arms out from under the belt. Michael had his head turned toward me. What with the dim light and shadows, I couldn't see whether his eyes were open or shut. He didn't move or raise a fuss, though, so I figured he must've fallen asleep.

After I'd pulled my arms free, I sat up and slipped the belt around to get at its buckle. I unfastened that, then put the belt where it belonged so I wouldn't lose my trousers.

Then I swung my feet down and took off my shoes. My notion, you see, was simply to dive overboard and swim for land. Would've been too dicey, trying for the skiff. But I'd take the life-ring along with me. And my shoes. I was busy tying their laces together so I could hang them around my neck. That's when a key rattled in the door lock.

Right quick, I scurried under my covers and pulled the shoes in with me. I shut my eyes, letting on to be asleep.

The door bumped shut. 'Rise up, maties,' Whittle said, just as cheery as you please. 'The time has come for my departure.'

I yawned and rubbed my eyes. 'Is it morning?' I asked, though I knew it wasn't.

'Why wait any longer? I'm eager to be on my way.'

Whittle stood with his back to the door. He wore his overcoat. It hung open. There was no blood on his sweater or trousers, nor on his face or hands. Both the knives in his belt had clean handles. I took all that for a good sign. It gave me hope, for just a bit, but then I figured he would've stripped naked for the butchery like he'd done that night in Mary's room. He always kept drinking water in the cabin, too, so he might've used it for washing. That sank my hopes some.

Michael sat up and looked at the door.

'Trudy's fast asleep,' Whittle said. 'Her assistance won't be necessary.' With a smile, he added, 'I rather imagine she'll be quite overjoyed when she awakens and learns of my departure. If we're very quiet about the preparations, perhaps we won't disturb her.'

I wished I could believe him.

He hadn't locked the door after coming out, but he stayed in front of it as Michael and I climbed out of our beds. I'd untied my shoe laces while he was talking, so he didn't catch on that they'd been laced together. I brought them out from under the covers with me, and put them on.

He kept his post at the door and ordered us about, his voice low as if he was being careful not to wake Trudy.

Earlier in the day, he'd loaded a large valise, filling it with clothes and loot. The clothes were mostly Michael's, as he was about the same size as Whittle and the father's duds were too big. The loot was all the money and jewels he'd found aboard the yacht, which was considerable. Michael, Trudy and her father, they'd been rich from the father's hotel business in New York City. They'd brought along tons of money, not to mention a scad of necklaces and earrings and brooches and bracelets and such so Trudy could fix herself up splendid for dress-up affairs. Whittle, he'd spent some spare time during the voyage hunting around for all the valuables. After finding what he could, he'd asked Trudy about hiding places where there might be more, and she'd obliged him by opening up some secret compartments. So he probably had every bit of it, now, in his valise.

Following his orders, Michael carried the case topside and I went up after him, empty-handed. He had Michael set it down by the stern. Then the three of us made our way forward.

It was a calm night, but mighty cold. Not another boat was in sight. A few lights glowed along the shore and inland. I sure wished I was there among them, and judged this might be as good a time as any for a swim.

But I held off, concerned about Trudy. Maybe Whittle hadn't killed her yet.

Maybe, instead of abandoning ship, I ought to have a go at throwing Whittle overboard.

I glanced back at him. He had a knife in his right hand. Not hankering to catch it in my belly, I went on after Michael to where the skiff was secured. Whittle used his knife to cut the ropes. Then he stood back and watched while Michael and I turned the skiff right-side up. We worked at it slowly, being careful not to raise any sound. Trudy was just beneath the deck from us, after all. Being quiet with the skiff seemed like a way to trick our minds into thinking she was only asleep.

We lowered the skiff over the side. Whittle walking in front of me, Michael behind, I towed the skiff by its bow line to the stern.

Whittle told me to tie it. While I did that, he told Michael to pick up the valise. I thought he aimed to have Michael climb down and load it into the skiff for him. But when Michael bent over to grab the handle, Whittle stepped in quick and slashed a knife across his throat. Michael straightened up quick and stood rigid, his mouth wide like he was mighty surprised. Blood squirted out of his ripped neck. Whittle danced out of its way and whirled toward me.

Well, I flung myself backward. The bulwark caught me behind the knees. As I pitched over the side, Whittle reached and clutched the front of my sweater. He tugged at it, trying to pull me up. But the sweater only just stretched, and I kept falling. So he shoved the knife into my belly. Or tried. Its point jabbed the back of my forearm, instead. I gave out a yell and kicked at him and he let got and I dropped headfirst.

My head missed the skiff. But my shoulder fetched it a hard thump that sent it scooting. I plunged down into the cold water between it and the starboard side of the yacht.

I was mighty shocked at how sudden he'd killed Michael and made his play for me. My shoulder hurt like it had gotten clubbed by a cricket bat. My arm hurt, too. And the water plain froze me. In spite of all that, I felt a trifle thrilled that I'd made it overboard alive. I'd gotten clear of Whittle, and that was what counted the most.

The ticket, now, was to *stay* clear of him.

So instead of popping up for air, I swam underwater to where I thought the yacht ought to be. I got my shoes off, then let myself rise, arms overhead. Sure enough, my fingers met the bottom of the hull. It was all slimy, and rough with barnacles. I kept under there, feeling my way around. When I found the rudder, it told me which way to go. I turned myself around and headed the other way.

Whittle likely figured he hadn't killed me. He'd be up there, waiting. So it didn't seem smart to surface where he might spot me.

I worked my way toward the bow, walking my hands along the hull and kicking a bit. The *True D. Light* had seemed awful tiny when we were out in the ocean getting knocked about by giant waves. Underneath it, though, with my air running out, it felt ten miles long. I reckoned my chest might explode before I got to the front of it.

Finally, though, the hull narrowed down to its prow. I let

my head come out of the water on the port side, gave a quick look around and didn't see either Whittle or the skiff. After breathing for a spell, I went down again and hid under the hull for as long as I could stand it. Then I came up for another breath and went down again. I must've done that twenty times, till once when I was up for air I heard the splash of oars nearby. Over on the other side of the prow. Well, I ducked under and held my breath forever.

Down there, I couldn't hear the oars. But I judged that Whittle was in the skiff, circling the yacht, scouting for me. Finally, I judged he must've had time to pass the bow, so I scooted over to the starboard side before bobbing up for air. He wasn't in sight.

No sound of oars, either.

I hung there for a while, then peeked around the end of the bow.

There was Whittle, a hundred feet off, rowing for shore.

CHAPTER FIFTEEN

On My Own

Whittle was almost to shore when I climbed the anchor chain and crawled onto the deck. If the water'd been cold, the air felt twice as bad. I didn't linger, but scurried along to the stern, keeping low in case Whittle might have an eye on the yacht.

Michael, he was sprawled out and still. Nothing to do for him. He was in the hands of Providence, now. So after a quick look to make sure Whittle hadn't turned around, I hurried below.

The heater was on, but it didn't give off enough warmth to stop my shudders. Real quick, I stripped off my duds and grabbed a towel out of a storage compartment. While I rubbed myself dry, I kept looking at the shut door to the forward cabin. I didn't want to see what was on the other side of it.

With a strip of sheet from my bunk, I bandaged my forearm. Then I put on some dry clothes. Didn't they feel just fine! They were the father's, and awful big on me, but I'd gotten used to wearing the dead man's things for I'd worn this or that of his almost every day of the voyage. I cinched in the trousers with a belt, and turned the cuffs up the way I'd always done. Then I got into his best shoes. Whittle had taken all Michael's spares, except the pair I'd had on when I went overboard. Those were at the bottom of the bay, and I didn't relish the notion of stealing the shoes off his body. So these would have to do, even though they fit loose.

Last, I put on the father's heavy coat.

That took care of getting myself dry and warm. There was nothing left but only to check on Trudy.

All tight and sick inside, I went to the door. I knocked on it. She didn't answer, so I rapped harder. Then I called her name a few times.

105

Nothing.

Well, I took hold of the door handle and tried to make myself turn it. I just couldn't, though. Pretty soon, I gave up.

Topside, I searched the dark waters for Whittle and his skiff. They were nowhere to be seen.

So what I did, I raised the anchor and set the mainsail. No easy job, but it beat taking a swim. At the helm, I steered for a piece of shore far away from where Whittle'd been headed.

I picked a long stretch of beach that didn't have any lights nearby. It took a spell to get there, but by and by I ran the *True D. Light* straight up onto the sand. She scraped along and stopped with a rough jolt.

Well, I rushed to the prow, all set to leap off and skedaddle before somebody might show up.

But then I got to thinking about Trudy.

I knew she was dead. But I didn't know *for sure*.

So I hurried down below again, and this time I didn't knock or call her name or give myself time to lose my nerve. I just swung the door open wide and looked in.

Even though I'd seen Whittle's work on Mary, it didn't make me ready for this.

With a yell, I spun around and heeled it, in such a lather to get away that I stumbled as I raced up the companionway stairs and barked a shin. I gave Michael a last look, and allowed he was lucky to be dead.

Then I dashed along the deck to the prow and jumped.

The beach knocked my legs out from under me. I landed on damp, cold sand, picked myself up quick and took just a few running strides toward the distant trees. Then I stopped.

Instead of rushing inland, I headed to the right.

Toward the area where Whittle must've landed his skiff.

All along, I'd reckoned it would take a miracle to survive the voyage. If the ocean didn't kill me, Whittle would do the job with his knife. Now I was clear of them both. Safe on land in America.

But Whittle was here, too.

Much as I wanted to be shut of him forever, it was me who had brought him aboard the *True D. Light*, me who had gotten Michael and the father murdered, me who had failed to save Trudy.

106

Walking brisk along that beach, leaving the yacht behind with its horrid cargo, I knew it was me who had to track down Jack the Ripper and put an end to him.

PART TWO

The General and His Ladies

CHAPTER SIXTEEN

The House in the Snow

I hadn't walked far before snow started coming down. Not much at first, but soon the night was just thick with big white flakes so I couldn't see more than a few yards in front of me.

It seemed like a good thing. If Whittle was lurking about, up ahead, he wouldn't have much luck at spotting me through the heavy downfall. Maybe I could sneak up on him.

I grabbed a chunk of driftwood to use for a club, and shoved a few rocks into the pockets of my coat. They didn't amount to much as weapons go. They'd do just dandy, though, if I could catch him by surprise.

Having such things gave me a sense of power that made me realize just how helpless I'd felt during those weeks on the yacht.

It sank in that I was actually free. Not a prisoner trapped aboard a boat. Not a lackey who had to obey orders and watch my step, always worried Whittle would punish Trudy if I didn't behave.

He couldn't hurt her now. He'd done his worst to her. As horrible as that was, it had taken away his only hold on me.

So I wasn't his slave any more. I was myself again, Trevor Wellington Bentley. Free. If I had a mind to do so, I could walk away and likely never set eyes on Whittle again.

If I had a mind to. Which I didn't.

The end of my slavery meant I was free to be a hunter. That was all I cared to be – a hunter of Whittle. I figured I'd stalk him forever, if that's how long it took.

By and by, I got to *hoping* he'd hung around the shore and seen me beach the *True D. Light*. I hoped he'd decided to lay for me. I hoped he might come leaping at me through the falling snow. Just let him. He would catch a couple of rocks in the face for his trouble, and once he was down, I'd bash his head to pudding.

All my eagerness for that skipped out on me, though, when I came to the skiff. The sight of it turned me cold and trembly. I filled my right hand with a rock and twisted around in circles, scared to death he might jump me, wishing the snow would let up so I could see him coming.

When nothing happened, I settled down some and gave the skiff a study. It had been dragged up the sand a few yards beyond the reach of the waves. It was empty except for the oars and a puddle of water that had collected near the stern. The puddle looked black. The snowflakes melted away when they fell on it, but otherwise the bottom of the boat, the bench seats and the tops of the oars all wore smooth, pale mats of snow.

I circled the skiff, looking for footprints. The only ones I found were my own. This near the water, the sand was stiff and hard, so Whittle wouldn't have left much in the way of impressions and what there might've been was hidden under an inch or more of snow.

As he'd left no tracks for me to follow, I put myself in his place and reckoned he had likely headed straight inland. He would want to put distance between himself and the bay, figuring the yacht might be found at daylight. What with the bodies on board, things could get hot for strangers in the area.

That goes for me, too, I realized.

It wasn't a comforting notion.

I put my back to the bay and started to march. Trekking over the dunes, my night in Whitechapel came back to me as clear as if it had been yesterday. The part about getting chased by the mob that mistook me for the Ripper. That had been an awful dicey time, and it had only been luck, mostly, that saved me. Well, I didn't need much imagination to see how I could find myself blamed for the killing of Trudy and Michael.

What if they grabbed me for it? How could I prove it was Whittle, and not me, who'd done such foul deeds? Maybe I'd end up swinging at the end of a rope.

When all that sank in, I allowed I had plenty more to worry about than tracking down Whittle.

The trick was to keep clear of everyone, at least until I could put some miles between me and the *True D. Light*.

112

It seemed like a mighty fine plan, but it flew all to smash the moment I came upon the house.

What I found, first, wasn't the house but a low stone wall that blocked my way. It stretched out in front of me for as far as I could see through the snowfall. My first thought was to pick one direction or the other and hike around it.

After all, the wall hadn't just grown out of the ground by itself. Someone had built it, and that meant there must be people nearby. I'd aimed to avoid people.

Then I figured that if Whittle'd come this way, he might've seen things different. What if he saw the wall as a sign that a house was close, and went looking for it? Maybe a house was just what he wanted – a place to get out of the weather and warm himself up, maybe have himself a good meal and a sleep. Maybe have himself a high time butchering whoever lived there.

Well, I climbed to the other side of the wall and went searching. I kept an eye out for footprints, but didn't find any. What with the darkness and the heavy falling snow, there wasn't much to see at all. Besides, Whittle'd likely had a good headstart on me. He might've passed through here before the snow'd hardly commenced to fall.

And everybody in the house – if there *was* a house and folks inside it – might be dead by the time I got there.

By and by, I figured there had to be a house. The area was planted with trees and shrubs, some of which gave me an awful start when they sort of loomed up and I took them for Whittle. There were some sheds, too. And a gazebo. And a walkway that only showed because some overhanging limbs kept the snow off its flagstones.

Finally, the house turned up. It looked to be made of stone, and maybe a couple of stories tall. Standing at the foot of the porch stairs, I could only see as high as an upstairs window, and that was dark. There didn't seem to be any light at all coming from this side of the house. The corners of its wall were out of sight.

I checked the porch stairs. The snow on them was thick and smooth, trackless.

I climbed three stairs, then got a sudden case of the fantods, so I backed down.

No point rushing things. The last time I'd gone sneaking into a stranger's digs, that's when I'd gotten mixed up with the Ripper in the first place. Seemed the wiser course to scout around before making up my mind as to whether I ought to try the house.

With that in mind, I headed off to the right. The windows along the ground floor were high enough so I didn't need to duck. They were all dark. At the corner, I turned and made for the front. The windows along this wall were dark, too. A couple of times, I stepped back and looked up. Didn't seem to be any lighted windows upstairs, either.

Well, it stood to reason. If a family was in there, they all would've turned in by now. I hoped they *were* asleep, and not slaughtered.

Whittle was mad, but crafty. Maybe he figured to play things safe, and not mark his arrival in America by killing folks straightaway.

Likely as not, though, he wouldn't look at it that way.

Pretty soon, I came to the front of the house and followed its long porch to the stairs in the middle. By now, it came as no surprise to find the windows dark. From the look of the snow on the stairs, nobody'd climbed up or down them for a spell.

I had a mind to walk the rest of the way around the place, but figured I was only just looking for an excuse to put off going in.

So up the stairs I went. The snow on them squeaked under my shoes. Under the porch roof, I put some white tracks on the floorboards, and stomped one foot to shake the clinging powder off my shoe and sock. The thump of it startled me considerable. I felt like a plain fool. Quiet and stealth were called for, not clean shoes.

A single thump shouldn't have been enough to rouse the household – if anybody was in shape to arouse. And if Whittle was in there, he only would've heard it if he had his ear to the front door, likely as not.

Anyhow, I stood still for a long while. Nothing came of the thump. But I wasn't eager to try the door. I set down my driftwood club and brushed some snow off my hair and coat. Then I bent down for my club, but decided not to take it in with me. If Whittle was inside, I'd have to make do with my rocks. Because he might not be. And I didn't fancy the notion of creeping inside a strange house with a weapon in my hand. I'd had a knife in my teeth when I climbed aboard the *True D. Light*, only to get myself laid into by an innocent chap who took me for a villain.

114

There's one thing about Trevor Bentley, he doesn't often make the same mistake twice.

So I kept my hands empty, the rocks in my pockets.

The door wasn't locked.

I eased it open and stood for a spell with my head in the crack. There wasn't much to see but only darkness. Nothing to hear but the tick-tock of a clock pendulum somewhere close by. So in I crept, and shut the door real soft.

It was mighty good to be out of the snowy weather. The air felt warm and friendly. It smelled a trifle old and stale like Grandmother's place near Oxford. It smelled of wood smoke, too. From a fireplace, I reckoned. And there was a bittersweet aroma that put me in mind of Daws the cabman. I remembered how he'd kept his pipe upside-down so the rain wouldn't put it out, the night I went to fetch Uncle William, and suddenly I felt mighty lonesome for home.

I would've given just about anything, right then, to be there with Mother.

I told myself this was no time to stand around feeling sorry for myself. This was dangerous territory, after all, whether or not Whittle was lurking about.

Keeping my eyes and ears sharp, I took to snooping about. Part of the time, rug was under my shoes. Other times, it was wooden floor. I moved slow, crouching some, my hands feeling ahead to warn me off collisions. I met up with an umbrella stand, a small table, a lamp, a couple of chairs. I only knew what they were by their feel. Somehow, I missed knocking any over. By and by, I found a newel post and stairway. The stairs seemed to be as wide as I was long.

It seemed smart to explore where I was before venturing into the upper parts of the house. So that's what I did. And before long, I found myself in a parlor. That's where the fireplace was. The fire had burnt itself down to glowing embers, but it gave the room some extra warmth and enough ruddy light for me to see I wasn't blind, after all.

Though the light was faint and left swarms of shadows, I saw right off that the room had walls and walls full of books. Where there weren't bookshelves or curtained windows, there were cabinets or paintings. The place was all aclutter. It had a sofa, and so many tables and lamps and chairs and so on that it seemed more like a storage room than a place for folks to spend their time.

Even though I worried some about what might be hiding

115

in the shadows, I wasn't eager to move on. I stepped over close to the fire, instead, and huddled down to feel its warmth better.

From somewhere behind me, a voice said, 'Chuck another log on there, fellow.'

CHAPTER SEVENTEEN

The General

Well, I jumped up so quick I near hurt myself, and swung around.

Off in a corner, a match flared. It showed a broad, wrinkled face with white hair curled all around it and a thick, droopy mustache. The old man was sitting in an armchair off to the side a ways. I must've walked right by him on my way to the fireplace.

He sucked the match flame down into his pipe a few times, and puffed out some smoke. 'Get that fire blazing,' he said. 'I only let her burn down because I was too comfy to get up and fool with it.'

He didn't sound like he meant me any harm. He sounded downright friendly, in fact. So I figured there was no good reason to hightail. I turned to the fireplace, moved the screen aside, added some wood onto the andiron, and puffed away with the bellows till the fire took. After putting the screen back where it belonged, I faced the old man again.

'Much appreciated,' he said.

What with the shimmery red light, I could see him better now. He was a husky fellow, all abulge under his flannel nightshirt. A blanket covered his legs. He sat there, looking at me, sucking on his pipe, just as calm as if I'd been invited into his parlor, not snuck in like a thief.

'General Matthew Forrest,' he said.

A General? That might explain how come I hadn't riled him.

'Don't stand there with your maw hanging,' he said. 'Introduce yourself.'

I let out a couple of noises like 'Uhhh, uhhh' while I tried to figure things out. He talked like a Yank, pretty much the same as Michael and Trudy, rather flat and clipped. Just a few words from me, and he'd know by my voice I wasn't any native. Then I'd have an awful piece of explaining to do. What I needed was a good string of lies about who I was and where I'd come from – lies that left out everything about Whittle and the yacht.

'What's the matter, cat got your tongue?'

I nodded, and suddenly hit on a plan. *Cat got your tongue?* Yes, indeed!

I commenced to frown and shake my head and touch my lips. Then I remembered how one of those rascals in *Huckleberry Finn* had let on to be a dummy. He'd wriggled his fingers and such, pretending it was sign language. So I had a go at that.

The General furrowed his brow. He tapped the bit of his pipe against a front tooth. 'I see,' he said. 'You're a mute. Not deaf, however. I knew a fellow name of Clay who suffered from just such a predicament. That was back in '74. A couple of Comanches laid their hands on him, cut his tongue clean off at the root. This wasn't more than half a mile from Adobe Walls. A buffalo hunter happened along, just afterwards, and picked off the savages with his Sharps. Saved Clay, but his tongue was already out. Being reluctant to part with it, he poked a hole in the tongue and wore it around his neck. Before long, the thing dried up like jerky. I hear he ate it, a year or two later on, to stave off hunger after he lost his mount and had to hole up in a cave for a week till the Indians cleared out.'

This General sure was a talker, which suited me fine. He rather put me in mind of Uncle William, the way he seemed to relish his grisly tale.

'I don't suppose the Comanches got yours,' he said.

Shaking my head, I stuck out my tongue so he could see I had one. Then I fingered my throat and let out a grunt.

'A problem with the voice box, eh?'

Nod, nod.

'That's a shame. However, it does give you a certain edge in conversational gambits.'

When he came out with that, I couldn't help but laugh.

'The Lord has seen fit to saddle me with not one but *two* women in my dotage, so your silence is mighty refreshing.'

Two women! That set off alarms in me. What if Whittle'd come in, skipped the parlor and missed the General, but found the gals?

I must've looked anxious and fidgety, because the General waved his empty hand in my direction and said, 'Oh, don't bother about them. They aren't likely to stray down and interrupt us. Once they've turned in for the night, they remain turned in. That's why I've taken to the habit of coming down for a smoke and a drink this time of . . .'

'I fear they might be in danger, sir!' I blurted.

So much for acting mute.

If the General was surprised to hear me talk, he didn't show it. He didn't sit still for a blink, but bounded out of the chair so quick it was amazing. 'Explain yourself,' he said. Turning his back to me, he dropped his pipe on a table and struck a match.

While he plucked the glass chimney off a lamp and lit the wick, I said, 'I followed a murderer tonight. He may've come here.'

The General didn't say a thing. He stepped past me lively with the lamp and snatched a revolver off the fireplace mantel. It was huge.

I bet he knew how to use it, too.

'Follow me,' he said. 'Look sharp.'

We hot-footed it out of the parlor, across the foyer and up the stairs. My heart pounded fierce. I hoped the women weren't dead, as that would be a sorry loss for General Forrest. But I sure hoped we'd find Whittle. Scared as I was of the man, I was keen to see him struck by lead. Five or six slugs in the chest would do him proper.

I fetched one of the rocks out of my coat pocket before we reached the top of the stairs. The General moved fast and silent into a hallway up there. I stayed close behind him. The lamp cast a glow that lit us and the walls on both sides, but left a long stretch of darkness ahead.

A runner on the floor kept our footsteps quiet, but boards creaked plenty. They would creak for Whittle, too, I judged, if he came sneaking along. But that didn't ease my mind much, so I looked over my shoulder every few seconds. When we walked past a couple of shut doors, I worried they might fly open and Whittle'd leap out. But they stayed shut.

The next door we came to, it stood open and the General hurried through. He didn't tell me to stay out, so I followed him, not hankering to be left all alone in the hallway. We rushed over to a big canopy bed. I could tell, right off, that

119

Whittle hadn't been at the woman because the covers weren't thrown off and she wasn't a bloody carcass. Only her head showed. It wore a bonnet.

The General's hands were full, what with the lamp in one and his revolver in the other, so he gave the mattress a jolt with his knee. The woman let out a moan.

'Stir your bones, Mable.'

She mumbled, 'Huh? Whuh?'

'We may have trouble. Get up now and come along, and be quiet about it.'

She rolled onto her back, caught sight of me and bolted up fast, clutching the covers to her front. She was a skinny, wrinkled old woman. Some white hair stuck out from under the edges of her bonnet. She blinked and worked her jaw.

'Who . . . ? What in heaven's name . . . ?'

'Shhhh,' the General said. 'Let's go.'

'Why, I never . . .' she mumbled. But she didn't waste any time. Throwing some sour looks in my direction, she scampered out of bed and shoved her feet into slippers. She wore a wool gown so long she had to hoist it a bit so the hem wouldn't drag the floor.

The General took the lead. I hung back and stayed behind Mable, figuring to guard the rear. She had a bit of a limp, but she moved along spritely.

She kept glancing back like she suspected I might knock her on the head with my rock.

Up the hallway a piece, we rushed into another bedroom.

The gal in this one must've been a light sleeper, for she sat up quick before the General got a chance to call out or knee her bed.

'Gracious sakes,' she said, 'what *is* going on?'

'Nothing at all, my dear,' the General told her. 'Nothing at all.'

She frowned, looking fairly perplexed. She was a fine, pretty woman, maybe ten years older than me, with sleek black hair that hung to her shoulders.

'Nothing?' Mable asked, giving the General a sharp look. 'Why, you've frightened me out of ten years' growth. Something had *best* be going on, you old fool. Who's this *child*? What's he doing in our home?'

'Trevor Bentley, ma'am,' I said.

'He came to warn us of a killer in the house,' the General explained.

120

'Oh, my,' the younger woman said.

'You stay here and watch the women, Trev.' With that, he headed for the hallway.

'Don't you dare leave us alone with this young rascal,' Mable blurted.

The General, he let on that he didn't hear her. He vanished with his lamp. We were in darkness for a bit. Then a match lit up the young woman. Sitting on the edge of her bed, she touched its flame to a lamp on her night table. She turned the wick up bright, and put the chimney over it, and blew out the match.

Mable went over to the lamp. She picked it up and held it off to her side as if she aimed to pitch it at me. 'I've dealt with my share of ruffians, fellow,' she said. 'Don't tempt me.'

'Settle down, Grandma,' the young one said, not at all snappish but soft and friendly. 'I'm sure Trevor doesn't mean us any harm.'

To show she was right, I tucked away the rock into my pocket.

'There,' she said. 'You see?' She stood up and went to her grandmother, and took the lamp. She set it on the table where it belonged.

She was a head taller than me, and slim and fine-looking. She wore a white nightdress that didn't quite reach to her ankles.

She gave me a smile that warmed me up considerable, then edged on past me and went for the door.

'I shouldn't go out there,' I warned.

She didn't heed that, but stepped out into the hall and looked both ways.

'Sarah, you get back in here this moment!'

Well, she stood out there ignoring me *and* her grandmother. I had to admire her pluck, but I was scared for her. So I heeled it into the hall. I had a mind to grab her and tow her back inside the room. Kept my hands to myself, though. Just stayed beside her.

We both studied the darkness.

I didn't know where the General had gone to, but I sure wished he'd show up quick.

'Come back in here and shut the door,' Mable sang out.

Sarah didn't answer. In a quiet voice to me, she said, 'I do hope Grandpa's all right.'

'I doubt the killer's in the house,' I said. I couldn't be certain, of course. I allowed it was a safe bet, considering Mable and Sarah hadn't gotten themselves butchered. But then again, he might've hidden out in another room for some reason. I figured there was no telling, when it came to Whittle. He might be creeping up on us even as we stood there.

Far off at the end of the hall, light came glowing from a doorway. Pretty soon, the general walked out behind his lamp and revolver. He didn't glance our way. He crossed to another door and entered a room.

'Let's go back inside,' I whispered.

She didn't answer, but just stood and folded her arms across her chest. I could hear her breathing sort of ragged. She was barefoot, and must've been mighty cold. Even though she had on a heavy nightdress, the chilly draft was likely chasing right up under it.

She put me in mind of Trudy, the night Whittle'd left her hanging. I thought about how I'd nearly frozen, myself, trying to brace her up. And then the way Trudy'd looked, dead, pushed itself into my head.

It made me just sick to think about. And it made me figure I could be a gentleman some other time. So I grabbed hold of Sarah's arm and said, 'Excuse me,' while I tugged her into the room. I dragged her clear of the door, let go, and threw it shut.

Old Mable, her mouth dropped.

Sarah frowned at me. 'That wasn't necessary,' she said, and rubbed her arm where I'd squeezed it.

'I'm quite sorry,' I said. 'Really, I am. But I shouldn't want Whittle to lay his hands on you. We're much safer, here.'

'Whittle?' Sarah asked.

'He's a horrid man, so quick with his knife we wouldn't stand a chance. He's likely not in the house, at all, but he might be. I don't know, really.'

'So *that's* what's going on,' Mable said, loud and triumphant. 'I knew it. I sensed it in my bones. A *killer* in the house. Why, he'll rue the day he crossed trails with Matthew Forrest.'

Well, she'd perked up in a way that was plain astonishing.

122

She grinned and rubbed her hands together. 'He's met his match *now*, this Whistle.'

'I certainly hope so,' I allowed.

Sarah didn't seem gleeful like her grandmother. She looked worried. 'He's not as young as he was in the Indian Wars,' she said. 'His hearing isn't what it used to be.'

'Nonsense. His ears are fit as a fiddle. He hears what he wishes to hear, and that's a fact.'

We all stood silent, then, watching the door and listening. I hoped Mable was right about the General's ears. As time went on, though, I got to worrying. The revolver wouldn't do much good if Whittle crept up behind him and slit his gullet. Then Whittle'd be the one with a gun.

I wished I hadn't left the General on his own. I could've watched his back for him.

'Perhaps I should go and help him,' I finally said.

'I'll go with you,' Sarah said.

'Now quit, both of you. Matthew is perfectly capable of dealing with this Whistle character.'

'Whittle,' I corrected her this time around. 'Roderick Whittle.'

'How is it that you know such a man?' Sarah asked me.

Well, things had gone too far for lies to serve much purpose, so I said, 'He brought me from England. We sailed together. He murdered the others on the yacht, but I escaped. He no doubt believes I drowned, or he would've lurked about to have another go at me. As he landed not far from here, I feared he might've come to your house. I crept in, myself, to search for him.'

'You came here to save us?' Sarah asked.

'Yes, ma'am.'

'That was awfully noble of you.'

Her words warmed me up considerable.

'Noble if he's not giving us a pack of lies,' Mable said.

'Grandma!'

'It sounds mighty far-fetched to me. Likely as not, he was fixing to rob or murder us till he ran afoul of Matthew, and then thought better of it and made up this ridiculous story to get himself off the hook.'

'I believe him,' Sarah said.

'Why, you're just like Matthew. You're both just as gullible as can be. It wouldn't surprise me a bit if . . .'

A sharp thump on the door made us all jump. 'Open up.'

It was the General's voice.

And wasn't I glad to hear it! I didn't waste any time, but rushed on over and opened the door.

CHAPTER EIGHTEEN

Forrest Hospitality

'I've scouted all the upstairs rooms,' the General said as he came in. 'There seems to be no intruder about, but the better part of wisdom says we stick together until I'm convinced he's nowhere in the house.'

'I don't suspect he exists this side of Trevor's imagination,' Mable allowed.

'He most certainly exists,' I said. 'It's quite possible he never came into the house, though. I haven't seen him since he rowed ashore. He may have gone in quite a different direction.'

Old Mable gave me a scathing look as if she'd expected me to come out with just such an excuse.

'It never hurts to err on the side of caution,' the General said. 'Come along.'

Sarah stepped into some slippers. Then she picked up her lamp. I held back, and followed the others into the hallway. We trooped downstairs to the parlor. It was a sight warmer than the rest of the house, and must've felt good to the women.

Mable plonked herself into the General's chair and covered her legs with his blanket. Sarah set the lamp on the mantel. Then she put more wood on the fire. After replacing the screen, she squatted down close to the blaze. 'Oh,' she said, 'it does feel wonderful.'

My eyes had been on her, not on the General, so I'd missed whatever he'd been up to. He took me by surprise when he stepped close to my side. 'Take this,' he said. He gave me a pistol. It was a tiny thing, not much bigger than my palm, with a barrel about three inches long. 'If the killer shows his face while I'm gone . . .'

'Matthew! Don't you *dare*! Take that away from him!'

'Hush!'

'I *never*!'

'This is a good time to start.' To me, he said, 'All you need to do is draw back the hammer, point, and squeeze the trigger. Go for the chest.'

'Yes, sir,' I said.

'You old fool! Don't you put a gun in his hand!'

Well, he acted like he didn't hear her. Taking his lamp and his big revolver, he hurried out of the parlor.

'Matthew!' she fairly squealed. 'Matthew!'

Sarah turned her face away from the fire. 'There's no call to be throwing a conniption, Grandma.'

I took a step toward the old woman, and she flinched up tight. She studied the pistol like it was a rattlesnake. Some drool trickled down her chin.

'You hold onto it,' I told her, and offered it by the handle.

She looked at me and blinked. She blinked a few times at the gun, then at me again. She wiped the spit off her chin. Then she reached out quick and snatched away the pistol.

'I shouldn't know how to use such a thing, anyhow,' I told her.

After that, she sort of slumped down in her chair. She cradled the little gun on her lap as if it were a cup of tea. Maybe she didn't know how to use it any better than I did, but I was more confident than ever that Whittle wouldn't turn up.

He hadn't come to this house, after all. That was a relief, but a disappointment, too. Since he wasn't here, the General wouldn't get a chance to shoot him. He was on the loose, and I wondered how I'd ever manage to track him down.

The longer I stayed, the farther away he was likely to get.

That was heavy on my mind when the General returned.

'The fellow must've bypassed us,' he said.

He saw that Mable had the gun, but he let the matter lie and didn't mention it.

'The thing for us now,' he said, 'is for the rest of you to turn in. I've taken the precaution of locking the doors. I'll keep on my toes and patrol the house till dawn. Sarah, show Trevor to a guest room.'

'I should be on my way, actually,' I said. 'He's out in the night, somewhere, and the sooner I find him . . .'

'Nonsense,' Sarah broke in.

126

'Nonsense is right,' added the General. 'I won't have you straying out in the snow.'

'We had the Great Blizzard last winter,' Sarah told me. 'Some four hundred souls perished.'

'This is no blizzard, but the snow's coming down heavy. You don't want to be out in it, Trevor. You'd freeze up like a statue.'

I reckoned that was true. And I sure didn't hanker to leave the warm house. I was loath to part from the General and Sarah, too. Mable wouldn't be any great loss. But I liked the other two and they were the first really friendly folks I'd encountered in longer than a month.

Besides, there was slim chance I'd be able to find Whittle tonight.

The General, he took the little gun from Mable. She gave it up without a fight. He handed it to me. 'Keep this with you.'

'Yes, sir.'

Sarah fetched her lamp off the mantel and said, 'Come along, Trevor.'

I bid the others goodnight. Together, we left the parlor and headed for the stairs. 'Do you have a home of your own?' Sarah asked.

'Yes, ma'am. It's nothing like this, of course. Mother and I have a flat in London, England.'

'Just the two of you?'

'There's Agnes, our servant.'

'We've had servants,' Sarah said. With a soft laugh, she added, 'They never stay long. Grandma makes life too unpleasant for them.'

As we started up the stairs, she asked, 'What of your father?'

'He was a soldier. He lost his life at the Battle of Maiwand.'

'Oh. I'm awfully sorry. Your mother is all right, however? She wasn't among those you mentioned who were murdered on the boat?'

'She was safe at home when last I saw her. I left her on an errand, actually. It was something of an accident that I found myself on the yacht.'

'Then she doesn't know what's become of you?'

My throat clogged up when Sarah asked that. All I could do was nod in reply.

127

'Well then, we shall take care of it first thing in the morning. I've never been blessed with a child of my own, but I can certainly imagine how terribly worried your mother must be.'

I managed to come out with a shaky, 'Thank you.'

We entered one of the rooms just past the top of the stairs. 'I hope you'll be comfortable here. We keep the room tidy for occasional guests – mostly Grandpa's old friends from the Point.'

I saw the big bed, and it looked grand.

Sarah lit up the lamp on the table beside it, then turned around to face me. 'I'm afraid we have no suitable clothing for a young man of your size. How old are you?'

'Fifteen, ma'am. I'll be sixteen next June.'

'You're so dear,' she said. Smiling kind of sad, she reached out and petted my cheek. 'I do hope you'll be in no hurry to leave us.'

My face heated up considerable, what with her stroking it.

'I'm quite glad to be here,' I murmured.

'Goodnight, now. Sleep well. We'll see you in the morning.'

'Yes, ma'am.'

'Sarah. Please call me Sarah.'

'Sarah.'

Leaning forward, she gave my forehead a gentle kiss. Then she turned away and left me alone. Out in the hall, she took a turn to the left, so I figured she was going on to her own room. I hurried over to the doorway and watched her, mostly to make sure she didn't get jumped even though I figured Whittle was far off somewhere in the night.

She just kind of flowed along, all graceful and elegant.

She put me in mind of my mother so much it made me feel peaceful and lonesome, both at the same time.

Once she was safe in her room, I went back to the night table. I set down the little pistol. Then I shucked down to just my sweater, which was dry and hung low enough to keep me decent in case I had to get up quick. I pulled back the bed covers, snuffed the lamp, and climbed into bed.

The sheets were silk. They felt slick, and mighty cold at first. After a spell, though, they warmed up.

The bed was so soft it snuggled against me. Not a bit like my bunk on the *True D. Light*. It didn't bounce and rock and pitch this way and that, either.

I hadn't felt so comfortable in ages.

Nor so safe.

Come morning, I woke on my own. I just lay there a while, nice and warm, mighty glad to be where I was and not aboard the yacht any more. But then I got to thinking about Trudy. That took the pleasure out of lazing in bed.

I climbed out, tugged the sweater down as far as it would go, and stepped over to a window. Well, the sight of all that snow took my breath away. We had snow at home, now and again, but I'd never seen so much of it. None was falling now. It must've come down all night, though, for there to be such a load. It hung all white on the branches of the trees out there, must've been a foot thick on the roofs of the sheds and such, and looked to be knee-deep where it was stacked against the brick wall at the edge of the property. What with the sky clear, all that snow glared so white in the sun that it stung my eyes.

I saw some other houses away off in the distance, and wondered if maybe Whittle'd chosen one of them. It seemed likely. Before the notion could take a good hold on me, though, I quickly reminded myself how the General kept a pistol handy. Maybe that was a common practice in these parts, and Whittle'd gone into a house fixing to do murder and gotten himself killed for his troubles. I hung on to that idea. It helped some, but not much.

I could see a sliver of the bay from my window. It was bright blue, with white-topped waves rolling toward shore. The yacht wasn't in sight, of course. I judged it might be seen from a different corner of the house, but it wasn't a thing I wanted to look at, anyhow.

'Good morning, Trevor.'

Startled, I dragged my sweater down, stretching it toward my knees. Then I turned around.

'I hope you slept well,' Sarah said, and walked straight in.

With the daylight, I saw she was even prettier than I'd thought. Her shiny black hair was pinned up, her face rosy, her eyes bright and happy. She wore a dress that looked like green velvet and had white lace around the collar and wrists.

'I . . . I slept quite well, thank you.'

She came walking right at me. Her eyes flicked down at my bare legs. 'You must be freezing.'

I wasn't freezing at all. I was broiling. Sweat was trickling down my sides under the sweater.

'I brought these for you,' she said. For the first time, I noticed she was carrying a robe and slippers. 'They belonged to my father. They're probably too large, but they'll have to do until we can purchase a wardrobe for you.'

She handed over the robe. I had to let go of the sweater. Before it unstretched too far, though, I shook open the robe and let it drape. She crouched in front of me and set the slippers down. I was mighty glad to have the robe hanging betwixt her face and me.

'Try them on,' she said.

I stepped into the slippers. They felt a sight better than the cold floorboards. But they were too big, just as she'd said.

'Is your father away somewhere?' I asked.

From the look of loss that filled her eyes, I wished I hadn't asked. 'He died in battle some ten years ago.'

'I'm sorry.'

'We have much in common, you and I. We both lost our fathers in war. Mine was killed by the Utes at Milk Creek.'

'Utes? Are those Indians?'

She nodded, and stood up straight.

Well, she seemed to be living in the house with just her grandparents, so I allowed I wouldn't ask about her mother.

'Slip into the robe and come along now,' she said. 'I've prepared a hot bath for you downstairs.'

A hot bath!

'Smashing!'

Luckily, she turned around and went for the door. I quickly plucked off the sweater. I got the robe on and tied its belt, then followed her into the hall. We went down the stairway, and she led me toward the rear of the house where I'd never been before. No sign of the General or Mable.

The kitchen was nice and warm with a fire in the stove. Off to one side, a door stood open. We went in, and there stood a tub chockful of water so hot, steam was rising off it.

'I'll go and fetch some of Papa's clothes for you,' Sarah said. 'They'll be too big, of course, but they'll have to do until we get you to a store.'

'Thank you,' I said.

I waited till she'd cleared out. She left the door open,

more than likely to let heat keep coming in from the kitchen. But nobody was in sight, so I stripped off and climbed into the tub.

The water near scalded me. It was dandy! I hadn't taken a proper bath since the Wednesday night before I'd set out from home. Not that I'd been a stranger to water in all that time, what with a few dips in the ocean and waves splashing me and getting myself showered by squalls so often. The sea water'd always left me salty and itchy. Every *drop* of water, whether it came from the ocean or the sky, had been just frigid.

So I was mighty glad to be in a tubful of hot water, even if it was sort of boiling me.

I lay there, just enjoying it for a spell. Then I soaped myself down and ducked under to get the suds out of my hair. When I came up for a breath, here was Sarah coming in with a bundle of clothes. The water was murky enough to hide my lower parts, thank goodness.

She put down a pair of shoes, then set herself in a chair with the other things on her lap and took to chatting with me. When she asked if I had any brothers or sisters and I said no, she allowed as how that was another thing we had in common. She'd been the only child of her parents. She went on from there, and told how she'd spent most of her early years in boarding schools because her mother had died of pneumonia when Sarah was only six, and her father had been a cavalry officer always on the move from one outpost to another out west until he wound up in Colorado and got himself killed by the Utes in seventy-nine. Later, she'd lived in Syracuse and taught at a girls' school until two years ago when her grandfather, the General, retired from the army. That's when she moved in here to live with him and Mable.

She said she cooked and cleaned house and did the shopping for them. As much as she appreciated them, however, she admitted she found herself lonesome for companionship of folks nearer to her own age. That's how come she was so glad I'd turned up last night.

I could see how it might wear on a person, spending night and day with nobody about except a couple of codgers. Even *interesting* codgers like the General would likely get tiresome if they were your only company, and I'd already noticed that Mable wasn't much fun at all.

Still, though, it seemed a trifle excessive for Sarah to be

enjoying her new friend while he sat naked in a bathtub.

She kept chatting along until my water lost most of its heat and I commenced to shiver. She finally noticed. Maybe my lips were looking blue.

She fetched me a towel, and said, 'You get dressed while I start breakfast.'

She went into the kitchen. I could see her through the doorway, but she wasn't paying any mind to me, so I climbed out and dried myself. I shut the door and used the toilet, then hurried into the clothes. From the size of things, her dead papa was taller and leaner than Trudy's.

Seemed like I'd never get shut of wearing dead father duds.

After rolling the sleeves and trouser legs out of my way, I joined up with Sarah in front of the stove.

It looked like she only had enough ham and eggs in the skillet for two.

'Where are Mable and the General?' I asked.

'I suppose they're sleeping. I heard Grandpa prowling about the house last night, and he probably didn't turn in until after sunrise.'

'It appears I came along on a false alarm,' I told her.

'Perhaps you were led here by Providence.'

I gave that notion some pondering, and judged she might be right. Taken all around, I was mighty lucky to still be alive. So maybe the Lord had plans for me. Likely, He aimed for me to send Whittle packing south for hell.

If that's what He had in mind, though, He could've done it Himself easy enough by sending the *True D. Light* to the bottom of the sea.

I would've gone down with her, of course.

So maybe there was more to all this than met the eye.

CHAPTER NINETEEN

The Yacht and the Horse

We ate a splendid meal of ham and eggs and rolls, all washed down with hot coffee. It was better than anything I'd tasted in a long time, considering we'd run out of eggs and fresh meat on the yacht after just a couple of weeks at sea. After that, we'd had only flour and potatoes that didn't come out of tins. I'd gotten a mite tired of it all.

I still had my mind on Providence, and was glad He'd sent me here for such a breakfast. I thanked Him in my head. While I was at it, I let Him know I'd appreciated the bed and bath, as well, and allowed He'd done a good job sending me to these people.

When we were done eating, I helped Sarah clear things. Then we stood at the sink together, her washing while I dried. Back home, Agnes had taken care of such matters. I didn't mind helping, however, and Sarah seemed to enjoy the job.

We'd no sooner finished than the General and Mable showed up. The General, he clapped me on the shoulder. 'That killer of yours must've known better and stayed clear of us,' he said.

'We were quite fortunate, then,' I told him.

'Fortunate.' Mable huffed. 'Never *was* such a scoundrel, in my opinion.'

If she wished to take a hike through the snow, I thought, I could show her a couple of bodies that might change her tune on that account. But I kept mum.

'We ought to alert the authorities,' the General said, 'so they can keep a look-out for him.'

'Trevor and I might take care of that while we're in town. He's in sorry need of new clothes, and we want to cable his mother in England so she'll know he's safe.'

'Nonsense!' Mable blurted. 'Send him off. We've got no use for him.'

'He's a child, dear,' the General told her.

'He's all alone in this country,' Sarah added, 'without a soul to look after him. Except us. The Lord guided him to our door.'

'Don't you go *Lording* at me, girl.'

'Trevor did us a fine service,' the General said. 'He came here to give us a warning. Besides, he seems a fine fellow to me.' He gave my shoulder another slap. 'Young man, you're welcome to remain under our roof for as long as it pleases you. So long as you behave yourself.'

'Thank you, sir.'

'I'll be *switched* if I'll have this rascal . . .'

'And you'll treat him *friendly*, dear, or I'll have to put you out in the snow.'

Well, she sank down on a chair and glowered at me.

Sarah took to fixing breakfast for the two of them.

By and by, I escaped and went upstairs. The General's talk about notifying authorities had unsettled me some. What with a couple of bodies in the yacht and nobody around to blame but me, I feared I might find myself in a spot of trouble.

At the end of the hallway was a window. I peered out. Down below were the rear grounds of the house, along with the trees and gazebo and such I'd roamed through last night, and the wall. Everything was piled high with snow. The sun had gotten itself swallowed by clouds, so the snow wasn't glaring white any more, but gray and gloomy.

Off beyond the wall, the land sloped down to the shore of the bay. I didn't see foot tracks anywhere. I looked to where the skiff should have been, but couldn't spot it. Likely as not, the snowfall had buried it.

Then I scanned along the beach to the right and braced myself. My heart took to pounding up a storm. I didn't much *want* to see the *True D. Light*, but that's what I'd come to the window for. I rather expected to find her crawling with local folks and constables.

The snowy beach stretched alongside the waves for about half a mile that I could see. Nobody was there.

The yacht wasn't there, either.

I stood peering out the window, searching this way and that, puzzling over the mystery, and then I spotted a ship far out on the rough, slate-colored water.

The sight sent a cold wind blowing through my bones.

I knew she was the *True D. Light.*

It must've been low tide when I beached her.

I hadn't bothered to drop anchor or reef the mainsail.

So now she was flying along with her sail full of wind, carrying Trudy and Michael on a journey to nowhere.

I got goosebumps all over.

Quick as I could, I rushed downstairs to the warm kitchen and live people.

We left the General and Mable to their breakfast. Sarah fetched me a pair of boots and leather gloves, a heavy coat and a hat. More of her dead father's things. She got bundled up, herself. Then we went out the front door and trudged across the snow to the stable.

It was on the left side of the house, where I hadn't seen it till now. It was plenty big. We hauled at the double doors. When they came open, they shoved swaths across the snow.

I looked in.

All of a sudden, I remembered the pistol the General'd given to me last night. It was still on the table by my bed. I felt a proper fool for leaving it there.

The stable wasn't exactly dark inside, but it wasn't bright by a long shot.

Sarah started through the doorway, but I grabbed her arm. She frowned at me – not like she was angry, only curious. 'What is it?' she asked.

'I shouldn't like to think that Whittle might be hiding in there.'

'He'd be silly, don't you think, to spend the night in a cold stable with a house so handy?'

How could I argue with that?

Still, though, I felt right jittery and kept my eyes sharp as we went inside.

I let go of her arm. She took hold of mine, though. Spite of what she'd said, she must've been worried.

We stopped before going in too deep, and looked around.

The place smelled like hay, mostly, but had a few other aromas that weren't so sweet. Near the front were a couple of carriages, one fancier than the other, and a sleigh that had two rows of seats. The walls of the place were all hung with tools and tack.

135

We walked in farther, to where the horses were. There were stalls to hold four of them, but the gate of the last stall stood open.

Sarah pulled up short and let out a quiet gasp. 'My Lord,' she said. She didn't release my arm, but dragged me along beside her. We hurried past the first three stalls. The horses, seeing us, snorted and snuffled. White plumes blew out of their nostrils.

The fourth stall was empty.

Sarah gazed into it, breathing hard, puffing out clouds of white. 'He's taken Saber,' she murmured. 'Wait here. I've got to tell Grandpa.'

She let go my arm and rushed off.

I wasn't keen on being left alone, but she was hardly out the doors before it came to me I needn't worry about getting jumped by Whittle. He'd come along last night, after all. It had been a mighty narrow call for the General and the women, for he must've been tempted to take over the house. He'd chosen, instead, to pinch a horse and light out.

It spooked me some, knowing he'd been here. But he was likely miles and miles away, by now. Any chap who would filch a horse on a snowy night, when he had a chance to hole up in a nice warm house, aimed to do some hard traveling.

In a way, it was good to know we were safe from him. It troubled me, though, that he'd gotten away. I had half a mind to grab a horse and chase after him.

More than half a mind, really.

It was what I ought to do.

But with such a headstart, and any direction to choose from except toward the water, he'd be near impossible to run down. Besides, there I would be in a strange land in the dead of winter, no money, no clothes but the borrowed ones on my back. And the folks here, they'd been awfully good to me. Making off with one of their horses would be a dirty play, and give Mable reason to bully the General and Sarah.

If all that weren't enough cause to hold me off, there was knowing that I'd miss out on my chance to cable Mother. She deserved to know, straight away, I wasn't dead after all.

So I gave up the notion of chasing after Whittle.

It seemed I was letting down everybody he'd killed, especially poor Trudy, but I judged I owed more to the living. The dead weren't likely to appreciate my efforts, anyhow.

136

Well, that led me to thinking about those Whittle hadn't killed *yet* – the ones he'd be butchering down the road a piece unless I stopped him.

They complicated things considerable, and I commenced to figure maybe I'd better take a horse, after all. By then, however, it was too late.

Sarah came striding along, frowning. She didn't have the General with her.

'Best not to tell him,' she said. 'If he finds out Saber's been stolen, he'll saddle up and ride off, and he won't come back empty-handed. He's too old for such shenanigans, but that's exactly what he'd do.'

We could go together! I thought.

Before I got my mouth open to suggest it, Sarah said, 'The way his health is, I doubt we'd ever see him again. But would that stop him? No, I hardly think so. Why, he would rather die and leave Grandma a widow than allow a horse-thief to get away from him.'

'He's certain to learn the horse has gone missing,' I pointed out.

'We'll leave the stable door open. Saber always did have a feisty nature. He's run off before. I'll simply explain that he was here when we set out for town. That won't throw Grandpa into such a tizzy as if he takes a notion that Saber's been stolen.'

Sarah wasn't just pretty, but had a sharp mind to boot. It bothered me that she was given to such trickery, but the way she had it figured, she was deceiving the general for his own good.

I told her the plan was quite clever.

She opened the gate of a stall that had a huge gelding inside named Howitzer. The name was embroidered in gold on his blue blanket. After pulling the blanket off him, Sarah walked him toward the front of the stable. There, I helped harness him to the sleigh.

Outside, snow was drifting down.

'Perfect,' Sarah said. 'It'll cover Saber's tracks.'

Well, Saber had no tracks that needed covering, as he was long gone. What Sarah meant was that the snow might hide the tracks Saber *would've* made, if he'd been here this morning and wandered off.

We stuck to her plot, and left the stable doors open.

Then we both climbed into the sleigh. Sarah sat down

close against me and spread a blanket across our laps. Then she picked up the reins, gave them a shake, called out, 'Gee-yup,' and off we went.

Sarah steered us away from the house. We glided past trees and a fountain with no water in it but that had a statue of Bacchus, who was sticking a grape in his mouth and wore nothing except for snow heaped here and there, and looked to be freezing.

We stopped at the wall's front gate. It was shut. Whittle must've taken time to dismount and close it after him, so folks wouldn't catch on he'd been here.

'I'll see to it,' I said as Sarah reined in.

'Leave it open a bit for Saber,' she told me, still keeping her mind on our ruse.

I hopped into the snow, swung the gate wide, and waited while Sarah 'gee-yupped' Howitzer then 'whoaed' him once they'd gotten to the other side. I left the gate standing open some, rushed ahead and climbed into the sleigh. It felt good to have the blanket on my legs again.

After we took a turn to the right, Sarah clucked a few times and Howitzer commenced to trot along at a smart pace. We fairly flew over the snow, the wind and flakes in our faces.

'Would you care to take the reins?' she asked.

'Smashing.'

I took the leather straps from her and gave them a shake. Howitzer checked over his shoulder, let out a snort of white steam, then faced the front again and kept on trotting. His hooves thumped quiet through the snow. The only other sounds came from him huffing, and the sleigh runners hissing along, the harness creaking and jangling, and bells on the harness tinkling out real merry.

It was all just uncommon peaceful.

'We'll be to Coney Island in no time,' Sarah told me, and gave my thigh a pat under the blanket. She smiled at me. Her cheeks were ruddy, her eyes moist from the weather. 'It's a shame you didn't arrive in the summer. People come from miles around. It's just so lively and gay.' She squeezed my leg. 'If you stay, you'll see for yourself. You *will* stay, won't you?'

Stay till *summer*? The notion stunned me. I didn't know how to answer, and wished she hadn't asked. By and by, I said, 'I shouldn't like to impose on your hospitality.'

'You'd be doing us a great favor. You could help with the chores and keep me company. We'd have a wonderful time.'

'It sounds splendid, really,' I told her. 'If it weren't for Mother . . .'

'I know. I'm sorry. You must miss her terribly.'

'I rather imagine she should like me home with her.'

'Does she have the means to pay for your return voyage?'

The question knocked me flat.

'The means?' I asked, though I knew precisely what she meant.

'Financially.'

My hesitation was all the answer Sarah needed.

'No matter,' she said. 'Stay on with us, and we'll pay you a wage. That way, you'll be able to purchase your own ticket home, and not work any hardship at all on your mother.'

She said it kindly enough, but it let the wind out of my sails, anyhow. All along, I'd known that getting home to England would be no easy trick. Most of the time, though, I'd been so worried about getting killed by Whittle or the ocean that I hadn't given much thought to the problem. When I'd considered what to do on the slim chance I survived, I'd always figured I'd find a way to get back, somehow, sooner or later.

Sarah's offer seemed to be the solution. All I needed to do was stay on long enough to earn the ship's fare. That sure seemed better than asking Mother to scrape up the funds. I reckon I should've felt mighty grateful. Instead, though, I had this kind of trapped feeling.

'It seems like a fine idea,' I finally said.

'Wonderful. We'll let your mother know of your plans.'

'You don't suppose Mable will object, do you?'

'Oh, she may whine and complain a bit. But we won't let that bother us.'

Well, by this time we'd left behind the few houses I'd been able to spot from my bedroom window. More came along, though. They got smaller, closer together. Pretty soon, they fairly lined the road. There were some street lamps, too, and I could see a town up ahead.

This looked to be the main street. Sarah took the reins from me, and slowed Howitzer. We went gliding past a few other sleighs, and some folks on horseback. I gave all the horsemen a study, not really figuring any of them was Whittle, but checking on them just the same.

Plenty of people were on foot, going and coming from various markets and shops and public houses. A good many of the establishments appeared to be shut, but some were open.

Just on the other side of a big hotel, Sarah pulled off to the side. We climbed down, and she wrapped the reins around a hitching post. I followed her onto a boardwalk and into a shop called Western Union. Nobody in there but us and a fellow behind the counter.

'I'd like a message sent to England,' Sarah told the chap.

'That's what I'm here for,' he said, real chipper. He slipped a form across to her and slapped a pencil down on it. 'Give me the name and address of the party she goes to. Put that right there.' He pointed to a space at the top of the form. 'Message goes here. And down here, I'll need your name and whereabouts if you'll be expecting a reply. We'll deliver it to you the day she comes in, if you live hereabouts.'

'We reside at the Forrest house,' Sarah told him.

Hearing that, he grinned. He had an upper tooth gone, right in front, and the remainder of his choppers looked just about ripe to follow its example. 'You're the General's granddaughter, then. And who's this young man?'

'He's our house guest from London,' Sarah told him.

'Trevor Bentley,' I said.

Sarah passed the paper across to me. I penciled in Mother's name and the address of our lodging on Marylebone High Street, London W1, England. While I puzzled over what to tell her, the fellow said, 'She's pay by the word, so you want to be brief.'

Well, they stood there waiting, so I wrote quick. 'Dear Mother, shanghaied to America, safe now. Will work for General Forrest and earn my fare home. Hope you are well. Your loving son, Trevor.'

Sarah handed it over to the fellow. After she paid him, he allowed we might get an answer in two or three days if the party chose to make a prompt reply. Said he'd have a boy deliver it to the General's house.

Then we were off. I felt mighty good about getting that cable sent to Mother, and thanked Sarah for it.

'It ought to lift a terrible burden from her heart.'

140

When she said that, I choked up some. My eyes watered, but I turned away so she wouldn't notice.

We waited for a rider to pass, then hurried across the street and went into a general store. It seemed we were in there forever, Sarah picking out this and that for me. We ended up with a whole passel of things – everything from a toothbrush to boots and house slippers, socks and longjohns and trousers, shirts and sweaters and a waistcoat, a jacket, even a nightshirt and robe. The whole pile cost her a bundle of money. But she hadn't more than got done paying for it than she hauled out her purse again and bought us each a licorice stick, a copy of the New York *World* for the General, and a sack of chestnuts for Mable.

We hauled our load on back to the sleigh, and it was a good thing there was only the two of us, or we never would've managed to fit it all in.

We boarded, and Sarah turned us around and we started heading back out of town.

She said, 'I hope we're not forgetting anything.'

I shook my head, even though I remembered we'd told the General we would stop at the constabulary and give information about Whittle. No point in reminding Sarah, though. If she'd forgotten, that suited me.

I couldn't see how it mattered. The *True D. Light* had carried off Michael and Trudy, so there weren't any bodies to account for. And Whittle, he likely hadn't stopped riding yet and wouldn't ever be showing up anywhere close to this town. So I didn't see any advantage, at all, to telling on him. It might only serve to stir up trouble for me.

When we got back to the house, the General forgot to ask if we'd gone to the authorities. He was too much in a frenzy about Saber getting loose. The three of us went outside and hunted high and low for the horse, till by and by the General allowed we ought to give up. Saber'd run off before, he said, and would probably wander back in his own good time.

I knew better, of course, but didn't set him straight.

CHAPTER TWENTY

Christmas and After

Two days before Christmas, a boy from Western Union came along with a telegram. It read, DEAREST TREVOR MY HEART IS FULL WITH NEWS THAT YOU ARE WELL STOP I LONG TO HAVE YOU HOME STOP WRITE TO ME AND STAY SAFE STOP I MISS YOU STOP ALL MY LOVE MOTHER

The message made me miss her something awful, so I sat down straight away in the General's study and wrote a long letter to her.

I scribbled on about what had happened to me after going to fetch Uncle William, and brought her all the way up to the present, telling her what nice people Sarah and the General were, and how I'd be working here at the house until I could afford a return ticket. Of course, I made no mention of a few items. Figured she was better off not knowing about me and Sue in the alley, or how I'd stabbed the whore's confederate, or about me hiding under Mary's bed when Whittle killed her, or even how he'd killed everyone on the boat except me. Knowing such matters wouldn't likely ease Mother's mind any.

I did tell her that Jack the Ripper was Roderick Whittle, and how he'd chased me to the Thames, and how I'd been his prisoner until we reached the shores of America where I escaped from him. She could pass the information on to Uncle William, and he could let the news out to everyone. It'd come as a great relief to the authorities – not to mention the East End whores – that Jack the Ripper would no longer be prowling the streets.

The next day, Sarah and I rode into town again. She sent me into the store with some money to purchase tobacco for the General while she took my letter to the post office for me.

The day after that, Christmas happened. It only made me

sad, mostly. I longed more than ever to be at home. It had always been a jolly time, with parties and caroling, a great feast at Uncle's house with goose and plum pudding and such, and getting ambushed under the mistletoe by folks I'd never let kiss me otherwise. We always had a Christmas tree on the parlor table all bright with tapers and fancy doodads. I wondered if Mother had put up a tree this year without me there, and thought how lonesome she must be. She wouldn't be getting my letter for a few weeks, but at least my cable must've perked her up some.

Christmas was pretty much like any other day at the Forrest place, only gloomier. We didn't even have a tree. According to Sarah, the General and Mable were down on Christmas because they had no family except her and didn't enjoy being reminded of the fine old times they used to have.

The General sat around morose in the parlor, smoking his pipe and drinking rum till he fell asleep at midday.

Mable, she went for a walk and disappeared. Sarah and I had to go out hunting for her. We found her about halfway to town, crouched down a ways off the road, digging in the snow. She gave us kind of a scatter-brained look and said she was aiming to pick some posies.

We loaded her onto the sleigh and took her home. Sarah told me this sort of thing had happened a few times before. Every now and again, the old lady would slip a cog and wander off. 'It's her age,' Sarah explained.

Back at the house, we tucked Mable into bed. The General was still snoring in the parlor. We hadn't gotten any chance to eat, so Sarah set to work on making some chowder.

We ate by candlelight in the dining room, just the two of us. Sarah could see I was feeling low, and tried to cheer me up. She poured us some red wine, and we 'Merry Christmased' each other and sipped at it. The wine tasted sweet and sent a warmth through me. But it put me in mind of the rum I'd drunk in Mary's room, and that reminded me of things that didn't improve my mood any.

After the chowder was gone, we kept sitting there and drinking the wine.

By and by, Sarah told me she'd be back in a minute and I should stay put. Feeling plain miserable, I helped myself to another glassful. Well, along she came hiding one hand behind her, and knelt beside my chair. I scooched it away from the table, and turned it toward her. 'Close your eyes,

Trevor,' she said. I shut them. When she told me to open, I looked and she was dangling a gold watch in front of me by its chain. 'Merry Christmas,' she said.

My throat clutched and my eyes watered up. I couldn't say a thing. She put the watch into my hand and I studied it. The timepiece was blurry, so I had to blink before I could make out the crossed revolvers engraved on its case.

'It's . . . grand,' I finally managed to stammer out. 'Thank you ever so much.'

'It belonged to my father,' she said. 'I want you to have it.'

'I shouldn't . . . really.'

'Certainly you should. You'll never know how much joy you've brought into my life. You must keep it always.'

'I . . . I do wish I had a gift to give you.'

'You might give me a kiss.'

With that, she uncrouched some. Hands on my knees, she leaned forward and turned her cheek to me. I kissed it. Then she faced me and looked me in the eyes.

'I know you miss your mother awfully,' she said. 'I do wish you *could* be with her, on this day especially.'

I nodded, and wished the tears would quit running down my cheeks.

'I doubt I'll ever be blessed with a child of my own,' Sarah went on.

'Oh, certainly you . . .'

She touched a finger to my lips. 'If I *did* have a son, I hope he would be as fine a young man as yourself.'

Then *she* took to weeping.

She sank to her knees and crossed her arms on my legs and buried her face and gasped and sobbed. I set my new watch on the table.

'Don't cry,' I said. 'It's all right.'

She kept at it. I patted her back and stroked her hair. Finally, she stood up. She straightened her dress and sniffled a few times. 'I'm sorry,' she murmured. 'I don't know . . .' And suddenly she was bawling all over again, even harder than before.

I got to my feet and put my arms around her.

We stood there, mashing each other tight, both of us sobbing to beat the band.

It took a while, but we finally got worn out and stopped our crying. We didn't let go of each other, though. It felt mighty comfortable to be hugging her, even though I knew she wasn't my mother and she knew I wasn't her son.

When we unclenched, she tried to smile. Her face was all red and slick with tears, her eyes ashimmer. She looked just lovely. 'Aren't we the silly ones, though?' she said. 'Carrying on that way?'

I didn't know what to say. Sarah brushed the tears off my cheeks with her fingertips. Then she kissed my mouth, real gentle and sweet.

Not long after that, I went on up to my room and turned in. Taken all around, it had been a mighty strange Christmas. I spent a while puzzling over things, but my head was all foggy from the wine and before I knew it I was asleep.

Sarah woke me up the next morning with a kiss. She took to doing that every morning. Each night she'd come into my room at bedtime. We'd usually chat a spell, then she'd kiss me goodnight and go on her way.

In between, we looked after the General and Mable. I helped prepare meals, clean the house, and care for the horses. About once a week, Sarah and I went into town. We took the sleigh sometimes, or a carriage when the road was clear. There in town, we always bought supplies and a copy of the *World*, and Sarah always fixed us up with licorice sticks. Sometimes, when the weather was good, we wandered over to the beach. A boardwalk was there, with all sorts of shops and booths and bath houses and pavilions and rides and such, but they were shut down for the winter. Sarah, she never failed to go on considerable about what a bully time we would be having there, come summer.

The way my savings were stacking up, a dollar each week, I could see I'd still be around through summer, and likely for a few summers more. I didn't know how much a boat ticket for England might cost, but it had to be dear.

Well, my spirits sank some whenever I thought about it. Mostly, though, I was fairly happy to be where I was. Sarah treated me real good. The General, he seemed to like having me around. Even old Mable warmed up to me. She bossed me something frightful, but didn't get snappish too often.

There were times when I went for whole days without giving a thought to Whittle. I figured I was safe, and he was far away somewhere. For all I knew, he might've gone and gotten himself killed. I sure hoped so.

Every time we came back from town with a new edition of

the *World*, though, I hunted through it. I checked each story, half afraid I'd find one about a butchery and know Whittle was up to his old tricks.

There were murders aplenty reported in that newspaper. Folks were forever getting themselves shot or bludgeoned or strangled or stabbed. For a while, though, I didn't find anything that looked like Whittle's work.

It was the middle of January when I came across a story about a woman 'of low character' named Bess who was found 'unspeakably mutilated' in a place called Hell's Kitchen. That sure set my heart to thundering. But I read on a bit, and the paper said a fellow named Argus Tate had been nabbed for it.

As the weeks went by, I found half a dozen more stories about women getting cut up. More often than not, it happened in Hell's Kitchen or Chelsea. I didn't tell Sarah why I was interested, but asked her about those places and she said they were in Manhattan, across the East River from us. When she let out that they were only just fifteen or twenty miles from us and you could cross the river by a bridge or boat, I felt rather squirmy inside.

You could get there in a *day*. Whittle could get *here* in a day.

Of course, it might not be him that was killing those gals. That's what I told myself. I had to tell myself that, because otherwise it'd be my duty to go after him. I allowed I'd stay where I was unless I knew for sure it had to be Whittle over there.

I kept on checking the newspaper, and always hoped nothing would turn up to make it Whittle for certain.

My studies of the *World* didn't take much time. In between chores and trips to town and such, I trekked through a good many of the books in the General's parlor. I read a heap of Shakespeare and Charles Dickens and Stevenson and Scott. I had a go at some tales by Edgar Allan Poe, but gave up quick on those, for they reminded me of when I'd tried to read one on the *True D. Light* and gotten woozy. I wanted no truck with anything that put me in mind of that yacht or Whittle.

The books I liked best were those about America. I read plenty of Mark Twain, and even got to finish *Huckleberry Finn*, which I'd left hanging the night Mother dragged

Barnes home drunk and I set off to hunt for Uncle William. I read all the *Leatherstocking Saga* by Cooper, and bunches of stories by Bret Harte. They gave me an awful hankering to see the Mississippi and the great forests and plains and mountains, and gold fields and the like. I longed to travel and have adventures.

Every now and then, I took a notion to light out for the West. I dreamed about it, but knew I was meant to stay with the Forrests until I could earn enough money for my return to England.

Besides, I heard tales from the General that made me glad to be safe in the civilized East.

After my goodnight kiss from Sarah, I often crept downstairs to the parlor and sat for hours with the General. We'd sit in front of the fireplace, him smoking his pipe, both of us taking sips of rum, and he'd talk on and on about his times with the Army.

He told me about West Point, and about Civil War battles, but mostly he liked to talk about his experiences during the Indian Wars.

Back on the yacht, Whittle had gone on considerable about going West and joining up with savages. If he'd had a chance to chat with Matthew Forrest, though, I reckon he might've sung a different tune. For one thing, most of the Indians were already killed or tame by now. For another, they did things to white men that would've made any reasonable chap eager to stay clear of them.

The General went on considerable about such horrors. I don't know if he just enjoyed trying to shock me, or if he *had* to talk about them. Maybe it was both.

Scalping seemed like a frightful thing, but that wasn't the worst of it.

Whenever the Indians had a chance to work on dead men, they stripped them naked and not only scalped them but packed them full of arrows and cut off their heads and arms and legs and privates and scattered such things about. It sounded just as bad as what Whittle'd done to Mary and Trudy.

The redskins didn't usually do such things to women, though, so Whittle had them beat there. They mostly hung on to the white women, and abused them, and kept them for slaves.

The General told me the two main rules of Indian fighting: don't let the heathens capture your women, and don't let them take you alive.

When women were at risk, you had to kill them. If it came down to one bullet left, and you had a choice of whether to plug an Indian warrior or your wife, why there wasn't any choice to be made. You shot your wife in the head.

He told me about a time when it looked as if the Sioux and Cheyennes might overrun Fort Phil Kearney, so the soldiers put all the women and children inside the magazine and left an officer with them who was supposed to touch off the powder and blow them all to smithereens rather than let the Indians take them alive. Fortunately, it didn't come to that.

He said the worst thing, next to letting them get their hands on women, was to let them take *you* alive.

One thing they liked to do was to strip a fellow naked and stake him out on the ground. Then they'd build a fire by one of his feet. When that foot was good and crisp, they'd cook the other, and then the legs and arms. They took their time about it, too. When they finally got tired of it all, they'd build a fire on the poor chap's chest and that would finish him.

Another favorite sport was to hang their captive upside down over a low fire. The head would cook real slow. By and by, though, it'd explode.

Sometimes, a white man would get turned over to the squaws. The General clammed up about what manner of games the squaws played on their prisoners, so I judged it must've been a sight worse than what he *had* told me. That was hard to imagine, though.

The upshot was, you'd rather be dead than captured.

If things got nip and tuck, you always saved your last bullet for yourself.

He told me about a time he found himself and his troops surrounded. He had a revolver for himself, but plenty of the others didn't. They only had rifles, so before the Indians came whooping down at them, every one of them tied a string around his rifle trigger and put a loop at the other end. That way, when it came down to the last round, they could put the rifles' barrels to their heads and use the toes of their boots to pull the triggers. Well, they got out of that scrape all right, but the General said it was common, when he came upon a massacre, to find whole passels of men who'd shot their own women and children, and followed it up with a bullet for themselves.

It made me sick to hear about such things, and to think about them afterwards. Putting a gun to your own head seemed mighty extreme, but for a man to shoot his wife and children or anyone else he loved – it made me shudder.

One time, I asked the General how he felt about it. He took a pull on his pipe, and let the smoke out slow, then said, 'There are many fates worse than death. Slow torture at the hands of the red man, that's one of them. Another is to lose those you love. A bullet in the brain-pan is quick and merciful next to either of those circumstances.'

I never told him about Trudy. But I spent considerable time worrying my head about the way she'd ended. Getting done by Indians was no worse than how Whittle'd butchered her. I took to feeling guilty about saving her life. If I'd let her hang or drown and not been so quick at jumping to the rescue, she would've been spared from his knife. The trouble is, I'd *known* it. Even while I'd been working to save her those times, I'd known she might be better off dead. But I'd gone ahead and saved her anyhow.

Maybe I didn't have it within me to do otherwise. But after hearing all the General had to say about saving a bullet for the woman, I knew I'd done wrong.

CHAPTER TWENTY-ONE

Losses

Early in April, on a rainy Tuesday afternoon, Mable went roaming off. She'd pulled such stunts five or six times before, always sneaking out of the house when the rest of us were busy. On this particular day, the General was snoozing by the fire and I stayed in the kitchen to keep Sarah company while she baked cookies. It wasn't till the cookies were done and we carried out a plate so the General and Mable could enjoy some hot ones that we noticed she'd gone missing again.

It always fell on me and Sarah to go hunting for her, as Sarah didn't want the General out in the weather for fear he'd come down with pneumonia or such. Besides that, he never worried much about his wife's disappearances.

I came back to the parlor after a quick search of the house and shook my head. 'She seems to have gone off,' I said.

Sarah winced.

The General swallowed a mouthful of cookie and said, 'Yes. There's been a palpable, refreshing silence for the past hour or so. My eardrums have greatly appreciated the respite.'

'Grandpa!'

'Oh, now, no need to worry your head about Mable. I believe she only takes her little jaunts for the fun of being retrieved.'

'It's *pouring* outside.'

'The rain'll do her good. She hasn't bathed in a fortnight.'

That was on account of me, I reckon. Sarah'd woken me up a couple weeks ago and after giving me my morning smooch, she'd said a hot bath was waiting for me. It had gotten to be a fairly regular thing. Every few days, she would prepare my bath bright and early so I could have it before the General and Mable got around to stirring. I'd go down and soak, then by and by she'd come along with coffee for both of us. She'd sit on her chair near the tub, and we'd have a nice chat while we sipped. Later on, she'd come over and scrub my back for me.

I'd found the business a trifle embarrassing the first few times, but that passed as I got used to it. Then I got to where I really looked forward to those baths.

Sarah took her baths on the days between mine. When she finished, she'd come into my room all fresh and rosy from the heat, her hair still damp. I always stayed in bed and waited for her.

It usually ran through my mind, while I was waiting, that maybe I could head downstairs and take coffee to *her*, and stay and chat and maybe wash her back for her. The notion made me feel a bit squirmy. It also put my mind at ease, though, for the way I got stirred up by thinking about Sarah in the tub made it clear Whittle hadn't ruined women for me, after all. I purely longed to go down and visit her, but I felt guilty about it. After all, Sarah was some ten years older than me and often put me in mind of Mother, so it didn't seem right.

I let her go on bathing alone, figuring if she wanted me to join her, she ought to ask.

It bothered me considerable that she never asked, but allowed she must have her reasons, so I never let on that our bathing ritual seemed a mite one-sided and unfair. Besides, whenever I *imagined* her asking, it wrecked my nerves so bad I judged I'd likely turn down the invitation.

Anyhow, on that particular morning two weeks before Mable wandered off into the rain, I put on my slippers and robe and hurried downstairs. Sarah had gone on ahead of me. I figured to find her in the kitchen, starting the coffee. But she wasn't there, so I waltzed on into the bathroom.

Mable must've thought the bath was meant for her.

She'd beaten me to it, but not by much. She wasn't in, yet. With one foot on the floor, she was holding on to the edge of the tub while she swung her other leg over the side. Of course, she didn't have a stitch of clothes on.

She hadn't seen me. I should've stepped out quick and silent, but I didn't.

Not that I took any pleasure from the sight of her. Not by a long shot. But I was so surprised to find her climbing into my tub that I just stood there, gaping.

Her face was all dark and wrinkled like old wood. So were her hands. But the rest of Mable, mostly, was white except for a passel of blue veins and looked maybe thirty years younger than her face. She was so skinny her bones showed through her skin. The way she was bent over, her breasts dangled. They were long and rather flat, and hanging so low the nipple of one rubbed the rim of the tub.

I saw all that pretty quick, and then I noticed her scars. When I saw those, I gasped. Must've been fifteen or twenty of them, though I never got a chance to count. Puffy pink scars, each about an inch long, on her rump and down the backs of both her legs. I'd pretty much gotten used to Mable's limp, but seeing all those nasty scars made me realize why she hobbled.

Well, the gasp gave me away.

Mable looked over her shoulder and let out a frightful squeal. I hot-footed into the kitchen. Safe outside the door, I called in, 'I'm frightfully sorry, Mable.'

'You'll *be* sorry when I lay my hands on you. Land *sakes*! A woman can't bathe in her own house! Sarah! SARAH!'

Sarah rushed into the kitchen. She saw me standing there flustered. Then she fetched a glance at the open bathroom door. Then her cheeks colored considerable and her mouth dropped. 'Oh, my,' she said.

Mable must've heard her. 'You get in here right *now* and shut the door! That horrid child's been *spying* on me!'

Sarah went into the bathroom and closed the door. I heard Mable rail on at her for a spell, and Sarah talking soft and reasonable, explaining the mistake. By and by, Mable settled down and Sarah came out.

She met my eyes. She was blushing fierce. 'It's all right,' she told me. 'In the future, we'll both need to be more careful. It must've been horribly embarrassing for you.'

'I do hope Mable will forgive me.'

'I made it clear that you had no intention of spying on her, and that the bath was intended for you.'

'I never . . . meant to look at her.'

'Oh, I know, I know.' Smiling a bit sadly, Sarah stroked my hair. 'After all, you've had every opportunity to spy on *me*, if your inclination leaned toward such things. You've never done that, have you?'

'Why, no. Certainly not.'

'I'm sure you haven't,' she said, but the look she gave me

was uncommon peculiar and set my face burning. Pretty soon, she said, 'You'd best have your bath another day.'

Then we went over to the sink, and Sarah pumped water into a pot. I added some wood to the stove, working up my courage, then asked, 'What happened to Mable's legs?'

She hoisted an eyebrow.

'I only glimpsed her for a blink, really, but . . .'

'Grandpa's never told you about that? All those nights you sneak downstairs and talk with him till all hours?'

I hadn't known Sarah was aware of all that. She'd done some spying herself, apparently.

'What happened to her?' I asked.

'If Grandpa hasn't told you, perhaps he'd rather you not know.'

'I suppose I might ask him about it tonight,' I said.

'Don't you dare. For heaven's sake, Trevor.'

'I won't, then.'

She set the pot of water on the stove to heat it. I figured she'd had her say on the subject of Mable's legs, but then she led me to the table and we sat down.

'It happened just after the end of the Civil War. Grandpa had been reassigned to a post in the West. He and Grandma were traveling there, just the two of them on horseback, when they were ambushed by a war party of Apaches near Tucson. Before they knew what was happening, Grandpa was shot off his horse. An arrow took him in the shoulder. When he fell, he struck his head on a rock. The blow rendered him unconscious, so he was completely unaware of all that happened afterward. I believe he's never forgiven himself for that, though it certainly was no fault of his. That's likely why he hasn't told you the story. He's never spoken a word of it to me, either. I only know about it because I once asked my father about Mable's limp. I've kept it secret from Grandpa that I know, and you must promise to do the same.'

'I promise,' I told her.

'What Mable did, she saw that Grandpa was down so she leapt off her mount and ran to his side. The way Papa told it, arrows were flying all about her. None hit her, though.'

'The Indians likely wanted to take her alive,' I said.

'That's exactly what Papa told me. And it seems to be the only reason they weren't both killed that day. What Grandma did, though, she drew out Grandpa's service revolver and emptied it at the Apaches. She got one of them, too. Then

153

she was empty, and the savages were closing in. Fortunately, her shots were heard by a squad of cavalry patrolling nearby. She didn't know that, though. Besides, the soldiers were still a distance off. Grandma didn't have time to reload, so she dragged Grandpa across the ground to a hole in the rocks. It was like a cave. She shoved him all the way in, but there wasn't quite room enough for both of them. She wedged herself into the rocks as best she could. Her legs and . . . hindquarters . . . wouldn't fit. I guess the Indians had plenty of time to rush in and drag her out, but they didn't do that. Instead, they stayed back and poured arrows into Grandma. They made a game of it. The way Papa told it, they were prancing about laughing and whooping it up and sailing arrows into her when the soldiers came riding in and scattered them.'

Well, that story changed my outlook on the General and Mable both. I could see why he'd never told me about it, and why he always went on the way he did about Indian tortures and how you had a duty to save your women even if it meant killing them. He must've seen it that he'd failed Mable. The Apaches hadn't taken her off, but they'd damaged her considerable, and the fact it didn't turn out worse was only due to luck. The whole thing made me feel sorry for the General, and like him all the more.

As for Mable, I never again looked on her as an obnoxious old nuisance, and felt rather ashamed for ever thinking bad thoughts about her. It was just bully, picturing her crouched at the General's side, blazing away at the redskins. Then she'd dragged him to safety, even though he was near twice her size, and caught a heap of arrows in the backside for her troubles. She was a heroine to me after I found out about all that.

Of course, I couldn't let on that I knew. But I treated her extra nice from that time on. More than likely, she laid it down to my blunder of barging into the bathroom, and figured I was trying to win myself back into her good graces. That wasn't it, though. The reason I turned so friendly was simply because I admired her awfully for the gumption she'd shown against the Apaches.

When the General mentioned that she hadn't bathed in a fortnight, I knew it had to be on account of me. It weighed on me some while I got into my slicker and hurried off to the stable with Sarah. I wanted to be Mable's friend, and not someone who gave her troubles.

We harnessed Howitzer to one of the carriages and set off in the rain toward town. That was the direction Mable always took when she wandered off. There'd usually been snow on the ground, the other times, so we'd worried about her freezing up. We'd always found her in time, though, and she'd never seemed the worse for wear. I figured she could handle some rain, so I wasn't much concerned.

Not till I saw her.

Mable was sprawled face down by the side of the road, on a stretch between their place and the house of the nearest neighbor. Even from a distance, I could see she wasn't moving. But I couldn't see the puddle till we reined in Howitzer and jumped down and ran to her.

It wasn't much of a puddle, actually.

No more than a yard around and a couple of inches deep.

But it had drowned her.

Or maybe it hadn't, and she'd keeled over dead and her face just *happened* to land in the water.

Either way, Mable was dead.

I hunched down and rolled her over. She tumbled, all loose, like she didn't have any bones. Her face was gray with muddy water. The rain cleaned it off, and fell into her mouth. Her eyes were open, staring. The raindrops splashed on her eyeballs, but she didn't blink.

'Oh, dear Lord,' Sarah murmured.

She closed Mable's lids, and then I picked up the poor limp body. Mable'd been a bit shorter than me, and skinnier. It surprised me, how heavy she felt. I managed, anyhow, and took her to the carriage and put her down across the rear seats. We climbed aboard, then turned for home.

We didn't say a thing. We didn't cry or carry on, either. I wasn't feeling any particular sorrow, just then. Mostly, I felt rather afraid and sick, and guilty we hadn't gotten to Mable in time to save her. And I dreaded how the General would take to the loss of his wife.

Much as he always complained about her, I didn't suppose he'd be glad to have her gone.

We left the carriage in front of the porch. Sarah, she went in ahead of me. I followed, holding Mable's body. We found the General in the parlor.

He rose from his chair. His mouth dropped open, then shut again. Not speaking a word, he stepped over to us and put a hand on Mable's cheek.

'I'm so sorry,' Sarah told him, her voice quivery.

'I appreciate your bringing her back to me, dear.' He gave me a sorry glance, nodded, and took the body from my arms. 'I'll put her to bed,' he told us.

We both just stood there, silent, while he carried her away. I heard the fire crackling and popping, heard the stairs groan under the General's slow footfalls.

Pretty soon, along came the gunshot.

We both jumped.

I looked quick at the fireplace mantel. The General's revolver was there, where he always kept it.

Sarah and I raced upstairs.

I knew what we'd be finding, but we had to go and see for ourselves, anyhow.

In the room, Mable and the General were stretched out side by side on their bed. It almost looked like they'd laid down for a nap, except for the bloody mess on the headboard behind the General.

He was holding one of Mable's hands.

His other hand hung over the side of the bed.

I didn't see any gun.

But he had a string looped around the toe of his right house slipper.

I stepped past the end of the bed. The string dangled down from his foot to a rifle on the floor, where it was tied to the trigger. The rifle must've been thrown off him by the recoil.

CHAPTER TWENTY-TWO

Mourning and Night

Sarah was their only surviving relation, but the General and Mable had a passel of friends she had to notify. About thirty of them showed up, mostly old men, some with their wives in tow. Just about all the men came in full dress uniform. They looked just splendid, sabers hanging at their sides, chests full of medals.

A service was held at the local Methodist church. One old fellow after another stood up front and eulogized the General and Mable. They had some mighty fine things to say about the couple.

When it came time to pay our last respects, we all lined up and filed past the coffins. Mable, she was rouged up pretty good and looked peculiar, but she was dressed in a fine satin gown like she was on her way to a party. The General looked ready to escort her there. A military ball, maybe. He was decked out in his uniform. He had more medals than most of the mourners put together. He'd shot himself through the mouth, so he didn't have any holes that showed.

I tucked one of his briar pipes into the coffin with him.

Sarah, she kissed each of her grandparents on the forehead.

They were planted in a graveyard behind the church. A powdered lady wearing more rouge than Mable sang 'Nearer My God to Thee' and then a skinny little soldier who looked older than dirt raised a bugle to his lips and played 'Taps'. It was a sunny afternoon, but we all watered the grass something awful.

When that part was over, everybody came to the house. There was more food laid out than I'd ever seen in one place. We all ate, and the men got liquored up. Later on, some of the folks cleared out. Others stayed on, though. Some

157

servants Sarah'd hired for the occasion made up guest rooms for them.

There wasn't a bedroom left for me, so I figured I'd settle down in the parlor. A drunk with a white beard down to his belt buckle snored on the sofa. I sat in the General's old chair. Its cushions were all sunken in from him.

The snoring wouldn't let me fall asleep, so I just sat there missing him and Mable, and wishing I'd known them better. By and by, I lit up one of the General's pipes. I figured he wouldn't mind. Back when he was alive and we'd sat up talking, he'd offered to let me smoke one. I'd always turned him down, but now I wished I'd smoked with him. When the pipe died out, I fetched the General's bottle of rum. That stuff always had a way of making me doze off. So I took a few sips of it, judging I'd need some help if I was to get any sleep at all.

I tucked the bottle out of sight quick when Sarah suddenly wandered in. She came silently through the parlor, her hair down and gleaming, her white nightdress ashiver with the firelight, floating soft around her. She looked just lovely.

Leaning down over me, she whispered, 'You don't want to spend the night in a chair.'

'It's quite all right, really.'

'I know a better place,' she said, and took my hand.

She hadn't brought a lamp along with her, so after we left the parlor we had to navigate our way in the dark. She kept hold of my hand, and didn't utter a sound as we climbed the stairs and started down the hallway.

I figured there must be a spare room, after all. But she led me to hers. She let us in, then shut the door real easy so as not to make a sound. Over by the bed, her lamp was burning.

'This should be much more comfortable for you,' she said in a hushed voice.

'It's *your* bed,' I told her.

'It's roomy enough for both of us.' With that, she went to it and stepped out of her slippers and climbed aboard. She pulled the covers over her, then scooched to one side. 'I brought in your nightshirt,' she said. Taking out an arm, she pointed to a chair by the wall. My flannel nightshirt was neatly folded on top of it.

Well, I didn't hanker to strip down in front of Sarah even if she had been a regular visitor during my baths. Those times, I'd been sitting in a tubful of water. So I doused the lamp before getting out of my funeral duds and slipping into the nightshirt.

I eased under the covers and lay on my back, close to the mattress edge so as not to bother her. The rum I'd drunk made my head a trifle foggy, but I felt so strange about being in the same bed as Sarah that I was wide awake. My heart wouldn't slow down, and I was shaking some even though the bed was warm and cozy.

By and by, Sarah's hand snuck over and found mine. She gave it a gentle squeeze. 'I'm so very glad you're here,' she whispered.

'This is vastly more comfortable than a chair, isn't it?' I said.

'You're all I have, now.'

When she said that, I feared she'd take to weeping. But she didn't. She rolled over warm against my side and said, 'Hold me. Please.'

So I turned and hooked an arm over her back, and she snuggled against me. 'It'll be all right,' I told her. I wanted to cheer her up. More than that, though, I needed to talk and take my mind off the feel of her. Sarah's head was tucked against the side of my neck, her breath tickling me. The way we were stretched out, she was pressing me tight all the way down to our knees. There wasn't a thing but our nightclothes between us. Her skin was hot through the cloth. I could feel every breath she took, and even her heartbeats.

'It'll be all right,' I said again, stroking her back. 'You'll see.'

Right off, I could tell that talking wouldn't do the job. I bent myself away from her and hoped she hadn't noticed the reason for it.

'Why,' I went on, 'I imagine you'll find yourself a husband in no time at all and you'll have a whole houseful of children.'

'If only that were so.'

'Just wait and see.'

'It's too late for me, Trevor. I'll never marry. I'll be an old spinster.'

'Don't talk that way. Why, I should think there must be *fifty* men in town who fancy you. There's Henry at the general store, for one. And the chap who owns the pharmacy. I could see just by how they . . .'

'I'll be twenty-seven years old, come October.'

'That isn't *old*. Besides, you're beautiful. I've not seen

159

another woman in the whole town who could hold a candle to you, in the way of looks.'

'You're so sweet, Trevor.' She kissed the side of my neck. It sent shivers down to my toes.

I tried not to think about that.

'If you should set your mind to it,' I hurried on, 'I've no doubt but that you could find yourself married before summer. No doubt at all. I'll help you. We'll pick out a fine chap for you, and . . .'

Her mouth got in the way. She gave me a kiss, but it wasn't the usual kind – brief and gentle. With this one, she mashed her lips against mine. Her mouth was open and wet, and she was breathing into me. It wasn't a way I'd *ever* been kissed before.

While our mouths were locked together, she took to squirming so that her body rubbed against me. I couldn't help but squirm, myself.

I'd never felt so fired up and strange. The nearest thing was my time with Sue in the alley, but she'd been a stranger and more my own age and we'd had more clothes on and she wasn't half as pretty as Sarah. Sue'd been after my money and such, too, whereas I didn't actually know what Sarah was after.

Taken all around, I felt tight and hot and fit to bust, but awfully confused and ashamed, too.

It went on for a spell, but finally Sarah unclenched me. I thought she was done. I felt awful disappointed, but mighty relieved, too. I wiped my mouth dry and fought to catch my breath.

She wasn't done, though.

She sat up and threw the covers off us. That was fine, for it had gotten mighty warm underneath them. But then she shucked off her nightdress. I could see her plain in the moonlight from the windows. Her skin looked pale as milk, and shadows smudged her face.

Kneeling beside me, she started to slide my nightshirt up my legs. I took her by the wrists.

'You'll be so much more comfortable without it,' she whispered.

I felt rather panicky, and searched for a way to call her off. 'The house is simply jammed with people,' I said, and suddenly wondered how come she'd waited for tonight, as we'd been alone in the house for a few days, ever since the bodies had been taken away. Maybe she'd needed this long to work up the gumption. Or maybe she'd only brought me in here to sleep, and hadn't planned on getting so friendly. 'What if someone should walk in?' I asked.

She answered that by climbing off the bed, crossing over to the door and turning the key in its lock. 'Now we're safe,' she said. 'We'll have to be careful when we leave the room tomorrow, is all.'

She came walking back to the bed. She crawled on, but this time she didn't kneel beside me. Instead, she straddled me down near my knees. I could feel the sides of her legs touching my skin. Her thighs were spread wide, and looked smooth as cream. She was dark where they came together. From seeing Trudy, I knew the dark place was hair. Above that, she was all pale and slender, a dot of shadow at her navel, and dark at the tips of her breasts. Her breasts were bigger than Trudy's, bigger than they looked when Sarah had clothes on.

She lifted my hands toward them and leaned in. Her breasts were almost out of reach, but not quite. She guided my hands over them. They were warm and moist, and I'd never touched anything so smooth. Not even satin or velvet or silk. The nipples didn't feel smooth. They were rumpled and puckered, with springy centers that stuck out. But something about them stirred me up even more than her smooth parts.

'You've . . . never been with a woman . . . have you?' she sort of gasped out.

'Not . . . in this manner.'

'Squeeze.'

I squeezed. Sarah writhed and moaned. But we were both sweated up pretty good by then, so my fingers slid around when they tightened on her breasts and it put me in mind of Whittle trying to pick up Mary's breast off the floor, and how it was all bloody and slipped out of his hand. Before I had a chance to stop myself, I jerked my hands back as if they'd gotten scorched.

Sarah flinched as if I'd struck her. 'Trevor?' Her soft voice sounded confused, hurt.

'I'm awfully sorry,' I said.

She said it again. 'Trevor?' All forlorn.

'They're lovely bosoms. Truly.' To prove it, I reached out for them. But my hands stopped short. I brought my arms

161

down to my sides. 'It's not at all your fault,' I murmured.

She gazed at me for a spell, not saying anything. Then she swung her leg clear and tumbled off. She rolled onto her back, pulled her pillow down and covered her face with it.

She just lay there sprawled in the moonlight, silent, motionless except for her breathing. Wasn't long, though, before she commenced to sob and whimper. Her misery just tore at my heart. But the way her breasts shook filled my head with more thoughts of Whittle. I couldn't help it, and even pictured him crouching over Sarah, slicing them off, cupping them up in his hands.

I hadn't laid eyes on him for months, yet here he was, tormenting me and Sarah both.

She'd had too much grief already. She didn't deserve this. I shut my eyes to keep them from her breasts, and stretched my arm across her belly and patted her side. She went stiff for a bit. Then she took hold of my wrist. I reckoned she was about to hurl it away, but all she did was hang on. Her belly kept jumping under my arm.

Finally, she calmed down. She sniffed and let out a sigh. Through her pillow, she said, 'Oh, Trevor. You're such a dear. Will you ever forgive me?'

'Forgive you? For what?'

'For making such a fool of myself.'

'You've done no such thing.'

She let go of my wrist. But I kept my arm across her and caressed her side.

'I'm not . . . I've only been with a man but once. And that was eight years ago. Ever since then, I've always behaved . . . like a lady. Until tonight.'

'You're a splendid lady,' I told her.

'Little better than a slut,' she said. This time, her voice wasn't muffled. I opened my eyes and saw that her head was turned toward me, the pillow hugged to her breasts. 'You had every reason to be disgusted.'

'Oh, but I wasn't. Not at all. Quite the contrary.'

'You needn't fib to me.'

'I found it all quite wonderful until . . .'

'Until?'

'Well . . .' It wasn't something I much cared to tell her about. My mouth got dry, and I could feel myself blushing all over.

'Please,' she said.

162

'It's rather unpleasant. Sickening, actually.'

'Trevor, tell me.'

There seemed to be no way around it. So I decided to tell her the truth. 'I'm afraid I've had some rather rum experiences in the matter of ladies' chests.'

She huffed out some air. It sounded very much like a sort of laugh. *'What?'*

'Whittle. Remember the murderer I told you about when I first arrived?'

'The man who stole Saber.'

'Yes. Whittle. He cut the breasts off two women. I saw them afterwards.'

'Dear Lord!' she gasped.

'When I . . . squeezed yours . . . I couldn't help but remember.'

'Oh, my Lord. Oh, Trevor.'

'So you see, it wasn't you.'

'You poor thing.' With that, she rolled toward me. I turned onto my side, and we hugged each other, the pillow soft and thick between our chests. She kissed me, but it wasn't like before. It was gentle and sweet and motherly. Right off, I knew I preferred the other sort.

What with the covers off and still being sweaty, I started to feel cold except for where the pillow was and where our bodies touched. Sarah didn't have a stitch on, so it must've been worse for her. I couldn't stir myself to fetch up the blankets, though, because it felt so peaceful to be laying with her that way.

I was glad I'd told her the truth. Now she knew I hadn't found anything wrong about *her*. There was more to it than only that, however. When you've got a dark secret, it doesn't seem quite so terrible after you've talked about it. Especially if the person you've told is someone as sweet as Sarah.

I took to thinking about the way things had gone for a while there before Whittle'd ruined it all.

By and by, I said, 'Of course, yours are still attached.'

She asked, 'What?' in that surprised, amused way she had.

'Your bosoms.'

'Yes, they are.'

'Perhaps if I should . . . become accustomed to them.'

'What?'

'Perhaps they wouldn't put me off.'

163

'I see.'

'Shall I have a go at it?'

She didn't answer, but I felt the pillow slide away. She tucked it under the side of her head. 'I'm to be your cure?'

'I do hope so,' I said.

She laughed softly, but then caught her breath when I curled my hands over her breasts.

That night, I got accustomed to attached ones. Whittle stood in my way for a while, but finally he skulked off and there was only just me and Sarah in that room. I held and caressed and squeezed those breasts of hers. I lifted them and shook them. I rubbed my face all over them. I felt their nipples press my eyelids. I licked and kissed and sucked.

Hardly got a good start on them before Sarah tugged the nightshirt off me.

She thrashed about and whimpered and moaned and hung on to my hair and gasped out my name over and over again.

We wrestled about considerable.

We were all over each other, touching everywhere, and I didn't feel shy once.

Then I found Sarah on top of me. Next thing I knew, her mouth was jammed against mine and her breasts were mashed to my chest and she took hold of me below decks. But not with her hands. I felt myself sliding into a tight, juicy place where I wasn't sure I ought to be. It felt bully, but Sarah acted like she was in pain, and that rather scared me so I tried to get out.

'It's all right,' she gasped.

'I'm hurting you.'

'No. No. It's where . . . I want you.' And then she shoved down and I went all the way in so far and deep it seemed I was getting swallowed up by her.

Well, I'd been feeling for a while like I might just bust. All of a sudden, that's exactly what I did do. I tried to pull out quick so as not to mess her, but she clutched my rump and wouldn't let me. I couldn't get out. I couldn't stop, either. Nothing to do but let it happen right inside her. The way she twitched and yelped while I unloaded, I figured she was even more upset than me.

When it stopped, I felt so embarrassed I wanted to die.

'I'm so awfully sorry,' I said.

She kind of relaxed, sinking down on me and panting like she was all tuckered out. She rubbed her cheek against mine, her hair making my face itch, her breath hot on my ear.

'I didn't mean to do that,' I told her.

'What?' she whispered.

'You know. *Do* that. *In* you.'

'It was wonderful.'

'But I've . . . gotten you full of yuck.'

She laughed softly, jiggling. 'It's not yuck, darling. It's your love. You've filled me with your love.'

'Was that . . . *supposed* to happen?'

'Oh, yes. Oh, yes.'

Well, that came as a considerable relief.

She went on kissing me. By and by, my love commenced to leak out of her. It syruped me up, and turned cold. But I didn't mind, for Sarah was heavy and warm and acting like I'd done her just the most wonderful favor of all time.

I felt pretty much the same about her.

CHAPTER TWENTY-THREE

Fine Times

Before you know it, we both got stirred up again and had another go-round. This time, I took the top. I rather knew what to expect, so I wasn't scared. The only surprise was that it didn't end so quick. I got plenty of chance to plunge about and appreciate things.

After we finished, we pulled the blankets over us and snuggled.

'I love you so much, darling,' she whispered.

'You're simply smashing,' I said.

She laughed softly, her sweet breath caressing my face.

'I only wish we'd had a go at this months ago,' I told her.

She laughed again, then squeezed me hard. 'We couldn't, of course. Not with Grandma and Grandpa in the house.'

'They needn't have known.'

'I couldn't bring myself to take the risk. They would've thrown you out of the house. Besides . . .'

She didn't go on, so I asked, 'Besides what?'

'I . . . feared that I might frighten you off. I couldn't bear the thought of losing you. That's what I thought I'd done tonight, lost you. When you pulled away from me.'

'It was only Whittle.'

'The cure seems to have worked.'

'Splendidly.'

'We'll have such fine times together.'

In the morning, I dressed and crept out of Sarah's room without being spotted by any of the visitors. Later in the day, the last of them departed.

The house was empty, but for the two of us.

We didn't talk about last night. We didn't carry on, either. But I could tell she hadn't forgotten about it. She acted different. She hardly ever took her eyes off me, and stayed a lot closer to me when we were doing chores and such. She touched me considerable, but not in any needful way – more like how she might touch her best friend. Also, she couldn't stop talking. She chatted on and on about this and that, and laughed at near everything I had to say.

I felt mighty grown-up and happy, though I got a bit nervous at times, wondering what was to happen next.

After our evening meal, we went into the parlor. She had me sit in the General's chair. Then she filled one of his pipes with tobacco. She lit it up, smiling at me as she sucked the flames down into the tobacco. When it was going good, she handed it to me. She sat at my feet and leaned back against my legs. I puffed away. Every now and then, I reached down to stroke her hair and she'd turn her head and gaze up at me.

The only light in the parlor came from the fireplace.

It all seemed uncommon peaceful and nice.

When the pipe went out, Sarah got to her feet and hauled me up. Humming a slow, peaceful tune, she started to dance with me. We stayed right in front of the fire. There wasn't much room, what with all the furniture, so we more or less kept to the same place, hanging on to each other and turning in circles.

It was cozy and a bit exciting, the way we held each other and glided about and sometimes kissed.

She hummed one tune after another. After five or six of them, she began to unbutton my shirt while we danced. We fumbled about and undressed each other and kicked our duds out of the way. After that, we went on dancing just like before. Only it felt quite different.

She was all smooth warm skin against me, sliding and rubbing. Sometimes, we danced far enough apart so our fronts hardly touched at all, just the tips of her breasts brushing my chest and me prodding her belly a bit. Other times, we mashed ourselves together. The hand I had on her back drifted down, and I took to holding her rump, which was ever so soft but flexed up firm with every step. She did the same to me.

Eventually, we gave up on the dancing part. We stood there squirming and kissing and caressing each other till we couldn't hold off any longer, and ended up on the rug in front of the fireplace.

We went upstairs after we were done, and had a fine time in her bed, and then fell asleep.

In the morning, she woke me with a kiss as she'd done so many times before. I opened my eyes to find her leaning over the bed, wearing her nightdress. 'Your bath is ready, dear,' she said.

She'd brought my robe and slippers into her room. She walked out, the same as she used to do. I put on the robe and slippers, went downstairs, greeted her in the kitchen, and got myself into the tub.

Like always, she brought the coffee in. I sat in the tub, sipping mine, while she took her usual seat nearby.

'We'll be going into town today,' she said. 'I need to see our attorney about a few matters.'

'An attorney?'

'He'll be turning over the estate to me.'

'The house?'

'Oh yes. The house, everything. I'm Grandpa's only heir, of course. He was very well off. Not that *he* earned a great deal. But he'd inherited a considerable sum from the family.'

'I'm quite glad to hear that. So then, you'll be able to continue on without financial worries.'

'None at all.'

I considered asking if she might raise my weekly pay a trifle, now that she was coming into a certain amount of wealth. That would've appeared greedy, however. Besides, such a request would only serve to remind her that I aimed to book passage for England if I could ever afford to do so.

Sitting in the bathtub with my coffee, I wished I hadn't thought about returning home.

I was not at all eager to leave Sarah.

Still, England was home and I sometimes missed Mother terribly.

I worried about her. She hadn't responded to any of the several letters which I'd posted to her during the past months. I'd received no message whatsoever other than the quick response to my cable just before Christmas.

It was perplexing, disturbing.

At times, I wondered if something terrible had happened to her. That seemed unlikely, however. Uncle William and Aunt Maggie no doubt knew my whereabouts and would've let me know if Mother had met with some sort of tragedy. But why hadn't she written to me? It seemed quite unlike her, and a day rarely went by that I didn't puzzle over the situation.

'Is something troubling you?' Sarah asked. I reckon my worry showed.

'It's Mother again, I'm afraid.'

She frowned and shook her head. 'You *should've* received a letter from her by now. It's strange.'

'I do hope she's all right.'

'Oh, I'm sure she's fine.'

'Then why hasn't she written?'

'She probably did. Maybe her letters were misplaced. Such things happen. You shouldn't let it upset you.' With that, Sarah set her cup aside. She came over to the tub, knelt behind me, and rubbed my shoulders. 'Any day now, the postman will come by with a letter from her. You'll see. But the main thing is, she knows you're in good hands.'

'I am that,' I said, and looked over my shoulder to smile at Sarah. My worries about Mother faded out, right quick. Sarah didn't have her nightdress on, any more. 'I say!' I said.

She laughed and kissed me. 'Never you mind,' she said, and took to soaping my back. I was used to that, but liked it all the more knowing she'd stripped down. When she finished my back, she reached around with both arms and slicked my front, which she'd never done before. Not just my chest, but my belly, too. Then lower down. She had to lean in pretty good for that. She nibbled the side of my neck while she was at it. Sent shivers all through me. And so did watching her hands. They were up to their forearms in the water, one sliding the soap bar while the other rubbed and stroked me.

'You are a thorough wench,' I said.

'One can't be too clean.'

'And does that apply to you as well?' I asked. Before she had a chance to answer, I scooped up water with my coffee cup and flung it over my shoulder. She let out a squeal that turned into laughter. Then she grabbed both my shoulders, pulled me backward and shoved, scooting me down till my head went under.

I came up gasping and blinking, just in time to watch Sarah swing a leg over the rim of the tub. She climbed right in with me. Kneeling between my legs, she took away the cup and handed the bar of soap to me. 'Finish the job you started,' she said, and laughed some more.

I was mighty glad to oblige her.

I soaped her up good, using both hands and taking my time about it. By and by, she quit laughing. She breathed heavy and moaned, and took to guiding my hands around. I'd been working mostly on her breasts, but she didn't want her southern section neglected, so she took my hands down there. After a bit, she was in an awful frenzy. I could say the same for myself, actually.

She didn't wait to rinse, but sprawled atop me, all sudsy and slippery.

Well, that came to a quick, wild finish. But we didn't stop. We carried on, thrashing and tussling and flopping about, taking breathers now and again to soap up places we might've missed earlier, soaping some of the same places, too, then commencing to splash around and join up all over again. It's a wonder nobody drowned.

The water was cold by the time we climbed out.

There was near as much on the floor as in the tub.

We dried each other with towels. Then I stayed and mopped the floor while Sarah made breakfast in the kitchen.

After the meal, we dressed and went out to the stable. There, we harnessed Howitzer to the carriage and headed off. Sarah let me handle the reins, as she knew I enjoyed it. That left her to hop down and attend to the gate. After closing the gate, she rushed over and checked the mailbox. I longed to see her reach inside and pull out a letter from Mother, but she returned empty-handed. Climbing aboard, she shook her head. 'I'm sorry,' she said.

'Perhaps the postman hasn't arrived yet,' I told her, though I knew it was already past noon. Back when the General was alive, Sarah had usually brought the mail to him before he'd finished breakfast. Though he and Mable ate much later than us, they'd get done by around eleven. So the postman had certainly come along by now, but with nothing to leave.

'Maybe tomorrow,' Sarah said.

Disappointed, I got us rolling.

Sarah stared at me, looking rather solemn. Pretty soon, she said, 'Shall I buy you a ticket for England?'

The merest whisper of a breeze could've knocked me over when I heard those words. I gawped at her.

'I'm able to afford it now, you know. Would it make you happy?'

'Do you mean it?' I blurted.

'Of course. If that's what you want.'

I gazed at her, struck dumb with surprise and gratefulness. The sun was out, shining on her face. She looked so beautiful it made my heart sore.

Much as I longed for home, the notion of going away from Sarah all of a sudden filled me with a sick, lonely feeling.

I'd been keen on Sarah since the moment I first saw her, the night I warned the General about Whittle and we stormed into her bedroom. It was likely Christmas night that I fell in love with her. After that, I would've been sorry to part with her. But now, what with all that we'd done since the funeral, I could hardly bear the thought of going off and never seeing her again.

'Would you come along with me?' I asked.

'What would your mother have to say about that?'

'I'm sure she'd be quite fond of you. You could stay with us. I'd show you all of London. We'd have a ripping good time!'

She shook her head. 'It's nice to think so, but . . . the difference in our ages. Your mother would be appalled. *Everyone* would be appalled.'

'They needn't know that we're more than chums.'

'We'd have to behave like strangers. We couldn't so much as hold hands or kiss, much less dance or share a bed . . . or bathe together.'

'Why, we would find times for such things.'

'No. I'm afraid not.'

'But Sarah!'

'It would be too horrible for both of us.'

'But how can I leave you?'

'I haven't *ordered* you to leave. I'm simply offering you the opportunity. The choice is yours.'

'I can't go without you.'

When I said that, her eyes watered up. She stroked my cheek and kissed me. 'You may change your mind, someday.'

I shook my head.

'If ever you do, tell me. We'll buy the ticket for you. Next week, next month, next year. You may grow weary of me, you know.'

'Never,' I said.

Soon after that, we reached the outskirts of town. Sarah gave me directions to the attorney's office, which turned out to be in his home. Before climbing down, she handed me a wad of money and told me I should go on and buy our supplies. She would find me when she was finished with the legal matters.

I left her, and headed for the markets.

I had a fair idea what we needed in the way of food and such, and set to gathering it. But my mind was all ajumble. Had I done the proper thing, refusing her offer? I felt as if I'd betrayed Mother. I felt, too, that Sarah had somewhat let me down. After all, she *could* go with me.

The more I puzzled over it, though, the more I saw she was right. Should she come with me, we'd be forced to keep apart. It would be awful.

So it came down to stay or lose Sarah, and I'd made my choice to stay. Bad as I felt about Mother, though, pretty soon I eased my mind about that. If Sarah hadn't offered to buy me a ticket home, why, I would've been staying anyhow. At least for several more months. The trick was to keep on saving my money till I'd earned enough for the passage home, and study the situation then.

I was feeling fairly comfortable about things by the time I'd rounded up our food and supplies. I loaded them into the carriage. Sarah hadn't returned yet, so I read the *World* while I waited for her.

CHAPTER TWENTY-FOUR

Slaughter

The story that changed everything wasn't in the issue of the
World which I read while waiting for Sarah to return from
the attorney's office. I turned from page to page, and gave
little thought to Whittle.

We went on about our lives, both of us mighty pleased
and content. The next couple of weeks were smashing. We
bathed in the mornings, and danced in the evenings.
Between all that, we ate our meals and cleaned the house,
worked on the grounds, took horseback rides, had picnics
here and there, went into town for supplies, and generally
had a fine time at whatever we were up to. It was wonderful
even when we only just talked. Sometimes, we did nothing
except sit about and read. Taken all around, we couldn't
have been much happier.

But then came the day we returned from town and I settled
down for a look at the newspaper while Sarah sat nearby
with a book of poems by Elizabeth Barrett Browning.

The story I ran across went like this:

TOMBSTONE ROCKED BY SAVAGE MURDERS

Tombstone, Arizona Territory, infamous for its history
of gunslinging desperados and marauding Apaches, was
stunned on 22 April by the early morning discovery of
Alice Clemons (42) and her two daughters, Emma (16) and
Willa (18), brutally slain in their room at Mrs Adamson's
Boarding House on Toughnut Street.

According to the *Tombstone Epitaph*, the three women
met their fate at the hands of person or persons unknown
sometime during the previous night. They were found by
the maid at 9:00 the following morning, whereupon the
unfortunate woman swooned at the grisly sight.

All who viewed the scene were shocked beyond measure.

'The room looked like a slaughterhouse,' averred Dr Samuel Wicker, who went on to say that all three women had been most horribly butchered and dismembered. Said Deputy Marshal Frank Dunbar, 'I've seen a few white men who got themselves carved up near as bad by the Apache, but these were ladies. Whoever done this is a monster, pure and simple.'

In addition to numerous unspeakable mutilations committed upon Mrs Clemons and her daughters, it has been reported that all three were scalped. This has led some to suspect that they did, indeed, fall victim to one or more renegade savages. Since the surrender of Geronimo to General Miles nearly three years ago, the citizens of Tombstone had experienced little or no difficulty with the redman. They had considered such troubles to have come to an end, and many are filled with dismay at the possibility that murderous Indians may be lurking in the area.

Not so Deputy Dunbar. 'A white man did this,' Dunbar avowed. 'He left bootprints in the blood. You don't catch many redskins shod in boots. He had a long stride, too, that puts him around six feet tall. If you don't count the likes of Mangus Colorado, your basic Indian's usually a short fellow.'

Be he redman or white, the vicious assailant remains at large and no witnesses have come forward with information about his identity. The people of Tombstone, so accustomed to acts of bloody violence, remain shaken by the unthinkable nature of this outrage perpetrated in their midst.

When I read that story, I felt like the world had caved in on me. I sat there stunned, my breath knocked out.

'What is it?' Sarah asked, looking at me.

'Whittle.'

She shut her book and leaned forward. 'What? They've caught him?'

I could only shake my head.

She set her book aside, came over to me, and took the newspaper from my shaky hands. 'Which piece . . . ?'

'Tombstone.'

She stood there, reading. Then she knelt in front of me, put the paper on the floor, and rested her hands on my legs.

'It might have been anyone,' she said.

'No. It was Whittle. I *know* it.'

'You can't know for certain.'

'He's doing precisely what he planned to do – go out west and cut up women. He even considered that his butcheries might be mistaken for the work of Indians. He hoped he might join up with a band of hostiles. And show them a few of his tricks.'

Sarah rubbed my legs gently while she gazed at me. 'You're not responsible for him. None of this is your fault.'

'I should've gone after him.'

'You did what you could, darling. You came *here* to save us from him. It would've been foolhardy for you to venture out again that night in the snow, and it was too late to chase after him by the time we found that he'd stolen Saber.'

'That's when I should've left.'

'No.'

'If I'd borrowed a horse and pursued him . . .'

'He was hours away by then. It would've been hopeless.'

'Hardly hopeless,' I told her, feeling just miserable. 'The man's got no nose. I could've asked about, tracked him down. I could've *got* him. But I didn't even have a go at it. I didn't want to have a go at it. I was safe and comfortable here.'

'Here is where you belonged, Trevor. I know how you feel, but it's never been your duty to stop him.'

'I don't know about duty,' I told her. 'But I had opportunities to kill him and failed. It's my fault he boarded the *True D. Light*. It's my fault he murdered the folks aboard her. It's my fault he ever came to America at all. Trudy and her family, and those Clemons women in Tombstone, they'd be alive today if it weren't for me. I've no doubt Whittle has killed others, too. Many others. Probably a whole string of gals between here and the Arizona Territory. They likely just didn't make the *World*, or I missed the issues that told of them. Maybe I did read about some of them, but talked myself into thinking it hadn't been Whittle's work. But this time, I can't deceive myself. Nobody but Whittle could've done this business in Tombstone. I'm afraid I must go after him.'

Sarah didn't say a thing for quite a spell. She only just held my legs and gazed at me real solemn. Finally, she said,

'It's no wonder that Grandpa took to you. You're so very much like him. Duty. Honor. Set the wrongs of the world aright, or die in the attempt.'

'I'm not the one who'll do the dying. That'll be Whittle's job.'

'Your mind is set, then.'

'I don't want to leave you, Sarah.'

'You *won't* leave me. Do you truly think I would let you go journeying off on such a campaign without me?'

That was the second time in a couple of weeks she'd thrown astonishment into me.

'You're joking,' I said. I knew she'd meant it, though.

She gave my legs a hard squeeze. Her eyes were afire with excitement. 'We'll go together. It may take a few days to make preparations. We'll need to close the house . . . hire a caretaker . . . set our finances in order . . .'

'But you're a woman,' I pointed out.

'I am indeed. I am also a Forrest, from a long line of soldiers and adventurers.'

'It's likely to be quite dangerous.'

'Whatever the dangers, we'll face them together.'

'I should do this alone.'

'Indeed?' She hoisted her eyebrows. 'You wouldn't return to England without me. Now you're suddenly eager to journey west alone? Why, the only difference is the direction of travel.'

'Going to England would not have put you in harm's way.'

'You would rather leave me here to fend for myself?' she asked.

'I'm afraid so. Yes. You'd be safe here.'

'I'd be lonely,' she said. 'I'd be destroyed. There would be nothing here for me except an empty, forlorn house. You *are* my life, Trevor. So what if we travel into danger? Better to face any peril, and perish if it should come to that, than to stay here without you.'

'It isn't that I *want* to leave you behind.'

'I know, darling. I know.'

Reaching out, I stroked her hair. 'I've seen what Whittle does to women. If he should lay his hands on you . . .'

'We won't allow that to happen.'

PART THREE

Bound for Tombstone

CHAPTER TWENTY-FIVE

Westering

We aimed to travel by rail, as that was the quickest way to cross such a distance.

So on top of making arrangements for the house, Sarah figured she had no choice but to sell off the horses. She knew that her attorney, Mr Cunningham, might be interested in them, so we went to his office together.

He was a heavy, cheerful fellow who put me in mind of old Daws, the cabman. That made me a bit lonesome for home, but the glooms couldn't stand up against all the excitement I had inside me.

After making up our minds that we'd hunt down Whittle together, Sarah and I had both found ourselves caught up in the thrill of it all. We knew it was a grim mission full of hazards, but that didn't seem to matter near as much as knowing we were about to set off on an adventure together.

Well, she explained to Mr Cunningham that she intended to escort me to Arizona Territory so I could join up with my father, a cavalry major stationed at Fort Huachuca, which wasn't too far from Tombstone. She could've made him a general, but I reckon she didn't want to lay it on too thick. She told him that she aimed to shut down the house and hire a caretaker. Then she asked if he might like to purchase the three horses.

Well, the upshot was that he offered to look after the horses instead of buying them. That way, they'd still be Sarah's when she got back from the trip. He also said he knew just the fellow to take care of the house, and would gladly handle the matter of hiring him.

Next, we went to the post office. There, Sarah arranged to have her mail forwarded to General Delivery in Tombstone. I mailed a letter to Mother, in which I told her about making a trip west and said she could write to me in Tombstone. I didn't mention that Sarah'd be with me. Nor did I say a thing about going in pursuit of Whittle, figuring she'd only fret if she knew the truth.

Done at the post office, we headed for the bank. Sarah loaded up on money.

That finished our town business. For the next couple of days, we set the house in order. Mostly, we cleaned and covered the furniture and got rid of perishables and such. When that was pretty much taken care of, we packed for the trip.

We wanted to travel light, so we didn't use trunks. I fit all my duds into just one valise. It took a couple more to hold Sarah's outfits. We figured to leave behind everything but our clothes and toilet articles. And weapons. Sarah slipped the single-shot pistol and some extra ammunition into her handbag. I threw the General's army revolver, holster, and a passel of spare bullets into my valise. We chose to leave the rifle behind. It wouldn't fit in our luggage. Sarah allowed we wouldn't want to be lugging it about, but I suspect she didn't want it around because of her Grandpa using it to shoot himself.

Mr Cunningham had hired a fellow name of Jim Henderson to look after the house. Henderson had dropped by a few times to talk with Sarah, and she'd arranged for him to ride us to the railroad depot in town.

It was the first day of May, sunny and warm and breezy, that we set out. At the station, we bid farewell to Henderson. Then we went to a ticket window and Sarah paid our fares to Manhattan. The train hadn't arrived yet, so we waited out on the platform with some other folks. Most of them didn't have any luggage at all. Others had little more than what they might need for an overnight stay. I don't suppose any of them were about to start on a journey as great as ours. I was so excited I could hardly sit still.

By and by, along came the howl of a whistle. I rushed over close to the tracks, and saw our train. It chugged around a bend in the rails, smoke belching from its chimney, just monstrous and wonderful. As it roared closer, I could feel the floorboards shaking under my boots. The engineer waved down at me from his high window, just as such chaps used to do when I was back in England standing by the tracks to enjoy the thrill of a passing train. I waved back to him. A moment later, the locomotive rolled by, clanking and hissing steam, followed by the coal car and a string of passenger carriages.

After they groaned and squealed to a stop, I went back to Sarah. A porter took our baggage, and we climbed aboard. Sarah let me have the window seat. Though I'd ridden many times on the underground and even gone by rail on holidays with Mother, I'd never felt near the thrill that coursed through me when this train commenced to chug along and leave the station behind.

I met Sarah's eyes. With a smile, she gave my hand a squeeze.

'Here we go,' she said.

After that, I kept my face pretty much mashed to the window.

It was glorious: the country, the bridge over the East River, the towers of New York City. But my aim here isn't to run along about all that; it's to tell you the story of my adventures.

The way I see it, an adventure is someone else's mishap.

Nothing much happened in the way of adventures for a spell, so I'll scoot along with my narrative and get to it rather quick.

What we did was change trains at Grand Central Terminal, then ride west toward Chicago in a Pullman car. The trip was bully. We spent plenty of time talking, meeting friendly people and such. We ate fine meals in the dining car, and slept at night in berths with hanging curtains. Whenever I could, I watched out the windows.

We sped along through towns and forests and mountains, crossed bridges over deep canyons and river gorges that gave me the sweats with notions of derailing, and raced across valleys where we zipped past farms and villages.

The nights were glorious. I spent many an hour in my berth, hidden away in darkness behind the heavy curtain, peering out at the moonlit land, wondering about the lives of all the strangers out of sight beyond the lighted windows of farmhouses and homes along the tracks. I'd just lay there, watching everything slip by while the train rocked me gently, wheels clickity-clacking over the rails, whistle sometimes letting out long, mournful hoots.

It was awfully peaceful, but it often gave me a peculiar empty feeling. A longing for I didn't know what.

Sarah wasn't the cause of it, I know that. She had the

lower berth, directly under me. At night, I'd wait a while and then poke my head out the curtain. When the coast was clear, I'd climb down and join her. We had some smashing times, but we had to be quiet about if for we`had let on to the other passengers that I was her servant. They would've been mighty shocked to see me sneaking down to her bed.

We never got caught, though. By and by, I'd kiss her goodnight and climb back up to my own berth, where I'd lay awake and gaze out the windows and feel strange all over again.

Before you know it, we arrived in Chicago. We spent the night in a fine hotel on the shore of Lake Michigan, returned to the depot the next morning and boarded a train that would take us south to St Louis.

After leaving Chicago behind, we went through just the flattest land you'd ever hope to see. Except for a passel of small towns with more grain elevators than you could imagine, there was nothing to look at but miles and miles of fields as far as the eye could see. Once in a while, there'd be a farm house and barn and silo off in the distance, but that was about it.

Finally we came to the Mississippi River. It took the breath right out of me. Here was the *Mississippi*! Mark Twain's river! We got closer and closer to it, and then we were above it on a bridge. I'd never seen the beat of it. I couldn't believe I was here, gazing down at the very same river where Mark Twain had been a steamboat pilot, where Tom Sawyer and Huck Finn and Jim had gone swimming and rafting. I couldn't see a paddlewheel, but there were ships aplenty, and I even spotted a couple of kids fishing off a canoe. I just hankered something awful to be down there with them.

Maybe I'll come back someday, I told myself.

And that's when it struck me why I'd been having those strange spells of longing. Because I was only just speeding along on the rails, glimpsing so many new places I'd like to explore, so many strangers I was never likely to meet. Glimpsing them and passing by, leaving them all behind.

There wasn't any way around it, though. Not if I wanted to reach Tombstone and track down Whittle.

Well, we stayed one night in St Louis, so Sarah took me to a restaurant on the shore of the Mississippi. Before returning to our hotel, we roamed along the river bank for a while. We watched boats drift by, all lit up in the distance, the sounds of voices and laughter floating soft across the water, sometimes the wail of steam whistles. It was just grand. I wanted to stay forever, but the wind stiffened and pretty soon a storm came along, chopping up the river and pouring rain down on us as lightning bolts split the sky and crashed all around. Drenched, we hot-footed it back to the hotel.

The next morning, the sky was clear again. We boarded a train that would take us across Missouri and Kansas to Denver, Colorado.

For days and nights, we headed west across the vast plains. Beyond the windows, I saw herds of cattle. And *cowboys*. When I saw my first cowboy riding his horse along a dusty trail near the tracks, I knew we'd reached the Wild West. The notion excited me something awful. But it scared me a bit, too, for it came as a reminder that we were traveling closer each minute to Whittle.

We were still a long way from Tombstone, though. We hadn't even reached Denver yet, and from there we'd have another few days riding south to El Paso. That would only take us into Texas, and we'd *still* need to travel farther west before getting into the Arizona Territory and finding our way to Tombstone.

Even if Whittle was still there, which I greatly doubted, we wouldn't be arriving for near a week after leaving Denver. So I tried to calm down and not think about him, and just fill myself with the wonders of rolling through the American West.

I saw cowboys aplenty. I kept a sharp lookout for them, and never got tired of seeing more. Now and then, I found myself hoping the train might get stopped and robbed by the likes of Jesse James. He'd gotten himself back-shot by a scoundrel name of Bob Ford six or seven years ago, so I knew we didn't stand much chance of enjoying a run-in with the James Gang. But I reckoned there were other outlaws available to have a go at us, and rather fancied myself plucking the General's revolver from my valise and engaging in some gunplay with them.

While I was on the lookout for cowboys and hoping for a hold-up, I caught sight of my first Indian. He sat astride a pony at a crossing, and looked just fearsome, feathers in his headband, face painted red, wearing a blue army jacket and leather leggings. What with all I'd read about the savages, and what I'd heard from the General and Sarah, my insides just squeezed up with fright. I was all set to make a grab for the revolver. But he didn't have a weapon that I could see. And the train was moving along so fast that he was out of sight in just a second or two.

I saw quite a number of Indians as we went along. None scared me like the first one, though. Some were mighty old, and some were squaws, and some were kids. Mostly, they looked rather poor and pitiful. It was hard to picture such creatures on the warpath, massacring settlers, taking scalps and torturing their captives.

Well, the Indian wars were over. They'd been beaten. At least that's what the General had led me to believe. He hadn't been quite correct on that score, as I was to find out later on, but that's a matter I don't aim to get into, not here.

By the time we pulled into Denver, I'd gotten fairly used to seeing both cowboys and Indians. They didn't thrill me quite as much as they'd done at the start, but I was still awfully excited about finding myself in the West.

We spent the night at a hotel near the depot. Early the next morning, we boarded the train that was to carry us south to El Paso, Texas.

Whenever we changed trains, we always found ourselves mixed in with a whole new bunch of passengers. We'd chat a bit with some of them, Sarah explaining that I was her servant. By and large, they seemed like decent folk.

This time, one of the passengers in our car was a man name of Elmont Briggs.

The trouble was ready to start.

CHAPTER TWENTY-SIX

Briggs

At just about the same time the conductor yelled 'All aboooard', Elmont Briggs came striding up the aisle. He appeared to be heading for the seats behind us, but stopped quick when he spotted Sarah.

She raised her face to see who was standing there.

For a spell, they stared at each other.

The fellow looked perplexed, but awful glad to see her. He was probably about Sarah's age, and had a face so pretty it looked downright girlish. It was clean-shaven, with reddish lips, a pert little nose, big blue eyes and pale brows. His wavy golden hair hung clear to his shoulders. I wondered if he might be a gal after all, even though he was dressed like a man. He was all decked out in shiny boots, black trousers and coat, and had a string tie around the neck of his shirt. A woman wasn't likely to dress in such a fashion. Besides, his chest looked flat. Then he spoke, and his low voice removed my doubts.

'Libby Gordon!' he proclaimed. 'I don't believe my eyes.'

'Pardon me?' Sarah said.

'It's *me*. Elmont Briggs.'

'I'm pleased to make your acquaintance, Mr Briggs,' she told him, sounding a bit amused. 'But I'm afraid . . .'

'You don't remember me? Yale? Class of '84. You accompanied James Bellows to the . . .'

'My name is Sarah Forrest,' she explained. 'I've never even *been* in Connecticut, much less accompanied a James Bellows to *any*thing. Obviously, you've mistaken me for this Libby person.'

'You're not Libby Gordon?' he asked, tilting his head to one side.

'No, indeed.'

'But . . . the resemblance is uncanny. Remarkable. I'm

dumbfounded.' Frowning, shaking his curly locks, he said, 'Please accept my apologies for intruding in such a bold fashion.'

'It's quite all right.'

I figured he would move on, now. But he stayed put.

The train started moving, though. As usual, it took off with a sudden lurch. Elmont staggered sideways. Even though he didn't seem to be in much danger of falling, he caught hold of Sarah's shoulder.

'Woops,' he said. Then he let go of it and grabbed the corner of her seat back. 'I only met Libby once,' he explained. 'I've never forgotten her, however. One does not forget such a vision of beauty. When I spied you sitting here . . . Such a shock. Such a delightful shock. But an error.'

Sarah's face was turned away, so I couldn't see how she was taking all this.

Elmont's eyes shifted over to me. He curled his lips. It was suppose to be a smile, I reckon, but it looked a mite sour. 'And would this fine young man be your brother?'

'My servant, Trevor.'

'You're traveling alone, then?'

'With Trevor.'

'I should very much like to join you. Perhaps we might sit together.'

'Perhaps you should shove off,' I told him.

Well, his pretty blue eyes bugged out and his face got scarlet. Sarah's head swung around. She looked as out of sorts as Elmont.

'Trevor!' she whispered.

'He's after my seat,' I snapped. *He's after you*, is what went through my mind.

'Is your boy always this impertinent?' Elmont asked.

'Bugger off,' I told him.

And Sarah slapped me across the face.

'What's the *matter* with you!' she snapped.

I just sat there, my cheek hot where she'd smacked it. The cheek didn't hurt much, but I felt like I'd been kicked in the stomach.

I felt a whole lot worse when Sarah stood up without saying another word and followed Elmont up the aisle.

She'd never struck me before. She'd never even spoken harshly to me. I doubt there were ever two people who got along any better together than me and Sarah.

Now, she'd not only struck me but gone off with Elmont.

She stayed with him, too. For a long, long time. Leaving me there alone and miserable. Couldn't she see that Elmont was a cad? What was wrong with her? How could she fall for his flattery like that? How could she abandon me? What if she doesn't come back at all, and takes up with him?

I almost got up to go looking for her. But I didn't relish the notion of seeing them together. They might be laughing. They might be holding hands. Or worse.

It sickened me to think about such things.

I couldn't stop it, though. I pictured his lips on her mouth, his hands exploring her body and sneaking under her clothes. In my mind, she didn't simply allow him such liberties, but led him along. And touched him in return.

I told myself they wouldn't dare. People would see. But the car wasn't particularly crowded. If the seats across the aisle from them were empty . . .

Well, she finally came back. She gave me a sharp look, then sat down.

'How could you speak to him that way, Trevor?'

'How could you go off with him?'

'He's a very nice man. You had no call to abuse him. You were awful.'

'I doubt there ever *was* a Libby Gordon. The cur took a fancy to you, that's all. He's a bloody liar.'

'You're acting like a child.'

Well, her slap hadn't stung me any more than those words did. I couldn't speak at all for a spell. Then I said, 'I'm a child and he's a man, is that it?'

'Don't be ridiculous.'

'He looks like a woman.'

'Stop it! For heaven's sake, Trevor.'

'Why did you go off with him?'

'I had little choice after your atrocious behavior. I can't *believe* you spoke to him that way. I've never been so embarrassed. What in the world possessed you?'

'I don't like him. Not one whit. He's a smooth-talking philanderer, that's what he is.'

'Ridiculous. You should be ashamed of yourself. Not only did you mistreat him, but you've misjudged him as well. The poor man lost his wife and child to smallpox last year.'

'I doubt it.'

187

'You're being impossible.'

'I shouldn't trust a word he breathes. He would quite obviously tell you *anything* in order to win your sympathies. Can't you see his intentions?'

When I said that, Sarah quit scowling. She gazed into my eyes, and pretty soon she smiled. Leaning against me, she whispered, 'Why, Trevor, you're jealous.'

'Not in the least.'

'You are!' She patted my leg. 'Oh, dear. What am I to do with you? Elmont's nothing to me. I've no feelings at all for him except as a friend.'

'He's after more than your friendship.'

'How can you say such a thing?' she asked, still talking soft. 'You don't know the man.'

'I know he intends to have you.'

'I hardly think so. If that is his intention, however, he'll be disappointed.'

Well, I wasn't feeling quite so down any more. Though it disturbed me that Sarah considered Elmont a 'friend', it seemed clear I hadn't lost her affections to him.

After a while, she said, 'I'm so sorry that I struck you, darling.'

'It didn't hurt.'

'Will you forgive me?'

'Of course.'

Then she whispered, 'You won't stay away from my bed tonight?'

'Why, I hardly think so.'

With my mind eased considerable on the score of Elmont Briggs, I took to watching out the window. In the early evening, however, came the chime of the dinner bell. 'Now don't get yourself into a tizzy again,' Sarah said. 'I asked Elmont to join us at our table.'

'Splendid,' I muttered.

'Please be nice to him.'

'I'll have a go at it.'

'Remember, you're supposed to be my servant. We can't have him suspecting the truth.'

We waited until most of the other passengers had cleared out of the aisle, then left our seats. Elmont was a few rows behind us, alone. When he saw us approaching, he stood up and gave Sarah a warm smile. The smile cooled some as he turned it on me, but I bobbed my head and said, 'I do hope you'll forgive my earlier rudeness, Mr Briggs. You bore such a remarkable resemblance to a scoundrel I once knew . . .'

Sarah gave me a sharp glance, so I shut my mouth.

'I accept your apology,' Elmont said.

He took the lead. The dining car was some distance back. At the end of each car along the way, Elmont would pull open the door for Sarah. Once she was outside in the noisy vestibule, he'd leave me holding the door, hurry around her, and get the next one. Which he always managed to shut while I was still between cars. He was mighty irritating.

The way Sarah let him get away with it, I got to feeling like she didn't care, one way or the other, if I was left behind. So I let it happen. When we finally came to the dining car and Elmont slammed the door in my face, I just stayed put. I stepped to the edge of the steel grille that covered the coupling, held on to the safety chain there to keep my balance, and stared off at the wooded hills. They were mighty pretty, what with the sun sinking low, but I was in no mood to enjoy the view.

I aimed to wait for Sarah to come along and fetch me.

But she didn't.

Having too fine a time with Elmont, no doubt.

It was windy and cold out there between the cars, so by and by I went on in.

Sarah and Elmont were seated across from each other at one of the dinner tables, Sarah talking away to him and looking happy. When she saw me, she waved me over to join them. 'What kept you?' she asked.

'I stopped for some fresh air,' I explained, feeling mighty let down.

'Where I come from,' Elmont said to Sarah, 'we don't eat with the help.'

'You're certainly an endearing chap,' I told him.

'Nor do we allow back-talk.'

'Behave yourself, Trevor, or I *shall* send you off.'

'Yes ma'am.'

After that, I kept mum. The waiter brought our meals along. I ate and watched Elmont, and listened to the conversation. He was just ever so charming. I reckon he and Sarah'd already found out plenty about each other, as they'd spent so much time together earlier. They didn't fill me in on what I'd missed, but I managed to figure out that Elmont was on his way to California, where he'd gone in with his brother to buy a fancy hotel on the beach at Santa Monica. To hear him talk, he was loaded down with money.

He invited Sarah to come and visit him there when she finished the visit with her father at Fort Huachuca. I had to smile at that, but Elmont didn't notice.

Sarah's father at Fort Huachuca?

I reckon she didn't consider Elmont *much* of a friend, not if she'd been telling him stretchers like that.

Though it amazed me that she'd fibbed to him, I was glad.

She allowed that she might consider a trip to Elmont's hotel, but maybe she didn't mean it.

I doubted he *owned* such a hotel.

The way it looked, lies were flying as thick as the gravy on my beef.

I knew what they were covering up, on Sarah's part.

As for Elmont's lies, I could only guess. The way I figured things, he didn't want Sarah to know he was using the last of his inherited wealth to ride the rails in search of a rich, available woman. And she was it.

Of course, I might've been wrong.

Maybe it was just my jealousy doing the thinking for me.

That's how I saw him, though.

I don't know that Sarah was smitten by him, but she sure did hang on his every word like she'd never encountered a fellow more fascinating and amusing. You could see he was aware of it, too. He had victory in his pretty blue eyes.

Matters turned worse after the meal. He invited Sarah to play cards with him in the parlor car. I started to follow them there, but Elmont said to me, 'I don't believe the lady will be requiring your services.'

'Go ahead and run along,' Sarah said.

Run along?

I heated up considerable. But I allowed that causing a row wouldn't help my cause any. It'd only serve to peeve Sarah. Besides, the way I felt betrayed by her – again – I wasn't particularly eager to keep her company. If she preferred a swine like Elmont over me, maybe she deserved him.

I cast a poison glare at Elmont, then went on my way.

Back in my usual seat, I sat alone and boiled. I tried to tell myself that Sarah was only just being kind to the man. But it wouldn't wash. In spite of what she'd said about considering Elmont no more than a friend, I'd seen enough to figure she was uncommon fond of him.

I had some awfully mean thoughts about her.

It got to seem like she'd only taken up with me in the first place was because I was handy. I was living in her house where she could get at me whenever she pleased. My age hadn't mattered much to her, then. And maybe the various men around town simply hadn't appealed to her, one way or another. I wasn't quite what she wanted, but I'd *do*.

Maybe she'd lied all along about loving me.

Maybe she'd lied about a whole heap of things.

She sure had told some stretchers to Elmont. And to every other passenger we'd spent any time with during our travels. Well, those fibs were understandable. We couldn't very well give out the truth about the two of us. The same goes for deceiving her attorney, Mr Cunningham, and any number of other folks.

Taken all around, though, she'd lied to just about everyone I'd ever heard her talking to.

Even the General.

Sitting there by my dark window, I recalled the time that Saber got hooked by Whittle. Instead of trying out the truth on her grandfather, Sarah'd come up with a fancy story about the horse running off on its own. We'd even left the stable doors and the front gate open to make it look good.

The more I thought about Sarah, the more it seemed like she never spoke the truth if she could come up with a lie that'd serve her better.

No telling how many lies she'd foisted off on me.

Why, I never could understand how a beautiful woman like Sarah was as unlucky with men as she'd always claimed. There she'd been, carrying on about how *old* she was and likely to end up a spinster – husbandless, childless, alone and pitiful.

Maybe she'd only said those things to win my sympathy.

She'd probably been with half the men in Coney Island, and thrown over each of them when a new fellow struck her fancy. The same way she was throwing me over for Elmont.

I felt like I'd been swindled.

For a while there, I plain hated Sarah and wished I'd never gotten tangled up with her. But then I got to thinking about all the fine times we'd had. The memories just carved me out hollow. Not the memories themselves, I reckon, but the notion that all the good things with Sarah were behind me.

Just for the sake of torturing myself even more, I hauled

out the gold watch she'd given me at Christmas. I opened it up and saw she'd been gone for nearly two hours. Then I snapped it shut and stared at the crossed revolvers engraved on its cover. *You'll never know how much joy you've brought into my life*, she'd said.

She'd brought plenty into my life, too.

Suddenly, I felt just rotten for all the mean thoughts I'd been having about her. She'd had good reasons for most of the lies I'd heard her tell. For all I knew, she'd never lied to me. Maybe she truly did love me, and loved me still. So what if she was spending time with Elmont? Why, I'd spent hours and hours with the General. The old man had fascinated me, but I sure hadn't *fallen* for him.

That eased my mind some, but not for long.

Elmont wasn't the General. He had designs on Sarah. He aimed to have her.

Even if all they did was play at cards and enjoy each other's company tonight, he was busy working on her. And he'd be having more chances tomorrow. And the day after that. On his way to California (if that's where he was really planning to go), he'd be traveling along our route and making sure he rode in the same trains as Sarah for the rest of the trip until we reached our destination at Tucson. Days from now.

I tried to tell myself that Sarah was bound to see through his smooth ways, sooner or later.

Maybe he'd make a try for her, and she'd spurn him and that would be the end of it.

But maybe he'd make his try, and she'd welcome it. After all, he was a man – not a child. Maybe Elmont was just the sort of fellow she'd always hoped to meet.

My thoughts were in a terrible whirl, so I was glad when Freemont the porter came along to make up the beds. After he was done, I went to the lavatory at the end of the car. I used the toilet, washed up and brushed my teeth, then walked down the curtained aisle.

I'd hoped Sarah might've come back while I was gone. Her berth was empty, though. I climbed into mine, got into my nightshirt and packed my clothes away.

Then I lay there in the darkness. The night outside didn't interest me. The gentle rocking of the train didn't soothe me. Nor did the regular clickity-clack of the wheels. When the horn hooted now and again, it sounded as mournful and lonely as my heart felt.

By and by, I got to wondering if Elmont had already managed to win Sarah's heart. I wondered if he'd already won her body, as well.

They might be together in his berth.

That notion hadn't more than entered my head when the curtains parted and Sarah looked in at me. I reckon I was glad to see her, but I felt tight and sick inside.

'I do hope you enjoyed yourself,' I said.

'Are you still in a mood?' She sounded weary.

'Oh, not at all. I'm quite delighted you prefer Elmont's companionship to my own.'

She reached in and stroked my cheek. 'I suppose I shouldn't have stayed away so long . . .'

'But you simply couldn't bring yourself to part company with Princess Charming.'

'For heaven's sake, Trevor.' She let out a long sigh, then backed away. The curtains fell shut.

I stewed for a spell, wishing I hadn't spoken to her that way. When you feel like you might be losing someone you love, though, you get rather crazy. You don't act sensible. You turn mean and wild, and make things even worse.

Well, I heard Sarah come back and settle into her berth.

I figured this was my chance to make matters right.

I waited a bit, then stuck my head out the curtains and checked the aisle. It looked like a long narrow canyon walled in by swaying shrouds, dimly lit by the gas lamps at each end. Nobody was in sight.

I climbed down to Sarah's bed. She pulled back the covers to let me in, but I just knelt on the mattress beside her.

My heart was pounding so hard I almost couldn't breathe.

'What *is* the matter with you?' she asked.

'Elmont Briggs.'

'You've no cause to be jealous. You're in my bed. Elmont is not in my bed.'

'Has he kissed you?'

'My God, Trevor!'

'Has he kissed you?' I asked again.

'Don't be ridiculous.'

'With his pretty red lips?'

'Do you honestly think I would allow him such liberties?'

'Would you?'

'You're talking nonsense. Now hush.' Reaching out, she slipped her hand beneath my nightshirt. It glided all warm

193

up my leg and gently took hold of me. 'I don't want to hear another word about Elmont.'

'I need to use the toilet,' I said.

Before she could say anything, I started to back my way through the curtains. She gave me a soft squeeze, then let go.

'Hurry back,' she said.

I started toward the rear of the car, wondering why I'd left her. It wasn't that I had any urge to use the toilet. That was just the first excuse that popped into my head. What I needed was to get shut of Sarah for a few minutes and settle down. Maybe take some fresh air. Clear my head and try to get Elmont out of it before going back to her and maybe saying things I'd have cause to regret.

When I walked past the curtains shutting off Elmont's area, an awful frenzy came over me. I had a notion to reach in and grab him. I wasn't quite sure which berth might be his, though. Would've been awful to intrude on a stranger. So I went on along to the back of the car, tugged the door open and stepped outside.

I wasn't the only one there.

Another fellow stood between the cars, his back to me, the wind tossing his long curly hair.

Elmont Briggs himself.

He hadn't looked around yet to see who'd come through the door. I should've gone back inside, returned to Sarah and savored knowing it was me, not Elmont, in her bed.

But I was just fifteen, and had more gumption than sense.

'I say,' said I. 'If it isn't the one and only Elmont Briggs.'

I had to pretty near shout so he could hear me over the noise of the wheels.

He turned around slow. He had a cigar between his lips, its tip glowing red in the wind. When he saw me, he plucked it out. He jabbed the air with it, pointing at me. 'Sarah's boy.'

'I'm nobody's *boy*, Elmont.'

'Has she sent you to fetch me?'

I stepped up closer to him. And sorely wished I had my clothes on. I was barefoot, my nightshirt blowing about like a woman's dress, the cold gusting up under it. I couldn't help feeling somewhat at a disadvantage. This was no way to be dressed when confronting a scoundrel.

'Speak up, boy. Does Sarah wish me to join her?'

194

'You're to stay away from her.'

'Am I?' He showed me his teeth. They looked gray in the darkness. I reckon he was smiling. Then he poked the cigar between them and gave it a puff.

I slapped the cigar out of his mouth.

He grabbed the front of my nightshirt, hauled me up against him and smashed his knee into my belly. The blow picked me clear off my feet. When they came down on the grille again, he was rushing me backward. He shoved me into the guard chain. Then he let go, ducked down and grabbed me around the legs. I couldn't do much more than catch hold of his hair before he hoisted me over the chain and pushed.

CHAPTER TWENTY-SEVEN

Farewell to the Train and Sarah

My grip on Elmont's hair didn't save me. Some came out in my hands, is all.

Then I was plunging headfirst, flapping and kicking, feeling the breath of the speeding train against my back. Time seemed to drag awful slow. It gave me plenty of chance to wonder what I might land on and whether I'd get myself cut in half by the wheels. I even had a chance to see my body sprawled out dead by the tracks, my nightshirt up around my chest. Seemed awful, making an indecent spectacle of myself that way.

Figured I might have time to arrange the garment, but I was still considering it when I struck the ground.

Not headfirst, though, thank the Lord. It was my back that hit. If my wind hadn't been knocked out already by Elmont's knee, the landing would've done it. I smacked down hard, but that wasn't the end of it. I bounced, and the ground was so steep it flung my legs up and somersaulted me. I tumbled and rolled for quite a spell, and finally came to a stop in some soft grass.

I lay sprawled there, hurting all over but happy to be alive. While I fought to wheeze some air into my chest, the clatter of the train faded down the tracks. Nobody must've seen me go overboard except Elmont, because it didn't stop. Pretty soon, the whistle tooted a farewell to me.

When I was able to breathe again, I got to my feet. I felt a trifle wobbly, so I didn't go anywhere but just stood where I was.

At the bottom of the railroad embankment. The high slope loomed over me, all rocks and weeds and bushes. From where I stood, I probably couldn't have seen the train even if it had still been there. All that remained of it was a distant rumble and some ragged tatters of smoke black in the moonlight.

Turning around slow and careful, I saw nothing except woods. Not a road or a house or a human being, nor the glimmer of a campfire.

I wasn't frightened, though.

I hurt too much to feel fear or much of anything else besides my hurts. My bones ached. My hands and knees burned, and so did parts of my back and rump. I'd been scuffed and scratched up considerable during my fast trip down the slope.

The nightshirt was clinging to my back. With dew, I hoped. I shucked off the shirt and held it out under the moonlight. It was shredded some. It looked mighty filthy, but I could only see a few dark spots that I took for blood. The better part of the dampness was dew, which came as a relief.

I put the shirt on, then made my way up the embankment. It wasn't a pleasant journey in bare feet, but a sight less distressing than the quick trip down it. When I got to the top, I sat on a rail to brush the grit and pebbles off my feet. The rail still felt a bit warm from the train going by.

The tracks stretched off into the distance, gleaming like silver.

I wondered what Sarah was thinking right then. She was likely all warm and snug in her bed, worrying about how come I was taking so long at the toilet. Maybe figured my supper hadn't agreed with me.

It was me who hadn't agreed with Elmont.

I could've kicked myself for knocking that cigar out of his mouth. Now he was riding along the rails with Sarah, all pleased with himself for removing a certain impudent servant boy.

With me out of the way, no telling what he might get up to.

He'd probably no sooner chucked me over the side than he'd gone looking for her.

No. Wouldn't do that. Too wily.

He'd want Sarah to fall asleep and not catch on till morning that I'd gone missing. Then he'd be at her full time.

It got me angry and miserable thinking about such things. Pretty soon, I realized I wasn't helping the situation by sitting on a rail. So I got up and started after the train.

The cinders hurt my feet. The wooden ties weren't a whole lot better. So I took to walking along the smooth iron of a rail. The only trick was keeping steady. Every so often, I'd fall off and do more damage to my feet.

But I kept at it. There was bound to be a depot up ahead, and likely a town. Just a matter of getting there. Of course, it might be twenty miles off. Or fifty. So long as I followed the tracks, though, I'd reach it sooner or later.

I tried to tell myself that Sarah'd be there waiting for me. The only chance for that was if she got worried and searched the train and figured out I was nowhere aboard. She might do just that. She sure wouldn't be able to get the train to come back for me, but she was bound to make it stop at the first station and let her off. Then she'd be shut of Elmont, and we'd be joining up again soon as I found the depot.

More than likely, though, Sarah'd drifted off to sleep. It'd be morning before she realized I was gone. By then, the train would be a few hundred miles south.

It was mighty depressing to contemplate.

But I judged things would turn out. All I needed to do was stick with the tracks, keep on heading for Tombstone, and we'd find each other by and by.

Unless Sarah decided to take up with Elmont, give up on me, and head off for parts unknown with the scoundrel.

That was out of my hands, though.

I tried not to worry my head about such things. The trick for me was just to keep on walking and find civilization.

The rail had been warm at first. But it cooled off pretty quick. Before long, it felt like ice under my feet. The wind picked up, too, and turned nippier by the minute. It slipped clean through my nightshirt, and tossed it about, and rushed up underneath it.

Finally, I took to shaking so bad and my feet were so numb that I fell off the rail every third or fourth step. I gave up on the rail, and hobbled along on the gravel and cinders and wooden ties. They weren't near as cold as the iron. My feet thawed out enough to let me feel every sharp thing they stepped on.

What I did was rip off my long sleeves and bind them around my feet. That helped some. I kept on going. No matter how far I trudged along, though, the tracks just kept on stretching out empty ahead of me and I never saw a thing except forests on both sides.

I allowed I'd likely freeze up stiff before I ever came to the next depot.

At last, I went down the embankment. It was mighty rough on my feet and hindquarters, but I got to the bottom. There, the wind wasn't so bad. Couldn't feel it much at all once I'd made my way into the trees and burrowed into the moist leaves. The ground was hard and lumpy. I still felt cold and miserable. But I fell asleep, somehow.

Morning improved matters considerable. I woke up to find warm sunlight shining down on me through the tree-tops. It felt so fine I just lay there, soaking up the heat and listening to the birds sing. Other than the birds and some bugs humming about, I heard a breeze rustling the leaves and a sound I couldn't quite place. It was a rushy noise like a strong wind. It didn't gust and fade like wind, though. It whushed along steady.

All of a sudden I knew it must be a river.

And me with my mouth as dry as sand.

I stood up quick, forgetting about my aches and pains. Right off, they reminded me of themselves. I let out a yowl. The way my feet felt, I might've been one of those fellows the General told me about – one of those captives who got staked down by Indians and had his feet toasted. The rest of me wasn't much better off. I stood there hunched over like a cripple. That didn't get me any closer to the water, though.

Finally, I straightened myself up. I turned toward the sound of the stream, and started to move. The first few steps were pure torture.

The pain was rather like a plunge in frigid water, shocking and horrid for a bit, but not so bad after you'd gotten used to it. Pretty soon, the pain eased off some.

I hobbled along, dodging tree trunks, ducking under low limbs, taking the long way around thickets and boulders and deadfalls in my way, sometimes pushing on through bushes that scratched my legs and snagged my nightshirt. Before long, I was breathless and pouring sweat. My night-shirt felt like it was pasted to my skin. The sleeves came off my feet a few times, and I had to stop and fix them before I could go on. Other times, I stopped for no reason other than to wipe my face and catch my wind.

At last, though, I came to the river.

What a grand sight! A lane of water thirty or more feet across, curling and tumbling its way over a bed of pale rocks. It was mostly shadowed by the trees, but here and there it shimmered with patches of sunlight.

I stood on the bank, gazing down at it, so struck with admiration that all my torments seemed to vanish.

This was *my* river. I'd trekked through the wilderness and discovered it. Me, Trevor Wellington Bentley, a lad from London. Like Natty Bumpo or Daniel Boone, I'd made my way over the trackless, uncharted land of the American frontier to find a secret wonder.

Battered as I was, I felt just bully.

It seemed as if nothing in the world existed except me and the woods and my river.

The rocks along the shore hurt my feet, but not my mood. Pretty soon, I stepped into the clear, rushing water. It was almighty cold! So cold I swear my feet hissed and steam curled off them. But they felt a whole lot better.

Crouching down, I scooped water into my mouth. One handful after another. It was the sweetest liquid that ever passed my lips. It was magical nectar. I felt like I was drinking mountain tops and sunlight and shadowy glens and a chill wind from the forest.

When I couldn't hold any more, I waded along through the currents. With every step, my stomach sloshed. I kept close to shore, and didn't stop till I came to one of the sunny places.

Hanging on to a boulder, I untied the sleeves and shook them out. I washed them, spread them out on the rock to dry, then did the same with my nightshirt.

The water froze me up frightful when I plunged in. It put me in mind of when I'd dived into the ocean to save Trudy. I hadn't thought about her much in recent times, and wished she hadn't snuck up on me now. A whole passel of bad memories started running through my head.

But they didn't last long. When I stood up and breathed the fresh air and saw the pale blue sky and the green trees and the river running along, all the horrible things didn't stand a chance. I was alone in the wilderness, nobody around to cause me troubles or worry.

The water didn't seem so cold any more. It felt soothing on my scrapes. I stayed in it for quite a while, paddling about and floating. Tom Sawyer himself likely never had a better time on the Mississippi than me in that river. I wished there was a Jackson Island where I could camp – but of course I had nothing to camp *with*. Even if I'd had matches for a fire, I had no food to cook on it.

200

My stomach, which was bruised on the outside from Elmont's knee, felt rather empty on the inside. That didn't worry me much, though. I allowed I could always find *something* to stave off starvation, one way or another. I'd worry about it later.

For now, I was mighty content.

I gathered my footwear and nightshirt, which were already dry, then waded over to a flat slab of rock hanging out from the shore. I climbed onto it and sprawled out. The sun warmed me up. Soft breezes with just a touch of coolness brushed along my skin.

I felt uncommon lazy. Everything seemed pretty near perfect, except I got to wishing Sarah was here with me. We could swim in the stream together, and lay out on the rock to dry. I got an awful hankering to see her stretched out in the sunlight, all bare and wet and shiny. See her and feel her and so on.

Well, of course we'd never get together again if I didn't start moving.

I was loath to stir myself, though. It would be a shame to leave my river. I wished I had a raft or canoe. Then I could just float along peaceful, take a drink whenever I got the urge, jump in to cool off when the sun got too hot, and have a fine time. That'd be a blessing for my feet, too.

But I had no raft or canoe, and didn't see how I could make one.

I could follow the river, hike along its shore or wade and swim if the terrain got too rough. That notion struck my fancy, and I nearly decided to have a go at it. But there was no way to judge where the river might take me.

Part of me didn't much care where it'd take me. I could just roam along forever, exploring. But mostly I wanted to join up with Sarah the quickest way possible, and that meant returning to the tracks.

I took one more swim. While splashing about, I wondered if there might be a way to carry some water with me. Of course, I had no container. I drank as much as I could hold, and pondered the problem.

The General once told me how the Apaches could carry around a huge load of water, enough to last a small party of warriors for days. What they'd do was kill a horse and take out its small intestine. They'd clean it out the best they could, then fill it up. When they had yards and yards of gut

201

fit to burst with water, they'd wrap it around a horse they hadn't killed yet, and be on their way.

Well, I didn't have a horse available. I'd spotted some squirrels and gophers and such, but didn't hold out much hope of catching one. Besides, the whole notion seemed a trifle gory for my taste.

Thanks to Whittle, I'd seen my share of intestines. I wanted no more truck with such things.

But I did hit on a plan, thanks to the General's story. After wrapping the sleeves around my feet, I soaked my nightshirt real good. Then I didn't wring it out or put it on. Instead, I draped it loose over my shoulders.

I started on my way, not at all happy to leave the river behind, but hoping it wouldn't wander far from the tracks so I might be able to find it later, if need be.

It was hot work, trudging back through the woods. The water in my nightshirt stayed cool for a while, and felt good the way it dribbled down my skin. Pretty soon, though, it turned so warm I couldn't tell the difference between the water and my sweat.

Finally, I came to the embankment. I scurried up, sorely missing the shade of the woods. The sun felt like fire, and the breezes had traveled elsewhere. I wished I'd just stayed at the river.

All burning and breathless and drippy, I stumbled onto the flat ground at the top of the slope. And sat on a rail. And squealed and leapt up when it scorched my rump.

After a wait to catch my breath and allow the pain to fade, I unslung my nightshirt and tipped back my head. I reckon I squeezed quite a lot of river water into my mouth. It was mixed with dust and sweat, but did wonders for my thirst. In my head, I gave thanks to the General for giving me the idea.

When I couldn't wrestle any more water out of the nightshirt, I put it on and started following the tracks. I'd learned my lesson, and stayed off the rails.

They were so shiny in the sunlight that they hurt to look at.

I walked between them, keeping my eyes on the gravel and cinders. I kept my ears open for trains, too. Another was bound to come along, sooner or later. For all I knew, several might've gone by while I was away. I probably would've heard them, but maybe not.

Anyhow, I didn't hanker to get run over. And maybe I could even get one to stop and pick me up.

The farther I walked, the surer I got that a train would whistle in the distance. From behind me. I'd turn around and wave my arms. It'd toot for me to clear out of the way, but I'd stay put so the engineer didn't have any choice but either to put on the brakes or splash through me. In my head, the train always stopped with a few feet to spare. The engineer and fireman, they leaped down to shout at me, but I acted quite meek and polite, explained my situation, and they settled down and asked me aboard. They gave me a ride to the next station, and there stood Sarah on the platform, thrilled to pieces and weeping for joy as I ran to embrace her.

It was a splendid daydream.

I played it out quite a few times in my head. Even improved on it, having the train approach from the front, heading north, with Sarah riding in the locomotive to keep a lookout for me.

Reality came back to me, though, when I spotted a bridge in the distance.

A bridge meant a gorge. A gorge might mean water. Maybe this was a place where my river cut across to the other side of the tracks. I was mighty cooked by then – wet on the outside and dry on the inside. The river was precisely what I needed to set matters right.

I hurried along smartly, eager to get there.

By and by, the rushy sound of water came along. This just had to be my river!

But I stopped dead, just short of the bridge.

The rail on my left was almost where it belonged. But not quite.

CHAPTER TWENTY-EIGHT

Desperados

The spikes meant to pin the rail down firm had all been yanked and scattered about. The rail was off to the side by half a foot.

The next train to happen along would wind up chewing earth. If it had much speed at all when it derailed, it'd likely pitch over and plunge into the gorge.

That's the first thing that ran through my mind. The second thing was how to stop the train in time to save all the lives certain to be lost in such a catastrophe.

I doubted my ability to repair the damage. The only other choice was to hurry up the tracks and have a go at stopping the train. But what if it came from the other direction?

I never got to thinking about the third thing. What it would've been, of course, was that somebody had *done* this to the rail.

Before I reached that stage of my thoughts, however, a gunshot barked. I jumped. And looked up from the rail to see a horseman charge up out of the gorge alongside the bridge. He came galloping straight at me, waving his pistol.

I chose not to bolt. After all, the only escape seemed to be a dive off the embankment. That was likely to bang me up considerable. And the fellow might shoot me. So I stayed put and raised my arms.

He slowed his horse to a trot, and reined it in just in front of me.

This was the closest I'd been to a real cowboy. Of course, I judged he wasn't an actual cowboy, but a desperado instead.

Not that he looked especially desperate. Other than the revolver in his hand, there was nothing fearsome about him. He wasn't ugly. He wasn't much bigger than me. He had a weathered, dirty face with a few days' worth of whiskers, and didn't seem to be much older than twenty. He was frowning, but not in an angry way. More like he was confused and rather amused.

Not saying a word, he gave his reins a shake. He walked his horse around me in a slow circle, studying me while I turned around to study him.

He was all decked out in a big hat with its brim turned up, a red neckerchief the size of a bib, and a bandolier chock full of cartridges that hung across his chest from one shoulder. His dusty old shirt was dark with sweat. Around his waist, he wore a belt with holsters on each side. The holster at his left hip was empty. The one on his right held a six-gun with its handle to the front. The holsters were tied down around the legs of his leather chaps. His boots had silver spurs that looked too fancy for the rest of his outfit.

After circling me a couple of times, he halted his horse and said, 'You fall outa bed or what?'

'I was thrown from a train, actually. I had a bit of a row with a fellow, and he chucked me overboard.'

'How come ya talk funny?'

'Do I?'

'Yup. You some kind of an easterner?'

'My home's in London, England.'

A corner of his mouth turned up. 'I'll be durned,' he said.

'Trevor Wellington Bentley,' I introduced myself, and held my hand out toward him.

Instead of shaking it, he touched the barrel of his revolver to the brim of his hat. 'Chase Calhoun, here.'

'Pleased to make your acquaintance, Mr Calhoun.'

'Well, don't get *too* pleased. I reckon I'll have to shoot you.'

All of a sudden, I felt mighty short of breath. But I managed to say, 'I do hope that won't be necessary.'

'Thing is, Willy, you got in the way. Me and the boys, we're fixing to hold up the express.'

He wasn't alone, then. That didn't come as any great surprise. Working the rail loose would've been a big job for just one man. I figured the rest of his gang must be waiting in the gully.

'You'll be causing a terrible wreck,' I explained.

'We can't rob the train without we stop it first.'

'You might send one of your compatriots up the tracks to wave it down. Otherwise, there's bound to be an awful loss of life. Women and children. I shouldn't like to have that on my conscience.'

205

'Well, you won't.' With that, he aimed the revolver at my face and thumbed back the hammer.

'I might be of some use to you,' I said.

'Don't see how.'

'I could ride with your gang, perhaps. I could run errands, perform chores, cook for you. I make quite a fine pot of coffee, actually. Why, there's no end to the things I might do to help. I might care for your horses. And I'm really quite an amusing chap. Why, I sailed across the Atlantic with a cutthroat worse than any ten train robbers, and he spared my life for no other reason than he didn't want to lose the enjoyment of my company.'

It was a stretcher, but I would've said just about anything to stop Chase from pulling the trigger.

'You sure run on,' he said.

'You seem like a fine fellow.'

'You're all right, too, Willy. I won't get no pleasure outa plugging you, but . . .'

'You certainly don't *look* like an Indian lover.'

He hadn't looked fearsome before. When he heard me say that, though, his face twisted ugly. 'Say your prayers.'

'If you shoot me, that's exactly what you are. No better than a bloody *Indian* lover.'

'My *folks* was massacred by the Sioux, boy!'

'And my best friend was General Matthew Forrest of the Fifth Cavalry.'

The hammer dropped.

Real slow, hooked by Chase's thumb.

'You knew General Forrest?'

'We were great chums. He took me into his home. I was present at his deathbed. Until last night, I was traveling in the company of his granddaughter, Sarah.'

'Well, let's see what the boys have to say. Move along.'

He rode alongside me as I walked to the edge of the gully. The bridge crossed a river, just as I'd figured. Over by the shore, the 'boys' were waiting. Chase dismounted, and led his horse down the slope, which wasn't steep enough to give me much trouble.

His gang stood by their horses and watched us come. Four of them, not counting Chase. A couple of them pointed at me and said things I couldn't make out, and laughed. The other two didn't seem amused.

'This here's Willy,' he said when we got close.

'Trevor, actually.'

'Whatcha wearing there, Willy?' asked one of those who'd pointed. He looked not much older than me. I found out later he was Chase's kid brother, Emmet.

'I was thrown from a train last night,' I told him.

'He's from England,' Chase said. 'Allows as he's a friend of Matthew Forrest.'

'General Forrest?' asked an older fellow named John McSween who had a big, droopy mustache that had some gray in it.

'I saved his life,' I said. Another stretcher, but I figured it couldn't hurt my cause.

'Don't see how the General'd *need* a lad the likes of you to save him,' McSween said.

'Why, a scurvy coward tried to back-shoot him on the streets of Coney Island,' I said. 'I called out a warning, and Matthew whirled around and emptied his revolver into the cad. Dropped him like an old boot, he did. Matthew presented me with a gold watch to show his gratitude. I would show it to you, but it's with the rest of my possessions aboard the train.'

'What're we gonna do with him?' Emmet asked his brother.

'Well, I was fixing to shoot him down, only then he took to claiming how he's a buddy of the General.'

A huge, red-faced fellow named Breakenridge said, 'Buddy or not, we can't chance him. He's had a good look at us.'

'I told him my name, to boot.'

'I reckon that settles it, then,' said a weasel-faced fellow with red hair. They called him Snooker, and I never learned his true name. 'I'll do the honors.' He pulled a Winchester out of his saddle holster and worked its lever.

Before he could swing the barrel my way, McSween clapped a hand on his shoulder. 'Hold your water there, pal. I rode with Matthew Forrest. This lad saved his hide, he's aces with me.'

'I don't reckon he's ever even *met* your General,' Emmet said. 'He knows he's in a fix. Likely just a pack of lies.'

'Can you prove you ain't lying to us?' Chase asked me.

'I could tell you how his wife, Mable, saved him from the Apaches and caught a dozen or more arrows in the backside for her troubles. She walked with a limp to her dying day.'

'She's passed on?' McSween asked.

'Yes, I'm afraid so. Matthew, too.'

'I'm right sorry to hear the news.' Turning to Chase, he said, 'I don't see as how it'd be right and proper to shoot this lad. He ain't fibbing. Mrs Forrest sure enough had a hitch to her gait. The story went, she got it fighting Indians when her and the General got ambushed.'

'I'd be honored to join the gang,' I said. 'You wouldn't need to split the booty with me.'

'We don't have a mount to spare,' Chase explained.

'Well,' said McSween, 'I reckon he might double up with me. Either that, or we oughta let him go on his way.'

'Where you trying to get to, Willy?' Chase asked.

'Tombstone. I was traveling there with Sarah Forrest . . .'

'Tombstone! Why, that's clear down in Arizona Territory. You won't get there riding with us.'

'It's a mite far to hike with nothing but rags on your feet,' McSween said.

'Actually, I was simply hoping to reach the next railroad depot.'

'How come we don't let him stay with the train?' McSween suggested. 'They'll get it running again, by and by. He can ride on along with it.'

'He knows us,' Snooker whined.

'I won't betray you. You have my word as a gentleman on that. However, I'm afraid the train won't be fit to take me anywhere. As I explained to Mr Calhoun, it's likely to be demolished in the crash.'

They all glanced about at each other.

'That's what he told me, all right,' Chase said. 'He seems to believe it'll run smack down into the gorge, here.'

'What does *he* know about such business,' Emmet muttered, scowling my way.

'We've derailed four trains already,' Chase said, 'and never a one of them crashed much.'

'Have you ever done it this close to a gorge?' I asked him.

'I'm afraid the lad has a point,' McSween said. 'Perhaps we ought've pulled the rail a hair farther off from the bridge. If she comes along under a full head of steam, who's to say but what she *won't* sail down here? We don't wanta be the ones to cause a wreck, you know.'

'They'd make it mighty hot for us,' Chase agreed.

'What we oughta do,' McSween said, 'is ride on up the tracks a distance and yank a rail there.'

'I'm sure it would save a number of innocent lives,' I said.

Snooker commenced to complain, and Emmet took his side. But Chase put an end to the protests when he pulled a watch from his shirt pocket. 'The express'll be along in fifteen, twenty minutes. We ain't got time to fool with another rail. What we'll do, we'll post Willy down the tracks so he can try and wave her down. She might brake for a boy in a nightshirt. That'll slow her down enough so she won't go over the edge.'

'He'll warn 'em, Chase.'

'I trust that he won't,' McSween said, giving me a friendly nod.

I nodded back at him.

Chase mounted up, then reached a hand down for me. I grabbed hold, and he hauled me up behind him. I lost the sleeve off one foot and had to squirm and kick some to get myself aboard. What with my state of dress, it caused considerable amusement for the audience below. Emmet and Snooker hooted and whistled and made remarks. McSween handed the sleeve up to me so I could put it on later.

I hung on tight to Chase as the horse carried us up the slope. I had saddle bags under me. They were leather, and hot from the sun, so they didn't feel good against my skin.

But I didn't mind the discomfort much. I was rather pleased with myself, actually. I'd managed to hang on to my life. It looked like the train might not crash, after all. And riding sure did beat walking.

I had my arms around Chase's waist. I gave some thought to going for his guns. They were in easy reach. If I was quick enough, I might be able to disarm him. Make him climb down. Then I could take his horse on up the tracks, meet the train and prevent the robbery altogether.

Why, I'd be quite a hero. I judged the railroad would likely be so grateful I might get a free ride all the way to Tucson.

I couldn't bring myself to try it, though. Too risky. But also, it seemed too lowdown. I didn't care at all for the rest of the gang, but I rather liked Chase and McSween. They'd put their trust in me. It just wasn't in me to do them dirty.

By and by, Chase said, 'I reckon this is far enough.' He

halted his horse and helped me to the ground. 'Have a try, Willy. But if she stops and you tell on us, folks are likely to end up dying. You'll be one of 'em.'

'I'll simply explain that I need a ride,' I told him.

Then he trotted off, raising dust. I tied the sleeve around my foot. By the time I got done, Chase was almost to the bridge. I watched until he rode down the slope and vanished.

More than likely, nobody had an eye on me. I was no longer in the clutches of the outlaws. And I figured they weren't likely to hunt me down if I took a notion to race down the embankment and hightail into the woods. I'd be shut of them, and free.

It wouldn't hurt them any.

Sure would hurt the folks aboard the express, though.

Besides, I'd be missing my chance to see a gang of real desperados rob a train.

So I stayed there by the tracks.

Pretty soon, a whistle tooted way off in the distance.

CHAPTER TWENTY-NINE

The Holdup

The train slid around a far-off bend, its chimney chugging out black smoke that hung above the whole train, thick near the front, spreading out some over the freight and passenger cars, rising higher and thinning out behind the caboose. In the distance as it was, the whole string seemed to be moving rather slow and quiet.

It got quicker and noisier, the nearer it came.

Pretty soon, the ground took to shaking under my feet.

I stayed between the rails and waved my arms. Well, the whistle howled and howled like it was shouting at me to get out of the way. The engineer, he leaned out his window and flapped an arm at me. Yelled, too, but I couldn't hear him.

The train kept on thundering closer and tooting.

Then it screeched. Steam hissed and spit from the locomotive, throwing out white clouds down low to the tracks. Sparks sprayed up from the wheels as they skidded over the rails.

I could see it wouldn't stop in time to miss me, so I jumped clear. Not a second later, the sun was blocked out by the great engine. I covered my ears to save them from the awful noise. Things got hot for my legs, but it didn't hurt too much. All wheezes and squeals, the train slowed to a halt.

I'd done it!

The engineer and fireman both jumped down. They came striding back past the coal car. They didn't look any too pleased.

'You hoping for an early grave, son?' the engineer asked. He was an older fellow dressed in overalls and a tall, striped hat.

The other fellow, the fireman, didn't say a thing. He stood in front of me with his fists planted on his hips, scowling. He was red and dripping sweat. He had more muscles than any man I'd ever seen before. His face had muscles.

'I'm afraid I fell from a train last night,' I said.

'You *fell*?'

The fireman shook his head. His eyes were squinted so narrow I wondered how he could see with them.

'Actually, a bloke picked me up and *tossed* me.'

The fireman grinned.

If I'd had any notion to warn these fellows they were on their way to a stickup, I lost it when I saw that grin.

'My fare was paid all the way to El Paso,' I explained. 'I should be most grateful for a ride.'

The engineer rubbed his chin and looked at my feet.

'Please, sir.'

After letting out a sigh, he said, 'I s'pose we can give you a ride to the next station, anyhow. Seeing as how we've already gone and stopped. I had half a mind to keep moving, but you looked so set on flagging us down, I suspicioned the bridge might be out. How's the bridge?'

'I shouldn't say that it's out. However, it did seem rather rickety. You'd be well advised to proceed with care.'

I heard somebody huffing up behind me, and turned around. It was the conductor, a little fellow, holding his cap down tight as if to keep the wind from stealing it. There wasn't any wind, but he didn't let the lack of it interfere. The gold chain of a watch swayed across the front of his waistcoat. One side of his jacket was swept back behind the revolver holstered on his right hip.

'What have we here?' he asked, giving me the eye.

'Take him on back with you,' the engineer said. 'He claims he got chucked from the southbound last night.'

'Natty attire,' said the conductor.

'Hurry,' the engineer said. 'We're losing time.'

With a crook of his finger, the conductor gestured for me to follow him. 'I'm much obliged,' I called to the other two, then hurried after the little man.

We were still walking along the right of way when the whistle blasted. A wave of rattles and clanks came running down from the front. The passenger car beside us jumped forward with a lurch. Then the one behind it did the same. Pretty soon, the whole string was creeping along.

The conductor stepped a bit closer to the tracks. We stopped and waited while the train picked up more and more speed. It still wasn't going particularly fast, though, when the caboose rolled by.

The conductor almost let it pass, then caught a handle and hopped onto the steps of the rear platform. As he scooted up, I grabbed hold and swung myself aboard.

We entered the caboose.

'Take a seat,' he said. I pulled a chair away from the cluttered desk, but he snapped, 'Not there. What's the matter with you?' Then he pointed me to a bench across from a potbelly stove.

I sat down on it. 'I'm much obliged for the ride,' I told him.

'Ain't my doing. I got work to do, so keep your mouth shut.'

'Yes, sir,' I said.

He sat at the desk and started working on some papers. And near fell out of his chair when all of a sudden the train braked. 'What in the nation!'

Glaring at me like it was my fault, he popped to his feet.

I shrugged, all innocent.

'What's going on?'

'I've no idea, really.'

Well, he rushed over to a window and poked his head out. Then he cried, 'Damn!' He shoved back from the window, snatched out his sixgun, and pointed it at me. 'You dirty bastard, you tricked us!'

'Don't shoot! Please! I'm not one of them.'

Some guns went off. The conductor, his eyes almost jumped out of his head. I've never seen a fellow so red in the face.

He thumbed back the hammer and let it drop.

I judged I was dead.

The hammer landed with just a clank, not a blast. I didn't wait for him to try again, but leaped off the bench and struck his gun hand. Not a moment too soon. I hadn't more than whacked it when he got off a shot. The noise slapped my ears, but the bullet missed me. I threw a punch into his belly. His air whooshed out, and he tumbled back against a wall. Slammed it pretty hard.

I twisted his hand till he dropped the gun, then used both my fists to lay into him. He didn't seem to have much fight left, but I was sore. I kept on pounding him. 'I'm *not* with

213

them,' I shouted while I punched. 'I *told* you that! Damn your bloody eyes!' Punch punch punch. 'And yet you tried to *shoot* me!' Punch punch punch. 'You'd no reason to *do* that!'

I went on railing at him and hitting him. But pretty soon I realized he wasn't in any shape to appreciate my efforts. I stepped back away from him, and he slumped to the floor and didn't move.

I picked up his revolver and aimed it at him. I had half a notion to shoot him. After all, he'd done his best to kill me and it was only pure luck that he hadn't put a slug in my chest. But then I got hold of my temper.

I was in enough trouble without plugging a railroad conductor. He'd mistaken me for one of the robbers, and I reckoned I could expect the same judgement from the engineer and fireman.

If I stuck around.

He got stirred up some when I commenced to strip off his duds, so I laid the barrel across his head. After that, he didn't give me any more trouble. I shucked off my nightshirt and the ragged sleeves I'd been wearing on my feet. Then I got into his trousers, socks, boots and shirt. They fit snug, but I reckoned they would have to do for now.

I buckled his belt around my waist and holstered the gun.

He was moaning some by the time I finished. I restrained myself, however, and didn't clobber him again.

I emptied out the pockets, not wanting to steal what I didn't need.

He was still stretched out on the floor when I rushed out the rear of the caboose. I jumped to the ground. The gang was near the front of the train. They all had bandannas pulled up to hide their faces, but I could tell one from the next because of their sizes and duds and such. I just caught a glimpse of Chase and McSween and Breakenridge as they climbed into the side door of a car.

Emmet, mounted, held the reins of all the horses. My friends the engineer and fireman were sprawled on the ground by the tracks, Snooker keeping them covered with his Winchester. He and Emmet were both watching the passenger cars, likely prepared to shoot at anyone who tried to interfere. They saw me coming. I waved to show I didn't mean any harm.

Between me and them were four passenger cars, most of

214

the windows open. Nobody seemed foolish enough to poke his head out, but I heard a lot of commotion from inside while I hurried along. There were angry voices, scared voices, a few folks crying and taking on like they figured they'd be getting themselves massacred.

I'd gotten past three of the cars when somebody stretched an arm out a window of the one ahead of me. The hand had a revolver in it.

Snooker and Emmet were both looking the other way, trying to see what was happening in the express car.

Ran through my head to shout a warning.

Judged it wouldn't help much.

I shouted, anyhow, but didn't leave it at that. All Emmet and Snooker got time to do was glance in my direction. By then, the conductor's sixgun was already in my hand. I let fly at the passenger's arm.

This was my first try with a firearm. When it went off, it near jumped out of my grasp. Of course, I missed the target. My bullet went high and knocked a hole through the upper part of the window. But I might as well have hit the arm, for it dropped the gun and jumped back out of sight, never firing a shot.

Emmet, he gave me a curious look with his head tipped sideways. Snooker winked at me.

I hurried along and picked up the passenger's revolver. It was a Colt .45 Peacemaker, the same as the conductor's. I holstered it, and shoved the conductor's gun under my belt.

Then I hurried on and joined up with Snooker and Emmet.

'Dang!' Snooker said. 'Ain't you the one!'

'Yeah,' Emmet said. 'Thanks.' Unlike Snooker, he didn't seem too friendly.

I couldn't help but smile.

In just the course of a few minutes, I'd been shot at, I'd beaten the conductor senseless, robbed him, and fired at a passenger. All those things shook me up considerable. So did knowing I'd joined in on the side of the outlaws. But I felt mighty pleased with myself, anyhow.

'I'm delighted I was able to help,' I said. 'The conductor was kind enough to loan me his weapon.'

Snooker laughed from under his bandanna. 'Appears he loaned you a sight more than his iron.'

'He was quite generous, really.' I stepped past the two

prisoners and nodded toward the express car. 'May I?'

'See what's taking so long,' Snooker said.

So I climbed aboard. Just in time to see Breakenridge fetch the strongbox a kick. He looked even bigger than I remembered him. Big and burly as a bear, but his kick didn't even shake the safe.

'Take more'n your boot,' McSween allowed.

'Well, *shitfire!*'

Chase had the drop on a fellow who looked scared and had a bloody hand clamped over his mouth. 'Didn't hardly recognize you, all dressed up.'

'I was forced to subdue the conductor.'

'Good for you, Willy!' McSween said.

'We've run into some trouble here,' Chase explained. 'The messenger, he won't open the box for us.'

'Can't,' the fellow said from behind his bloody fingers.

'That's what he claims. Says it's a through-safe, locked in Denver and can't be opened till El Paso.'

'I don't reckon he's lying,' McSween said.

'Hey!' Breakenridge called from somewhere in the dark near the front of the car. 'Here's the ticket.' He came back with an ax. 'Stand clear, buddies!'

We gave him some room. He hefted the ax over his shoulder and swung it down. It chopped against the safe with a terrible clamor, and bounced off. The door stayed shut. The blow did little more than leave a scratch on the box's steel top. He had another go, with the same result.

'Too bad it ain't made out of logs,' McSween said.

Breakenridge paid no attention, but gave the box about ten more licks. He might've kept at it all day, but the ax handle finally broke. The head flew up and whistled past Chase's face.

'Lord sakes!' Chase blurted.

'We ain't getting into it,' McSween said.

Breakenridge gave it another taste of his boot, then flung the ax handle off into the darkness.

'We might take the safe with us,' I suggested. 'Given enough time, we should be able to . . .'

'Tried that once,' Chase said.

'Let's just see what we can get off the passengers,' McSween said. 'Better than going off empty-handed.'

Chase jabbed his gun into the express messenger's chest.

216

'You stay here. Poke your head out, and we'll oblige you by blowing a hole through it.'

'Yes, sir,' he said between his fingers.

We all climbed down. Breakenridge, who was winded and sweaty from his labors with the ax, slid the door shut.

Chase explained the situation to Snooker and Emmet.

'We could've got in it easy if we'd only just brought us along some dynamite,' Snooker said, sounding whiny.

'Right,' Chase told him. 'And got our own selves blowed to Kingdom Come.'

'Farney never knew what-for about the stuff. He was the stupidest ass to ever . . .'

'Don't speak ill of them that's gone,' McSween said.

'He wouldn't *be* gone if . . .'

'Well, we don't *have* dynamite, so leave it lie. Let's just gather up what loot we can from the passengers and be on our way.'

'I want in on it,' Emmet said.

'You stay with the horses,' Chase told him.

'Let *him*,' Emmet said, nodding at me. 'I always gotta mind the horses. It ain't fair.'

'We didn't come here to shoot people,' Chase said.

'I won't shoot a soul!'

'So long as a soul doesn't happen to cough behind you,' McSween said.

That brought him a sharp glance from Emmet.

'Y'all gonna hold that against me forever? It just ain't fair. No fair! All I ever get to do any more is hang on to the reins and wait around while everybody else has the fun.'

'Give the boy another chance,' Breakenridge said.

'A feller already tried to plug us out a window,' Snooker added. 'Willy took a shot at him and . . .'

'Missed,' Emmet said.

'Got close enough to scare him off. But what I'm saying, we don't know but what we might run into a feisty passenger or two. If it comes down to gunplay, couldn't hurt none to have Emmet along.'

Chase seemed to think it over for a spell. Then he nodded his head. Looking at me, he said, 'You'd have to watch our prisoners here. Think you can handle them?'

'I managed the conductor, and he had the benefit of a

firearm.' I patted the handle of the revolver I'd taken off him.

'You might have a call to shoot one of these fellers,' McSween said. 'Have you got the sand?'

'They'll either lie still, or meet dire consequences.'

'Good enough for me,' Chase said. 'All right, Emmet. But mind your weapon. Nobody's to get ventilated without he pulls down on us and asks for it.'

'You got my word.' Looking mighty happy now, Emmet climbed down off his horse and handed all the reins to me.

Then the whole gang hurried off on foot. They stayed in a cluster, talking among each other, then split up alongside the first two passenger cars. When they were in position, they pulled their revolvers. All at the same time, they rushed up the stairs. Chase and Emmet entered the lead car, front and back. McSween and Snooker went in the front of the next, Breakenridge the rear.

They hadn't more than got inside when gunshots thundered. Some folks shrieked and others commenced to bawl. Then I heard Chase call out, 'This is a hold-up, friends. Settle down. We don't aim to hurt you. We don't want nothing but your money and watches. Just hand 'em on over to my pal when he comes by. We'll get done right quick, and you can be on your way.'

I didn't suppose they'd be on their way any too soon, not with the rail out. From where I stood, though, I could see that the engine had stopped short of the ruined section of track, and hadn't derailed at all.

'You're starting down a hard road, son,' the engineer said.

I looked down at him, sprawled there on the ground beside the fireman. They both had their heads turned, their eyes on me. Neither of them made a move to get up, but I switched the load of reins into my left hand and unholstered the Colt.

'You don't want no part of these doings,' the engineer told me.

'If I'd taken no part in these doings, sir, your train would presently be a heap of debris at the bottom of the gorge. It was my idea to flag you down.'

'If that's the case, I'm mighty grateful.'

'Your conductor took me for one of the outlaws and tried to shoot me down.'

'That's no call for you to turn to a life of crime, son. I ain't asking you to let us go or nothing of the sort. All I'm

218

saying is you shouldn't ride off with this bunch. You ride with outlaws, you'll wind up eating lead or swinging at the short end of a rope. That's a plain fact. What you wanta do is bid 'em a fare thee well and stay here. We'll see to it you get a fair trial.'

Up till he mentioned the fair trial, he near had me.

'I do appreciate your concern, sir. However, I'd rather prefer to take my chances with the gang. They haven't shot at me once, whereas your law-abiding conductor never gave me so much as the benefit of a doubt before he fired upon me.'

'You're making a bad mistake, son.'

'Perhaps. Now you lie still and leave me in peace.'

'Leave him in peace,' the fireman said. 'He's a dead man, but just don't know it yet.'

'Shut your mouth.' I pointed my Colt at it. He grinned, then rested his face on his crossed arms.

Pretty soon, Chase and Emmet trotted down the stairs from each end of their car. Emmet had his gun in one hand, a valise in the other. He hadn't gone in with the valise. I wondered if it might be full of loot.

It looked a lot like Whittle's leather bag. Whittle's loot hadn't been money and watches, but parts taken from Mary.

Watching Emmet and Chase hurry on to the third passenger car, I remembered myself walking along the street so long ago on that cold, rainy night in Whitechapel. Following the Ripper. It came to me how, if I'd only just let him go and not rushed in to save that whore, I never would've found myself standing here in league with a band of robbers.

If I'd let him go, the whore'd be dead. But Trudy and her father and Michael, they'd likely still be among the living. I never would've met up with Sarah. I wondered if the General and Mable might still be alive, but judged they wouldn't be. Me being at the house probably hadn't done them any harm. But Sarah wouldn't have traveled west if not for me, so whatever might come of that would be my fault. Whatever Briggs might do with her.

The ladies in Tombstone, and whoever else Whittle might've killed in America, they wouldn't be dead if it weren't for me. Maybe more women in London would be, though.

Finally, it ran through my head that it was me who'd caused the train not to derail and crash. If I hadn't interfered

219

with Whittle that night, I'd be home with Mother right now and the train would likely be a heap of rubble at the bottom of the gorge, all sorts of passengers broken up and dead.

It was enough to make me dizzy, thinking about all the folks whose lives had either been saved or lost, or only just changed considerable, for no other reason than because I'd taken a notion to follow Whittle and stop him from butchering just one whore.

It's mighty confounding, in life, how so much good and harm can get set into motion by just a single lad who only meant to do the proper thing.

Now, I'd thrown in with a gang of outlaws.

I couldn't see much good coming of that, but it sure beat the notion of standing trial.

Anyhow, I waited, bothering my head, but not completely lost in my thoughts. I stayed aware enough to make sure my prisoners behaved and the horses stayed put, and to kind of watch the train. Chase and Emmet weren't in the third passenger car for long when the others jumped down and hurried along to the last car before the caboose. I was too busy with my other thoughts to wonder about the conductor. He never showed his face, though.

When the bunch started heading back, all the deep thinking deserted me. They had my full attention. They carried three satchels among them, so they must've done rather well. They walked slow, keeping their eyes on the windows till they got past the passenger cars.

'Any trouble?' Chase asked me.

'Not at all. And you?'

'It went slick as grease.'

They emptied the satchels into their saddle bags, then took their reins from me and mounted up.

McSween brought his horse over close to me. 'You done a fine job, Willy. Climb on aboard.' He reached down to give me a hand.

'Don't do it, son,' the engineer warned. He seemed a good fellow who wanted to save me from a bad end.

Emmet laid a bullet into the dirt no more than an inch from the engineer's nose. It threw up dust into his eyes.

I grabbed hold of McSween's hand. He swung me up behind his saddle.

As we galloped toward the bridge, every last one of the band pulled his gun and took to firing into the air. They shouted out whoops and banged away at the sky. Hugging the steed with my knees, I unlimbered both my Colts and let fly.

It was simply bully!

But part of me was listening and counting.

The sixgun I'd taken off the conductor, it fired four times.

CHAPTER THIRTY

Shooting Lessons

We went charging to the bottom of the slope and didn't stop when we came to the water, but raced downstream, staying in the shallows near the shore. We splashed along right quick for a while, then slowed and took it easy.

McSween and I were at the rear. Some of the others were laughing and talking up ahead, but what with the rushy sounds of the water and the hoofs plopping and such, I couldn't make out a thing they said.

We must've put quite a few miles between us and the train before we finally rode up onto the bank and dismounted. I untrapped my feet from the tight boots, waded into the water and helped myself to a drink while the others tied their horses to some bushes and pulled off the saddle bags.

By the time I joined them, they'd dumped the loot into a heap. They were sitting on the ground, busy separating the watches from the money. I sat down by McSween.

Well, looked like they had enough watches to open up a shop. They had a good big pile of coins, too, and a bundle of greenbacks.

'It don't appear we've struck it rich,' Breakenridge said.

'Should've let *me* try the messenger,' Snooker said.

'I stuck my iron through his teeth,' Chase told him. 'If he could've opened up the safe, he would've.'

'Poor fellow wet himself,' McSween said, and commenced to roll a smoke. After he got it fired, he offered his makings to me.

I thanked him, and took him up on the offer. The others got busy counting the money and didn't notice how I fumbled about with the tobacco pouch and paper. Otherwise, they'd have had a good laugh on my account. It required quite a bit of work, but I finally had myself a crooked cigarette with tobacco leaking out its tip.

McSween, who'd been watching the count, looked over at me. He only glanced at my cigarette, then plucked it from my mouth. Just as nimble as you please, he flipped it open, took his pouch and tapped in some more tobacco, then tongued the paper, rolled it, tightened it up and smoothed it out.

I was in the midst of saying, 'I'm more accustomed to a pipe,' when he poked the remade smoke between my lips.

'There you go,' was all he said. Then he lit it for me.

'Thank you so much,' I said.

We sat there and smoked. By and by, the others finished counting. All together, they'd taken a total of $985.36 from the train passengers.

'Well,' McSween said, 'it's better than we done last month at Pueblo.'

'Just by a hair,' Chase said.

'We had to divvy up that eight ways,' Breakenridge pointed out. 'This time, we only got the five of us.'

I wondered what had become of the other three. Maybe they'd simply moved on. But maybe they'd been shot or captured. Had Farney been one of them – the fellow who'd blown himself up with dynamite? I didn't think I ought to ask.

'Six,' McSween said.

Breakenridge gave me a surly look. 'He ain't one of us.'

'I don't see it that way, Meriwether,' McSween told him.

Breakenridge bristled. It appeared he didn't care to hear what must've been his Christian name. But he kept his mouth shut. Big and powerful as he was, he apparently knew better than to tangle with McSween.

'What do you say, Chase?'

'You needn't give me any,' I spoke up. 'It's quite all right, really.'

'Seems to me,' Chase said, 'the kid deserves a cut. He handled the conductor for us, tended to the horses, kept the prisoners from acting up.'

'Took a shot at that damn hot-head passenger,' Snooker added.

'And missed,' Emmet put in. He did like to remind everybody of my poor aim.

'He done fine,' Snooker said.

'We'll cut it six ways,' Chase said. And that's what they did. I ended up with $150.00. I did some calculating and judged I'd been shorted to the tune of about fourteen dollars, but I didn't let on.

This was far and away more wealth than I'd ever had in my whole life.

McSween picked out a watch for me. It wasn't near as fine as the one Sarah'd given to me, but I accepted it.

'What'll be done with the other watches?' I asked.

'We'll sell 'em off when we get to Bailey's Corner,' Chase explained. 'We got a feller there gives us a good price on 'em.'

'Bailey's Corner?' I asked.

'That's about a week's ride from here,' McSween told me. 'We'll head on down there and kick up our heels.'

'Whooee!' cried Snooker, who apparently fancied the notion of kicking up his heels.

McSween slapped my shoulder. 'We'll fix you up good, Willy. Get you outfitted proper.'

'Smashing,' I said.

After that, Chase dumped all the watches into a saddle bag. I got back into the tight boots. Then we mounted up and rode across the river. We left it behind us, and pretty soon we left the woods behind us, too. Hour after hour, we rode along over rocks and dusty yellow earth that glared with the sun, hardly a tree anywhere to give us shade. The only things that seemed to grow out here were cactus and scraggly little bushes. They were mostly in blossom, it being May.

May or not, the sun felt almighty warm. Nor was my seat behind McSween's saddle too comfortable, particularly as my bum had gotten itself scuffed up the night before. Aside from that soreness, I ached in my legs and all up my back from riding so long. I was hungry, too. These fellows hadn't eaten since the time I'd joined up with them.

I took to thinking that the life of an outlaw had its drawbacks. Would've been a lot easier on these fellows to take regular jobs as store clerks or such, instead of tackling robberies so they had to spend their time on horseback riding mile after mile.

But they'd sure made themselves a load of money for their troubles. So had I.

My pockets were just stuffed to the brim with greenbacks and jangling coins.

I didn't feel quite right about my new wealth. After all, it had been stolen from folks who'd likely worked hard to earn

224

it. I didn't see a convenient way to return it to them, though. It might as well be in my own pockets, instead of split around among the others in the gang.

Besides, I judged that I deserved some recompense. It might be looked upon as repayment for the favor of saving all those folks from a nasty crash. Not only that, but one of those law-abiding folks – the conductor – had tried to murder me. I hadn't even done a thing wrong. But did that stop him? No, sir. I'd be dead with a bullet in my chest if his gun hadn't misfired. I figured $150.00 was about fair pay for playing target for that rascal.

By the time I had it all parsed out, my regrets about the money seemed foolish. Taken all around, maybe I deserved more than what I got.

I still do feel that way, mostly. I can't bring myself to feel ashamed of taking my split. It was wrong, of course. But my conscience has plenty of awful doings to work on without fretting over what I gained from a robbery that wasn't my fault, anyhow.

Sometime late in the afternoon, a jackrabbit made the mistake of showing itself. It no sooner hopped into view from behind a bush than Snooker leaped from his horse, whipped out his Winchester, and tried to draw a bead on it. The hare was pretty far off by the time Snooker fired his first shot. His bullet *whinged* off a rock. His next kicked up dirt. Well, that rabbit dodged four shots. But the fifth threw it tumbling. Snooker yelled, 'Whoooee!'

'Fine shot!' McSween called to him. 'Reckoned you'd get it right if you tried long enough.'

The remark didn't seem to bother Snooker. He just grinned, then slid his rifle into its boot, swung himself onto his horse, and galloped out to where the hare lay on its side. His horse hadn't even stopped moving before he hopped off. He hit the ground at a run, snatched up his prize, leaped into his saddle and came racing back toward us, whooping and hollering and swinging the dead critter over his head by its ears. When he got closer, you could see blood spraying out. It sprinkled Snooker considerable, but he didn't pay it any mind.

I figured the hare was meant to be food, and Snooker would want to dismount and clean it. We'd all have a chance to get off the horses. I was mighty eager to stand on my own feet and stretch and take a rest from the misery. But Snooker joined up with us and we kept on riding.

He cleaned his game, sure enough. But he stayed in his saddle to do it, holding the hare off to the side and carving away at it with his knife. Watching the guts drop out and fall to the ground, I was put in mind of Whittle. I turned my head away and studied the back of McSween's shirt.

By and by, Emmet shouted, 'Mine! I got it!'

He went racing after another rabbit, reins in his teeth, his hands full of iron. He blazed away just twice. His first slug tore off half the critter's head. His second, fired at near the same instant, took it in his rear and knocked it sideways.

It was the most splendid bit of shooting I'd seen up to that time.

'Astonishing,' I muttered.

'Seen worse,' McSween said.

'I certainly wish *I* could shoot in such a manner.'

'Well, ask him real sweet, and maybe he'll show you a thing or two.'

I decided to do precisely that.

Later in the afternoon, we stopped near a creek where a stand of cottonwoods grew and there was some grass. Chase sent me off to gather firewood while the rest of them saw to their horses. When I returned with an armload, they were arranging their saddles and bedrolls under the trees. McSween said I could borrow his saddle blanket for the night. So I took that and spread it out to air.

I hadn't more than laid it on the ground when McSween called to Emmet. 'The lad here purely admires your talent with the Colts. You oughta take him over yonder and learn him a few tricks.'

My face heated up. But I said, 'I'd be quite grateful.'

Emmet, he grinned. 'You think I'm good, do you?'

'Quite the best I've ever seen.'

'You're a regular John Wesley Hardin,' Snooker said. 'I can sure outgun you any day of the week with both eyes shut.'

'If you could slap leather as good as you flap your gums, you'd be a wonder to behold.'

At that, Emmet took the opportunity to slap leather. Both guns seemed to jump into his hands. They came up cocked and ready. But he didn't let the hammers drop. He just grinned at Snooker, who hadn't gone for his at all.

Snooker's hand had darted to his face, not his holster.

Pulling his fingertip out of his nose, he studied what he'd found up there and said, 'You beat me fair and square, you little booger.'

Emmet laughed, lowered the hammers with his thumbs, and holstered the weapons. Then he squatted down, felt around inside one of his saddle bags, and came up with a box of ammunition. 'Come on along, Willy,' he said.

The others stayed behind. We walked down along the creek a ways. Then Emmet stopped and nodded toward a dead stump on the other side, about thirty feet off. 'Watch here,' he said.

After setting the box of cartridges on the ground, he stood loose, arms hanging at his sides, and stared over at the stump. 'That's an hombre there that's fixing to poke me full of lead. Now, I just can't count on him missing. From what I've seen, most fellers can't shoot any better than you do, but I can't *count* on that, you see? So I wanta plug him before he gets to take a crack. That's what the quickdraw's all about. As a general rule, the man that clears leather and gets off the first shot's gonna be the one that walks away. Here goes.'

Emmet snatched out both his Colts. In a flash, they came up cocked and level and spat lead. His bullets thunked into the stump, throwing out little clouds of dust and wood.

'Ripping!' I said.

'They don't come much better,' Emmet told me.

'Have you been in actual gunfights?'

'Why, I should say so. I've killed four men.' He seemed right proud of the accomplishment.

Not wanting to appear the complete novice, I said, 'I've killed one man, myself.'

He narrowed an eye at me. 'You?'

'Oh yes, quite. A bloke had a go at me in London, and I dispatched him with a knife.' Actually, I was never certain the man had died, but he'd told me he would. That seemed good enough for the purpose of bragging.

The way Emmet looked at me, he couldn't figure out whether I was lying or not. But he said, 'A knife won't do you no good at all out here. Any man that's worth his salt packs iron and ain't afraid to use it. You gotta be quicker than the next guy, or you just won't last. And you gotta hit what you aim at.'

He stepped aside, then nodded at the stump.

I let my arms hang, the way I'd seen him do. Then I went for my Colts. The one in the holster came out clean, but I had a spot of trouble with the one in my belt. By and by, I got them both up and cocked. I pulled the triggers. The hammers clanked.

Emmet snickered.

'Ain't *you* the gunfighter?'

My face heated up something awful. 'I'm terribly sorry.'

'Terribly dead, that's what you'd be if that was more than an old dead tree over there.'

'I'm afraid my irons are empty.'

'I noticed that.' Laughing some, he picked up the box and opened it. 'You don't hardly need two Colts just now. You'll be lucky to handle one good enough to count.'

'Yes, sir,' I said. I jammed the conductor's pistol down my belt, then helped myself to some ammunition.

Then stood there with my sixgun in one hand and cartridges in the other. Stood there and stared at them and sweated.

Emmet grinned at me. 'What're you fixing to do with 'em?' he asked.

'Slip them into the gun, is it?'

'That's the idea.'

What I did, I took a cartridge between my thumb and finger and tipped the barrel up and puzzled over the matter. I'd handled the General's weapons, but I never had occasion to load them. I simply didn't have a clue as to how I might go about it. Sliding a round down the muzzle didn't seem the proper way. The bullets had to get into the cylinder, somehow. I was still trying to figure it out when Emmet suddenly commenced to split his sides.

He acted like he'd never seen anything funnier. He laughed so hard he couldn't stand up straight and his eyes filled with tears. Every now and then, he'd gasp out a word or so. An 'Oh, Lord!' or a 'Never in my born days!' or a 'Wish the boys was here!'

The boys *wasn't* here, and mighty glad I was for that. Though I suspected they'd be hearing about me.

Emmet went on busting himself with gaiety and tears while I worked on my problem. He was still at it when I found a little door behind the Colt's cylinder. It opened sideways, and showed me a used shell. I shook that one out and replaced it with a fresh round. Then I turned the cylinder and repeated the trick. I put in six cartridges and shut the door.

Emmet hadn't noticed at all. He'd worn himself out. He was bent over, holding his knees and gasping when I fired into the air.

The noise jerked him up straight. He gazed at me. His red, wet face grinned. Then he applauded.

'I'm not a total dunce, really,' I said.

Shaking his head, he rubbed his eyes and took some deep breaths. Finally, he said, 'Now that you're loaded . . .' and then wheezed and took on again. Finally, he got control of himself. 'Let's see . . . let's see if you can hit anything. Oh . . . they do work so much better . . . with bullets in 'em.'

Well, I stuck my arm out straight, pointed my Colt at the stump, and pulled the trigger. The gun blasted and jumped. Through the ringing in my ears, I heard a quiet thud. A puff exploded off the stump.

I'd hit it dead center!

'I say!' I blurted.

Emmet looked at me and wiped one of his eyes. 'Only thing is, you took all day to do it.'

I holstered the Colt, rubbed the sweat off my hand onto the leg of my trousers, then tried for a quickdraw. I snatched the gun up quick. It no sooner cleared leather than I thumbed back the hammer. I brought the barrel up fast, pointed it in the general direction of the stump, and let fly.

My bullet sang off a rock just to the right of the stump.

Emmet, he didn't laugh or say a word.

I had another go. This time, I hit the stump.

Twice more, I unlimbered that Colt with all the speed I could muster and got off my shots. Both of them poked holes in the target.

Emmet looked at me, frowning some.

I took a deep breath, feeling pleased with myself and more than a trifle surprised. The air smelled strong with gunsmoke. It seemed a fine aroma.

'I did rather well, wouldn't you say?'

'You ain't hopeless,' he told me.

I reloaded, slapped leather, and pounded another hole into the stump. Out of six tries, I only missed twice.

Emmet didn't seem particularly happy about my progress. He watched me, narrow-eyed, while I loaded up again. When

229

I finished and holstered my weapon, he stepped over so we were shoulder to shoulder, both facing the stump across the stream. 'On the count of three,' he said. 'One. Two.'

He said, 'Three,' and I pulled. So did he. His Colts blasted, and the roar of them was still in my ears when my shot followed. His slugs smacked the stump not more than a blink or two before mine did the same.

Then he eyed me again. 'I don't much like getting my leg pulled, kid.'

'Pardon me?'

'Acting like you ain't got the first notion how to handle a sixgun . . . like you didn't know how to *load* the damn thing. Making a fool outa me the way you done.'

Seems like I was *forever* getting myself wrongly accused of this or that.

'Why, I've never fired a weapon before today, much less had an occasion to fill one with bullets. Never.'

'Bullsquat.'

'It's the honest truth.'

'You've had your laugh on me.' He put away his Colts, then picked up the ammo box and headed back for camp.

I caught up with him. 'Actually, I apprenticed in gunmanship under no less than Wild Bill Hickok.'

That got him to look at me. 'There you go again. He's been sleeping in sod since seventy-six.'

Some calculating showed me I was no more than about two when Hickok died.

'I'm a spot older than I look,' I told Emmet.

That got him to laugh.

'Who really showed you?' he asked.

'No one but you, actually. I never in my life fired a shot until this very day when that fellow stuck his arm out the train window.'

He gave me a puzzled look. There was some wariness to it, but not much anger.

'I'm not having you on,' I said. 'Believe me. If I'd known what I was about, I most certainly wouldn't have humiliated myself in the matter of loading bullets.'

He took to smiling again when I reminded him of that. 'Land, I've never seen such a thing.'

'I suppose you'll tell everyone.'

'It's just a shame they wasn't there to see it for themselves.'

CHAPTER THIRTY-ONE

My First Night in the Outlaw Camp.

Back at the camp, a big pot of stew was bubbling on the fire. The smell set my mouth to watering.

McSween was busy stirring the mixture, Chase bringing in some more firewood, Snooker cleaning his Winchester, Breakenridge resting on the ground with his back propped up by his saddle, busy at nothing.

'How'd it go?' McSween asked.

'Well,' Emmet said, 'we had us quite a time.'

'Glad to see nobody's wounded,' McSween said.

'You all sure missed a show,' Emmet announced.

With everybody looking on, he drew one of his Colts and plucked a cartridge from his gunbelt. 'This right here's how Willy went to load up,' he said. Holding the pistol in front of his face, frowning and sticking his tongue out a corner of his mouth as if he were trying very hard to think, he poked his bullet into the muzzle. 'I say,' he said, mimicking the way I talk, 'isn't this how it goes, really?'

'No!' Snooker squealed. 'Did he?'

Well, I hadn't and Emmet knew it. But I judged he might like me more if I didn't spoil his fun.

'Sure as I'm standing here.'

Snooker and Breakenridge, they both whooped it up considerable. Emmet, too, though not as hard as he'd done in the first place. 'Yep!' he went on. 'Just what he did!' Chase didn't laugh, but sort of grinned with one corner of his mouth and shook his head at me.

McSween glanced my way, then looked around at the others. He didn't seem amused, but rubbed his whiskery cheek. 'Well,' he said, 'no call to make sport of the lad. He didn't know no better.'

'It just beats all!' Snooker blurted.

'Well, that's what *I* reckoned,' Emmet said, calming down

some. 'But then he figured out where the bullets go, so I picked myself up off the ground and watched him try to shoot.'

'Hope you took cover,' Snooker said.

Emmet gave my arm a squeeze. 'Show 'em, Willy.' With the pistol in his other hand, he pointed to a tree off beyond the campsite. 'See if you can put one in there.'

'Don't plug the horses,' Snooker said.

The horses, they were way off to the other side, and not in any danger at all no matter how bad a shot I might be, unless I turned halfway around.

But I didn't figure I *was* a bad shot. Quite the contrary. I was feeling just brimful of talent.

'Hold on, there,' Breakenridge said. He wanted to be standing up so he wouldn't miss the fun.

While he got to his feet, Snooker made quite a show of scampering around behind me. 'Think I'm safe here?' he asked.

'Quit your funnin' the lad,' McSween told him. He unsquatted and turned to watch me.

They *all* watched me.

'Are we quite ready?' I asked.

'Just take her easy,' McSween said. 'Spite of what Emmet likely told you, quickest draw in the world don't matter worth a hill of beans if you miss what you're aiming at.'

'Don't blow your toes off,' Snooker warned.

I pulled and fired. Bark jumped off the tree trunk.

The laughing stopped.

'I'll be,' McSween muttered. 'That's some mighty fair work, Willy.'

Emmet said, 'I learned him real good, huh boys?'

'Where'd you learn to shoot like that?' Chase asked me.

'Over by the creek.'

'He claims he never fired a gun till today,' Emmet explained.

'That the honest truth?' Chase asked.

'Yes, sir,' I said.

'Jesus wept,' Breakenridge said.

'Just don't let it swell your head up,' McSween told me. 'There's a whole lot more to life than being handy with a sixgun. Not that it don't help. But it can get you into scrapes if you don't watch yourself careful.'

'McSween knows plenty about scrapes,' Chase said, and sounded serious.

'That's a fact.'

'I don't suppose I'm quite good enough to start taking on real gunfighters,' I said.

'Glad to hear you say it,' McSween said. 'And you're right. You got loads of natural talent, looks like, but what you gotta do is hone your skills. And learn what you can from those of us that's been around.'

'Thank you. I'd like to learn whatever's necessary.'

McSween and Chase, they'd treated me fine pretty much from the start. But after my demonstration with the Colt, the others warmed up to me. All of a sudden, I was no longer an outsider. They talked to me and joked with me, just like I'd been with the gang forever. It made me feel welcome and happy.

Long about dark, the stew finished cooking. McSween scooped out gobs of it into tin cups, and we all sat around the fire to eat. The rabbit parts were mixed in with beans and onions. A morsel of food hadn't passed my lips since the previous night aboard the train, so I consumed the stew with great relish.

I can't recollect ever enjoying a meal more than that one. Not only did the hot stew taste wonderful, but I was among five new friends who were actual western desperados – actual train robbers. Me. Partnered up with a gang of outlaws.

Good fellows, even if they did ride on the wrong side of the law. Good fellows who figured I had the makings of a gunfighter.

For a while there, I forgot about all my aches and worries. I hardly felt like myself at all. Trevor Wellington Bentley seemed like a stranger I'd left behind. I was Willy. A hard-riding ruffian good with a Colt, caught up in a grand adventure. It was ever so bully!

After we got done eating, I volunteered to take the pot and cups down to the creek. I went off by myself and cleaned them. The night was lovely, all atwinkle with stars, a full moon glinting silver on the water and making all the rocks and bushes look like they were brushed with milk. The creek gurgled along, quiet and peaceful. I could hear the boys talking off in the distance. Some birds were warbling. A coyote howled.

I don't know as I'd ever been quite so happy to be right where I was.

When the supper things were clean, I set them on a rock and dried my hands. I stretched. I filled myself with air that smelled a bit of woodsmoke. Then I snatched out my Colt. Didn't fire, though. The night was too calm for gunshots. I didn't want to stir up the boys, either.

The iron felt heavy and good in my hand.

I holstered it. 'Don't make me ventilate you, hombre,' I whispered. 'Go for your iron, and you'll be sleeping under sod.' The hombre in my head didn't listen to reason. I slapped leather. 'Pow!'

Well, I was having myself a fine time, so I kept at it for a while. By loosening my belt so the holster didn't hang so high, I was able to draw faster. Each time I pulled, though, the gun lifted the holster off my leg a bit. I could see why Emmet and the others tied theirs down. What I needed was a rawhide thong, but I didn't have one.

Not wanting the others to catch on that I'd been practicing, I tightened up my belt again before gathering the utensils and heading back to the fire.

They were passing around a bottle of whiskey. I took my place by McSween's side. He handed me the bottle, and I swigged some, then passed it over to Chase.

'Emmet tells us you killed a feller,' McSween said.

'Only one,' I said, recalling that Emmet had claimed four for himself. 'And you?'

'None that didn't ask for it.'

'Mine asked for it, I reckon. He attacked me, and I did no more than defend myself.'

'Did the law take after you?' Emmet asked.

'Indeed, I found myself pursued by Bobbies and an awful mob. If they'd caught me . . .'

'What the tar are them Bobbies?' Snooker wanted to know.

'Why, they're constables. Policemen.'

'So they had a posse on your tail,' Chase said. 'Been in the same fix our own selves from time to time. How'd you get shut of it?'

'I nipped into a courtyard and hid.'

'This was over there in England?' McSween asked.

'Yes, sir. If I hadn't stabbed that bloke, I'd be there still.'

'So you lit out?'

'Actually, I ran afoul of Jack the Ripper.' None of the boys acted like they'd ever heard of him, but they seemed mighty interested in my tale. So I plugged on, only taking breaks to hear all the things they had to say and to answer questions and to swallow some whiskey whenever the bottle came around.

I explained how the Ripper'd skulked about the East End, murdering whores. Then I told how, after escaping from the mob, I'd taken shelter in Mary's room. How I'd been right there under her bed when the Ripper butchered her. I told about following him afterwards and attacking him.

'That showed a heap of gumption,' McSween said.

'Why, I couldn't allow him to slay the poor woman. I only wish I'd killed him then and spared the world from further woes. If I'd had a Colt in my hand, he'd be in Hell where he belongs.'

I told about stabbing him in the back, and how it hadn't appeared to damage him much at all. The boys took on quite a bit over my removal of Whittle's nose. But they settled down and listened as I described the chase and my plunge into the Thames.

About then, Breakenridge fetched a new bottle from his saddle bag, and we started in on it. I was feeling mighty fine.

After I explained what happened to Trudy's father, Snooker allowed the old man got no worse than he deserved. 'He shouldn't't've busted your head, Willy boy.'

'It goes to show what comes of making wrong estimations in regard to another feller's intentions,' McSween added.

I went on with my story, telling about our trip to Plymouth, the death of the Irishman, then about our voyage across the Atlantic. Why, the boys seemed purely spellbound as I told of how we fought our way through rough seas and those terrible storms.

I was just full of myself and liquor and the joy of having an audience that hung on my every word. I was in rare form. But I got the yacht all the way to Gravesend Bay before I realized I hadn't mentioned much of anything about poor Trudy – only that she'd been aboard and cooked for us. Nothing about the ways Whittle had tormented her, or how she'd been the one to throw the Irishman's head overboard, or how I'd saved her those times from hanging and drowning.

I hadn't left such things out of my story on purpose. They'd simply stayed inside me. And I was glad of that.

Some of the fun leaked out of me when I recalled all that had happened with Trudy, and how she'd ended.

I drank some more whiskey, almost dropped the bottle, but caught it in time. Then I handed it over to Chase.

'We were anchored offshore, that night. I was quite sure Whittle wouldn't let us live. I knew we had to take drastic steps if we were to save Trudy. Michael, however, wanted no part of it. The bloody coward.'

I do have some recollection of calling Michael a bloody coward.

Then it was suddenly morning. I found myself wrapped in a blanket near McSween, sore all over, my head just afire with agony. I grabbed my head to keep it from coming apart. That helped some.

It wasn't quite sunup yet. The others were still snoozing away.

I lay there with my pains and tried to think back. I couldn't remember turning in. For a while, I couldn't remember anything at all that had happened after coming back from the creek and sitting down by the fire. Then bits and pieces started showing themselves. Pretty soon, I recalled what had gone on up till I reached the part in my story where I called Michael a bloody coward.

Beyond that, it was all blank.

Had I passed out? Or had I gone on with my tale? For a while, my worries hurt more than my head, for I feared what I might've told about me and Sarah.

It didn't feel good at all, lying there, so I sat up. My boots were by my head, along with my belt and holster and both guns. I sure couldn't recall taking them off.

Over on the other side of them the grass was matted down with once-used stew. Had I done that?

I checked my clothes. If I'd lost my supper, at least I'd gotten none on me.

Oh, I felt a proper fool.

My mouth was so dry I could hardly swallow, so I got into the boots and went over to the stream. I drank till I couldn't hold any more, then washed up and sat on a rock and hung on to my head.

I had half a notion to wander off, for I sure didn't look forward to facing the boys.

I stayed there even after I heard their voices.

Finally, I worked up my nerve and went back to the camp.

McSween had the fire going. He looked at me and smiled. 'Glad to see you ain't dead, Willy.'

'I rather wish I were.'

'Know how it is.'

I appreciated McSween's kindness. Chase came along, and didn't make sport of me, either. Emmet and Snooker and Breakenridge, however, had themselves a fine time at my expense. I felt too sick to care much. From their comments, I gathered that my story hadn't progressed much beyond telling how I'd beached the yacht and gone along the shore looking for Whittle. I'd got a bit rowdy, at that point, and jumped to my feet and yelled, 'Show your face, you bloody cur! I'll put a slug where your nose use to be!' Then I'd pulled my Colt, dropped it, bent over to pick it up, and would've fallen into the fire except that Chase leaped and caught me.

In spite of my ill health and humiliation, I was mighty glad I'd passed out and never had a chance to blather about me and Sarah.

Well, I survived all the joshing the boys handed out. With some breakfast in me, I felt a spot less sick. But then it came time to mount up. I took my usual place behind McSween. We left the camp behind, and I commenced to experience the most frightful agony as the horse rocked and swayed under me.

By and by, I thought I might lose my breakfast. So McSween let me climb down and walk. Right away, I felt better. The way the horses ambled along, I had no trouble at all keeping up with them. My boots pinched, but not too bad. Every so often, I'd give my feet a rest and ride for a spell. Mostly with McSween, but also with Emmet and Snooker. I couldn't stay on any of their horses for long, though, without feeling woozy. Then I'd jump down and walk some more.

The day seemed to drag on forever.

Finally we stopped and made camp. By then, I wasn't feeling horrible any more, just sore and headachy. Emmet and Snooker tried to talk me into some shooting, but about the last thing I wanted was to hear gunfire. 'I'd rather not, really.'

'There'll be plenty of time for practice,' McSween said, 'when Willy ain't feeling so poorly.'

So they let me off the hook.

After supper, we sat around the fire and the boys passed around a bottle of whiskey. When it came to me, I took one whiff and winced. The others drank, though.

They asked me to go on with my story. Actually, I would've preferred to hear about their adventures, but they insisted, so I went ahead.

I told about finding Whittle's skiff, hiking through the snow and sneaking into General Forrest's house. McSween, he'd been a trooper in the General's command, and asked a passel of questions about him. I talked considerable about the General and Mable, but didn't say much about Sarah. Only that we got to be friends, and how, after the deaths of her grandparents, I'd stayed on as her servant until I read about Whittle in the newspaper and we headed west.

Not a word about our baths or dancing or any such thing.

Even though I mostly kept mum about Sarah, I took to missing her something awful. I tried not to let it show.

When it came time to tell about Briggs, I had to bend the truth considerable. Otherwise, they would've seen it was jealousy that got me into trouble. I let on that Briggs had been rude and ornery to Sarah, and pestered her till I had no choice but to deal with him. Finally, it came to getting myself tossed off the train.

'The next day, I climbed on back up the hill and followed the tracks. I thought Sarah might disembark, don't you know, once she discovered that I'd gone missing. Perhaps she would be waiting for me at the next station down the line. But then I met up with you chaps. I haven't a clue what to do next, actually, other than ride along with you.'

'We're pleased to have you, Willy,' Chase said.

'You've all been mighty good to me.'

'Seems to me,' McSween said, 'like you've got business elsewhere.'

'I do hope to find Sarah.'

'You don't wanta be showing your face around no railroad depots,' Chase said. 'Not for a spell, leastwise.'

'No, I should think not.'

'Not unless you're looking for a chance to use your Colts on something more lively than a stump,' Emmet said.

'You ain't likely to find her, anyhow, walking the rails,' McSween told me. 'By now, your Sarah's either turned around and headed for home, or gone on down the line figuring you might catch up to her at Tombstone.'

'Least if she hasn't been interfered with by that Briggs feller,' Chase added, which didn't make me feel any better.

'I reckon Tombstone is where I need to go. Even if Sarah's not there, it seems the best place to start my search for Whittle.'

'Well,' McSween said, 'you can't go nowhere till we get you a horse. Best thing's to stick with us till we get to Bailey's Corner. You can buy a good mount there and rig yourself up for the hunt.'

CHAPTER THIRTY-TWO

Dire Threats

The next day, I got my horse.

I'd been taking turns riding double with some of the boys, and was mounted behind Emmet when he pointed and said, 'Over yonder.'

I leaned sideways and looked past him. Off to the right, at some distance, a pair of horsemen were headed in our general direction. These were the first strangers we'd come across since lighting out from the train.

Emmet reined in, and the rest of the boys caught up with us.

'Not enough of 'em to be a posse,' Breakenridge said.

'If we had a posse after us,' Chase said, 'it wouldn't likely be coming from the east.'

This talk of posses unsettled me some. Nobody'd mentioned, until now, that we had any reason to worry about such things.

'Don't matter who they are,' McSween said. 'Thing is, there's only just the two of 'em.'

McSween took the lead, and we headed for the strangers. When we got within hailing distance, he waved his arm and called out, 'Howdy, boys!'

One nodded. The other touched a finger to the brim of his hat. They were riding side by side, going slow as if they weren't in any rush to get somewhere. From the looks on their faces, they were neither glad to meet us nor unhappy about it. They didn't rightly have expressions, at all. They just watched us approach.

The older of the two was a slim fellow with grim eyes and a mustache that was just as black as his outfit. His hat was black, same as his string tie and frock coat, trousers, gunbelt and boots. I didn't care at all for the looks of him.

The bloke he rode with wasn't just younger, but heavier.

He looked as if the heat didn't agree with him. His face was red and sweaty, his shirt collar open, his tie hanging loose. He had a black coat like his friend, but it was tied down behind his saddle.

I wondered if they might be a pair of preachers or undertakers, dressed in black that way.

If it'd been up to me, I would've passed them by.

But McSween rode straight toward them. 'Hate to be a bother,' he said, 'but you boys look like you've got a horse to spare.' The last word wasn't out of his mouth before a Colt was in his hand, cocked and pointed at the skinny fellow.

Emmet, Chase and Breakenridge all pulled at once. On both sides of me, hammers went *snick-clack*. Snooker took a while to come out with his Winchester. He worked its lever and shouldered it.

Both the strangers hoisted their arms.

'Climb on down,' McSween said.

They dismounted and stood beside their horses. Each had one hand in the air, the other holding reins.

'Willy, get on over here.'

I slid off the back of Emmet's horse and walked toward the two fellows. The way they glowered at me, I rather shriveled up inside. But then their eyes turned to McSween as he swung to the ground. He stepped in front of them, one at a time, and took their pistols. They never said a word to him. The fat one, his chin was trembling. The mean one looked like he wanted to bite McSween.

After collecting their sidearms, McSween fetched their rifles out of the saddle scabbards. He handed one of the Winchesters to me, then toted the other weapons over to a thicket of prickly bush and tossed them in among the nettles.

Coming back, he said, 'Let's have your boots off, friends.'

They sat on the ground and tugged their boots off.

'Try 'em on, there, Willy.'

'I'd rather not, actually.'

'Go on, now. You need a pair what fits, don't you?'

Well, this didn't seem a good time to argue the matter, so I gathered the boots. I sat down with my back to the fellows so I wouldn't have to look at them, then pulled off the boots I'd taken from the conductor. I tried on the new ones. The first set felt too tight, the second too loose. The loose boots belonged to the fat chap. They felt a sight better than what

I'd been wearing, but I had no wish to keep them on. They were hot and juicy inside so I felt like my feet were sliding about in swamp slime.

So I yanked them off and shook my head. 'They're altogether too large,' I said, and got into my old familiar boots.

'Well, that's a shame,' McSween said.

I carried the boots back to their owners and dropped them.

'Too bad, friends,' McSween told them. 'You lost out on a sale.'

'A sale?' the fat guy asked.

'Why, we ain't here to rob you. Nosirree. Willy here, he'll pay you fair and square for what he needs.' After saying that, McSween checked the horses over pretty good. He looked inside their mouths, ran his hands down their legs, studied their hoofs, and such. Then he came around front and said to the thin fellow, 'He'll give you eighty dollars for your mount, friend. Throw in an extra ten for the tack, and ten for the Winchester. Willy, you owe the man a hundred dollars.'

I wasn't eager to do it, but figured I hadn't much choice. So I counted out my money. I stepped closer to the man, who was still on the ground with his legs stretched out. He just glared up at me. I tossed the money at his feet.

'You take my horse, boy, and I'll kill you sure.'

A chill started to rush through my bones, but then I flinched as a couple of gunshots bashed the silence. The slugs missed him. They kicked dust onto the legs of his black trousers.

'You best watch your tongue, mister,' Emmet said. I looked up at him in time to see smoke drifting away from the muzzles of his Colts.

McSween drew his own pistol. Crouching, he aimed it at the fellow's face and thumbed back the hammer. 'You wanta take back them words?'

'Take 'em back, Prue,' the fatty blurted. 'They'll shoot us both sure.'

'It's *my* horse.'

'No call to threaten a boy's life,' McSween told him. 'He's my buddy. You look like the sort to follow through on a thing like that, so I reckon you either repent your words or die right here.'

'Prue! Good God, man!'

Prue, he looked fit to bust. Not scared at all, but just in a rage, all red in the face, his breath hissing through his gritted teeth.

'What's it gonna be?'

Prue took to nodding.

'What's that?'

'I take it back.'

'How's that?'

'*I won't kill him.*'

'I don't reckon I believe you. Goes against my grain, though, to shoot a man down in cold blood. So I'll tell you this. Listen good. We ain't taking nothing we ain't paid for. We're leaving you a horse and your weapons. No law says we gotta, but it wouldn't be right to do otherwise. You keep that in mind. We treated you fair and square. Now, if you or your pal take it into your heads to come after us, know this. Next time I catch sight of either one of you, I'll figure you come to make good on your threat to the lad. Lead'll fly. It's that simple.'

After having his say, McSween unsquatted and holstered his gun. He led the horse forward between the two men. While I held the reins, he unloaded the bedroll, saddle bags and such so we wouldn't be taking anything we hadn't paid for.

Then I mounted up and slid my new Winchester into its scabbard.

I was awful shaken by the whole affair, but it did feel good to be sitting up high in the saddle of my own horse.

We rode off at a trot. I wanted to dig my heels in and light out fast, but the others just weren't in that much of a rush. Except for me, Snooker was the only one who even looked back to keep an eye on those fellows.

They were watching us. Not even heading for the bush to retrieve their guns.

Well, I reckon they were too smart for such a play.

If they'd fired just a single shot, I've no doubt at all but what McSween would've wheeled around and led the gang in a charge.

The pair was still in sight when we slowed our horses to a walk. Me and Snooker were at the rear. I rode over closer to him and said, 'Do you reckon they'll be coming after us?'

'Never can tell. I'd rest a sight easier if McSween'd shot

'em. Now we're gonna have to watch our backsides.'

'They don't seem at all worried, do they?' I asked, nodding toward the others.

'Them rascals is nothing we can't handle. Just gotta watch they don't take and bushwack us. If they do that, though, they'll wind up dead. We ain't a bunch of gals, you know.'

'I rather suppose you've dealt with worse rascals,' I said.

He gave me a weasely grin full of sharp, yellow teeth. 'None that's still above ground.'

'Who's the best of the lot?'

Patting the stock of his rifle, he said, 'Why, I reckon I could knock the left eye out of a gnat at a hundred yards in a sandstorm. Chase and Emmet, they're mighty sharp with their sixguns, though they can't hold a candle to McSween. You take Breakenridge, now, he's having a lucky day when he can hit the *air*. But I once seen him get shot twice by a card sharp, then lay one punch that turned the bastard's head clean around backwards. They never bothered to untwist him, either. Saw him in his casket.'

'Which side up?' I asked.

Snooker laughed. 'Face and ass!'

'You're having me on.'

'It's the plain truth, just ask Breakenridge.'

I thought I might pass on that, as Breakenridge wasn't one for talking much and generally seemed rather solemn. 'Is that how he came to be on the wrong side of the law?'

'Oh, he got himself acquitted on that one. A fair fight, you know. The way I hear it, he was just a kid in Missouri when he laid an ax into his schoolmaster on account of the fellow called him a name. Went home to fetch it, first. Then came along with it and chopped him up right there in front of everyone.'

'I say,' said I. 'What did the schoolmaster call him, do you know?'

'Called him Meriwether.'

'But that's his name, isn't it?'

'He don't care to be reminded of the fact.'

'I heard McSween call him that.'

'Well, I reckon McSween can call him anything he likes.'

'They're great chums, is it?'

'Not hardly. They only just tolerate each other. But Breakenridge, he knows you don't fool with McSween.'

'That dangerous, is he?'

244

'Only if you rile him.'

'He seems quite friendly, really.'

'Oh, he's as sweet as pie, mostly.'

'Is he the leader of the gang? I'd rather assumed it was Chase, but . . .'

'Chase pretty much runs things. But he don't run McSween. It'd been up to Chase, I reckon we would've let them fellers alone, back there, and you'd still be riding double. Looks to me like McSween took a notion you oughta have a horse of your own, that's all. He thinks highly of you, Willy.'

Well, it didn't come as a surprise to hear that, but it made me feel mighty good.

'With a friend the likes of him, you ain't got much to worry about. He'll look after you and see no harm comes your way.'

Later on in the day, McSween broke off from the rest of us and rode to the top of a hill. Up there, he raised a pair of field glasses to his face. He studied the direction we'd come from.

I met up with him at the bottom. 'Are they after us?' I asked.

'Didn't see no sign of 'em. I spect they knew better, though I wouldn't trust that one feller no more than a rattlesnake.'

'What if they should come?'

'Be some gunplay.'

'Perhaps we shouldn't have taken the man's horse.'

'He acting up on you?'

'Not at all. He's quite fine, really.' I patted the horse's neck, and he glanced back at me and nodded like he appreciated the kindness. 'I just don't want any troubles to come of it.'

'Don't worry yourself about that, Willy.'

The rest of the boys had started moving again. We rode along behind. McSween didn't seem in any hurry to catch up with them.

'Got a name for him?' he asked.

'I should imagine he already has a name.'

'Has he whispered it to you?'

I laughed.

McSween rolled a smoke. He lit it up, then handed his makings across to me. I'd had some practice since my first go at it, back when we'd divied up the loot. So I made myself a smoke that wasn't too crooked or leaky. I lit up, and passed the makings back to him.

'You oughta give him a name,' he said.

'He doesn't feel as if he's actually *my* horse.'

'Why, sure he is. You paid for him fair and square. All you're missing's a bill of sale. Fraid I didn't think of that. If it'd make you feel better, I'll do you one up myself when we make camp. We'll let on like I sold him to you. Not that anyone's likely to raise a fuss about it.'

'Other than the owner, do you mean?'

'You heard what I told him, didn't you?'

'Yes.'

'Well, I don't say such things but what I mean 'em.'

'So you'll actually shoot him if you ever see him again?'

'That's the long and short of it, Willy.'

'What if he sees you first?'

'You sure do worry your head over things.'

'I shouldn't like to see you get shot.'

'Many a man has tried.' He flicked his smoke away and pulled off his hat. While he held that in one hand, he stroked his mustache with the other. Then he gave his long hair a few flings with his fingers. 'You see all this-here silver?'

Both his mustache and his hair were mostly black, but streaked with plenty of shiny strands.

'Know what it is, Willy?'

'Gray hair, is it?'

'Silver. Precious silver. It's the pay you get for staying alive. The longer you go without getting perforated by various rapscallions and Indians – or scalped – the more you collect. All you gotta do is take a gander at a man's head, and you can get yourself a fair estimate of his worth. You see much silver up there, you know he ain't easy to kill.' He flapped his hat back down onto his head. 'What I'm getting at, you shouldn't be spoiling your good times fretting about me. What're you gonna call your horse?'

I gave it some thought. 'Perhaps I ought to name him Meriwether.'

When I said that, McSween laughed harder than I'd ever seen him do before. He didn't take on like Emmet over my reloading, gasping and weeping, but he sure did laugh up a storm. After he'd settled down some, he said, 'That's purely rich, Willy. Don't you do it, though. That old boy's a mite touchy about his name.'

'How does General sound?'

'After Matthew Forrest? I reckon he'd be right proud.'

'General it is, then. Howdy, General,' I said. The horse bobbed his head up and down as if he liked the new name.

Once I'd named him, he did seem to be more mine. I suddenly felt fonder of him just because of it. I knew I'd actually stolen him, no matter what sort of light McSween wanted to put on the doings. But I told myself that General was better off with me. Just by looking at the previous owner, you could see he had a mean streak. I had no doubt but what he'd mistreated General whenever he got the chance. So I pretty much stopped feeling bad about stealing him, though I never got past worrying that the fellow might come after us.

By and by, it came to me that I was all set up, now, to travel on my own. I had myself a horse, a rifle, two pistols, a bit of money. No reason, really, not to bid the gang farewell and head for Tombstone to seek out Sarah and Whittle.

I just wasn't eager, though, to take that step. Partly, I reckon, it was for fear I might run afoul of the pair we'd robbed. I didn't hanker to be alone if that should happen. Thing is, I didn't hanker to be alone at all.

So I figured to ride along with the boys, at least till after we got to Bailey's Corner.

For the next few days, we kept an eye on the territory to our rear. Nobody appeared to be following, though.

Each evening, after finding a place to camp, Emmet and I wandered off for shooting practice. He gave me some rawhide to tie down my holster, and that helped considerable. I got quicker on the draw, and my aim improved.

A couple of times, I asked McSween to come along with us. He never did, though, until the final evening before we rode into Bailey's Corner.

'You've come along real good,' he said after watching me pull and fire. 'That feller Whittle, he's gonna rue the day he crossed your trail.'

'If I'm ever able to find him, perhaps.'

'I've got half a mind to join you for the hunt,' he said.

'Do you?'

Emmet gave McSween a look as if he figured the chap had gone daft.

'Yup. Half a mind.'

'That would be smashing!'

'Fact is, I used to be a fair hand at tracking redskins. Might be I could help you run down this Whittle and put him to rest.'

'Why on earth you wanta do such a thing?' Emmet said.

'Not much sport in robbing trains.'

'It's what we *do*.'

'Seems like maybe I've done enough of it for a spell. It'd feel good to take a rest from it and get in on a good chase.'

CHAPTER THIRTY-THREE

Trouble at Bailey's Corner

Nothing more was said about McSween's notion to help me track down Whittle. I got to worrying, later on that night, about whether he'd meant it or not. After the others had turned in and McSween was standing first watch, I crawled out of my blanket and went looking for him.

We'd been posting lookouts ever since we took Prue's horse, as a precaution against ambush. There'd never been any sign of Prue or his friend, but McSween had said we shouldn't count them out. 'It's when you quit watching for trouble,' he said, 'that it most always sneaks up on you.'

It took me a few minutes to spot him. He stood in a shadow between two high, moonlit boulders off beyond the campsite. He had his back to me.

I was trying to walk quiet, mostly as it was night and I didn't care to disturb the stillness. So sudden it shocked me, McSween whirled around and grabbed iron.

'Don't shoot!' I whispered. 'It's me!'

'I *know* it's you. If I was fixing to shoot, it'd be done with by now.' He holstered his Colt. 'You got a lot to learn, Willy, or you ain't likely to grow no silver.'

As I walked closer to him, he said, 'Many a feller's died before his time for no better reason than he walked up behind the wrong man. I knowed a marshal in Tucson shot his best friend dead in just such a manner. Heard him sneaking up, turned and let fly. Put three slugs in his buddy and only just saw who he'd killed by the muzzle flashes.'

'That's awful,' I said.

'Happens plenty. What you wanta do is keep your distance and call out, make sure he knows who you are.'

'Yes, sir.' After a bit, I asked, 'How did you know it was me?'

'Them tight boots you got on. Your gait's got a hitch to it

cause of how they pinch your toes.'

'You must have frightfully good ears.'

'They've had a share of practice. So how come you're up and about?'

'Will you actually help me to search for Whittle?'

'I might do just that very thing.'

'It would be splendid.'

'Well, I spent some time down there, know the territory. Ran with Al Sieber and his boys back in eighty-two. That's when we took on Nan-tia-tish. Then it was Geronimo and Nachite raising hell. Chased them all through creation. I reckon there ain't a canyon or a cactus between Fort Apache and the Torres Mountains that I ain't met up with, one time or another.'

'I'm not familiar with those places, actually.'

'You don't need to be, cause I am.'

'Have you been to Tombstone?'

'Many a time.'

'You'll be able to help me find it, then?'

'Why, sure. Lead you straight to it. She's a far piece west of here, then a ways south. Shouldn't take more than a couple of weeks to get there, once we start out.'

'When shall we start?' I asked.

'Let's just wait and see. We wanta spend us some time at Bailey's Corner and live it up some, you know.' He smiled, pale teeth showing under his mustache. 'You don't wanta start off on a long journey with too much cash weighing you down. It'd only serve to tire the horses.'

'Will the others come with us, do you suppose?'

'That'll be up to them. Much as I'll likely miss the boys, I reckon we'd be better off shed of 'em. First thing you know, they'd be hankering to pull a holdup. We don't want none of that. Can't hunt a man proper if you gotta keep a lookout for lawmen and posses and the like. It'd only serve to interfere with business. Sides, they'd slow us down.'

'I'd hate for you to leave them on my account,' I said.

'High time I pulled out. I been putting it off too long already.'

'Then, you're not doing it only because of me?'

'Let me tell you a thing or two, Willy. Chase is the only feller in the bunch that has a lick of sense. Them other three, any one of 'em could end up dragging us all into some kinda mess. Breakenridge, he's got a temper so hot he'll kill a man for looking at him sideways. Emmet's got an itch to swap lead with any feller that gives him half an excuse. Snooker's got himself a streak of yellow that makes him worse than either of 'em. He's a back-shooter, and he ain't particular who he does it to. You ride with boys like that, you always gotta watch 'em and try to keep a rein on 'em, but sooner or later they're gonna draw you into some mighty deep trouble. I been with this bunch for a couple of years, now, and we been lucky. But luck has a way of petering out on you. Best to get shut of 'em.'

When I think about what happened later, it seems funny – in an awful sort of way – that McSween said such things just the night before we went into Bailey's Corner. He'd sure been right about luck petering out. But he couldn't have been more wrong about Breakenridge or Emmet or Snooker being the cause of our trouble. McSween himself was the one who brought it down on us all. Because of me.

Prue and his friend must've been tracking us the whole time after we 'bought' the horse. They'd been smart enough to keep well out of sight, so we never saw hide nor hair of them, nor suspected they were on their way. They didn't show up until our second night in town, and they showed up with help.

We were having us a farewell supper at the Silver Dollar Saloon, drinking beer and eating steaks, all sitting together around a corner table. I was feeling mighty fine. I'd had a good sleep the night before in a hotel bed, I'd had two baths and a haircut, I'd been eating good meals for the better part of two days, my wealth had increased by fifteen dollars due to the sale of the stolen watches, and I was decked out in a brand new outfit.

I was mighty proud of my outfit. The whole gang, except for Breakenridge, had helped me pick it out the day we got into town. Dressed up the way I was, I felt just like one of the boys.

I wore a pair of dandy boots that didn't pinch, spurs that jingled every time I moved my feet, comfortable trousers, a blue shirt like McSween's, a leather vest, a red bandanna that dropped around my neck, and a splendid beaver hat. The pride of my new gear was a gunbelt with a big silver buckle, loops across its back for ammunition, and holsters at each hip. Both holsters had tie-downs. They held the Colts I'd acquired at the train.

251

I knew I looked bully. Quite the desperado. But I near choked on my last swallow of steak when Emmet said, 'We gotta make sure Willy don't ride outa here tomorrow a virgin.'

Snooker let out a whoop. 'Let's take him on over to Sally's!'

Last night, they'd all gone to Sally's, but I'd let on that I had a bellyache, and got out of it. It hadn't been much of a lie, for the notion of 'visiting the ladies' had indeed turned me queasy.

'I'd rather not, actually,' I said.

'Feeling poorly?' Emmet asked.

'Why, there ain't nothing to it,' Snooker said. 'No call to be scared.'

'I'm not at all scared,' I protested, though such talk was giving me an awful case of the fantods. In my head, I found myself back in that East End alley with Sue the whore. Much as I'd been thrilled by that encounter – up till she attacked me – the notion of taking up with another person of her sort upset me considerable. 'I'd rather not, is all.'

'He's plumb terrorized,' Emmet said.

'Oh, leave him be,' Chase told him.

'Gals isn't nothing to be scared of,' Snooker went on. 'They's just the same as fellers, only they got nicer parts.'

'It can be a mite trying, first time around,' McSween said. I judged he was coming to my aid, but then he disappointed me. 'What we'll do, we'll have Sally fix you up with a sweet young thing that'll treat you right.'

Once again, Sue came to mind. I shook my head.

'It don't *hurt*, you know,' Emmet said.

'I'm quite aware of that,' I blurted. 'Me and Sarah . . .' Well, I shut my mouth quick. But not quick enough.

'You and Sarah?' Emmet asked. 'The General's daughter?'

'Granddaughter,' I corrected him.

'Well, shooey,' Snooker said.

'If that don't beat all,' McSween said, smiling some.

My face felt like it was burning up. 'I'm quite fond of her, really,' I muttered. 'I shouldn't like to . . . have a go . . . at someone else.'

'Don't wanta betray her, is that it?' McSween asked.

'Why, she don't ever have to know,' Emmet said.

'Still . . .'

Snooker said, 'I bet she's gone and taken up with that

feller on the train you told us about, anyhow.'

That remark changed my embarrassment to anger. 'Bugger off,' I snapped.

Snooker's eyes got wide. 'What's that?'

'Let's settle down, boys,' Chase said.

'What'd he say to me?'

'Bugger off and sod you.'

'*What?*'

'Are you deaf?'

'Willy,' McSween said, real low.

Snooker leaped up from the table so fast his chair fell over backward. Other folks in the saloon stopped what they were doing and turned to watch us. 'Why don't you and me step outside, kid?'

I jumped up, myself, figuring to accommodate him.

McSween was next to spring to his feet. 'Now the both of you quit.'

Snooker jabbed a finger at me. 'He cussed me, John! I got every right to . . .'

'What makes you guess he cussed you?'

'Why . . . he . . . I don't rightly know *what* he said, but it was a cuss.' Glaring my way, he asked, 'Weren't it?'

'Bloody right.'

'You see?' he asked McSween.

McSween didn't answer. What he did was yank both his Colts and let fly.

'*Jesus!*' Snooker yelled through the explosions.

But the bullets weren't aimed at him.

Someone cried out.

I turned my head in time to see Prue, pistol in hand, stumble backward with a shocked look on his face and three holes in his white shirt. On both sides of him were men with badges. As they went for their guns, Snooker spun around and pulled. Emmet shouted and blazed away from where he sat. I snatched out my own Colts. Though I loathed the notion of killing a lawman, I knew I had to help my friends. Before I got the chance, both lawmen flopped to the floor without ever firing a shot. Only Prue's fat friend was still standing. He'd been shielded for a spell by Prue's body, which knocked into him as it pitched backward. Now he was raising a double-barreled shotgun. About seven or eight slugs all punched him at near the same time. It was an awful thing to watch. They smacked holes all over his belly and chest, one poked through his throat, and another broke his front teeth and sent blood spouting out his mouth. His shotgun went off, and would've blasted the floor except that Prue's face was in the way.

The roaring quit. I looked around and saw nobody who appeared ready to join the fight. The other folks in the saloon were mostly flat on the floor or crouched under tables.

When I turned to check on the boys, I could hardly see them through the clouds of gunsmoke. They were on their feet, hands full of iron, glancing this way and that as they stepped clear of the table.

McSween, reloading, said, 'I reckon we wore out our welcome.' The way my ears rang, I almost couldn't hear him.

'Anybody else wanta try us?' Emmet yelled.

Nobody answered.

McSween holstered a gun just long enough to drag some money from his pocket. He tossed the greenbacks onto the table to pay for our meal, then drew again.

Chase led the way out, me and McSween backing ourselves through the doors to watch those in the saloon.

A few folks were gathered on the walk, but they rather shook their heads at us and kept their hands a safe distance from their holsters. We stepped down to the street. A few horses were tied at the hitching post there, and I figured we might take them and hightail.

That wasn't what the others had in mind, though.

I stayed with them. What we did was walk across the street toward our hotel. I kept figuring we'd get shot at by someone, but not a single soul tried. We made it clear to the other side of the street without any gunplay, and walked into the hotel.

'What are we *doing*?' I asked McSween.

'Clearing out.'

Apparently, however, none of the boys was in any big rush to get on with it.

We got some wary, curious looks in the lobby, but no trouble.

Then we were up the stairs and going into our rooms. Mine was shared with McSween and Breakenridge. As soon as McSween got a lamp burning, we set to gathering our gear. I heard some yelling from outside the window. My mouth was parched, my heart thumping fit to explode. But

McSween and Breakenridge seemed mighty cool as they stuffed this and that into their saddle bags.

We stayed together in the room until all three of us were ready. Saddle bags draped over our shoulders, bedrolls roped across our backs, Colts holstered and rifles in our hands, we stepped into the hallway.

Nobody there.

A couple of minutes passed, then the others came out of their room.

'Reckon there's a back door outa here?' Chase asked.

'The front door suits me,' McSween said.

I shriveled cold.

Just as calm as you please, McSween and Chase strode side by side to the head of the stairs and started down. I kept next to Emmet, behind them. Breakenridge and Snooker followed us, watching the rear.

That stairway seemed just endless. It was all I could do to stop my shaky legs from giving out.

We didn't see nobody at all in the lobby.

McSween and Chase didn't hesitate for a blink, but stepped right out the front door.

Well, we paraded straight down the middle of the street. It was empty except for us and the horses and carriages along both sides. But it seemed that everyone in town had their eyes on us. Doorways and windows were packed with silent watchers.

I heard some horses shuffling their hoofs, snorting, letting out a whinny now and again. A piano was playing a lively tune nearby. Off in the distance, a dog was yapping. Other than that, about the only sounds came from us – our boots thumping soft on the dusty street, our spurs clinking, the leather of our gear squeaking and groaning.

It was a mighty long walk.

I judged that, any second, a volley would roar out and we'd all be dropped in our tracks.

Didn't happen, though.

Finally, we came to the livery stable at the far end of town. The proprietor, a fellow named Himmel, had seen us coming and had already sent his boys to fetch our horses. McSween settled accounts with him. Then we spent just forever, it seemed, fumbling about with our bridles and saddles and such. McSween finished before me, and mounted up. While I worked at tightening General's cinch, he sat up there high on his saddle and rolled himself a smoke.

I tied down my saddle bags, tied down my bedroll and slipped my Winchester into its boot. By the time I got done and climbed aboard, the others were all mounted and waiting for me.

We rode out onto the street.

What came next shouldn't have surprised me, not after what I'd seen of the gang so far.

There we were, at the very end of town. We had no reason at all to ride in the opposite direction.

That's just what we did, however.

McSween dug in his spurs, pulled both Colts, and charged, spitting lead at the night. For a cautious man proud of his silver hair, he sure had himself a keen interest in gawdy exits.

We all followed him, yelling and blazing.

If we were shot at, I never heard the gunfire through all our own commotion.

We were still on our saddles, none the worse for wear, by the time we left Bailey's Corner behind us.

CHAPTER THIRTY-FOUR

The Posse

The hard way we rode, only stopping now and then to let the horses catch their wind, I judged that the boys didn't figure we were in the clear.

Finally, I had to ask. I put the spurs to General and caught up with McSween. 'Do you reckon they're coming after us?'

'That's a good bet, Willy,' he said, looking over at me. 'You know them two lawmen that was fools enough to side with Prue? They was town deputies. I don't know the one, but the other was James Brewer, brother to the sheriff, Ike.'

'Well, where was *he*, then?'

'Ike? Don't rightly know. I gave him all kinds of time to take a crack at us. Wanted him to try, but he never showed. Sure would've been a blessing to kill him then and there. Way matters stand, we gotta figure he'll lead a posse after us.'

'What are we to do?'

'Whatever we gotta.'

We kept on riding through the night. I spent plenty of time remembering how the train engineer'd tried to talk me out of joining up with these boys, and wished more than once that I'd heeded his warning. It was far too late for that, though. In the course of a week, I'd helped rob a train, I'd stolen a horse, and I'd stood with the gang in a shootout that left four men murdered. I was no better than an outlaw, myself. And now McSween judged we had a posse coming for us, so I figured I might end my life just as the engineer had predicted, either shot or swinging from a rope.

It made me feel plain sick to think about.

I kept looking back over my shoulder. Behind us was nothing but moonlit desert.

Maybe a posse *won't* come, I told myself.

I couldn't take much comfort from hoping that, but I did

finally calm down. What helped my nerves was knowing I was with the boys, and they weren't likely to let any posse have its way with them. No, sir. I wouldn't be getting myself shot or hanged long as I stayed with McSween and Chase and Emmet and Snooker and Breakenridge – and the engineer be damned.

My optimism lasted till just after dawn.

That's when we halted near the top of a rise and spotted the cloud of dust a few miles to our rear. I couldn't see anyone back there, just dry washes and piles of rock, cacti and stunted trees, and all that blowing yellow dust.

'Aw, shit,' Snooker said.

Chase glanced at McSween. 'Fifteen, twenty of 'em?'

'Least twenty, I'd say.'

'Aw, shit,' Snooker said again.

'Who'd think a town that size,' McSween said, 'could come up with that many fellers eager to get their toes turned up?'

'Reckon we oughta split up?' Chase asked.

Oh, I didn't care for *that* notion. Not one whit. Goosebumps went scurrying up my back like a troop of spiders with icy feet.

'It'd thin 'em out,' Breakenridge said. 'I'd sure rather have four or five on my tail than all of them.'

McSween commenced to roll a smoke. After giving it a lick, he said, 'We put our heads together, maybe we can figure us a *better* way to thin 'em out.' He lit up. Smoke curled away from under his mustache as he smiled. 'Get my drift?'

He offered his makings to me.

Dry as my mouth felt, it would've likely caught fire if I'd had a go at smoking. I shook my head.

'Are you saying we ought to attack them?' I asked.

'Seems a fine idea to me,' he said.

'Jesus wept,' said Breakenridge.

Chase gazed off at the dust cloud, which seemed to be closer to us already, and rubbed his chin. 'Let's do it,' he said.

'Hot damn!' Emmet blurted.

Snooker and Breakenridge didn't appear to enjoy the notion, but they didn't speak against it.

'How you doing, Willy?'

We sat atop our mounts, all by ourselves, waiting.

'Not at all good, actually.'

'Can't say as I blame you,' McSween said. 'Not feeling too spry myself, if the truth be known. Sorry we pulled you into this.'

'It was my own choice.'

'My own blamed fault. I just knowed I should've plugged Prue and the fatty back when we took the horse. Just gave 'em credit for more sense than they turned out to have.' He lifted his bandanna and mopped some sweat off his forehead. 'This is what comes of having a generous nature.'

'It is a shame they showed up when they did,' I said.

'You never know. At least we ain't got them to worry about no more.'

'I'd rather have dealt with those two on my trail than a whole crowd.'

He laughed softly. 'Well, there ain't gonna be a crowd much longer.'

I looked over my shoulder and was glad to see that the gap between the piled boulders was still empty. The low thunder of hoofbeats sounded louder and louder.

'What you might wanta do,' McSween said, 'is dig in your spurs and light out.'

'That's what I *intend* to do.'

'It's right now I mean.'

'Now?'

'That's what I'd like you to do, Willy. Go on and skedaddle. No point in you being in on this. At the best, you'd only bloody your hands. At worst, you'd end up killed. Go on, now. We'll handle this here posse. Things work out, I'll catch you down the trail.'

'I'm not a bloody coward,' I told him.

'Why, I know that.'

'It's only because of me that we *have* this posse after us.'

'That's no call for you to stick with us.'

'It's all the call I need,' I said, talking quite a heap braver than I felt.

'Reckon it's too late, anyhow,' McSween said.

I was still watching the gap. It was still empty. But now the thunder was so near I almost thought I could feel the air quaking.

'This is it, Willy,' McSween said. He shouldered his Winchester and thumbed back its hammer. 'Ride fast, keep low, and shoot straight. And God be with you.'

'You, too,' I told him. It came out no louder than a whisper.

A lone horseman rode through the gap. His head was turned. He seemed to be talking to someone behind him, though he was too far off for me to hear his voice. McSween's rifle spoke. The fellow pitched backward. His horse reared. He fell off, but one of his feet got hung up in a stirrup. The horse scampered to the right, dragging him.

'Hightail!' McSween yelled.

We didn't linger. We hunched and dug in and bolted.

From behind us came shouts. 'There!' and 'Bastards!' and 'Get 'em!'

It was Whitechapel all over again, a mob after my blood, only this time they had guns.

They blasted away at us.

Bullets whinged off rocks, buzzed past my head. I kept an eye on McSween racing alongside me low in his saddle with the wind shoving his hat brim up. He didn't look like he'd been hit yet. So far, I'd been lucky, too. I figured a slug was on its way toward my back. I waited for it to whack me, but all I could feel was General dashing like mad, the hot wind rushing into my face so quick it wanted to choke me.

The mouth of the pass hadn't seemed like more than a stone's throw away when me and McSween had picked our spot to wait for the posse.

But that stone's throw seemed more like a mile now that the mob was on our tails, spitting lead.

I wished I hadn't been so eager to play bait.

None of the others had volunteered for the job, however, and I'd figured McSween shouldn't have to go it alone.

Even though it *was* his own daft idea.

'You don't never wanta try this trick on the redskins,' he'd said. 'Why, hell, it's *their* trick. You take your white foiks, though, they fall for it every time.'

I'd neglected to ask him how many redskins got themselves shot dead while leading their pursuers into such traps.

At long last, we galloped between the boulders at the mouth of the pass. The gunfire slackened off a bit, so I raised my head and glanced about. I didn't see hide nor hair of the boys up there among the rocks. What if *they'd* lit out? The notion shook me. But I reckoned they weren't the sort to pull such a dirty stunt.

I took a chance and looked back. Here came the posse, two at a time, racing at us down the narrow pass, only the pair in front firing. The rest had quit shooting so they wouldn't hit their own.

Me and McSween kept riding just as fast as our mounts could carry us.

The boys kept waiting.

If they were here.

Suddenly, puffs of smoke bloomed on the canyon walls as four guns crashed and four men tumbled off their horses.

McSween cut to the left. Rifle in hand, he hurled himself to the ground and dashed behind a clump of rocks. I reined in General, snatched out my Winchester, and leaped down to join him.

He was already scurrying up the slope. I followed, rather hoping it might all be over before we found a proper perch.

It sounded horrid. The canyon just roared with gunfire. Horses squealed and whinnied. Men shouted, cried out.

They came to kill us, I told myself.

Too soon, McSween picked himself a rock. It was big enough for both of us. We rose up behind it and shouldered our rifles.

Down below was mayhem. Dead men. Dead horses. A few fellows rode breakneck for the mouth of the pass in a panic to escape. Others stayed. Of those that stayed to fight, some simply crouched in the open and returned fire, some scampered up into the rocks, some hunkered down to take shelter beside their fallen mounts, and a few rode in their saddles, shooting this way and that as their horses wheeled and bucked.

McSween's rifle deafened my ear. One of the men on a circling, snorting horse keeled over sideways.

I levered in a cartridge myself and sighted in on a fellow who was squatting next to a dead man. He'd lost his hat. He was bald. His head was down while he worked at reloading his pistol.

I spent a fair amount of time lining him up in my sights. It beat looking at the carnage. McSween kept on firing quick.

The way I judged matters, my fellow was just a law-abiding citizen doing his duty. Maybe he was a shopkeeper,

261

or the like. Maybe he had a wife and children. If I shot him, I'd be no better than a murderer. On the other hand, I wanted McSween to figure I was doing my level best to help the situation.

So I eased my barrel over some, took aim at his weapon, and squeezed the trigger. Missed. My bullet raised some powder off the shirt of the dead man.

My fellow finished reloading. He looked up toward me and McSween, swung his pistol toward us, and caught a slug in his forehead from McSween's rifle.

I didn't feel too sorry about it, but was glad I hadn't been the one to kill him.

With him dead, I had no choice but to search out another target.

The only fellow still moving down there had a wounded leg and was hobbling toward a skittish horse. Just as he got to it, he fell. But he latched a hand on to one of the stirrups. The horse lit out for the mouth of the pass, towing him. It was a big white stallion. I levered a round into my chamber and aimed toward the man's feet. I figured to try for one of his boot heels. But then there wasn't any point, for the stallion caught lead. It stumbled sideways and stepped on him. It missed him when it toppled over. Before the man could move – if he had it in him to move – he got smacked by three or four slugs.

After that, the shooting stopped. The quiet seemed mighty unnatural. Other than the wind and the ringing in my ears, all I could hear were the cries of wounded men and horses.

We climbed down to the bottom of the pass. All of us did, that is, except for Breakenridge. Snooker'd been near him on the slope, and said he'd been killed.

Keeping our guns ready, we wandered among the fallen. It turned out there were nine dead and seven wounded. Ike Brewer, the town sheriff, was among the dead.

We disarmed the wounded to avoid surprises, then gathered enough horses for them. Those too hurt to ride, we tied aboard their saddles. We sent them through the mouth of the pass, figuring that the few who'd escaped from our ambush would likely see to them.

When they were gone, we climbed up a slope and found Breakenridge. A bullet had gone into his right eye, and he was awful to look at.

Nobody seemed particularly upset about the loss of him.

He hadn't been the friendly sort, after all. If the others felt the same as me, they were mostly feeling glad it was him instead of themselves that had gotten killed.

It took four of us to tote him down to the bottom. Snooker held our rifles for us. I helped out by lugging one of Breakenridge's legs. He was huge and heavy. We were mostly all worn out by the time we got done.

We spent a while rounding up our horses. Then we hoisted Breakenridge up across his saddle, and tied him so he wouldn't fall off.

We rode south out of the pass.

Early in the afternoon, we unloaded Breakenridge in a dry wash and covered him with rocks. Chase read some words over him from a Bible he took from his saddlebag. Then we split up what was left of Breakenridge's loot. We kept his horse as a spare, and rode on.

All through the day, we kept a watch behind us. There was no sign that the remains of the posse was coming after us. McSween allowed it was a good thing we'd shot Ike in the ambush, as he'd been a stubborn fellow who wouldn't have given up. The way he saw it, the rest of the bunch likely figured they'd got off lucky, and were hurrying on back to town with the wounded.

I hoped he was right about that, but not because I was scared of the posse. It would take more than whatever handful had survived the trap to do us any harm. I just hoped they wouldn't show up because I didn't want any more of them to get killed.

I was feeling mighty lowdown and miserable about the slaughter back at the pass. We hadn't any choice to speak of. It was them or us. But there just wasn't a way to put it in a light that eased the burden. I hadn't shot anyone, but I'd helped bait the trap. And the posse never would've come after us if we hadn't stolen Prue's horse. It all stemmed from that.

Four men in the saloon and nine at the pass, and Breakenridge – not a one of them would've gotten killed if I hadn't made a choice to ride with the gang.

Fourteen men.

That got me to thinking how Trudy and her father and Michael had also died on account of me. No way I could blame myself for the General and Mable, but they'd taken me into their home and they'd ended up dead, too.

263

It seemed like nobody was safe around me, like I carried a curse that got folks killed.

Just a matter of time, I judged, before my curse would wipe out McSween and Chase and Emmet and Snooker.

If I stuck with them.

Much as I wanted McSween to help me track Whittle, I finally made up my mind to ride out alone. I sure would miss him. But I'd miss him more, and take on a new load of guilt, if he came along and got killed for his troubles.

I didn't let on about my plan. During supper that night, the boys discussed splitting up. Chase and Emmet figured they'd go east in the morning, Snooker said he thought he'd head up to Denver, and McSween allowed as how he and I would make for Tombstone. I acted as if that suited me.

Later on, we all turned in except for McSween, who had first watch. I lay in my blanket, waiting. When it came my turn, I pretended to be asleep. McSween knelt and shook my shoulder. 'Time to play sentry, Willy,' he whispered.

I yawned, rubbed my eyes, and gave him a good show of waking up. McSween crawled into his blanket while I pulled my boots on and strapped on my gunbelt.

'Come sunup,' he said, 'we'll hit the trail for Tombstone.'

'Splendid,' I said, and felt badly about how he might feel in the morning when he saw I'd lit out.

I wandered off past the others. I climbed a pile of rocks and sat down at the top, figuring to wait an hour or so. The sky had clouded up. With the moon and stars hidden away, there wasn't enough light to see much. That would work to my advantage when it came time to sneak into camp for my things.

Sitting up there, darkness everywhere, I soon found that the notion of riding off alone had lost some of its appeal. It was a mighty big wilderness. A fellow might lose his way. Worse, a fellow might run afoul of thieves or cutthroats. Or Indians? The Indian wars had ended, so everyone said, but that didn't mean every last savage was accounted for.

I hadn't worried about such things while I'd been with the boys; I'd always had them to rely on. In a while, I'd be leaving them behind.

I can take care of myself, I thought.

But it would be a blessing to have McSween at my side.

There was really no call to sneak off without him.

Then I thought, if I don't get shut of him, I'll get him

killed. I don't want him to die on my account like all those others.

By and by, it came time for me to go if I was going.

I stood up.

Fire spit at me from off in the dark. A boom pounded my ears. A slug nipped my side. Startled more than hurt, I took a quick step backward and my boot found nothing but air. Crying out, I fell. Rocks jabbed and poked me as I tumbled down. I kept figuring one might split my head open, but that didn't happen.

I came to a stop on my back, my legs hoisted up by a boulder. The ground under me shook with pounding hoofs.

Earlier that day, I'd felt sorry for the poor folks we'd ambushed. Now, I suddenly wished we hadn't let a single one of them get out alive.

McSween had said they wouldn't come. Not with Ike dead. But he'd been wrong.

And somebody'd *shot* at me.

From beyond me came shouts of alarm from the boys. They were mixed in with the thumping of hoofs and warwhoops that came from our attackers.

I kicked my legs down and got to my knees as a bunch of horsemen charged through a break in the rocks, their guns ablaze.

I patted my sides, figuring I must've lost my Colts in the fall. But they were snug in their holsters. For just an instant. Then they filled my hands.

I shot two blokes out of their saddles straight away.

Then McSween got hit. I saw him in the muzzle flashes, both his pistols blasting as slugs smacked his chest, knocking him backward. At least three men caught his lead and dropped from their horses before he went down.

I don't believe I witnessed the ends of Chase or Emmet or Snooker.

My eyes weren't watching for them.

My eyes were on the horsemen as they dashed this way and that, yelling and firing, some riding at me with their guns aroar.

I used only my right hand, as I'd had little practice with my left. I never moved my legs at all, but stood there at the edge of the campsite, aiming and firing. When my hammer came down on a used shell, I dropped that gun and switched to the other.

Before you know it, that one ran out, too.

I went to reload, and thought it strange I hadn't been killed yet. I just hoped I could get it full of bullets and take down a few more of the bastards before they got me.

But when the cylinder was full and I raised my arm to continue killing, I couldn't find a target.

I fired once, anyhow, to scatter the horses.

As they hurried off, the moon came out. Its pale light came down. In front of me, shrouded by drifting gunsmoke, was a field of twisted bodies.

They weren't all dead.

Some men lay there, writhing and moaning.

I checked on them. They weren't McSween or Chase or Emmet or Snooker.

I shot them.

At daybreak, I covered my friends with rocks. I read out loud from Chase's Bible.

I let the men from the posse lay where they'd fallen. There were eleven.

I set all the horses free except General. I gathered money, food and ammunition, as there was no advantage to leaving such things behind. Then I saddled up General and rode out.

PART FOUR

Plugging On

CHAPTER THIRTY-FIVE

Ishmael

The wound I'd taken in my side while standing watch didn't amount to much, just a gouge across my ribs. More than once, I wished whoever'd taken the crack at me had been a better shot.

I knew I wasn't fit to go on living.

The third or fourth night after the shootout at the camp, I decided to blow out my brains. It seemed a proper way to stop myself from doing more harm in this world.

I'd built a fire, which was only to keep me warm as I hadn't cooked a meal or eaten much of anything since the shooting. I sat down beside it and put a Colt to my head. Then it seemed maybe I ought to leave a letter behind.

A letter for who, though? Mother? Sarah? Neither of them was ever likely to see my last message, left out here in the middle of nowhere.

Maybe somebody would find it, sooner or later, and send it along. I couldn't count on that, though. Every day, I'd been riding west, putting my back to the sunrise and heading for the sunset, and not once had I met up with a human being. That suited me. But it didn't allow much hope of anyone finding my note.

What would I write in it, anyhow? That I was the curse of death to everybody I met? That I'd turned bad and killed men? Wouldn't serve any useful purpose for Mother or Sarah to know such things. Better to let them go on wondering what had become of me than to weigh them down with the grim truth.

So I gave up the notion of leaving a message.

I thumbed back the hammer and was all set to squeeze the trigger when General gave a snort.

The sound reminded me that he was hobbled for the night.

He would die if I went and shot myself without releasing him first.

I only aimed to kill myself, not General.

So I holstered my gun and went to him. He looked over his shoulder. 'You'll be quite better off without me, chum,' I explained, and gave his neck a pat.

Then I crouched down and untied the hobble.

'Get on, now.' I smacked his bum. He trotted off a bit, stopped and looked back at me.

It was no concern of mine. He was free. He could stay or go, as he chose. I judged he'd move on once I'd finished putting a slug into my brain pan.

I walked back to the fire, sat down, and drew my Colt. As I pulled back the hammer, I remembered how the train conductor had tried to shoot me dead, only his gun had misfired.

It hadn't been a bad round, as it had gone off just a while later when I was riding away with the boys, shooting at the sky.

I'd counted the misfire to be a rare piece of luck.

I didn't look at it that way now. It had been the worst kind of luck, leastwise for the gang and the men that came after us in the saloon and the chaps of the posse. All those fellows were dead because of one misfire.

Well, it wasn't likely to happen twice.

And if it should, I had me four more chambers full of bullets in the one gun, five in the other. (Emmet had taught me not to travel about with a round under the hammer, and only to load that chamber for target practice or troubles.) There wasn't enough luck or magic or whatever in this world to stop them all from doing their job.

A miracle wouldn't be saving me this time.

I judged the misfire *had* been a miracle, of sorts. Pretty much as if I hadn't been meant to get killed.

Pondering over that, I saw how I'd squeaked by and survived dicey situations over and over again ever since the night I set out for Whitechapel.

There was the ocean, which should've either swallowed me up or froze me solid long before I ever reached the shore of America.

There was Whittle, who'd butchered so many folks but not me.

Getting chucked off the train by Briggs could've been fatal, all by itself.

Chase had threatened to shoot me. I gave that some thought, though, and allowed it shouldn't count. He'd likely been joshing, and never actually intended to do such a thing.

The conductor, though, had certainly had a go at me and failed.

Not a bullet had touched me during the gunfight at the saloon. Of course, I don't believe that Prue or the others got off a single shot, so maybe that shouldn't count, either.

But the posse men had taken a great many cracks at me, particularly when McSween and I were leading them into the ambush.

Later on that night, a fellow had creased my side. If he'd been half good with his gun, he would've killed me sure.

All that made for quite a string of close shaves, but then I'd come through the massacre at the campsite without taking a hit. Mighty perplexing, when you consider I only just stood there and didn't take cover and the bullets flew so thick and everyone but me bit the dust.

Just call me Ishmael.

I lowered the Colt onto my lap and gazed at how its black steel gleamed in the firelight.

'And I only am escaped alone,' I whispered.

Had to be a reason.

Had to be a reason I'd survived such a passel of narrow calls.

The reason had to be Whittle.

I was meant to live long enough, at least, to put him in the ground.

That's how I figured it, anyhow.

And that's how come I decided not to shoot myself, that night, after all.

CHAPTER THIRTY-SIX

Strangers on the Trail

Once I made up my mind to go on living, I still didn't feel any better about being the cause of so many deaths, but I did all of a sudden find myself hungry.

General had wandered off, so I had to chase after him. I brought him back to camp and hobbled him. Then I cooked myself up a pot of beans.

When I got done chowing them down, I set up the tin can and some sticks on the rocks around the fire. Then I stepped back, pulled and fired.

My first shot knocked the tin flying.

I holstered and drew and went for the sticks.

When that gun was empty, I practiced with the other. Left-handed. It came out clumsy for a spell. More often than not, I hit my fire or bounced my bullets off the rocks. But I got better, by and by.

Blazing away, I remembered a chap the boys used to call Willy. Willy'd considered it a great adventure to ride with desperados, smashing fun to slap leather and fire away at stumps and sticks and cans and such.

I found myself rather missing Willy.

He was dead.

He'd died with McSween and the rest of the gang.

He'd died young, and never got the chance to return home to his mother or to find his sweetheart, Sarah.

Tough break, that.

I don't rightly know who I missed more, Willy or McSween.

McSween, I reckon.

I used up a whole lot of ammunition, taking turns with both hands, and killed me a heap of kindling.

Then I turned in.

* * *

The next morning, I came upon a wagon trail. It appeared to be leading west. I was tempted to stay clear of it, for I didn't relish the notion of meeting up with travelers. But the trail would be a sight easier on General than the rough terrain we'd be crossing. We'd make better time on it, and it was bound to take us somewhere.

Seemed a better way to find Tombstone than if I just kept to the trackless wilds and hoped for the best.

So we took it.

Soon enough, some travelers came along. I spotted a couple of horsemen riding toward me. While they were still a good piece in the distance, I gave some thought to steering General off the trail so as to avoid them. But then I judged it might rouse their curiosity. Better just to act natural and pass them by.

Funny thing was, much as I wanted to be clear of these two strangers, I didn't feel any fear of them. Not even when they were close enough for me to see how ornery they looked. One had a pinched, pointy face that put me in mind of Snooker. The other had a droopy eyelid. Both had the same sort of lazy, smirky ways in how they stared at me.

'Howdy,' I said, and touched the brim of my hat.

'Howdy back,' said the bloke with the droopy lid. I nudged General to go around him, but he raised a hand. 'Hold her up there.'

I did as he asked. Then I dropped the reins over the saddle horn to free my hands. 'Yes sir?' I asked.

The one with the pointy face laughed. 'Yes *sir*. Ain't he got manners?'

'He's pretty, too. Just as pretty as a girl.'

'I betcha he *is* a girl!'

They appeared to enjoy the bit of wit.

'You got titties in there?' The one winked his bad eye in the direction of my shirt, and grinned. 'Give us a peek.'

'Ride on, fellows.'

'Why, she's shy.'

'I'm shy on patience,' I said.

'Now you be nice. Angus and me, we haven't had us a girl in near a month.'

'And she was ugly.'

'Ugly but willing.'

They both laughed.

'I'm not a girl,' I said.

273

Well, they glanced at each other and laughed all the more.

'That don't make no difference,' Angus of the half-mast lid finally said to me. 'Know what I mean? Now, you just climb down off your horse, there, and get shed of them duds.'

I didn't move.

'You do what Angus says!' snapped the other.

'If you'd like me to oblige,' I said, 'you'd best fill your hands.'

All of a sudden, they turned uncommon serious.

They glanced at each other, silent and smirkless, then turned their faces toward me.

'Have a crack, chaps,' I said. 'Or ride on.'

They both spent some time studying me out. I saw their eyes flick about, taking in my holstered Colts, the torn and blood-stained side of my shirt, my hands resting atop my thighs, and my face. They took quite a spell on my face.

Then Angus said, 'We didn't mean nothing, mister. Only just having us some fun.'

The other bobbed his head. 'We'll just be moving along. Adios, now.'

They split apart and rode past me.

I turned General around, as I didn't aim to get back-shot.

Angus and the other rode off slow at first, neither one of them glancing back. Then Angus, he put the spurs to his horse. His friend did the same, and they both hightailed.

I rode on, puzzling over matters. It seemed odd the way they'd backed down. What seemed odder, though, was that I didn't feel much of anything. They'd had it in mind to use me like a woman, I reckon. But I hadn't been scared, the whole time. Nor had I felt any relief when they'd given up the notion and gone away.

Comes right down to it, I'd just as soon have shot them both.

I didn't *wish* I'd shot them, though.

I just didn't care, either way.

Late in the afternoon, a covered wagon turned up. It was heading west, same as me, but going so slow that I was bound to overtake it.

A blanket draped the rear opening, so I couldn't see how many or what manner of folks the wagon had in it.

Whoever they might be, I wanted no truck with them.

I figured to ride by quick, and urged General to a trot.

274

But when we came alongside the wagon, I saw how its canvas side was painted up with pictures of red bottles floating this way and that among words that said:

DR JETHRO LAZARUS
PURVEYOR OF THE WORLD RENOWNED
GLORY ELIXIR
'Good for what ails you.'

There was plenty more to read, so I slowed General down to an easy walk.

Toward the rear was a notice that said you could buy one bottle of the Glory Elixir for a 'mere dollar'. Toward the front, it said:

GLORY ELIXIR
GUARANTEED TO VANQUISH
whooping cough
palsy
sour stomach
boils
feminine complaints
arthritis
runny bowels
gangrene
rattlesnake bite
gaseous embarrassments
dropsy
dizziness
DEATH

The Glory Elixir's list of cures rather amused me till I saw that final one. Death. That one took me by surprise and took the fun out.

I put my spurs to General, figuring to get shut of such nonsense.

As we hurried by, I took a gander sideways at the driver. He was all alone at the front.

'Say there, young fellow!'

'Good day,' I said, and left him behind.

'Cowards die many times,' he called after me.

Well, I didn't rightly know what he meant by that. And I judged he could call me a coward if he pleased. What got me

275

to rein in General was that I recognized the words.

As the wagon rattled closer, I met the old man's eyes and said, 'The valiant never taste of death but once.'

He smiled real cheerful. 'A man of learning. Delighted to make your acquaintance. Dr Jethro Lazarus, here.'

'Trevor Bentley.'

'Who hails, no doubt, from the land of the Bard.'

'Quite true,' I said.

'Would you care to join me at the helm?' He patted the seat beside him.

Well, he looked peculiar but harmless, a heavy chap with a red nose and white beard, his head topped with a bowler hat that had two white feathers swooping up from its band, one at each side. Golden hoops hung from his ears. He wore a leather shirt that shivered all over with fringe. It was cinched in around his huge belly by a beaded belt. He didn't wear a pistol, but a rather large knife was sheathed at his hip. His trouser legs were tucked into high moccasins that nearly beat his shirt for all their fringe.

I judged the sensible thing might be to stay out of his reach.

Besides, a blanket draped the opening behind him, so I couldn't see into the wagon. No telling who might be back there, laying low.

'I'll keep to my mount, but thank you for the offer.'

'I'm on my way to Tucson, myself,' he said. 'What about you?'

It didn't seem wise to tell him my plans. 'Just touring about, I reckon.'

'Beware the heathen, barren place of lawless men and savage race.'

'Not Shakespeare, is it?'

'Lazarus.'

'You're a poet, then?'

'Poet and purveyor of the Glory Elixir.'

I wanted no truck with his Glory Elixir, so I asked, 'Did you encounter a pair of rascals, earlier?'

He let out a soft chuckle.

'I do hope they did you no mischief.'

'They beat a quick retreat at the sight of my friend, Buster.' He reached down by his feet and hoisted a shotgun. Its barrels were cut off short, just in front of the forestock. 'Buster.'

I half expected him to point it at me, but he stowed it away.

'Buster's sent many a miscreant to glory,' he said. 'When he gets done with them, they're well beyond the aid of my Elixir.'

I couldn't help but smile at that. 'Doesn't it vanquish death, then, after all?'

'Why, it most surely does, Trevor. However, the vital revivification of the deceased is greatly impeded by the destruction of his anatomy. That is to say, it don't work worth spit if I've blown off the bastard's head.'

Now that I'd been hauled into this talk of death and the merits of Lazarus's flim-flam Elixir, it all didn't seem so grim. 'If a bloke's anatomy wasn't destroyed some,' I allowed, 'he wouldn't likely be dead in the first place.'

'All depends, my friend. Depends on how much is intact and how much is demolished.'

'If a chap's dead, he's dead. This Glory Elixir of yours won't change that.'

'There are more things in heaven and earth, Horatio . . .'

'I might look like a fool, Dr Lazarus, but I don't regularly think like one.'

Well, he pulled back on the reins and halted his team.

'I tell you what, Trevor. Just suppose I give you proof, right before your very eyes, that my Glory Elixir has the power to raise the dead?'

'Reckon I'd purchase a bottle,' I said, shaking my head. He couldn't prove any such thing, and I knew it. Still and all, as he climbed down and I followed him toward the rear of the wagon, I found myself wondering whether I could backtrack to the place I'd buried McSween and the boys. And I wondered if they were shot up too much for the Elixir to work on them. Then I wondered if I should buy enough to raise the other eleven. That'd be the proper thing to do, but I judged they might try to shoot us all over again, and then I took a mind to kick myself for allowing such thick-headed notions. No amount of Glory Elixir could fix any one of those fellows.

Be that as it was, I'd worked up a powerful curiosity to see the old fellow's proof.

He let down the gate at the back of his wagon, then crawled in under the blanket. The wagon shook some as he scurried about inside. Then came a scrapy, dragging sound.

'Lend me a hand,' he called from inside.

I dismounted. By the time I got done tying General to a bolt at the back of the wagon, the blanket was abulge with Lazarus. He jumped to the ground, hauling at the end of a wooden box. A pint bottle of Elixir was standing atop the box, its red fluid sloshing about.

He stopped pulling, grabbed the bottle, and tossed it to me. Then he went on dragging. More and more of the box slid into sight.

'What have you there?' I asked, though I could sure see what it looked like.

'A casket. Be a good lad and take the other end.'

CHAPTER THIRTY-SEVEN

Lazarus and the Dead Man

My curiosity shrank some. I didn't hanker to see what might be inside the casket. But I slipped the bottle into my pocket and did as he asked. When I got close, I had to hold my breath so as to avoid the sickening aroma in the air.

My end of the box was so heavy I near dropped it, but I managed to hang on until we got it lowered into the dust behind the wagon. Then I stepped back a few paces to get clear of the odor.

The hard work must've tuckered out Lazarus, for he sat down on the casket. He plucked a kerchief out of his trouser pocket and mopped his brow.

'You have a corpse in there, do you?' I asked.

He answered with a wink.

'Be a good lad and pass me the Elixir,' he said.

I handed over the bottle. He uncorked it, took a swig, and sighed. 'Good for what ails you. Have a drop yourself,' he said, and held it toward me.

I shook my head. 'I reckon I'll move on. I've seen my share of dead folks.'

'Nothing to fret yourself over. He's in passable shape. He don't even stink much, long as you stand upwind. It was only two days ago I cut him down.'

'Cut him down?'

'He's a fellow who threw a long rope and wound up at the end of a short one.'

'Threw a long rope?'

'A rustler. Cattle. Only his luck ran dry, and he was strung up by the ranch hands that nabbed him. I arrived upon the scene purely by happenstance, in the very nick of time to watch him swing. It was a stroke of wonderful good fortune. Very difficult, you see, to find a healthy subject for revivification.'

He took a few more swallows of the Elixir. 'A lynching's just the thing. If a fellow's hanged proper from a gallows, you see, his neck gets itself snapped. Stretched considerable, too. That's if he don't drop too far and get his head popped off altogether. Either way, the fellow ain't fit. I've brought back a few that had their necks busted, and they pretty much put off my customers, how they stumbled along with their heads all wobbly. But you take a feller that's gotten lynched, he's generally been choked to death so his neck's in fine shape. That's how it went with this one. Choked. Strangulated.' He rapped his bottle against the top of the casket. 'Right off, I knew I had to have him. The ranch boys didn't want me to take him, as they preferred to let him dangle as a lesson for others of his ilk. But I paid them a dollar, and they allowed me to cut him down.'

Lazarus raised the bottle again, took one more sip, then corked it. Smiling at me, he said, 'This fellow here, he'll be dandy once he gets a taste of the Glory Elixir.'

'I shouldn't think so.'

'Shall we give it a try?' Lazarus stood up. He handed the bottle to me.

The lid was only just laid across the top of the casket, not nailed down. The old man bent over it and took hold of the edges. I figured if I aimed to skedaddle, now was the time. I just stood there, though. He had me hooked. I knew he couldn't bring a corpse back to life, but I sure wanted to see how he played out his bluff.

Then he frowned at me and straightened up again. 'Only one problem,' he said.

'Indeed, I should think there might be at least one.'

'I've been fixing to save this fellow for demonstration purposes after I got him to Tucson. I can't lose him now for just one sale.'

'Then you wish me to buy more than one?'

'A revivification oughta be worth five bottles.'

'I'll purchase ten if he's truly dead and he comes back to life.'

'That'll cost you ten dollars. Are you traveling with enough?'

His question put me off even more than the prospect of seeing a dead man inside the casket.

I suddenly knew the name of his game.

He had no intention of revivifying the corpse.

280

He hadn't been inside the wagon for long, but long enough to slip Buster into the box alongside the body.

'I have ten dollars to spare,' I said.

'You sure?'

'Open it up.'

'By and by,' he said. 'We have one other small matter requiring discussion.'

'Yes?'

He toed the casket. 'Like I say, I aim to use him at Tucson. He won't do me no good at all, alive and kicking. So I don't want you causing a fuss when it comes to rekilling him.'

'Certainly not,' I said.

'I'll need to strangulate him, you see. It won't be a pretty sight.'

'It's quite all right with me,' I said, knowing it wouldn't come to that.

'What I'm saying, Trevor – don't get overly fond of him.'

'Not likely,' I said.

He bent down over the casket again. As he shoved the lid off, I switched the Elixir to my left hand, dropped my right to my sixgun.

Lazarus didn't reach inside, so I didn't pull.

I stepped closer, holding my breath to keep out the awful stench.

No sign of Buster.

Just a dead man.

A skinny chap who didn't look to be much older than thirty, wearing boots, dungarees, a dirty plaid shirt and a noose. The noose was loose around his neck, the looped bundle of the hangman's knot resting atop his chest and the cut end of the rope dangling off to the side. His neck looked as if it had been polished with boot black. His tongue was black, too. It stuck out from between his teeth. His face had a nasty grayish color. There were pennies on his eyes to hold the lids shut. I was relieved to find his eyes covered, but thought it a spot peculiar that the pennies hadn't fallen off, what with how the casket had gotten jostled about.

Lazarus gave each penny a flick. They skittered away and rolled about the bottom of the box. The eyes stayed shut.

'Would you care to do the honors?' he asked.

I shook my head, and handed him the bottle of Elixir.

Lazarus uncorked it with his teeth. He spat out the cork. It missed the dead man's face.

281

'You might prefer to stand back, Trevor. These fellows can get awful frisky.'

I was happy to oblige. I stood back and breathed again. The stink was still there, sour and sweet at the same time, but if I moved any farther off, I wouldn't be able to keep a close watch.

I stayed ready, just in case Lazarus had tucked Buster out of sight underneath the corpse.

The first thing he did, he tucked the black tongue inside the fellow's mouth where it belonged. He pulled down on the jaw to make a bigger target, then commenced to pour Elixir out of the bottle. Some of it missed, splashing the gray lips and running down the whiskery cheeks. But some found its way into the mouth. I saw that his teeth were gray, which seemed a mite peculiar. But then the Elixir dyed them red.

Lazarus quit pouring.

The dead fellow just laid there.

I took myself a deep breath, then held it and stepped up close. Standing directly above the corpse, I could see a little pool of Elixir down there inside his mouth. It didn't appear to be going anywhere.

He gulped.

I flinched and jumped back.

With a whiny noise, he sucked in air. Then he let it out with a loud sigh.

He licked his lips, then opened up as if he hankered for another dose.

Lazarus obliged him.

The fellow's Adam's apple bobbed up and down. He swallowed just as fast as Lazarus could dump Elixir in.

'That should do him.' Lazarus uncrouched himself and rushed backward.

I moved away some, and breathed again.

I didn't rightly know what to make of all this, but I was sure keen to see what would happen next.

What happened next was, the fellow let out a squeal that made my hair rise. Then he bolted up, buggy-eyed and wheezing, grabbed the edges of his box and leaped to his feet. He looked down at himself. He glanced at Lazarus, then at me. Then he cried out, 'Whoooeeee!' and commenced to clap his hands and prance about on the floor of his casket. 'I'm saved!' he yelled. 'Lordy, Lordy, I'm *saved*!' Well, he hopped over the side and bounded toward me, weeping and laughing.

I was just too shocked and perplexed to get clear of him in time. He grabbed me and hugged me and kissed my cheek. And didn't he stink! I shoved him off, and he went skipping over to Lazarus and gave him a slew of hugs and kisses.

Lazarus acted more friendly toward him than I'd done. I reckon he was used to such doings. Instead of trying to free himself from the creature, he hugged him and patted his head. 'No call to take on,' he said. 'You're fine. You're just fine, young man.'

'I was *hung*! I was dead and *gone*!'

'You've been revivified,' Lazarus explained, giving him another hug. 'You've been returned to the land of the living with the aid of my patented Glory Elixir.'

'Glory Elixir?'

'Good for what ails you.'

'Glory! Glory hallelujah!' He broke away from Lazarus and I feared he might come after me again, but instead he dropped to his knees and hoisted his arms into the air. He gloried and hallelujahed for quite a spell.

He was still at it when Lazarus stepped around him. He walked toward me, looking solemn and thoughtful. 'You've witnessed the miracle,' he said.

'Witnessed something.'

He laid an arm across my shoulders and led me toward the wagon. 'It's truly a wondrous thing to behold, the restorative power of the Glory Elixir. It revives the dead! Just imagine the curative miracles that such a fluid works on the living, such as yourself. Why, with *ten* bottles at your disposal, I've no doubt but what you'll find yourself fit as a fiddle for a century at the very least.'

We stopped at the rear of the wagon, and he climbed in.

While Lazarus was out of sight, I turned my attention to the other fellow. He was still on his knees, but he'd quit acting strange. His face had the same dingy gray hue as when he'd been dead, which was odd. Now that he was breathing again, seemed like his skin should've taken on a healthier color.

When he saw me looking at him, he smiled.

'How'd you like being dead?' I asked.

'Not much,' he said.

'If you don't care for it, you'd best hurry off. Lazarus aims to rekill you.'

'Trevor!' Lazarus shouted from inside the wagon.

'I thought he ought to know, actually.'

The revived fellow wasn't smiling any more. But he wasn't lighting out, either.

'You'd best skedaddle,' I warned him.

He just stayed kneeling there.

Lazarus crawled backward, dragging a wooden box out through the blanket. 'Why'd you want to tell him such things?' he asked. He sounded a trifle peeved.

'Well, don't worry yourself. He's still here.'

After climbing down, Lazarus called to him, 'The lad's joshing you.'

'Oh, I know that, Jethro.'

Dr Jethro Lazarus rolled his eyes heavenward. Then he pulled a bottle from the box, just as if nothing had gone amiss. 'There's one,' he said, and handed it to me.

'You *told* me you intended to rekill him,' I said.

'Don't mean *he* has to know it.'

'He'll know it quickly enough when you have a go at throttling him.'

'I'll make it quick and painless.'

'Tell you what, I'll make it quicker.' Well, I swung around and tossed the bottle into my left hand and slapped leather with my right.

Lazarus yelled, 'No!'

His buddy yelled, 'Don't!'

Then my Colt was blazing, blasting up dust all around him. He sprang to his feet. He dodged about.

'Hold still!' I shouted.

He froze and reached for the sky.

'Please! Don't! Don't shoot!'

'No call to fret,' I told him, and took careful aim at his chest. 'Dr Lazarus'll revive you.'

Lazarus chuckled. 'I do believe we've been found out.'

'He's fixing to plug me!'

Shaking my head, I holstered the Colt.

The dead fellow looked quite relieved. He came toward us, watching me careful. Along the way, he dug a hand into a pocket of his trousers and dragged out a sort of rodent by its tail. It looked as flat as if it had gotten stepped on. He

284

gave it a fling and it thumped into the casket. 'How'd he catch on?' he asked Lazarus.

'You called me by my name, dummy.'

'It was more than that,' I said, rather pleased with myself. For the first time since the big shootout at the camp, I didn't feel horrible. I found myself smiling. 'Why, do you two frauds actually *fool* folks with your game?'

'More often than not,' Lazarus said.

His partner came up to us. Even without the dead critter, he didn't smell any too fresh. 'I'm Ely,' he said, and stuck out his hand.

It was the same hand he'd used to rid himself of the rotten carcass, so I didn't shake it but touched the brim of my hat instead. 'Trevor Bentley,' I said.

'Glad you didn't poke me full of lead. Care for a licorice?' He dug into his other pocket and came out with a stick.

It put me in mind of Sarah, and how we always ate just such candy when we visited town. I felt a little pull of sadness, but that passed as I realized Ely'd used the licorice to blacken up his tongue and lips. It had darkened his teeth, too. I'd seen they were gray, which hadn't seemed right. Death shouldn't do that to a man's teeth. I hadn't caught on, though.

'No thank you,' I told him, not wanting any truck with something he'd handled. 'I don't wish to turn my tongue black.'

They both laughed some at that. Ely tore off a piece of licorice and commenced to chew.

'Bootblack on your neck, is it?' I asked.

Lazarus clapped me on the shoulder. 'You're too quick for the likes of us.'

'And how is it you made your face such a color?' I asked Ely.

'Ashes,' he said. He licked a finger in spite of it being one that had plucked the dead thing from his pocket, and took a swipe at his face. A path of gray came off. He had ruddy skin underneath. He grinned like he'd shown me a secret of the universe.

'You two blokes certainly went to a fair piece of trouble on my account.'

'A sale's a sale,' Lazarus said. 'No hard feelings, I hope.'

'Well, you put on a lively show. Did you try it out on that

pair of rascals that came along before me?'

Lazarus shook his head. 'I'm afraid we missed the opportunity. They rode up on us too quick. Had a chance to spot Ely.'

'You don't travel along in the casket, then?' I asked the deceased.

He grinned, chewing and showing me his licoriced teeth. 'Gets a mite close in there.'

'I should think so. A mite smelly, too.'

'Oh, Ely don't mind the smell.'

'Nope,' he said, and bit off another piece of licorice.

'You two certainly do beat all.'

'Now,' Lazarus said, 'how many bottles of the Glory Elixir do you suppose you might like to purchase?'

I still held a bottle of the stuff. I shook it, and watched the red fluid slosh about. 'What's it made of?'

'Secret herbs and spices from the Far East, guaranteed to . . .'

'Quit having me on, now.'

'Gin and cherry syrup,' Lazarus said.

'Is it, now?' Well, I believed him. I uncorked my bottle, took a sniff, then drank some. It tasted mighty fine and sweet, scorched my throat, and heated up my stomach. 'And what does it cure, actually?'

Lazarus laughed. 'Sobriety.'

Though I had a vivid recollection of my bout with a hangover following too much whiskey with the boys, I judged that some Glory Elixir might be a fine thing to sip now and again. But then I figured Ely might've had a hand in filling the bottles. Real quick, I lost my thirst for the stuff.

'Suppose I pay you a dollar for the show, and you keep your Elixir?'

Lazarus scowled and rubbed his beard. Pretty soon, he said, 'I tell you what. You keep your dollar and ride along with us. Scout up ahead. Then you let us know quick when someone's coming along so Ely can get himself set for a demonstration. We'll pay you handsomely for your services, give you ten cents on every bottle sold. How does that appeal to you, Trevor?'

I gave it some thought, then said I'd do it.

I went on over to General, mounted up, then waited while they loaded the casket into the wagon. It was good to be out of smelling range of Ely.

When they got the wagon moving, I rode on ahead.

They were quite a pair of rascals. They'd livened me up considerable with their antics.

For a while there, I aimed to follow the plan and scout ahead for them. It'd be a treat to see them have a go at tricking some folks.

I figured I might travel with them all the way to Tucson. They seemed like good company, if you don't count Ely's aroma.

I could see how we might get to be chums.

But chums of mine don't last.

If I stayed with them, they were bound to end up dead. Same as everyone else.

So I chose to spare them.

I was some distance ahead of their wagon by then, so all it took was to quicken General's pace. By the time I looked back, they were out of sight.

CHAPTER THIRTY-EIGHT

I Get Jumped

Later on that same day, another wagon came along. This one had a man and woman up front and a boy about my own age riding a mare alongside. I considered warning them not to be fooled by Lazarus and Ely, but chose to let them look out for themselves. If they were fools enough to fall for such a swindle, they deserved it. Besides, I judged it'd be lowdown of me to ruin business for those two chaps.

All I did was say 'Howdy' as I rode by. The woman acted like I wasn't there at all, but the man and boy watched me close as if they feared I might be a desperado looking for a chance to gun them down.

Lazarus and Ely weren't likely to have much luck with this crowd.

Nobody else came along. When the sun got low, I put some distance between me and the trail. I found a sheltered place in a dry wash. After seeing to General, I did some shooting practice. Then I made myself a fire and cooked up a can of beans.

Now that I'd regained my appetite, the beans didn't seem altogether satisfying. They filled me up, but I had an awful hankering for fresh meat.

After supper, I felt like having a smoke. Didn't have any makings, though. They were back at the old campsite with the rest of McSween's things.

I turned gloomy, remembering McSween.

So I pulled a whiskey bottle out of my saddle bag. It had belonged to Breakenridge. I'd taken it, along with the gang's ammunition and money and some other supplies, even though I hadn't the heart to take McSween's tobacco and paper.

I uncorked the bottle and worked on it. It didn't have the good, sweet taste of the Glory Elixir. But it had never been touched by Ely, either, so that was a clear advantage.

The whiskey didn't perk up my spirits much.

I quit while I still had my wits about me, and turned in.

The next day, I returned to the trail. I still had a hunger for fresh meat, so I kept my eyes open.

There were birds about, magpies and hawks mostly, but a gunshot was likely to blow such a thing to smithereens if I was lucky enough to hit one. McSween had told me once that rattlers made good eating, but not a one showed itself. I figured that was for the best, as I wasn't keen on the notion of chowing down a snake.

I did spot a few gophers or prairie dogs. They'd poke their little heads up out of holes, I'd dismount and have a crack at them with the Winchester, miss, and go on my way again.

It was starting to look like I'd be eating beans from here to the next town. But then, long about noon, I caught sight of a jackrabbit as it hopped away from behind a boulder about fifty yards off.

I lit out after it.

The critter led me a merry chase, but I closed in, slapped leather, and shot from the saddle. My first bullet knocked its brains out.

Feeling mighty pleased with myself, I dismounted and fetched my knife. It had been Snooker's knife, which he'd always worn on his belt. I carried it in one of my saddle bags as I hadn't figured out a good way to wear it, what with having holsters at both hips.

Anyhow, I unsheathed the knife and gutted the hare and cut off its head and skinned it. I couldn't see much advantage to waiting, so I built a fire and cooked it up on the spot. It smelled just splendid as it sizzled away. By and by, the outside turned a lovely golden brown. I took my meal off the fire, then had to wait for it to cool down.

I ate the hare right off the spit and it tasted simply delicious. When about half was gone, I judged it'd be a fine thing to save some for supper. So I wrapped the remainder in a cloth and put it into a saddle bag along with my knife.

Then I climbed onto General and we headed back for the trail.

We were almost there, passing through a gap between some boulders, when my head got clobbered. Whatever it was thumped me solid through the crown of my hat and shook my brains. I couldn't see anything but red as I tumbled sideways and bounced off some rocks. After I hit the ground, my vision came around in time to let me watch General prance so as not to step on me.

I tried to sit up, wondering what had struck me. Just then, someone leaped off the top of a boulder and landed in my saddle.

General, spooked, reared up on his hind legs. The stranger yelped and pitched backwards, boots kicking at the sky, and came crashing down on top of me. My air blew out. The wound in my side felt like it burst open.

The rascal sat up quick, so I snatched a handful of shaggy hair and tugged. Out popped a grunt that sounded like it came from a boy no more than seven or eight years old.

I'd been attacked by an *urchin*?

It crossed my mind that he seemed mighty big for his age – more my own size. But I had no doubt he was a child. So I figured I shouldn't shoot him unless I had to.

Instead of going for my gun, I kept him held down atop me by the hair and used my right hand to punch him in the side. He grunted and flinched each time I struck a blow, but that didn't slow him down. He squirmed and twisted and finally sailed an elbow into my side. It found my wound.

The pain turned me weak so I lost my grip on his hair and he went to sit up. I grabbed for him, but only caught shirt. He wasn't ready to let that stop him. He strained against it, groaning. I heard a rip and the shirt came down off one shoulder. Then my arm got knocked away by an elbow and he scurried off me.

Without a glance back, he stumbled to his feet and made a dash for General, who was watching us from just beyond the gap.

I sprang up and gave chase.

'Stop or I'll shoot you!' I yelled.

He didn't stop.

I didn't shoot.

I just didn't have it in me to plug a kid. Besides, I was quicker on my feet and gaining on him, so it wasn't called for.

He was still a few strides short of General, yellow hair all abounce, shirt flapping behind like a cape, when I dived and caught him around the legs. He went down hard, breath whumping out. We both skidded through the dust. General scampered clear.

But the kid wasn't done yet. He squirmed and kicked, got his legs free, and smacked a boot heel into my head.

Well, that pretty much shredded my temper.

'Damn your bloody eyes!' I shouted and grabbed the boot that had kicked me. On my knees, I gave it a rough pull. It didn't come off, but dragged him closer. Then I twisted that boot. Crying out, the kid flipped over onto his back.

If you're a sharp reader, it won't come as any surprise to find out that the kid was no boy at all.

I wasn't reading about the situation, though. I was living it, and let me tell you, I couldn't have been any more surprised if he'd turned out to be a circus monkey.

For a while yet, I still thought I'd caught a boy.

He no sooner rolled onto his back than I dropped his boot and charged ahead on my knees, all set to pulverize this kid who'd attacked me and obviously aimed to steal my horse. But the way the shirt was sprawled open, I couldn't help but see he had what appeared to be a pair of smallish bosoms.

I'm not always a quick study.

What I thought, just for a bit, was that the lad had a deformity. Maybe he was some brand of freak or he had himself a disease that made him swell up in such a fashion. I'd once read in a book about the bubonic plague, which caused people to grow lumps on their bodies. Maybe what this kid had were buboes.

That notion gave me pause, for I didn't relish catching a dose of the plague.

My pause was all she needed.

She couldn't go anywhere, as her legs were trapped under me, but she bolted upright and swung a fist into my face.

It knocked me off to the side.

We tussled in the dust, me too stunned to put up much fight, and next thing you know, she was on top of me. She sat across my hips, unleashing a flurry of blows that battered my face considerable.

She had a savage look on her face. It was a pretty face, though, and I decided she likely *was* a girl, after all. So those were breasts, after all. Not deformities or buboes. They were sweaty and bouncing about as she lit into me, but I couldn't work up much interest in them.

291

Girl or not, she had to be stopped.

I tried to go for my guns, but her legs were in the way.

Finally, I managed to catch her wrists. They were slippery, but I held on. She jerked her arms in a frenzy, huffing and grunting. 'Quit it!' I shouted. 'Stop! I'll . . . have to . . . hurt you.'

'Hurt *me*?' She rather sneered it out, then pulled her wrist up and bit my knuckles.

I yelped and let go. Before she could take another swing at me, though, I threw my fist at her chin and got lucky. As her head snapped sideways, I bucked and shoved her. She tumbled off me. I scrambled to my knees and pulled a Colt and pointed it at her face.

'Don't you move!' I gasped.

She was propped up on her elbows, ready to have another go at me. But when she saw the gun, she sank back down onto the ground and lay there, panting for breath. Blood trickled from a corner of her mouth.

Her shirt hung wide open. Her tawny skin glistened in the sunlight. I could see reddish smudges on her side where my punches had landed.

Her blue dungarees had gotten pulled clear down past her hips during the fight. Some gold hair curled out over where they buttoned shut.

I reckon she saw how I was studying her, for she hiked the trousers up to her waist and shut her shirt. 'You think you're gonna meddle with me . . . you better think again. You'd have to shoot me first.'

'I've every right to shoot you,' I said. 'You tried to nick my horse.'

'Well, he's all yours.' She propped herself back up again with her elbows. Her shirt slipped open some. She checked to see how much. It left a bare strip down the middle of her chest and hung off the sides of her belly, but it kept her breasts covered so she didn't fool with it. She was still breathing hard. She blinked sweat out of her eyes, and stared at me.

'You don't need to go on lying there,' I told her.

'It gives me less room to fall if you kill me.'

I couldn't help but let out a laugh when she said that. The laugh made my head hurt worse. I felt around up there and found quite a bump above my right ear.

My whole face felt tight and sore from the drubbing she'd

given me. I checked my right hand. It had a passel of dents from her teeth, but she hadn't broken the skin.

'You sure did me some damage,' I said. 'But I don't suppose I'll kill you.' I holstered my weapon, then added, 'Just leave my horse be.'

'You aim to let me go?' she asked.

I didn't rightly know *what* to do with her.

While I gave it some thought, she sat up. Didn't get off the ground, though. She crossed her legs and watched me.

'Can't let you go,' I said. 'You're no better than a horse thief.' I couldn't help but recollect that I was the same. 'Besides, you bashed me about quite a bit.'

'No more than what you bashed me.' With that, the back of her hand rubbed a dribble of blood off her chin. She frowned at it, then showed it to me. 'You see?'

'I took quite the worst of it, actually.'

'You sure do talk peculiar. Anybody ever tell you that?'

Well, that set me to blushing. 'There's nothing at all peculiar about how I talk, thank you.'

'Oh yes there is. What are you, a Yankee?'

'I come from London, England.'

Her eyebrows went up. 'I'll be danged,' she said. 'An Englishman. If that don't beat all.' Her eyebrows came back down, and she was suddenly frowning. 'I didn't do that to you, did I?'

'What?'

'Your side there.'

I raised my arm and looked down at where the posse bullet had ripped my shirt. The cloth was bright with fresh blood. 'It was healing up quite nicely before you ambushed me.'

'Someone go at you with a knife?'

'It's a gunshot wound.'

'Let me see,' she said, and got up. I watched her close, wary of tricks. On her feet, she tried to fasten her shirt. Its buttons were gone, though, so she pulled it shut and tucked it into her trousers. Then she came on over to me.

'You'd best behave,' I warned her.

'I just wanta see.'

Well, I wasn't fool enough to pull up my shirt and give her a chance at my Colts. So I took them both in my hands, then raised my arms.

She stopped straight in front of me. Her eyes were level with my own, and green as emeralds. I hadn't seen them up

293

close like this. They were so sharp and clear they gave me a squirmy feeling inside.

'You sure are a caution,' she said.

'I don't intend to get myself ventilated by a girl.'

That brought a smile to her face. I saw her lips were dry and cracked. There was a cut at one corner, which I judged must've been caused by my fist. The cut had a drop of blood on it. Her teeth were straight, and shiny white.

'I ain't ventilated a soul all day,' she said.

Then she took hold of my shirt with both hands. It was pretty much untucked from the fight. She hauled out the remainder and hoisted it up. Bending over some, she peered at my wound.

'Why, it's only a scratch, mostly. I bet you just walked too close to a thorny bush.'

'They must have rather big thorns where you come from.'

'Don't they just,' she said. Then she leaned in closer and blew on my wound, which I knew to be more of a furrow than a scratch. Her breath felt pretty good. She did it again.

'What are you doing there?' I asked.

'You picked up some grit and it don't wanta blow off. You got some water, I'll clean it for you. Otherwise, you might just fester up and die.'

'I shouldn't like that to happen.'

'Well, go get your water.'

She let my shirt fall and stepped back. She had a look of mischief in her eyes, so I judged she was up to one trick or another. 'Wait here,' I said. Then I holstered my guns and hurried off to fetch General.

I gave some thought to making the girl come with me. More than likely, she had no intention at all of cleaning off my wound, but aimed to light out.

I rather hoped she might do just that. Run off and hide. I didn't know what to do with her, anyhow, if she stayed. She had already caused me a spot of trouble. The sooner I could get shut of her, the better.

So I took my time going after General. He'd wandered off a piece. I found him nibbling some leaves off a bush, and let him work on it for a while. Watching him, I had a mind to mount up and ride away. If I did that, I'd be clear of the girl whether or not she'd decided to vamoose. Only problem was, my hat had gotten knocked off when she clobbered me off my saddle and I didn't aim to leave it behind.

Besides, I was curious.

Maybe I was more than that.

The hat was the excuse I gave myself, though.

After a while, I took the reins and walked General back through the rocks. Along the way, I found my hat and picked it up. Its crown was caved in some, but the dent popped right out when I gave it a poke. I knew better than to wear my hat, what with the sore lump on my head, so I hung it over my saddle horn.

A few more steps took me past the rocks. The girl was leaning back against a boulder, arms folded across her chest.

'You didn't dodge off,' I called. Didn't quite know how I felt about that.

'Where would I go?' she asked.

'You aren't afraid of me, then?'

'Oh, that beats all.'

'Perhaps you ought to be, you know,' I said, and lifted down my water bag.

'You're *just* a boy.'

'Used to be one.'

She watched me come toward her. Even though she didn't smile or smirk, she had a sassy look about her face. 'And how old *are* you?' she wanted to know.

'How old are you?'

'I asked you first.'

'Older than you, I suppose.'

'Ha.'

'I'm nineteen, going on twenty,' I told her.

'You're a liar's what you are.' She reached out and grabbed the water bag. 'I bet you're no more than thirteen.'

'Eighteen,' I said.

'More likely twelve.' She unplugged the pouch, tipped back her head and commenced to gulp down my water.

She had a tiny, pale scar under her chin. Her neck was smooth and shiny, same as the skin that showed between the edges of her shirt. Staring at those places, I all of a sudden lost my urge to squabble with her.

'Actually, I'm closing in on sixteen.'

She lowered the pouch and smiled. 'That sounds more like the truth.'

'It is the truth.'

'Truth is, I've got you beat. I'll be seventeen come October.'

'So you're sixteen.'

'Older than you by a country mile. Go on and take your shirt off.'

She helped herself to another swig while I started to work on the buttons. 'What's your name?' I asked.

'What's yours?'

'Trevor. Trevor Bentley.'

'Mighty hifalutin.'

I finished with the buttons and pulled my shirt off. 'I told you mine,' I reminded her.

'Give.' She wiggled her fingers at my shirt.

I handed it to her. She bunched up the tail and soaked it with water.

'What sort of name *should* I have?' she asked. She pushed herself off the rock, stepped closer to me, and reached the wet cloth toward my wound. 'Pick up your arm.'

I raised my arm, forgetting to take my Colt with it. By the time I caught the mistake, she was already patting the cloth against my raw gouge. She was gentle about it, too. With both her hands full, she'd have trouble going for either of my guns, so I tried not to worry about it.

'You want me to guess your name, then?' I asked.

'Bet you can't.'

'Rumplestiltskin.'

She laughed softly. 'Yep. You got it on the first try. That's Rump for short.' She stopped swabbing my wound and gave the shirt to me.

As I put it on, she stepped back and slipped the strap of my water bag over her shoulder.

'Saw you cooking up a jackrabbit,' she said. 'You give me some, I'll tell you who I am.'

'You've already told me, Rump.'

'You don't wanta see me shrivel up and die,' she said, and walked on around me.

Here we go again, I thought, figuring I might have to throw her down. But she didn't try to mount General. Instead, she gave my horse a few pats, then opened the saddle bag and pulled out the remains of my hare. Turning around, she smiled and said, 'Much obliged.'

'That's my supper.'

'Not any more, I reckon.' She unwound the cloth I'd wrapped it in. 'Or are you gonna shoot me?'

'Do you always do just as you please?'

'Pretty near.' She bared her teeth and ripped a chunk out of my hare. Her eyes closed. She chewed a few times and sighed. Then she tore off another chunk and worked on it. Some juice dribbled down her chin. She wiped it off with the back of her hand, then opened her eyes and said, 'Mighty fine, Trevor.' Her words came out sounding thick and mushy. 'It's gonna be a pure pleasure riding with a feller that's such a good cook.'

'You have a notion to ride with me, do you?'

'Name's Jesse. Jesse Sue Longley.'

CHAPTER THIRTY-NINE

Pardners

'Which direction are you traveling?' I asked, figuring this might let me off the hook.

'None in particular,' said Jesse Sue Longley.

'Why, you must be going *to* somewhere.'

'Ain't going *to* anyplace. Just *away* from where I been.'

'Where's that, then?'

'That's my nevermind.'

'It's my nevermind if you aim to ride with me. What is it you're running away from? Have you got someone after you?'

Her eyes narrowed. 'Nobody's after me. What about you? How'd you get yourself shot?'

'That's *my* nevermind,' I said.

She smiled. 'Looks like we're even, huh?'

'Looks that way. Far as I know, though, I'm in the clear. Those who caused my troubles aren't looking for me.'

'I can say the same,' she said.

Mine were all dead. From Jesse's manner, I couldn't help but wonder if maybe hers were dead, too. Instead of putting me off, the notion made me feel like we had more in common.

'Where is it that you don't want to go?' I asked.

'Only just Texas.'

'Well, that's not where I'm going.'

'I knew that. I saw you on the trail. You was heading the wrong way for a feller bound for Texas. Not as it would've mattered if I could've nabbed your horse.'

'How'd you get out here, at all, without a mount of your own? Did you walk the whole way, or . . . ?'

'Do I look like an addlehead?'

'Not at all.'

'I should say I'm not. No, sir.' She dipped her head down and brought it up sharp as if agreeing with herself rather

298

fiercely. Even though she had a frown on her face, something in her eyes stayed amused – like she was up to some brand of mischief. She'd pretty much had that same glint in her eyes all along. It seemed fitting the times I knew she was having me on, but times like now it didn't rightly belong there and seemed peculiar – as if she carried a secret knowledge inside that maybe set her apart from whatever was actually going on.

'I had me a horse,' she said, 'till yesterday when a dang rattler spooked him and he threw me. He run off, and I ain't seen him since. Sorriest excuse for a flea-bitten nag I ever *did* see. Lost him, and everything I owned but the clothes on my back. Lost me a good Sharps rifle,' she added, as if that were an especially sore point.

'A spot of bad luck, that.'

'Worse luck for the rattler.' A grin came up, matching the usual gleam in her eyes, and she patted her tummy.

'You *ate* it?'

'Killed it first. Stove in its ugly head with a rock.'

'The same as you did to me?'

'Well, your head ain't so ugly, and I didn't stove it in.'

'You certainly had a go at it, didn't you?'

'I only just meant to knock you off your saddle,' she protested. 'If I'd aimed to kill you dead, you'd be stretched out in the dust before now.'

'I doubt that.'

'Not me.' She bent over, hitched up a leg of her dungarees, and snatched a knife out of her boot top. It was just about the biggest knife I'd ever seen, the blade near as long as my forearm. She tapped its point against my chest. 'This here's my Bowie knife,' she said.

I gazed at it, and felt myself shrink and get cold here and there. She'd had that awful weapon all along. If she'd used it instead of the rock, she could've split my head open. She hadn't even gone for it when we were fighting hard on the ground, and there'd been moments when she'd had the chance. She'd *chosen* not to pull it and gut me.

'Why didn't you use it?' I asked.

'Makes a terrible mess,' she said, and slid it back down into her boot. Standing up straight in front of me, she lost her smile. 'I didn't have any call to kill you. I just needed a horse to ride on.'

'I'd be pleased to have you ride along double with me,' I told her.

'Much obliged,' she said.

She gave me the water pouch. I took my hat off the saddle horn and hung the pouch there by its strap. I needed both hands to mount General, so I put my hat on and winced as it squeezed the lump on my head. Then I reached down. Jesse took hold of my hand, and I gave her a tow as she swung up behind me.

'Mind?' she asked.

Before I could inquire what she meant by that, she plucked the hat off my head. 'Lost mine down a canyon two days back,' she explained.

'It seems you've lost a good deal.'

She slapped my shoulder. 'Gained more than I've lost, pardner.'

I let her wear my hat.

She slipped an arm around my waist, and we rode on over to the trail. It was strange, having a girl behind me, hanging onto me, sometimes brushing up against my back. I rather enjoyed it, actually.

After I'd seen that Bowie knife, I couldn't help but trust her. I couldn't help but like her, too. She was tough and had more gumption than any gal I'd ever run across. Even though she'd tried to steal General and she'd hurt me some, I judged she must have a good heart or she would've cut me open.

She was awful pretty, too.

I took to feeling glad she'd jumped me.

Maybe we'd stay together all the way to Tombstone.

But by and by she said, 'I sure could do with a smoke.'

The words were rocks that crushed my joy.

'I haven't any makings, I'm afraid.'

'Too bad.'

Too bad. Quite.

She's bound to end up as dead as McSween, I thought. Dead as everybody else who's crossed my trail.

There was only one way to save Jesse. I had to get clear of her, and soon.

But I'd told her she could ride with me, and the notion of going against my word didn't set well. Besides, it wouldn't be right to leave her alone in the wilderness without a horse and supplies. So I was stuck with her, at least for now.

Glad to be stuck with her, too, though it worried me.

I'll just have to see that she *doesn't* get killed, I told myself.

The trick was to keep her alive, and let her stay with me till we came to a town or met up with some folks who might be willing to take her off my hands.

We rode on and on. Sometime late in the afternoon we came up behind a buckboard pulled by a pair of mules. It was still a ways off when I saw it had a boy in the back, a man and a woman in the driver's box. This looked like an outfit that might not mind an extra passenger.

The kid was maybe eight years or nine years old. He sat amidst of a jumble of luggage and supplies, so I judged the family likely had food to spare. I couldn't see how they might object to taking Jesse along if I paid them for their troubles.

But it didn't seem right to foist her off on these folks without warning, so I said, 'I should think this family might be pleased to have your company. Perhaps we'll ask if they'd be willing to let you travel with them.'

She didn't answer. Pretty quick, though, she smacked the back of my shoulder.

'Say, now!'

'Dirty sidewinder.'

'You'll be better off.'

'I'm just fine right here, thanks all the same.' Then she fetched me another smack.

'Quit that.'

'You ain't gonna drop me off with a passel of strangers. Get it outa your head.'

We were just drawing up on the buckboard, the kid waving, the man and woman in front both turning around to see us, when Jesse called out 'Gee-yup!' and gave General a whap on the rump. He took off with a lurch. I had half a mind to pull in the reins, but instead I let him trot on until we'd left the bunch a ways behind us.

General settled down to a walk.

'I don't see why you had to do that,' I said.

Jesse didn't talk for a spell. Finally, she said, 'I thought you and me was pardners.'

'You'd be better off with those folks.'

'How do you know that, Mister Smarty? How do you know the pa – if that's what he even is – don't take a horsewhip to his wife and boy eighteen times a day just to exercise his arm?'

'It wouldn't have hurt to have a talk with them. They

might've been quite friendly.'

'How come you're so all-fired hot to throw me off on someone else?'

'I don't care to see you hurt.'

'You fixing to hurt me?'

'Why, no. Certainly not. The problem is, you're likely to *get* hurt if you stay with me. You just won't last, not unless you get clear while there's still time.'

'Why's that?'

'I don't know, actually. But I've left behind me an awful string of dead folks.'

'You got a sickness?'

'Nothing more than bad luck.'

'Well, that eases my mind. You near had me scared. I saw a feller caught himself a dose of the rabies, one time. He took to cavorting down the street all wild-eyed and slobbering. You never seen such a sight. He went to bite old lady Jones, and Sheriff Hayes dropped him stone cold dead. That was in El Paso three years back. Saw it happen with my very own eyes. They say it was a dog bite. You get yourself bit by a rabid hound, you might just as well cash in your chips then and there. That's what I'd do, blow out my own brains and call it quits. You don't want to make a fool outa yourself, foaming all over tarnation and snapping at folks so they have to shoot you.'

'You won't catch rabies from me,' I told her.

'When was the last time you got yourself bitten?'

'Earlier today, actually.'

She let out a laugh and slapped my arm, but not hard. 'Smarty.'

'I do hope I won't commence to slobber and snap.'

My hat suddenly got shoved down onto my head. 'Ow!'

'You better wear it for a spell. The sun's getting to your brain.'

I lifted it some so it wouldn't squeeze my bump. We rode on for a while, then Jesse said, 'So what was it that killed off such a string of folks?'

'Mostly guns and knives.'

'But you ain't the one that done 'em in?'

'I didn't kill my friends. But plenty of them ended up dead on account of me, so it's much the same thing.'

'How'd you manage all that?'

'It's rather as if I led them into trouble, you see. Not that

302

I did such things on purpose. But those folks got killed, anyhow. I'm afraid the same might happen to you.'

'Well, don't go worrying about me.'

'I can't avoid it, actually.'

'You won't get me killed, so quit bothering your head about it. When my number comes up, it won't be on account of you. It'll be my own dang fault. You can bet on that.'

'It *shall* be your own dang fault, quite right. It'll be your stubborn ways. I've warned you fair and square.' I turned General and looked back down the trail. The buckboard was still a distance off, but getting closer. 'You ought to reconsider.'

'Nope. I'd a sight rather take my chances with your bad luck, which I don't believe anyhow, than join up with them folks.'

'You claimed you're not addleheaded.'

'That man, he'd take after me. It's what men do.'

'He's married, Jesse.'

'That ain't likely to stop him. He'll just bide his time till he can get me alone, maybe tonight when his woman's sleeping or maybe he'll just go and try me right in front of her eyes. Some fellers ain't particular who watches.'

'You're daft.'

'I know what I know. It'll happen, sure as you're sitting there. And then I'd be forced to give him a taste of my knife. More than likely, the widow'd lose her head when she saw how I'd carved her husband. Wouldn't matter that he was no good and better dead. He was her husband and the father of her boy, so she'd throw a fit and grab a gun and shoot me. Then *I'd* be killed. And you know what? Every last bit of such a sorry business would be all *your* fault for passing me off on these folks.'

I twisted around on the saddle and gazed at her. She looked grim, but had the usual spark of mischief in her green eyes.

'When was it now,' I asked, 'that you kissed the Blarney stone?'

'What're you getting at?'

'I've rarely heard such malarkey.'

'Malarkey?'

'Outrageous nonsense.'

'You just don't know nothing at all.'

General stepped off the trail without any urging from

303

me as the buckboard closed in on us. But he needn't have bothered. The fellow with the reins brought his mules to a stop in time to miss us, even if we hadn't moved.

'Vahs iss dee problem?' he asked. I'd run into a German or two back home and took him for one because of the odd and spitty way he talked.

Before I could answer, Jesse said, 'No problem.'

He scowled at her. He looked like a hard man. Maybe Jesse hadn't been far off the mark with her notion that he enjoyed taking a horsewhip to his family. The gal beside him kept her head down as if she was bashful. She wore a white linen bonnet. I couldn't see her face at all. The boy in the rear of the wagon watched us, but kept mum.

'Iss dis your sister?' the fellow asked me.

'She lost her horse,' I explained. 'I've been giving her a ride.'

'Allzo,' he said, whatever that meant. One of his dark eyebrows climbed up his forehead. 'Vee take dis froyloyn. She komm mit, yes?'

At that, the gal raised her head. Her face was all ablush. She was working her lower lip between her teeth and she stared at Jesse with a jittery look in her eyes.

Well, then she shook her head just a bit. It wasn't much of a shake, but enough so the man noticed it. He spat some words at her. They didn't make any sense at all to me, but she cringed and dropped her head.

Now that she was taken care of, he gave me a sly grin and said, 'Vaht vant you for her? I give you dee five dollar, yes?'

'I don't reckon so,' I said.

'Nine?'

'He wants to *buy* me, Trevor.'

'She isn't for sale,' I said.

'But yes. Vee feel?'

Jesse snapped, 'Nobody lays a hand on me, you damn polecat!'

Scowling fierce, he lurched to his feet there in the driver's box, jabbed a finger at her and hissed, '*Shee*son!'

The word wasn't out his mouth before I had a Colt in my fist.

He gave it a glance, frowned some, then came back at me with his oily grin. 'Ten dollar?'

'Bugger off,' I said, then wheeled General around and put in the spurs. We galloped on down the trail till a rocky bend put the buckboard out of sight.

Pretty soon after we'd slowed down to a walk, Jesse pushed her head against me. Her hair tickled the back of my neck. 'Sure glad you didn't sell me off to that pig,' she said.

'I wonder if he might've gone up to twenty.'

She bumped her head against me fairly solid. A bit later, I heard a few sniffles. It crossed my mind she might be crying, but that didn't seem likely. Not Jesse.

Just in case she might still be worried, though, I said, 'You can ride with me for just as long as you like. I won't try to give you away again. Or sell you, either.'

She leaned more of herself against my back and wrapped both her arms around my middle. She gave me a squeeze, then said, 'See that you don't.'

CHAPTER FORTY

The Damsel in Distress

Later on, we came to a shallow creek that crossed the trail. Even though we still had some daylight left and could've gone on, it usually doesn't hurt to camp by water. I'd had no trouble yet with running low. It was dry country, though. If we moved on, no telling when we might run into another place with good water.

Other folks were likely to have the same notion. I didn't want company, and figured Jesse felt that way, too, so we followed the creek north till we were a good distance from the trail.

We found a fine spot that had high piles of rock on two sides, and even a few scrawny trees. They'd give us shade till the sun went down, and block out some of the wind that usually stirred up cold at night.

As I unsaddled General, Jesse said, 'You just stay here and don't you dare come looking for me. I'm going upstream for a spell.'

She wandered off. I stayed where I was, finished removing all my gear from General, set down the sack of oats for him, and groomed him while he ate. When I got done, Jesse still wasn't back yet. I let General wander down to the creek, but didn't follow him.

The reason Jesse had warned me off, I judged, was so she'd have privacy for bathing. It stirred me up some, thinking about that. I took a notion to climb the rocks and spy on her. It seemed like a lowdown thing to do, though. Besides, she might catch me at it and get riled.

So I hauled my saddle into the shade under a tree and leaned back against it to make myself comfortable. A soft breeze was blowing. I closed my eyes and listened to the birds. It was uncommon peaceful and nice. I might've drifted off to sleep except that my mind wouldn't let go of Jesse.

306

I kept remembering how she'd looked when we were fighting, her shirt open as she threw punches at me. And how she'd looked later, sprawled on the ground. She might be in the creek right now without a stitch on. It was almost more than a body could stand.

I pictured how she might look, all bare and wet. Quite a bit slimmer than Sarah, not near as curvy, more like a boy. I wondered what her breasts might feel like. They weren't near as large as Sarah's. They'd looked like they might be hard, but then I recalled how they'd jiggled some while she swung at me. So they couldn't be terribly hard. Likely not as soft as Sarah's, though.

I recalled my first night in Sarah's bed, and how she'd cured me of being put off by breasts. Then I was thinking about the other fine times I'd had with Sarah. There'd been the dancing and the baths and all those other times we'd ended up having at each other. But there'd been the rest of it, too. Trips into town, horse rides and picnics, and the pure pleasure of just being with her – talking or reading, doing chores or sharing meals.

Pretty soon, I was missing her something terrible.

If only I hadn't seen that story about Whittle in the newspaper, we might still be at the house.

That set me to thinking about our railroad trip, and I got angry remembering Briggs. If that no-account hadn't thrown me off the train, we'd be together yet.

But he had thrown me off.

And I'd joined up with the gang.

It seemed likely that I would never see Sarah again. No telling where she might've gone to, by now. Maybe she'd traveled on to California with Briggs. I sure hoped not. But if she was fool enough to get pulled in by the likes of him, she deserved no better.

It made me feel ornery, thinking that way about her. I told myself she was too good for him, too smart for him. What she'd probably done was turn around and gone home to Coney Island. I hoped so.

That way, I would be able to find her again after I'd finished my business with Whittle.

Except I won't, I thought.

Till now, I hadn't given it much real thought. But I'd known, way in the back of my mind, that me and Sarah were finished. It finished between us the night I shot down those posse men.

After that, I was no longer fit for her.

Sarah and even Mother herself were good women. I was no better than a murderer. Best for all concerned if I never saw either one of them again.

I judged they'd be better off without me, anyway, on account of how they'd likely end up killed.

The same went for Jesse. But I was stuck with her.

I recalled how she'd put her arms around me there on the trail after we'd left the German behind. It seemed clear she was growing rather fond of me. I couldn't deny that I'd gotten fond of her, too.

She was full of gumption and her sassy ways appealed to me. Even if she'd been an ugly thing, I would've enjoyed her company. But she was awful pretty. Too pretty.

If I didn't watch out, I might find myself purely infatuated with her. That wouldn't do, at all.

I won't allow it, I told myself.

I'll only take her as far as the next town.

I won't spy on her. I won't touch her. I won't even think about her being a girl.

She's just someone who needs a ride.

My job's keeping her alive long enough to leave her behind.

After making up my mind about that, I felt somewhat better about the situation. I felt pretty near gallant. Jesse was a damsel in distress, me a knight determined not to lose my heart to her and only to fulfill my mission of delivering her to a safe haven.

With that settled, I figured it might be time to rouse my bones and start a fire. So I opened my eyes, and there was Jesse watching me. She sat nearby in a patch of sunlight, barefoot, arms resting across her upraised knees. Her ankles were wet. Water dripped off the cuffs of her dungarees. Her blue shirt was damp and clinging to her. It wasn't tucked in, but she'd used her belt to hold it shut around her waist. Her face glistened with specks of water. Her short hair wasn't fluffy any more, but lay against her head in thick, golden loops. A few of those hung across her brow. Two on the sides curled down in front of her ears and came to points.

In short, she looked wet and fresh and altogether splendid. She looked so fine it put a lump into my throat.

I could see it wouldn't be an easy task to keep my wits

and not take a powerful liking to her.

The gleam in her green eyes and how she smiled didn't help at all.

Sitting up, I said, 'You could get yourself shot, you know, sneaking about in such a manner.'

'Bunkum,' she said.

'There was a lawman I heard about, he ventilated his best friend when the bloke walked up behind him unannounced. It happens all the time, actually.'

'This must be my lucky day.'

'I'm quite serious.'

'Well, next time I find you sleeping, I'll be sure and pelt you with a stone.'

'I wasn't asleep.'

'Then you should've heard me coming. Ears no better than that, it's a wonder you've lasted.' A drop of water slid off one of her curls. It trickled down her eyebrow, so she wiped it away with the back of her hand. 'So then, you were playing possum.'

'Not at all,' I protested.

She narrowed her eyes. 'You were up in them rocks having a gander at me. Saw me coming back, so you scampered on down and let on like you'd spent your time dozing.'

A blush heated my face.

'Ah-ha!' She didn't seem angry, but pleased with herself for finding me out.

'I did no such thing,' I said.

'No call to fib about it.'

'It's the truth, Jesse. But you go ahead and think what you wish. I'd be quite a wealthy chap if I had a dollar for every time I've been wrongly accused of this and that. It's as ordinary as daylight.'

'Liar. I seen you.'

'Did not.'

'Did, too.' She pointed a thumb over her shoulder at the rocky height behind her back. 'Right up there. So you might just as well fess up.'

All of a sudden, the bottom seemed to drop out of my stomach. I jumped to my feet, pulled a Colt, rushed past Jesse and went charging up the slope.

'What in tarnation?' she called after me.

I paid her no heed, but raced upward, leaping higher and

309

higher, my mouth gone dry, my heart thudding fit to bust. I wasn't so much scared as outraged. Some bloody scoundrel had gone and spied on Jesse. He'd watched her bathe in the creek. No telling why he hadn't gone on down and attacked her. Maybe he aimed to bide his time and take us by surprise later on. Well, he wouldn't get the chance.

I bounded over the top of the rocks, all set to shoot him dead.

And that's just what I would've done, but he wasn't there.

I wandered about, searching behind every rock, peering into crevices, circling around the few tangles of mesquite thick enough to hide a man. By and by, I judged he must've skedaddled.

From my perch, I had a mighty fine view of the creek. Anyone up here would've had just such a fine view of Jesse. I was in a fit to shoot him. But he wasn't down by the creek, nor hurrying down the slopes. I studied the low land all around us, but couldn't spot him or any horse other than General. There were hiding places everywhere, though. Dry washes, boulders, jutting heaps of rock, cacti and bushes and a few stunted trees. Not many places for concealing a horse, though a man on foot could disappear in any of a thousand places.

I might've stayed up there longer, hoping he'd show himself, but then it came to me that I'd left Jesse alone.

What if he'd circled around?

What if he'd jumped her?

Quick as I could, I hurried along the top of the rocks till our camp came into sight. There stood Jesse, arms folded across her chest, gazing up at me. And wasn't I glad to see her!

Before starting down, I scanned the area. Nobody appeared to be lurking about. I could see the wagon trail off in the distance, but nobody was in sight on it.

'He got away,' I called, and commenced to make my way toward the ground.

'Who got away?' Jessie asked.

'The bloody cur that *spied* on you!'

She frowned some. 'He wasn't you?'

'Certainly not. Did he look like me?'

'Well, I didn't see him up close. He was only just peeking down outa the rocks.'

310

'We'll have to keep a careful watch,' I said, and leaped to the ground in front of her. 'I shouldn't have let you go off by yourself. That was a bad mistake.'

'Well, nothing come of it.'

'Not this time. From now on, we'd best stay together.'

'I need me some private times, Trevor.'

'What you need is me standing guard. No telling where this fellow might be, or what's on his mind. I don't aim to see you attacked or killed for the sake of your modesty.'

'I can take care of myself, I reckon. Just let me take along your Winchester, I'll get along dandy.'

I couldn't see a good argument against that. She ought to be fairly safe, armed with the rifle. 'Perhaps that'll do,' I told her. 'We ought to stay together, regardless, unless you're fixing to . . . bathe or the like.'

'Sounds good to me.'

She got into her socks and boots. Then we roamed about the area, gathering stray bits of wood and roots for our fire. I kept my eyes open for the stranger, and also for game. Neither appeared.

Jesse seemed uncommon quiet the whole time.

After we made our fire, she kneaded some flour into dough, jammed wads of it onto sticks, and cooked them over the flames while I heated up a pot of beans.

After we finished our meal, we took the pot and spoons over to the creek. That's when I noticed how still and quiet things seemed. The air had a yellowish cast to it. Looking off to the west, I saw that the sun was gone behind somber mountains of cloud.

'Do you suppose we'll have a storm?' I asked Jesse, who stood nearby with the rifle.

'Could be. Just as likely not. Doesn't appear as how they get much rain in these parts.'

We didn't pay it any more mind. I cleaned off the pot and spoons. Afterward, we spent a while scouting about to gather more fuel. When it got too dark to see, we quit that. We led General back to camp, and I hobbled him so he wouldn't go wandering off too far during the night. Then we sat down by the fire.

Jesse still wasn't talkative. Pretty soon, I asked, 'Are you worried about that chap you saw in the rocks?'

'You might say that.'

'He hasn't shown himself yet. Why, I suppose he dodged

311

off long ago. All the same, we'll need to take turns standing watch. Can't have him sneaking up on us while we sleep, you know.'

'Oh, he ain't likely to sneak up on us.'

'One can't be too careful. It's when you're least expecting trouble . . .'

'I never did see him, Trevor.' She flung a stick, rather briskly, into the fire. It hit and tossed up a spray of sparks. 'I didn't see nobody. I only just let on.'

I gaped at her, flabbergasted.

'That's the way of it. I'm right sorry I went and got you so worked up about him.'

'He wasn't there at all?'

'Nope. I figured sure you must've climbed up top to goggle at me and you'd fess up once I claimed I saw you.'

'I *told* you I'd done no such thing.'

'Well, who'd admit it?'

'I'm not one to go about lying.'

'Me neither. Not as a general rule. But I wanted to catch you out.'

'Why should I *care* to goggle at you?' I blurted.

'You know why.'

I certainly did know why, but I wasn't about to admit it. So I kept mum.

By and by, Jesse said, 'I seen how you look at me, Trevor Bentley.'

My face heated up, but I doubt it was noticeable in the firelight. 'Malarkey,' I said.

'I don't blame you none for it. You're just a feller. They can't help that sort of thing.'

'You're roaming up the wrong trail, Jesse.'

She narrowed her eyes at me, and a corner of her mouth turned up. 'Why, you can go on denying it till your face turns blue, I know what I know.'

'Seems to me that you hold quite a high opinion of yourself.'

'I sure do. That's a fact. A mighty high opinion. That's how come I don't allow myself to get jumped on by every lowlife sidewinder that takes a fancy to me.'

'I've *not* taken a fancy to you.'

'Sure have.'

'Am I a lowlife sidewinder, then?'

'Don't reckon you are.'

'Thank you kindly, ma'am.'

'That don't mean I'll let you jump on me.'

'I've no intention of jumping on you, actually. You're the one who's done all the jumping on folks, so far.'

She let out a soft laugh. 'Long as you leave the jumping to me, we'll get along fine.'

We went quiet after that, and just sat there watching the fire for a spell. Then the wind kicked up, so Jesse fetched my blanket. She brought it back, sat down beside me, and wrapped it around both of us. I scooted closer to her and our arms touched. That earned me a wary glance.

'Quite sorry,' I said.

'Oh, never mind. It ain't your fault I'm touchy.'

'Whose fault is it, then?'

'Chester Frank and Charlie Gunderson and Jim Dexter, I reckon. Bobbie Joe Sims and Karl Williams, Bennie Anderson, Danny Sayles, Hank Dappy, Ben Travis, Billy "One-Eye" Cooper.' She took a deep breath, then went on, 'Randy Jones, Ephram and Silas Henry, Reverand Haymarket, Jack Quincy. Did I mention Farley Hunnecker?'

'I don't believe so.'

'Well, then, Farley too. And Gary Hobbs, Dix Talman, Robert E. Lee Smith, a dimwit called Grunt – I never caught his real name. Then there was "Sweet Sam" Bigelow and . . .'

'By Jove,' said I. 'How can you recall such a string of names?'

'You ain't likely to forget the names of such swine.'

'What did they *do* to you?'

'It ain't what they did, it's what they *tried* to do.'

'Every *one* of those chaps?'

'There's more. You didn't let me finish.'

'They *all* tried to . . . have a go at you?'

'One way or another. See, I didn't have no one to look out for me. I reckon that was partly the trouble. My ma, she passed on when she gave birth to me, and my pa was a damn drunk. He tried me a few times himself, but I learned him better.'

'Your own father?'

'He was just as low as the rest of 'em. Lower than most. But it was Clem Catlow that was the last straw. Clem was big as a tree, a boxer. He rode into town to fight Irish Johnny O'Rourke, one of our local boys, and KO'd Johnny in the

313

first round. Same night, he followed me when I went to walk home. I worked in the kitchen there at the Lone Star Steak Emporium on Third Street. Anyhow, he stumbled along after me and sweet-talked me some. I gave him a piece of my mind, but he wasn't one to be put off. Finally, he took hold and hauled me into an alley. I says to myself, "It's him or me." I'm a mighty tough scrapper.' She looked at me and hoisted an eyebrow.

'You are that,' I said.

'But I knew I weren't no match for Clem Catlow. One good whack, and he'd likely knock my head crooked. I yelled and begged, but it weren't no use. He threw me down and took to ripping off my duds, so I had no choice but to kill him.'

Just when she said that, thunder rumbled through the night. It sounded some ways off, but we frowned at each other.

'You *killed* him?' I asked, whispering as if to keep the storm from hearing my voice and coming after us.

'Tore him up with my Bowie knife. Let me tell you, it was no easy job squeezing out from under him afterwards, either. But I managed it. Then I ran on home and got my things together and saddled up Pa's horse and lit out.'

CHAPTER FORTY-ONE

The Gullywasher

'I stabbed a man myself,' I told her. 'It was in an alley, too.'

Jesse looked at me. 'No,' she said.

'Yes, indeed. He and others had a go at robbing me. Then I was pursued by a mob and . . . Why, I would be in England yet if not for that.'

'Ain't it strange? I'd still be in El Paso, I reckon, except for taking my knife to Clem in that there alley. Looks like you and me are two of a kind.'

'I suppose we are.'

Smiling, she bumped her shoulder against me.

Along came another grumble of thunder. It sounded closer than the last.

'Tell me more,' Jesse said.

'I should hardly know where to start.'

'Start at the start. We got all night.'

I gave it some thought, then commenced my story where it rightly began, with Mother bringing the drunken Rolfe Barnes into our flat. When I told about him laying into her with his belt, Jesse let out a hissing noise. 'I know just his kind,' she said. She seemed quite pleased about the way I'd bashed him with the fireplace poker, but allowed as how I should've finished the job.

I plugged along with my tale. Jesse seemed mighty interested, and asked questions about this and that and made comments. All the while, the thunder got noisier and closer and lightning sometimes brightened up the sky. Still, the rain stayed away.

I came to the part about Sue, but didn't let on that she was a whore. According to me, she was simply a stranger who offered to guide me to Leman Street. I told how she'd led me into the alley.

'And you went along with her?'

'I hadn't any choice, actually.'

'What'd you suppose she aimed to *do* in there?'

'It might've been a shortcut, you know.'

'Sounds to me like you were looking to have yourself some good times.'

'Not at all!'

'You got no call to lie, Trevor.'

Right then, the sky lit up bright as noon. Thunder crashed. Rain came pouring down on us. We leaped to our feet, hoisted the blanket over our heads to keep us dry, and rushed over toward the rocks. Along the way, I snatched up my saddle bags and Winchester.

Earlier, I'd spotted a place where a big flat slab jutted out. We raced up a bit of a slope to get there, ducked under the overhang, and huddled down with our backs against a rock wall. I propped up the rifle by my side, hugged the saddle bags to my chest. I was wearing my sixguns. Jesse was wearing my hat. What we'd left out in the weather was my saddle, bridle, bedroll, water pouch, and some other odds and ends that we shouldn't be needing till after the storm.

With our feet pulled in, we were out of the rain. But it gushed down on both sides of us, and in front. Our campfire flickered a few times. Then the last of the flames were pounded out, and all I could see were a few pale wisps getting whipped away by the wind. After that, there was nothing to see except shades of darkness.

There sure was plenty to hear, though. Water splashed down from the overhang so loud we might've been hunkered behind a cataract. The wind wailed and howled like a banshee coming for the dead. Somewhere out in the darkness, General was stomping the ground and letting out frightful squeals and whinnies.

I purely ached to help him. There was no place to give him shelter though. He'd just have to get by the best he could. The rain was only water, after all, and not likely to hurt him any. He ought to survive if he didn't get struck by lightning or panic so bad as to hurt himself.

Still, it pained me to hear him carrying on. He was mighty spooked.

In a lightning flash so bright it stung my eyes, I saw General rear up on his hind legs. The way I'd left him hobbled, I feared he might pitch over. But he came down safe just as the blackness shut him off from sight.

A roar of thunder came next, so heavy and loud it shook the air.

I gave some thought to rushing out and cutting General loose. I could borrow Jesse's knife, or dig my own out of the saddle bag. But then I judged he would run off and we might never see him again.

Jesse stirred beside me. I looked at her. She was just a dim shape, but I could see enough to watch her take off my hat and set it atop her upraised knee. Just about then, a flash lit her up. She turned her head and smiled at me. She rolled her eyes upward. She said something, but a cannonade of thunder killed her voice and the dark came back.

After the thunder stopped, she shouted, 'Don't this beat all!'

'I do hope it doesn't last!' I yelled back at her.

It wasn't much use, trying to talk.

By and by, she snuggled closer against my side and slipped an arm down low across my back. She rested her head on my shoulder.

If it hadn't been for the horrid noises of the storm and knowing General was out there scared half witless, I might've found myself rather pleased to be huddled with Jesse in such a fashion. As it was, I couldn't work up much interest. I was just too nervous about the chaos raging around us.

But she did feel good and warm where she pressed against me. I put an arm around her, and that felt even better.

As bad as the storm was, we were safe and mostly dry. Lightning couldn't hit us. Nothing at all could hurt us, I judged.

Except for what might happen to General, there was no call to be fidgety about our predicament.

Much as I tried to tell myself that, however, I couldn't get shut of a nasty feeling of dread that had me cold and shaky inside.

'Are you scared, Trevor?' Jesse asked. Her face was near enough to mine that I could hear her plain in spite of the noises.

'Are you?'

'I asked you first.'

'What's to be frightened of?'

'You're all a-tremble,' she said.

'Not at all.'

'Are, too. Is it the storm?'

317

'I'm not afraid of any old storm.'

'You ain't scared of *me*, are you?' She reached over and patted my stomach.

'What are you doing?' I asked.

'Not a thing. Don't get worked up.'

All of a sudden, my bum was wet. A chill scurried up my spine.

Jesse and I gazed at each other in the darkness.

'Uh-oh,' she said.

I slapped my hand down at the ground beside me. It splashed up water.

This didn't make a lick of sense. We were on a slope. Not much of a slope, to be sure, but enough of one so we shouldn't have water rising around us.

'It's me for the high ground,' Jesse said, jamming my hat onto her head.

As she scurried out from under our shelter, dragging the blanket after her, I grabbed hold of my Winchester and saddle bags. Then I plunged through the curtain of water spilling off the ledge and was drenched in a blink.

On my feet, I swung around and spotted Jesse. She was already in the clear, perched on a boulder off to the right. I waded toward her, water sucking at my boots, and climbed up some rocks till I got up there beside her.

'A real gullywasher!' she yelled.

'We ought to . . .' My voice went dead as an awful roar filled my ears. The roar wasn't thunder. I didn't know what it might be, but I didn't like it. 'What's that!' I shouted.

'Flash flood?'

'We'd best . . .'

'What about General?' she yelled.

Before I could think to answer, Jesse threw down the blanket, slipped the Bowie knife out of her boot and leaped off the boulder. I knew just what she aimed to do – cut the hobble so General could make his escape. It was what I should've done myself, but she'd beaten me to it.

Now she was gone. I couldn't see or hear her. There was just the darkness and the downpour and the awful noise roaring closer. I dashed up to some higher rocks, threw down my rifle and saddle bags, dropped my gunbelt, and hurried back to where Jesse'd jumped from. Just as I got there, lightning ripped across the sky.

In its jittery glare, I spotted General a few yards off. He

was up to his elbows in the swirling dark flood. The flash lasted just long enough to let me see Jesse burst up out of the water beside him, raising her Bowie knife.

Well, I leaped as the dark came back. Landed on my feet and commenced to trudge through the currents, reaching out for Jesse and shouting her name. Not that she could hear my puny voice through the bedlam of thunder and that *other* noise which sounded like a locomotive barreling toward us.

Just when I wondered if I could ever reach her, the water suddenly went down. Splendid! I thought, feeling it slip away till it wasn't more than ankle-deep. I splashed on ahead, got brushed by General as he bolted past, and then collided with Jesse. We both went down splashing, her on top.

She pushed herself off me. I sat up. Another flash of lightning came along just then. I saw her bending over, hair in her face, shirt drooping open. She reached for me with one hand while the other pushed the knife into her boot. And then a wall of water loomed up behind her.

'No!' I yelled.

I didn't see it smash Jesse, for the lightning quit. I darted my hand toward where she'd been, touched something that might have been her hand, then got myself slammed down by the monster wave. It shoved me along the ground, picked me up, tumbled me head over heels, scraped me against the rocks, bounced me off this and that. Fearing my brains might be dashed out, I hugged my head with both arms. Not a bit too soon, either. I'd no quicker covered up than a blow numbed my elbows and jammed my arms together so tight I thought they might crush my head.

I didn't know it just then, but the mighty wave had hammered me into the rocks not very far from our shelter – head first into a narrow gap.

It was a nice bit of luck, though I hardly considered it so at the time. I figured my arms were busted and I *knew* I was trapped. My arms and head were wedged in tight, the water piling over me, pushing at me, twisting my legs and shoving me up as if it aimed to snap my spine. Of course, I couldn't breathe. But that seemed like a minor problem, as I judged the wave would likely break me to pieces before I could ever find the opportunity to drown.

Then it quit trying to kill me.

Like a grizzly deciding to chase after tastier prey, it let go and raced off.

As the water receded, I sucked in a chestful of air. My knees came down on something solid.

Without the wave ramming at my back, it didn't take much work to squirm myself free. That's when I saw the blocks of stone with the gap between them, and realized how lucky I'd been. If the gap hadn't caught me, no telling where I might've been swept off to.

It didn't seem likely that Jesse'd met with the same brand of luck.

The moment she entered my head, I forgot about all my hurts. I got to my feet, rather unsteady, and turned around to look for her. The rain was still coming down in a deluge. What with that and the dark, I couldn't see a thing below me.

Pretty soon, though, the sky lit up. Where we'd been camped was a wild, surging river. All but one of the trees was gone. I caught a glimpse of the rocky slopes just before the lightning blinked out. No sign of Jesse.

The thunder took a while in coming, so the storm seemed to be moving on.

Off in the distance was the freight train noise same as I'd heard when the bloody wave was approaching. I was all set to scamper for higher ground, but then noticed that the roar was fading, so stayed where I was and waited for another lightning flash.

When it came, I looked again for Jesse on the rocks. If she was there, the short burst of brightness didn't give me enough time to spot her.

So I took to searching.

I was none too steady on my legs. They didn't hurt as much as my arms, but they were awful sore and wobbly. The rocks were slick and, except when lightning came, I couldn't see where I was going. I fell a few times, and once even tumbled down into the water. Didn't quit, though. Kept at it, searching low and high, criss-crossing the slope time and time again. Finally, there was no more point. Jesse was gone. That huge damn wave had carried her off.

I climbed on up to where I'd dropped my guns and saddle bags. They were high enough that they hadn't gotten swept away. I strapped on my belt, then just sat there in the rain.

Jesse hadn't been with me even one full day.

CHAPTER FORTY-TWO

The Body

Some time during the night, the rain stopped. I didn't notice
when it happened, though I never did fall asleep. Just sat
there, mulling over Jesse, hating it that I hadn't grabbed her
before she could jump down to cut General free, remembering how she'd looked just before the wave took us, remembering *everything* about the hours she'd been with me, and
all the while missing her, aching for her to be alive and come
back.

Over and over again, I pictured Jesse under water, trying
to fight her way to the surface but always being towed down
deeper by the rough current, running out of breath so her
lungs burned, getting hurled along, tumbled, smashed
against rocks, torn asunder until she was dead. Even after
she was dead, the flood wouldn't leave her be, but rushed
her limp and broken body down through the endless desert
beyond where I could ever find it.

A few times, that night, I heard Jesse call out my name.
But I knew it was only the wind howling its agony through
the night, and not Jesse at all.

Once, she came to me. She sauntered out of the dark, hair
shaking in the wind, shirt flapping behind her, a smile on
her face and a merry spark in her eyes. 'Can't get rid of me
that easy,' she said, and my heart swelled up with joy. Then
a bolt of lightning ripped through the clouds and I saw she
wasn't there at all and I wept.

That wasn't the only vision I had that night. In the other,
I was carrying her dead body in my arms. All the region's
kites were swooping down at us. They were going for her
eyes, her lovely green eyes, no longer alight with mischief,
but flat and dull. As my arms were full, I couldn't fight off
the buzzards. One of the big, stinky things finally perched
on her chest, so I bit off its head. I left the carcass in a heap

321

on top of Jesse as a warning to the others. They stayed away, and finally Jethro Lazarus came down the trail in his wagon. He was just the man I'd been looking for. I hailed him, and said I needed to buy a bottle of the Glory Elixir. 'Sold my last bottle no more than a hour ago,' he explained. I cried out, 'No!' Lazarus grinned and shook his head. 'You had your chance to buy some, lad. It's all your fault.' I shrieked, 'No!' again and slapped leather and shot him.

Except I didn't shoot Lazarus. My slug whinged off a boulder no more than six feet in front of me and I wasn't lugging Jesse's body along the trail, at all. I was sitting in the rain, all by myself among the rocks.

Those were the two visions I had that night. They weren't dreams or nightmares, as I was awake when they came to me. After getting over the upset about each of them, I took to wondering what they might mean. They might be omens or premonitions, maybe. But I didn't rightly believe in such malarkey. More than likely, they meant nothing. They were only just my mind going sour on me from too much weariness and grief.

It wasn't till the sun came up that I noticed the rain had stopped.

The sunlight put a new slant on things.

I took a notion that Jesse might not be dead, after all. *I'd* survived the flood. Maybe she'd lived through it, too. It was a slim chance, and I knew it. But even if she had perished, as seemed likely, I needed to hunt for her, bury her decent if I could find her body.

Getting myself off the ground was no easy trick. Some of me was numb, the rest ungodly sore. But I made it to my feet, then stretched this way and that to get the kinks out. I felt like somebody'd taken a sledge hammer to my elbows and shoulders. They were stiff and achy, and I swung my arms around until they limbered up, then practiced drawing my Colts a few times. Once I got my arms working decent, I bent over low enough to pick up my saddle bags and rifle.

Then I turned around and gazed down the slope. Our campsite was dry except for a few puddles which mostly seemed to be in holes where the trees had been uprooted and carried off. The rocks we'd used for a fire ring were gone, along with every trace of burnt wood and ashes. The flood had also carried off my saddle, bridle, bedroll, everything.

Nothing moved down there.

I called out Jesse's name. She didn't answer. I called it out again and again, but the only sounds came from the breeze and a few birds and the creek rushing by.

The creek, off beyond the rocks, looked more like a river now. It was swollen up to ten times its regular size, rough and muddy, sweeping bushes and sticks along toward the south.

I commenced to climb down, groaning some with each step, and was about to jump from the bottom boulder when a whinny came through the quiet.

It was the sweetest sound I could've heard just then, other than Jesse's voice.

It came from the left, so I snapped my head sideways. The pain in my neck fetched a wince out of me, but I had to smile at the sight of General off in the distance. He was no more than a hundred yards away, nibbling the leaves off a bush.

I got about halfway there before he noticed me, nodded and whickered and came wandering over. He seemed no worse the wear for the last night's near miss. After greeting him with some fond words and pats, I swung my saddle bags across his back and led him over to a rock. Using that to give me some height, I had little difficulty climbing onto him. With my rifle in the crook of one arm, I gripped his mane with my other hand and turned him toward the water.

We followed the shore, me calling out Jesse's name and studying both sides of the river. The sun was starting to heat things up, so steam drifted off the damp ground and the water. The mist wasn't thick enough to hide much. It rather gave me the creeps, though. What with the stillness, the limbs and such rushing by on the dirty river, the dead critters here and there along the banks and the white shroud hanging over it all, I felt like I was riding through a wasteland fit for a nightmare.

The flood seemed to have killed everything it met. I came upon the remains of birds, snakes, gophers, and even a three-legged coyote, all of them washed up along the shore. They had flies buzzing about them. A buzzard was working on the coyote.

Once, a dead burro glided by on the river.

Much as I wanted to find Jesse, I took to dreading the notion. She was bound to be dead, same as all these animals. I didn't care to see her that way. It was my duty to keep on

323

looking, though. Mostly, I hoped I might beat the buzzards to her body.

Soon after the mist burned off, I spotted a pair of white legs sticking up out of a tangle of tree limbs at the other side of the river. The sight made me want to curl up and die.

The tree was still in the water, but jammed tight among some rocks. All I could see of the body was its legs. They were bare, which made me wonder what had become of Jesse's boots and dungarees. Maybe they'd been tugged off by the currents, or maybe she'd had time to pull them off so they wouldn't sink her. One leg pointed straight at the sky. The other hung sideways at the knee.

The look of that broken leg made it all worse, somehow. Bad enough she was dead, but it pained me even more to see how she'd been ruined.

As she was across the river, I figured I was likely to drown trying to reach her. Didn't much care, though. I couldn't ride off and leave her there. If I got drowned, so be it.

I stopped General upstream a ways, dismounted, and shed my clothes. Then I raced into the water. It splashed up, wrapped around my shins, and climbed higher until I couldn't run any more, but only trudge along. It was a mite chilly, though not cold enough to bother me much. The current shoved at me. I was near halfway across and still on my feet when a branch came scooting along. I had to backstep to keep it from hitting me. As it slid by, I grabbed hold and let it tow me downstream till I was just above the caught tree. Then I let it go and got sucked down. I was shoved and tumbled for a bit. When I finally got my feet planted firm on the bottom and stood up, I found myself just below the tree. The water was no higher than my waist.

Leaning into the current, I worked my way back to the snagged tree. Its trunk was half submerged. I hung on to the top side of it and stood in the water, catching my breath and trying not to look at the legs. I could see them out of the corners of my eyes, though, off to the right. Even after I was breathing easy again, I stayed put. I just didn't want to do what had to be done.

Finally, I judged as how waiting wouldn't make it any easier.

So I boosted myself up onto the trunk and crawled along its top, crawled straight for the legs and couldn't help but look at them. They were scratched and bruised. They had an awful bluish-gray color. The leg that dangled sideways from its knee was the closer of the two, and made me wish I could've come from the other side.

The body was stuck in the fork where the trunk branched out. It was caught at the waist, actually. More than just her legs were out of the water. Those parts had been out of sight, hidden by some branches, until I'd climbed onto the trunk. I wished I couldn't see them now, but there was no way around it.

They put me in mind of the time I'd walked in on old Mable about to climb into the bath tub. I was seeing what I shouldn't. Shame got mixed in with all the other miseries I was feeling.

Jesse'd been mighty riled yesterday about the notion that I might've spied on her at the creek. I'd hankered to do just that. Now, here I was. And here she was.

The sight of her private areas made me feel sick and sad and guilty.

The tuft of hair down between her legs was dark, not shiny gold the way I'd imagined it might be. Her rump was heavier than it had seemed when I'd watched it through the seat of her dungarees. Close up, she didn't look near as good as I'd supposed.

All at once, I caught on to how I was studying her and how I was disappointed she didn't *look* good. If I'd felt lowdown before, now I was no better than a snake.

A sidewinder, that's what Jesse would've called me.

I got to my feet so quick I almost fell on her, but found my balance in the nick of time. Standing with one foot on each side of the fork, I bent over picked up the broken part of her leg. It felt wobbly, the skin tight and cool. Holding that leg by its ankle, I reached out and caught hold of her other ankle.

I brought her legs together and gave them a pull. But she was still wedged in tight. I had to move in closer, stepping out along the branches. I had to hug the legs against my chest and push with my body. It was horrible. I was naked. I couldn't keep my own legs together and still keep my footing, so I had to shove at her with my chest and belly and couldn't help but rub her with my lower parts. I sure did wish I'd kept my trousers on.

I shoved and tugged upward and finally she came unstuck, so quick I wasn't ready for it. All of a sudden, she jumped upward. I yelped and let go of her legs and waved my arms and pranced, but it was no good. I tumbled sideways through a thicket of limbs and plunged head first into the river.

Before the current had a chance to rush me away, I grabbed a chunk of rock on the bottom. That halted me till I could plant my feet.

Just as I started to stand up, something pounded against me and knocked me down again. I knew it might be Jesse, so I flung my arms around it. As soon as I pulled it in against me, I knew it was the body, all right. I had it by the waist, and felt its back against me.

As we got rushed along, I kept heeling the bottom, trying to stop us with my feet. But we kept being towed along backward. I reckoned I might drown if I didn't let go of her so I could break the surface and find a breath. I just couldn't do it, though. Figured I'd rather drown than lose her.

That's how it might've ended, too, but somehow we got swept toward the shore. Just when my chest felt ready to explode for want of air, my bum slid over some rocks and sunlight heated my face.

I scurried out from under the body, wheezing, blinking to clear the water from my eyes, and grabbed hold of her under the armpits and stumbled backward, dragging her toward the shore.

That's when I saw her breasts. I was hunched over, staring straight down at them. The first thing I thought was that they'd swollen up huge from soaking in the river so long. I also figured the water – or death itself – had leached the color out of them. These looked as if they'd never been darkened by sunshine, whereas Jesse's had been pretty near as dark as her face.

The hair on the head of the corpse didn't seem right, either. Too dark and straight and long.

Still, I figured this had to be Jesse. I was only just troubled by her odd appearance.

I bent lower and looked at the face. I was seeing it upside-down. It was an awful shade of purple and the lips looked almost black. The mouth was drooping open. The eyes were shut, but one lid was rather sunk in, as if it had no eye underneath it.

I studied the face, *knowing* this was Jesse, trying to find something familiar about the hideous visage.

326

All of a sudden, ice chased up my back.

I cried out, 'Yeeah!'

I dropped her and staggered back a few steps, shocked, appalled. I'd been hauling at a stranger!

Not a stranger, exactly.

But not Jesse.

The German's wife.

The river started to swing her away. I sure didn't want to touch her again. Not this awful dead thing that wasn't Jesse. I wished I'd never handled her at all.

But I'd brought her along this far, and it didn't seem right just to let her go. So I splashed after her and grabbed an arm and commenced to pull her toward shore.

It gave me an awful case of the fantods, touching her. Now that she wasn't Jesse.

When I almost had her ashore, I squealed out another yell.

For she wasn't alone.

In her other hand, she held the hand of a boy. The kid who'd been riding along behind her in the buckboard. Her son, more than likely.

She'd had him all along, must've. Even when she was pinned, legs up, in the fork of the tree. He'd been under there, clutched in his mother's dead hand.

It was purely amazing and awful.

I dragged the woman, and she kept her grip on the boy. They both came out of the river and onto the dry rocks.

Neither one of them wore a stitch of clothes. Neither did I, for all of that. But I knew how come I was naked.

I sat nearby, gazing at them, wondering. Trying to figure out what had happened to their clothes, but mostly imagining how their final moments must've been, the mother clinging to the boy's hand as they both got carried to their deaths by the monster wave.

I wondered what had happened to her eye. A stick had likely poked it in. I hoped she was already dead when that happened.

The boy didn't appear to be banged up or maimed, but I didn't get near enough to study him. I wished I'd never seen him or the woman.

I gave some thought to burying them. It seemed the decent thing to do. Pile some rocks atop them, maybe. If I went to do that, though, it'd mean getting in close and seeing more of them. I'd already seen more of these two than I could hardly stand.

Besides, there was no telling where the man might be. He was probably as dead as this pair. I scanned about. There was no sign of him or his wagon or his team. They'd likely been swept far off downriver. But suppose he'd lived through it? He might come wandering along and find me, naked as the day I was born, mucking about with his woman and boy. And me with my guns across the river.

Wasn't worth the risk.

He'd seemed like a mean sort of bloke, and I didn't hardly know these people anyhow. They meant nothing to me, and they weren't likely to notice, one way or another, whether I covered them over or not.

I got to my feet and brushed the grit off my bum.

Then I bent down and took a stone in each hand and walked over and set them down on either side of the woman's head. Much as I wanted shut of these two, I just couldn't leave them sprawled out bare and dead for the vultures that were sure to come.

I roamed about the shore, gathering more stones and hauling them back and setting them down beside the woman. I figured I would start with her, and get to the boy afterwards.

I hadn't been at it more than a few minutes, though, when I happened upon my own beaver hat. The sight of it, resting atop a boulder off in the distance, just about knocked my breath out. I rushed over and picked it up, then searched around for Jesse and called her name.

She didn't answer.

Alive or dead, she was nowhere to be seen.

I put the hat on my head. It hurt me some where she'd clobbered me with the rock the day before, and suddenly I just had to find her. It was foolishness to waste time covering a couple of strangers while Jesse was somewhere, maybe dead and needing a burial, maybe alive and hurt and needing help. Bloody foolishness.

So I ran to the river and waded in.

CHAPTER FORTY-THREE

I Find Jesse

Though the current was still quite swift, the water never rose much above my waist and I was able to stay on my feet all the way to the other side.

I raced along the shore to where I'd left my duds, got into them quick as I could, strapped on my gunbelt, picked up my rifle and saddle bags, then hurried on over to General, who was having himself a drink, and climbed onto him. It was tough to do, what with a rifle in one hand and him without a saddle, but I flung myself aboard, grabbed his mane and hauled his head around. Then I dug in my heels and we were off at a gallop.

Why the all-fired rush, I'm not quite sure. Somehow, it was on account of finding my hat. It had been on Jesse's head, last time I'd seen her. It made me reckon she might be nearby, though there really wasn't a good reason for believing any such thing. Nearby, and needing me. I had to find her straight away. Every second mattered, or so it seemed to me though I'll be blamed if I know why.

General fairly dashed along the river bank, hooves thundering, mane afly. We hadn't made such speed since the time we were with McSween, the posse giving chase. That time, though, I'd had a saddle under me. Now all I could do was hang onto his mane one-handed and grip his sides with my legs and hope for the best.

What with the rush and the way it all jarred me, I couldn't get much of a look at the shores. It crossed my mind that we might race past Jesse and leave her behind. The notion didn't worry me, though. I simply knew we'd find her, and soon.

And it happened just that way.

The river took a turn to the east, and we no sooner galloped around a bluff near the bend than straight in front of us was a buckboard overturned with its wheels in the air and Jesse sitting on the ground, leaning back against it.

Alive and watching me come.

Golden hair, golden skin agleam in the sunlight.

Wearing her boots and dungarees, and no shirt.

I wanted to let out a whoop, but anger and alarm got mixed in with my joy.

Her legs were tied together at her ankles. Her arms were stretched overhead, roped to the wheel rim.

Nobody else seemed to be about.

I pulled General to a halt, leaped down and rushed for Jesse. 'Where is he?' I asked.

'Went off to hunt for his family.'

'Keep a lookout.' Crouching, I propped the rifle up against the buckboard. Then I reached for the top of Jesse's boot, figuring to use her knife on the ropes.

'He took it off me. Don't reckon I'd be in this fix if I still had my Bowie knife.'

With a glance over my shoulder, I saw that General had wandered off a piece. My knife was in the saddle bags across his back. Not wanting to waste time, I commenced to pluck at the bundle of knots by Jesse's wrists.

'Figured you was drowned,' she said.

'I thought the same of you.'

'Came right close to it. Grabbed ahold of a tree and rode it like a raft.'

'Was it the German who got you?'

'Varmint found me sleeping. He's got himself a Henry. Poked me awake with it. Figured I'd slice him anyhow, so I went for my knife and he jammed the damn muzzle halfway through to my backbone.'

'Bloody swine,' I muttered. The last of the knots came loose. Jesse squirmed her hands out of the coils while I backed away toward her feet.

Smack in the center of her belly, just under her ribcage, her skin was bruised bright red and purple from the muzzle of the Henry rifle.

She lowered her arms. She rubbed her wrists.

'How long has he been gone?' I asked, and started on the knots between her boots.

'I ain't been keeping track of the time, Trevor.'

'What did he do to you?'

'Brung me here, what do you think?'

'Did he hurt you?'

'Oh, he was just as gentle as a lamb on Easter Sunday. What's the matter with you? Sure he hurt me.'

'He took your shirt?'

'The flood got that off me. If it hadn't, he would've. Put his hands all over me, the dirty snake.'

The last bit of knot was too tight. I couldn't work it loose with my fingers, so I hunched down low and went at it with my teeth. The feel and taste of the rope put me in mind of when I'd chewed Trudy's knots aboard the yacht. I suddenly remembered all that had happened to that poor woman, and how useless I'd been when it came to saving her.

Jesse broke into my thoughts, and I was glad to have them stopped. 'The damn sidewinder was happier than a thirsty tick on the hind end of a hound dog. Should've seen how he pawed at me. Put his damn mouth all over me, too, once he had me tied good. Don't know how come he didn't go on and do the rest of what he wanted. Just stopped and grinned and said, "Vee haff you later, yah? I must Eva and Heinrich find." '

The knot came apart in my teeth. I unhunched and pulled at the rope.

'Then he wandered off downstream,' she said.

'He should've gone upstream,' I said. 'That's where they are.'

'You seen 'em?'

'They're dead.'

'That oughta suit him. I reckon he aimed to shoot his wife, anyhow, if she wasn't drowned. He was looking mighty peculiar and sly when he went off.'

I flung the rope away and stood up. 'We'd best light out before he . . .'

Jesse made a quick grab for the Winchester. Just as she shouldered it, a gunshot blasted the stillness. A section of one spoke on the wagon wheel exploded, throwing splinters into her hair. I was whirling around grabbing iron when she fired.

Her bullet took out the German's knee. He was standing in the open about forty paces south of us, levering a fresh round into his Henry. The slug smacked his trouser leg and drilled through. Blood splashed out. He squealed and lurched backward. When he came down on the hit leg, his knee folded.

That's when my first bullet hit him. It punched his forearm.

The stock of his rifle jumped and knocked him in the chin. His head flew back. He flung out his arms. The rifle started to fall. I put a bullet into his stomach. He was still up, but going down fast. Before he hit the ground, I laid three slugs into his chest. He landed flat on his back and jerked about and shuddered. Then a rifle went off behind me. The bullet got him under the jaw. He flinched and went still.

Turning around, I found Jesse was standing, the Winchester at her shoulder as she worked the lever. She sighted in on the German, but only just stood there and didn't fire. By and by, she lowered the rifle. She looked at me. Her green eyes were wild and fierce, and didn't show a bit of the fun that had nearly always been there before. She took a deep breath. When she let it out, I could see her shoulders tremble some.

'Are you all right?' I asked.

She nodded. Then she clamped the rifle stock tight under her arm. It rather flattened the side of her breast and pushed the whole mound outward a bit. The sight stirred me up. I didn't let on, though, and looked away quick.

We walked over to the dead German. We stood above him and gazed at him, not saying anything. I went about reloading. My hands shook.

'You'll need a shirt,' I said.

'You shot his full of holes.' Jesse squatted beside him, set down the rifle, and pulled her Bowie knife out of his belt. She shoved its blade down the side of her boot. Then she commenced to unbutton his shirt. It was drenched and red. 'Reckon I can wash off the blood.'

'You can wear mine, if you like.'

'This one'll do me fine.'

After the buttons were open, I wrestled the body up and slumped it forward over its outstretched legs. I held it that way while Jesse pulled off the shirt. Then I let it down. We went to the shore and Jesse crouched on a rock and scrubbed the shirt.

I watched her.

We'd just killed a man. I'd just spent a good part of the morning with the dead woman and her son.

I'd spent the night figuring Jesse was dead.

But here she was, alive and washing the blood off a shirt.

I felt rather dazed and sick, sore with pains all over my body.

But standing there, watching Jesse, I felt quite wonderful. Her dungarees hung low on her hips. Her moist back glistened in the sunlight. It was smooth and slick, though scratched and bruised here and there. The bumps of her spine pushed out at her skin. Her shoulder blades slid about. Some damp ringlets of hair curled against the nape of her neck. I could see the side of one breast, and watched how it jiggled just a little as she worked. Sometimes, the nipple brushed against her knee.

When she finished, she stood up and shook open the shirt and raised it toward the sky. The worst of the blood was gone. Only some rusty stains remained. 'Good enough,' she said. Turning around to face me, she swept the shirt behind her back and pushed her arms through its sleeves.

'You don't mind wearing a dead man's shirt?' I asked, knowing how it was. I'd spent a lot of time in the clothes of dead men.

'After what he done to me – and what he was *fixing* to do? I *like* it.'

She fastened the buttons. The shirt was far too large for her. As she went to roll up the sleeves, she looked down to study herself. Her skin showed behind the bullet holes. The nipple of her left breast poked out through one of them. When she saw that, she laughed. 'Shoot,' she said. 'Reckon we better trade off, or you'll wear out your eyes staring at me.'

'That one's quite fetching, actually.'

With a playful smirk, she showed me her fist. 'Give,' she said.

So we both shucked off our shirts and traded. The German's was wet and cool. It felt good on my hot skin, but gave me a squirmy feeling.

I followed Jesse back to the body. She took the dead man's belt. It had cartridges in loops for his Henry and his revolver, but no holster. His Colt was tucked into a front pocket of his trousers that was lined with leather. Jesse cinched the belt around her waist, checked to see that the revolver was loaded, then pushed it down under the belt at her left hip, butt forward for a cross-draw.

'Too bad he don't have no hat,' she said.

'I'll let you wear mine.'

She looked up at it, squinting against the sun. 'Where'd you find that?'

'Oh, it washed ashore.'

As I reached for it, she said, 'No, you keep it on your own head. I already lost it once for you. Anyhow, I've got me an idea.'

She pulled her knife and slit a leg of the German's trousers all the way up the side. She cut it off from around his thigh. Being none too careful, she gashed him once. The blade opened a raw pink furrow in his skin.

She sliced and tore at the cloth, getting it to the proper size, then wrapped it around her head and tucked in the loose end. When she finished, the bundle of checkered cloth atop her head resembled a turban.

Still, she wasn't done with the German. She pulled off his boots, checked inside them, and tossed them aside. Then she went through his pockets. She found a folding knife, a handful of coins, and a leather pouch.

'This is for you,' she said, and tossed the knife to me.

She kept the money.

She opened the pouch. Inside was tobacco, cigarette papers and matches. She grinned up at me. 'Let's have us a smoke.'

She got to her feet. I picked up both the rifles and we wandered over toward the buckboard.

'Are they dry?' I asked.

'He never got his feet wet,' Jesse said. 'Told me as how he was up in the rocks when the flood hit. Carried off everything but him.'

We sat down and leaned back against the wagon. Jesse rolled herself a cigarette. She passed the makings to me, and I did the same. She waited for me to finish before striking a match, and used it to light both our smokes.

She drew in on hers, and sighed. 'What ever come of all that there bad luck you was telling me about, Trevor?' The glint was in her eyes again.

I was sure glad to see it. I felt uncommon fine to be sitting there next to Jesse, having a smoke, nobody about who might cause us harm, the sky cloudless and blue.

But I reckoned there'd be trouble ahead.

'I shouldn't be calling the flood *good* luck. Not this morning's business, either.'

'Whatever befalls you is good luck if you come through it kicking. We come through it right handy, appears to me.'

'We lost everything.'

'Didn't lose General. Nor your saddle bags and guns. Didn't lose each other, either.' She reached over and gave my leg a pat. 'Fact is, we gained us a good Henry rifle and a fair .45, a folding knife, a handful of change, and some fine smokes. A gunshot shirt, too,' she added, and nudged my side with her elbow.

'We lost my water bag,' I told her.

'That don't amount to much.'

'It'll amount to quite a good deal if we try to carry on down the trail.'

'You sure are a worrier, Trevor Bentley.'

'It helps me stay alive.'

'We'll do fine, long as we stay here. I'm too tuckered out for travel, anyhow.'

'I didn't sleep all night, myself.'

'Let's get us some shut-eye.'

'Now?' I nodded toward the body.

'Oh, he ain't likely to cause no trouble.'

'He'll draw scavengers.'

'Then let's get shut of him.'

After finishing our smokes, we went over to the German and dragged him by his heels to the river. We waded out a few paces, then let him go. The current sailed him off.

We washed our hands and returned to the buckboard. We hefted it up on its side. All the cargo was gone, but that came as no surprise.

We gave the wagon a shove. It crashed down on its wheels. One wheel was busted before we started and another gave out when it fell. They were both at the rear, so the wagon had quite a slant. But it was dandy for our purpose. We crawled into the shade underneath it and stretched out.

Me and Jesse, side by side.

We lay there and looked at each other for a spell. She eased an arm over and took hold of my hand.

We were safe. We were together. I figured we had some tough times ahead of us, but everything seemed just fine right then.

I drifted off to sleep.

335

CHAPTER FORTY-FOUR

Mule

Waking up, I was all hot and groggy and felt like I'd been asleep for a month. Jesse wasn't beside me any more. That worried me and cleared my head. I rolled over and crawled out into the blazing sunlight.

Not only had Jesse gone missing, but so had the Henry rifle.

I figured she might've wandered over to cool off at the river. General was there, taking a drink. But I couldn't see hide nor hair of Jesse.

At the shore, I looked up and down the river.

No Jesse.

Nobody else was in sight, either, which came as a relief. We sure didn't need any more trouble, not after all we'd been through.

More than likely, she'd taken the rifle to do herself some hunting.

I got shed of my hat, gunbelt and boots, but kept my shirt and pants on so they'd get wet and keep me cool for a while afterwards. Besides, I didn't fancy being naked on account of Jesse might come back and see me that way.

Then I waded into the water. It wasn't racing along furious any more, and had shrunk down considerable to where it was only about three times as wide as it had been before the storm. Nothing dead appeared to be drifting my way, so I had a drink. After that, I swam and floated about, enjoying the coolness.

I'd just climbed onto a rock, figuring it was time to go searching for Jesse, when the bray of a mule caught my ears.

It came from downstream.

The mule wasn't in sight yet, but the sound made me think it must be hidden by the outcropping about fifty yards south of me. Fearing there might be more than a mule, I ran

336

for my gunbelt. No sooner was it buckled around my waist than the mule hobbled into view. Behind it walked Jesse, prodding it along with her rifle.

The mule was having a rough time, grunting and braying as it struggled forward on three legs. It kept its left foreleg off the ground. The way the hoof wobbled, I judged the poor mule's leg was broken at the knee.

I got into my boots and hat while Jesse nudged the mule closer along the shore.

'Look what I found us,' she called.

'He won't do us much good, being lame,' I said.

'I don't aim to ride him,' she said. 'This old boy, he'll keep us in meat for a week.'

'You want to *eat* him?'

'Gotta put the thing out of his misery, anyhow. No use letting him go to waste.'

I couldn't come up with any good argument against that.

We stood him close to the water's edge. Then Jesse shot him in the head. I was glad she didn't ask me to do it. I'd plugged my share of men, but they'd all been fixing to kill me or my friends. This mule hadn't done any harm. I felt sorry for it. From the look on Jesse's face when the mule dropped, she wasn't too happy, herself, about shooting it.

After setting the rifle down, she commenced to roll up her sleeves. 'You go on and build us a fire.'

She pulled the Bowie knife out of her boot and knelt down beside the carcass.

I hurried off, glad to get away. Instead of scrounging about for bits of wood, I broke up some of the buckboard. Jesse still had the German's tobacco pouch with the matches. She was up to her elbows in blood, though, so I fetched matches out of my saddle bag. I found Snooker's big knife in there, too, and used it to split some kindling.

I made a neat pile of wood, and fired it up.

The notion of eating mule didn't set well with me. But meat was meat. While I watched the flames rise, I recollected that General Forrest had told me how the Apaches were more inclined to eat horses than ride them. They had an appetite for mules, too. According to him, though, they weren't above eating rats. He sometimes called the Apaches 'gut-eaters'. That didn't speak well for their taste in vittles, but I allowed as how I'd rather eat mule than rat just about anytime at all.

With such thoughts in my head about the Apaches, I suddenly recalled their trick of using horse guts for storing water.

The flood had taken our water pouch.

We couldn't leave the creek behind if we didn't have us a way to carry water. It ran from north to south, so following it wouldn't get us any closer to Tombstone.

We might head upstream, find the trail and wait for strangers. Somebody was sure to come along, by and by. Then we'd need to borrow, buy or steal a container.

It seemed a mighty roundabout and dicey way to handle the problem. Better, by a far sight, to avail ourselves of the mule's innards.

I picked up my knife and went on over to where Jesse was busy carving. She'd already cut us a couple of steaks off the critter's flank, and was slicing long, thin strips off the thigh.

'We'll have us these tonight,' she said, prodding one of the steaks with her knife, 'and jerk the rest.' She nodded, quite pleased with herself. She had a smear of blood across her brow. I reckon she'd rubbed a hand there to deal with an itch.

Not being any too eager to commence my task, I helped her cut some more strips.

When we had quite a passel of them, we carried all the meat on over to the fire. We ripped a plank from the buckboard, cut it into a few long poles, and fashioned them into a rack. With that in place, we draped the strips rather high over the fire to let them smoke.

Back at the creek, we washed up. Jesse didn't seem aware of the blood on her forehead, so I dampened the front of my shirt and wiped it off.

Looking me in the eyes, she reached up a wet hand and smoothed some stray hair across my brow. Then she curled the hand behind my neck, eased me closer to her, and kissed me on the cheek. My face heated up. I felt myself go all mushy inside.

I had a good notion to take her in my arms and have a go at kissing her mouth, but she stepped away quick and said, 'Reckon we oughta float the mule down the stream before it ripens on us.'

My wits were still rattled. I just gaped at her.

She swung out a hip and tipped her head sideways and studied me. She had a frown on her face, but her eyes gave it away that she was amused, not annoyed. 'What's the matter with *you*?'

'Not a thing, actually.'

'You never been kissed before?'

'Not by you.'

'Well, don't let it spoil your day. Come on, now, let's send the mule off to join the German. Then we'll cook up them steaks and . . .'

'I'd prefer to eat first. We've already washed our hands, after all.'

'Won't take a minute. Then we'll be shut of the thing.'

'I'm afraid there's a rather messy job that needs to be done before we dispose of the mule. It's likely to ruin my appetite.'

'What're you talking about?'

'We can fashion a water bag out of the guts.'

She only just stared at me, scowling.

'I know it's rather appalling, but if we clean the intestine properly . . .'

'Where'd you ever come up with such a notion?'

'The General once told me about it.'

'Your *horse*?'

'No, certainly not. General Matthew Forrest, an old Indian fighter. It was a trick the Apaches used.'

'Sure wish *I'd* thought of it.'

She was just full of surprises. 'You think it's a good idea, then?' I asked.

'It's just bully, that's what I think. You're right, though. We oughta eat before we settle down to meddle with the thing's innards.'

With that, we headed on back to the fire. The strips hanging in the smoke had already darkened some. Their drippings fell into the flames, popped and sizzled. Mule or not, the aroma set my mouth to watering.

I added some wood to the fire. Then we cut a couple of sticks from the side of the buckboard, whittled points on the end of each one, and poked our steaks onto them. Jesse held both the steaks over the flames while I removed the whiskey bottle from my saddle bag.

It was about half full.

I held it up for Jesse, sloshed the whiskey around, and watched her smile.

'This should help the steaks go down a spot better,' I said.

Then I sat on the ground and took over my own share of

the cooking. It wasn't long before the slabs of meat were good and crispy on the outside. We swung them away from the flames, waited till they quit smoking, plucked them off their sticks, and commenced to rip into them with our teeth.

If I hadn't known my steak was mule, I would've known anyhow that it sure wasn't beef. It was tough and stringy and had an ornery flavor.

After a couple of mouthfuls, I was mighty appreciative of the whiskey.

I took a swallow and offered the bottle to Jesse.

She used one hand to take the steak away from her mouth. With the other, she wiped the grease and soot off her lips and chin. Looking at the bottle, she chewed real hard for a spell. She rolled her eyes upward, and kept on chewing.

I grinned. 'How's supper?'

'I've eaten worse,' she judged, her voice a bit muffled. After a grimace and a swallow, she took hold of the bottle.

'This is better than rattlesnake?' I asked her.

She had herself a sip, and gave the bottle back to me. 'Didn't say that.'

We both took to laughing. Then we ate more mule and drank more whiskey. The more whiskey I drank, the better the mule tasted. Not that the critter ever did quite reach the stage where it gave me any great pleasure in the eating.

I was glad to swallow the last of it and be done.

'What we should've done,' I allowed, 'was spare the mule and eat the German.'

Jesse laughed so sudden and hard that it sprayed her last mouthful into the fire. I looked on, mighty pleased with myself till she commenced to choke. Then I pounded on her back. She took turns coughing and laughing for a while. When she finally got herself under control, her eyes were teary, her nose running. I fetched the bandanna out of my pocket. It was still moist from my swim in the creek. She used it to clean herself, then stuffed it into a pocket of her dungarees.

'Didn't want it back, did you?'

'Consider it yours,' I told her.

'You dang near killed me.'

'I'm bound to kill you sooner or later,' I said. 'I gave you fair warning yesterday, didn't I?'

When I said that, it took some of the fun out of matters. Not just for me, but for Jesse as well.

She looked at me somber. 'You're a good man, Trevor Bentley. Don't go running yourself down that way. Now let's go and gut ourselves a mule.'

'Let's finish the whiskey first.'

We passed it back and forth a couple of times. When it was empty, I held it up and said, 'I don't suppose this will hold enough water to suffice us on the trail.'

'If you've got a few more like it.'

'Only the one, I'm afraid. Though I did have an opportunity to purchase ten bottles of Glory Elixir a couple of days back.'

'Glory Elixir?' she asked, getting to her feet.

'Good for what ails you.'

Then I told her about my encounter with Dr Lazarus and Ely while we went over and got to work on the mule. She seemed to enjoy the tale, and telling it helped take my mind off our ghastly task.

Not that it was all that ghastly for me.

Jesse took it upon herself to slit open the mule's belly and haul out the guts. Mostly, I stood guard. I wasn't exactly worried that intruders might come along, but keeping watch gave me a reason to avert my eyes from the mess.

The few times I did look, it put me in mind of poor Mary in her Whitchapel digs and poor Trudy the way she'd been the last time I saw her on the yacht. What with all my other troubles, it had been some time since I'd given much thought to Whittle.

I wondered how many more women he'd butchered since those luckless ladies in Tombstone. And where was he now? And how was I to go about tracking him down?

It wouldn't be an easy trick, but I judged there was no advantage to worrying about it. For now, what mattered was to take care of a day at a time and get us safe to Tombstone.

'How much of this do we want?' Jesse asked.

I figured it was time to join in. We cut off two sections of intestine, each about a yard long, and stretched them out along the ground. They looked like a pair of slimy fire hoses.

We mashed them flat to empty them, then laid them across a rock by the creek.

After shucking off our boots and socks and rolling up our trouser legs, we picked up the guts and waded in.

We held them under the surface so water flowed in one end and out the other. Kept them under for a long time.

341

When we judged they were as washed out as they were likely to get, we tied a knot at one end of each and filled them up till they were swollen and heavy. Then we twisted them shut at the other end and lugged them back to the fire. With short pieces of the rope that the German had used to tie Jesse, we bound the twisted ends.

We hefted the bloated tubes onto the buckboard, stepped back, and grinned at each other.

'Looks like we got us traveling water,' Jesse said.

'I'm quite surprised it worked, actually.'

CHAPTER FORTY-FIVE

No Rain, Storms Aplenty

The sun went down while we packed some innards back inside the mule and dragged it to the water. We watched it float off toward the south, then washed ourselves and the knives. We carried our things back to the fire.

We added some more wood and sat there, warming our bare feet.

'It's a shame we drank up all the whiskey,' I said.

'We can have us a smoke.'

So we rolled cigarettes and used a brand from the fire to light them up.

'Hope it don't rain,' Jesse said.

Rain seemed mighty unlikely, so we had us a small laugh about her quip. Then we just sat quiet for a spell, enjoying our smokes. When our feet were dry, we got into our socks and boots. I broke some more wood off the buckboard to keep the fire going. Jesse took the whiskey bottle over to the creek and came back with it full. We passed it back and forth.

I watched as she unwrapped the turban from around her head. She folded it, then rubbed her scalp and fluffed up her hair, which shone all golden in the firelight. 'You never got to tell me about that feller you knifed in the alley,' she said. Then she pulled the hat off my head. She stuffed her cloth inside, and set my hat aside. 'Let's hear all about it.'

It seemed like days ago that I'd commenced the tale of my adventures, only to get stopped by the downpour. It seemed like years ago that I'd been led by Sue into that East End alley. I spent a few moments collecting my memories, then took up the story where I'd left it off last night.

This time, we didn't have any storm or flashflood. Nothing interrupted. We sat by the fire, sometimes adding wood to it and sometimes having a sip of water, while I talked and talked. I didn't stop with the fight in the alley, but went on and told about taking refuge in Mary's digs, about Whittle and the ocean voyage and my escape from him at Gravesend Bay. I gave Jesse pretty much the same version as what I'd told McSween and the boys around the campfire that time I drank myself into a stupor and fell down. I went easy, though, telling about the murders. I only said Whittle'd cut the women's throats, and didn't let on about the way he'd butchered them.

She asked questions now and again. Mostly, she just listened. About the time I had me and Sarah on the train heading west (of course, I didn't tell her that we'd been more than friends), Jesse stretched herself out along the ground and rested her head on my lap.

'Shall I quit now?' I asked.

'Nope. Just getting comfortable.'

So I plugged on, lying considerable about the trouble with Briggs, but coming back to the truth once he'd pitched me off the train. I told how I'd met up with the gang and got pulled into the robbery, all about 'buying' General and the shootout at Bailey's Corner, how we'd led the posse into a bushwhack, and finally about the attack on our camp.

'Nothing much happened after that,' I finished, 'until you came along and brained me.'

'I sure am sorry about all your friends,' she said. 'That was a mighty hard thing. But you oughta not go blaming yourself. McSween's the feller that took General.'

'Only on account of my needing a horse. If I hadn't chosen to ride with the gang . . .'

'Blame Briggs, then. He's the snake that chucked you off the train. Or put the blame on Whittle. You got no call to be ashamed of anything you done, Trevor. Why, you'd still be home in England and wouldn't none of it have happened except you took on Whittle to save that gal. The one he was fixing to kill on the street there. That's how I see it, leastwise.'

'I see it that way myself, sometimes,' I told her.

'It ain't rightly your fault Whittle killed them folks on the boat. Nor even that you shot up the posse. Those boys aimed to kill you, plain and simple. Wasn't no better than murder, how they rode in and shot up the gang. The wonder's that you lived through such a passel of close shaves.'

'I just wish none of it had happened at all.'

344

That was sure the wrong thing to tell Jesse.

She opened her mouth, but didn't say anything. She just gazed up at me, her eyes shiny with firelight.

'What?' I asked, a bit slow at seeing my mistake.

She shook her head, then got to her feet and stomped off toward the creek.

I went in the other direction and relieved myself, wondering what had put the burr under Jesse's saddle. She'd turned as chilly as the night air, and it didn't make a lick of sense.

Back at the fire, I looked around and spotted General. I recalled how I'd nearly lost him and Jesse both in the flood on account of hobbling him, so it seemed best to leave him free. He wasn't likely to wander far.

By and by, Jesse came along.

'We oughta break up some more wood and keep our meat smoking,' she said. 'Sides, gonna be a cold night less we keep the fire up.'

So we commenced to rip some more planks off the buckboard and hack them to pieces with our knives.

'It's a shame we lost our blankets,' I said.

'Well, you only lost the dang things cause you was fool enough to leave home. Should've stayed there with your ma.'

'Oh?'

'Yep. You would've gone and missed out on every last one of the nasty mean things that's come your way.'

'Oh,' I said. Now, I was commencing to catch on to the nature of the problem.

'Yep.'

We carried our loads of wood over to the fire and dropped them into a heap.

Jesse wiped her hands on the front of her shirt.

'I don't regret *every*thing,' I said. 'I'm quite glad that I met you.'

'That so? Well, you oughta just keep it in mind when you go to wishing you'd stayed home. How do you reckon I feel, you say such things? And after I gone and kissed you, too.'

When she said that, I stepped right up to her and put my arms around her and pulled her close against me and kissed her on the mouth. I rather expected her to shove me away. She didn't do it, though. Instead, she moaned and squeezed me tight. I couldn't rightly believe my luck. I was actually holding Jesse in my arms, kissing her mouth, and she wasn't fighting me off. It was bully.

But then Sarah came into my head. I took to feeling guilty. She'd given herself to me, heart and body. And here I was, taking up with the first pretty gal who'd come my way.

She's more than just a pretty gal, I told myself. She's Jesse Sue Longley.

I might never see Sarah again, anyhow.

Besides, she seemed like part of my past, part of the life I'd left behind when I took up with the outlaws. She'd never met the train robber, the horse thief, the murderer. The boy she'd known was dead and gone. She'd likely have no use for me.

With Jesse in my arms, I had no more use for Sarah, either.

Best to forget about her.

Jesse pulled back and looked me in the eyes. 'What's troubling you?' she asked.

'Nothing at all.'

'Don't you fib to me. What is it?'

I just shook my head. I tried to hug her again, but she held me off.

'Time we got us some sleep,' she said.

'But Jesse . . .'

She didn't say anything, but pulled the German's pistol out of her belt. Stepping past me, she fetched the folded trouser leg from inside my hat.

'I don't kiss liars,' she said, and lowered herself to the ground by the fire. She set the Colt nearby, then eased herself down on her side and tucked the cloth mat under her head to use as a pillow.

Well, I was feeling too riled to sleep. I sat across the fire from Jesse and stared at her.

'I'll keep watch,' I said.

'You don't need to watch *me*.'

'I'm no liar, Jesse.'

'That so.'

'If you must know, I had to do some thinking about Sarah Forrest.'

'Stead of me.'

'Because of you. I needed to set matters right in my mind. You see . . . we were somewhat more than friends. I lived with Sarah for several months, and after the General and Mable were gone, we . . . we rather took up with each other. That's all.'

346

'That's all, huh?'

'I'm sorry.'

'Betcha wasn't sorry when you was bedding her.'

'I'm sorry now.'

After a while, Jesse said, 'Where you reckon she's at?'

'She might be anywhere. Maybe she returned to her home in New York.'

'Maybe she's waiting for you at Tombstone.'

'It doesn't matter, actually. I don't want to see her again.'

Jesse was silent for a spell after that. She lay motionless, curled on her side, an arm tucked under the pad beneath her head, her eyes open and staring at me from the other side of the fire.

Finally, she said, 'Don't go and throw her over on account of me.'

'You're not the reason. I made my decision before you ever came along.'

'That so.' She said it calm and snide.

'Bloody hell!'

'No call to curse.'

'You're enough to drive a person daft!'

'It ain't me that had my way with Sarah.'

'And I suppose you're just as innocent as the day you were born? You told me yourself about all the blokes who've had *at* you.'

'Didn't a one of them *get* me.'

'That so,' I tossed back at her.

'Yep. And I aim to keep it that way.'

With that, she shut her eyes. It was just as good as if she'd walked away.

I had half a mind to throw a stick at her. The other half wished I was hugging her. She was just the most infuriating woman that ever crossed my path.

My plan, from the start, had been to get shut of her at the first opportunity.

The sooner the better, I thought. All she does is make me crazy.

But the notion of parting with her made me feel cold and empty inside. I recalled how miserable I'd been after the flood, thinking her dead, and my joy when I found her.

Found her hogtied by the German.

Hadn't been for me, he would've had his way with Jesse for sure. She wouldn't be so high and mighty after that, and hold it against me about Sarah. Maybe I shouldn't have been so quick to rescue her.

Well, thinking such a thing made me feel awful lowdown, so I took it back and judged I was glad I'd saved her in time.

I wanted to stop thinking about her altogether. Sleep ought to do that. So I added more wood to the fire, then unstrapped my gunbelt and stretched out. The ground felt mighty hard. The fire kept the cold off my front, mostly, but it was no use at all for warming my backside.

Maybe we should've skinned that mule and made us a blanket from its hide.

The mule was long gone, though. No advantage to bothering your head about what you might've done different.

I lay on my side, curled close to the flames, and commenced to ponder all the things I might've done different if only I'd known what was to come.

It all ended up with this – from the time I'd set out for Whitechapel on that night so long ago, any different sort of move that might've saved me or the others from grief would've likely changed the direction of my life so that I never would've turned up where I was when Jesse bounced the rock off my head.

Maybe that would've been for the best, I told myself.

Didn't believe it, though. I judged I'd go through it all again for the chance to join up with Jesse.

I must've fallen asleep, for I woke up. It was still night. Colder than before. So cold I was shivering. What must've stirred me awake was Jesse adding wood to the fire. She was crouched at the other side of it, taking sticks from the pile and feeding them to the flames. She wasn't looking at me. I kept mum and shut my eyes. And pretended to be asleep even when she lay down behind me and snuggled in close and wrapped an arm across my chest.

I was purely astonished by her behavior.

It came into my head that this might not be happening at all. Maybe I was having myself another fantasy, like those last night. Or maybe it was a dream.

Jesse sure felt real, though.

Her warmth seeped through my clothes. Her breasts pushed against my back. I could feel her heartbeat and every breath she took.

By and by, she kissed the nape of my neck.

'Possum,' she whispered.

Rolling over, I hugged her and kissed her mouth.

She didn't let me kiss her much, though. She said, 'Don't get no funny ideas, Trevor. It's just too dang cold over there by my lonesome.'

'I see,' I whispered.

'Don't make me use my Bowie knife.' The warning was no sooner out than her lips covered mine.

She was likely joshing about the knife.

I didn't want to risk riling her, though. We kissed and squirmed some, but I took care to keep my hands from straying anyplace that might offend her.

Later on, she lay still with her face buried against the side of my neck.

She seemed to be asleep.

But then she murmured, 'This ain't working out.'

'What have I done?'

'It ain't you, this time. It's the ground. I just can't find me a way to . . .'

'Here, then.' Holding Jesse against me, I rolled onto my back. 'How's this?'

She didn't answer at first. She lay still, then shifted about some. She gently pushed my knees apart and eased her legs down between mine. Her hands curled over my shoulders. She lowered her face against my cheek.

'Am I squishing you?' she asked.

'Not at all.'

'This is real nice.'

It was and it wasn't. Her hair made my face tickle so I had to scratch now and again. Her chin felt like a rock digging into my collar bone. But those were minor bothers. It was wonderful to feel her stretched out atop me, heavy and warm. A spot *too* wonderful, actually.

Before you know it, a certain part of me commenced to push at Jesse.

It upset me considerable. But Jesse didn't speak up or slap me, so I judged she must be asleep.

I quit stroking her back, squeezed my eyes shut, and tried to make my problem go away.

Jesse moaned a couple of times. She squirmed, which didn't help at all. By and by, though, she lay still and commenced to snore.

I went through a mighty rough spell, what with the way she felt on top of me and knowing she was asleep – and all

349

the temptations that ran through my head. But I kept a tight rein on myself. Somewhere along the way, I fell off to sleep.

CHAPTER FORTY-SIX

We Carry On

When morning came, I woke to find Jesse sprawled out beside me. She lay on her back, an arm across her eyes to block the sunlight.

I took a quick look about. The fire had died. The mule meat above it had shrunk considerable and dangled from the rack like several lumpy, leather belts. General was standing motionless, head down, a few yards beyond the rear of the buckboard. No sign of any intruders.

Satisfied that all was well, I turned toward Jesse again and crossed my legs and studied her.

She looked peaceful and beautiful, spite of her mouth hanging open.

A warm breeze made her hair stir ever so slightly. It wasn't blowing enough to move her shirt. Her shirt had gotten itself twisted around her somehow. It was drawn tight against her chest. With every breath she took, her breasts seemed to strain at the cloth.

Lower, some of the buttons had come open and her shirt was spread apart, leaving her belly bare all the way down to where her dungarees hung about her hips.

It made me hurt to see the awful bruise. It had a dark ring in the center from the muzzle of the German's rifle. Around the ring was a purple smudge. I was glad we'd killed the varmint.

Below the bruise, Jesse's skin looked smooth and velvety. It was spread over with a golden fuzz too fine to see at all if you didn't look close. You didn't need to look close to see the locks that curled out from under the waist of her dungarees. They gleamed as they swayed in the breeze.

I had an urge to kiss the wound, to caress her, to run my hand over her silken belly, ever so lightly. I wondered if I should be able to feel the fuzz. I rather ached to touch the curls and slip my fingers through them.

But caution won out.

She was bound to pitch a fit if she should wake up to find me pawing her.

Afraid that temptation might overcome prudence in the long run, I stole to my feet, picked up my gunbelt and hurried on down to the creek. I pulled off my boots and waded in.

I spent a while swimming and floating, then sat on a rock to let the sun dry me. I felt just bully.

And better yet when Jesse crept up behind me. Far as I knew, she was still asleep. All of a sudden, she wrapped her arms around me, pressed herself against my back, and kissed my ear.

'Whoever you are,' I said, 'you'd best not let Jesse Sue Longley catch you.'

'Why's that?'

'She's the jealous sort. And quite the scrapper. If she should find you chewing on my ear, she'd likely bash you senseless.'

'Chewing, huh?'

So then she did take to chewing on my ear. It felt mighty strange. I got all goosebumpy, and squirmed until she quit.

'Ain't mule,' she said. 'But tasty.'

Holding on to my shoulders, she stood up. 'How's the water?'

'A trifle chilly. Rather refreshing, though.'

Jesse stepped around to the front of the rock. She had left her boots behind, the better for sneaking up on me, no doubt.

'Should I leave?'

'No call for that,' she said, and jumped into the creek. She waded out till the water was waist deep, then turned and smiled. 'It's right nice,' she said, sinking down. After ducking her head, she cupped some water to her mouth and drank. 'Don't take a notion to come in,' she warned. 'Just stay where you are and keep an eye out for strangers.'

I checked about. Nobody in sight. When I looked again at Jesse, she had her shirt off. She was crouched low so that the water covered her almost to the shoulders. It was fairly clear, though. Below the surface, everything looked shadowed and wavery.

She mopped herself with the shirt, then draped it over her

back and flung the sleeves around her neck so she wouldn't lose it.

'Would you like me to hold that for you?' I asked.

Instead of answering, she sank down, filled her mouth, then came up and squirted at me. The spout fell short. It splashed the rock in front of my crossed legs.

'I say! Don't get me wet! I may have to come in and throttle you.'

'You stay where you are, Trevor Bentley.'

With that, she took off her dungarees. She held them off to the side. The current lifted them, stretched them out, filled their legs.

'Don't lose them, now.'

'If I lose 'em, I'll have to take yours.'

I laughed. But my laughter rather got caught in my throat as Jesse's free hand commenced to rub at her body. I thought it might be best to look away. But Jesse knew I was here, knew I was watching, and had glanced down often enough to know what could be seen through the water.

Obviously, she didn't object to my watching.

She watched me watch, her eyes all bright with their mischief.

A game of sorts. Perhaps a test. Or maybe nothing of the kind. Perhaps she'd simply grown to trust me, to care for me enough that she no longer felt it necessary to bathe in private.

Below the water, her body was blurred and shimmery. Still, I could see her hand gliding up and down her legs, then delving between them before she went about cleaning behind herself.

All the while, she watched me.

When she finished washing, she stayed crouched down, her chin just touching the water. 'Am I as pretty as your Sarah?' she asked.

Right then, I couldn't pull a picture of Sarah into my head. Didn't need to, though. 'Oh, yes, quite. You're far more beautiful.'

'Figured,' she said, and nodded.

'You're also considerably more conceited.'

'That so.' A grin came up that near-about split her face. 'Too bad. It's me you're stuck with, pardner.' Laughing some, she struggled back into her trousers. Once they were fastened, she stood up and waded toward me, her shirt still draping her back, its sleeves around her neck like arms ready to choke her.

She gleamed in the sunlight. Water dribbled down her skin. Her breasts bounced and shook ever so slightly. They had goosebumps, and the nipples stuck out proud. Drops of water fell off them as she climbed onto the rock in front of me.

Kneeling there, she smiled with just one side of her mouth. 'Watch you don't wear out your eyes.'

'What do you expect me to do with them?'

'It ain't polite to stare.'

'And is it polite to parade about . . . shirtless?'

'Feels good. If I was a feller, I don't reckon I'd wear one much at all. It's all cause of the dang tits.' She scowled down at them. 'You're lucky you ain't got any.'

This was some of the most peculiar talk I'd ever heard. Not that it surprised me much, as it came from Jesse.

'Gotta keep 'em covered all the time . . .'

'Not that you do so.'

She shook her head and kept frowning at them. 'They're only just *me*. Same as my face or hands. I don't all the time gotta wear a mask and gloves, do I?'

'It's different.'

'That's for durn sure. It beats me why, though. Shouldn't oughta be, do you think?' Before I could come up with an answer, she plugged on. 'They're a plain nuisance. Men always gawping at 'em. Grabbing if they get half a chance. That damn German went and *sucked* on 'em. How come he didn't latch onto my shoulder instead? Or my forehead?'

'I don't exactly know, Jesse. It's that there's something rather splendid about breasts.'

Saying the word set me to blushing fierce.

'Well, it don't make a lick of sense.' She pushed against her breasts, mashing them against her chest. 'How's that?'

Lucky hands, I thought. But kept mum, judging she might not appreciate a remark of that caliber. Besides, I doubt that any comment at all could've squeezed through my throat at that moment. I was flustered and stirred up something awful.

She jerked her hands away and the breasts came springing out. They looked a bit red.

354

'Sometimes,' she said, 'I've got half a notion to cut 'em clean off.'

Whittle's work slammed through my mind. 'Bloody hell!' I blurted. 'Don't you ever say that!'

She gaped at me, startled. 'Land sakes! What's the matter with you? I was only just joshing.'

'There's nothing at all funny about it!'

'Settle down, settle down.' She took hold of my shoulders, looked me in the eyes. 'What is it? Trevor?'

I shook my head.

'Tell me. We're pardners, right?'

'It's Whittle. He . . . he didn't only cut their throats. The women I told you about. He carved them up terribly. And . . . and he cut off their breasts.'

Jesse's hands tightened on my shoulders. She didn't say anything, but just knelt there in front of me, hanging on. By and by, she leaned closer until her forehead met mine. 'I'm ever so sorry I said such a thing,' she whispered.

'If he should ever get his hands on you . . .'

'He won't.'

'He'd cut yours off. Then you'd get your wish.'

'It ain't my wish. I was only just joshing.'

I lifted my hands to Jesse's breasts. I held them gently, feeling their chilly wetness, their slickness and weight, the press of their nipples. She didn't stop me. Instead, she eased herself lower against my hands. Then she kissed my lips.

'We ain't never gonna kill Whittle,' she finally said, ''less we hit the trail.'

Then she kissed me again, leaned back and unwrapped the shirt sleeves from around her neck. Reaching high up behind her, she pushed her arms into the sleeves.

As she fastened the buttons, I realized what she'd just said. '*We* aren't going to kill Whittle,' I told her. 'It's *my* duty, and I won't have you involved in such an enterprise.'

'That so.'

'Quite.'

We got to our feet, climbed down from the rock, and Jesse watched while I strapped on my gunbelt.

'You ain't going nowhere without me,' she said.

'Eager to get yourself butchered, are you?'

'You might just need me, you know.'

'I don't need you dead.'

355

'Same goes both ways. How you think I'd like it, you went off and got yourself killed? I'll *tell* you how I'd like it – not much. So I'm sticking with you. Better get used to the notion.'

Well, I could see no advantage to arguing. With most women, you might as well try and argue with a stump. And Jesse was worse than most that way.

'Whatever you say,' I told her.

She gave me a look so I knew she wasn't fooled. But there was more to her look than that. It seemed to say, 'Just you go ahead and *try* going after Whittle without me.'

Back at our campsite, we gathered up the strips of jerky. We each chewed on a piece while we wrapped the rest in a rag and tucked it into one of the saddle bags. It didn't taste near as ornery as I figured it might, but chewing so hard made my jaw sore. We washed it down with water from the whiskey bottle.

After that, Jesse cut the traces off the buckboard. She mucked about for quite a long spell, and managed to fashion a bridle for General.

We slipped it over his head, then harnessed the swollen tubes of water onto his back with more straps from the traces. When those were in place, there wasn't room for more than one rider. But we didn't have much choice in the matter, as we needed the water.

We strung the two rifles together with a rope tied around the stock of each, and hung them across General's back.

Finally, I put on my hat and Jesse wrapped the German's trouser leg around her head like before.

She mounted up.

We started off northward alongside the creek, me walking.

I felt rather sorry to leave our camp behind. Never mind we'd killed the German there. It was the place where I'd found Jesse alive, against all odds, where we'd worked together and solved a passel of problems, where we'd quarreled and settled differences, where we'd laughed and kissed and held each other, where we'd become somewhat more than 'pardners'.

It was our place by the creek. Its upside-down buckboard was still in sight when I already took to missing it.

But we couldn't stay there forever.

Whittle was waiting for me.

He would always be waiting for me, giving me no peace,

until I'd found him and put him down.

We knew the flood had washed away the trail, so I sat by the creek while Jesse rode in search of it. I felt mighty lonesome and jittery after she was gone. I worried and worried.

By and by, I noticed a tree off beyond the other shore. Its stump was jammed into a familiar nest of rocks. It was the very same tree where I'd found the German's wife and boy, though the water'd gone away and left it on dry land.

The sight of it turned my insides cold. I wished I hadn't recognized it. But there it was.

I turned my eyes away quick before they could search out the bodies that I'd left on the bank downstream. I knew they were there somewhere. Sure didn't want a look at them.

At last, Jesse came riding back.

I was mighty glad to see her.

'Found it!' she called. 'Still a ways off.'

We followed the creek for a while longer.

By and by, we crossed to the other side and caught up to the trail about a hundred yards farther west. That much of it had gotten itself swept out by the flood.

We followed it, taking turns riding General, sometimes both of us walking to give him a rest. When we got hungry, we ate jerky. We satisfied our thirst, and General's, with water from one of the gut tubes. Neither the food nor the drink was much to brag about, but it took care of our needs.

The first day, we didn't meet up with any other travelers. To keep it that way, we made our camp a good distance from the trail. The next day, we met a man from Bisbee who'd come up by way of Tombstone. He caused us no trouble, but told us how to get to Tombstone, and we were glad to hear that our destination was only sixty or seventy miles off.

For the next three days, we made our way in the direction he'd told us. We managed to shoot some game so we had a few meals other than mule jerky, we found enough fresh water to keep our gut bags full, and we encountered more travelers but no trouble.

Jesse didn't shuck off her shirt again, the whole trip. Not in front of me, leastwise. I reckon she kept it on so I wouldn't be reminded of Whittle.

I thought about him plenty, anyhow. The nearer we got to Tombstone, the more he crept into my head. If Jesse'd skinned off her shirt a few times, I likely would've spent a heap less time worrying about him and more time feeling good. But she didn't, and I stayed clear of the topic.

We never did get us a blanket. We managed to keep warm at night, anyhow, snuggling together on the ground. Even though Jesse didn't allow me to take liberties with her, not even to touch her as I'd done by the creek, the nights were quite wonderful.

I got to wishing we wouldn't find Tombstone, at all.

But long about sundown of our third traveling day after meeting the Bisbee man, we looked down from a rise and found a town sprawled in the distance, maybe no more than five miles off.

'I reckon it's Tombstone,' Jesse said. Then she slid off General's back, stretched, and rubbed the seat of her dungarees.

We stood side by side, gazing at the far-off town. There wasn't much to see. A pattern of streets, rows of buildings near the middle and a bunch of other buildings scattered about the area. It was too distant for us to make out any of the people there.

Jesse stopped gazing after a while. She handed the reins to me and wandered over to a rock, where she sat down with her back to the town. She unwrapped her turban. She used it to wipe her sweaty face.

'Well,' she said, 'looks as how we made it.' She gave me a rather grim, one-sided smile. 'What'll we do when we get there?'

I led General closer to her, and found myself a rock. It felt all-fired good to sit down after so much walking. 'We'll have ourselves a splendid meal in a restaurant,' I said.

Her smile brightened some. 'Tired of mule?'

I made a snorty 'Hee-haw,' and she laughed.

'What I'm hankering for's a bath,' she said. 'I could use some fresh duds, too, before I sit down to a meal.'

'I'll buy you a fine dress.'

'Buy a dress, and you can be the one that wears it. Ain't gonna catch me in any such getup.'

'I'd certainly like to see you in one.'

'Ain't about to, so you'd best forget it.'

'You are a woman, you know.'

'None of my doing. I'd a sight rather be a man.'

'I'm quite glad you're not one.'

'Oh, I sure do know that.'

I flustered some when she said that, but I was so hot and sweaty she likely couldn't notice. 'Well, I don't aim to *force* you into wearing a dress.'

'Couldn't if you tried.'

'I suppose you'd take your knife to me.'

I expected a snappy retort, but instead she frowned down at her boots. 'I wouldn't cut you,' she muttered. 'You oughta know that.'

'I know.'

She hung her head and rested her elbows on her legs.

'Are you all right?' I asked.

'Nope.'

'What is it?'

She shook her head.

'Jesse?'

She looked up at me. Her green eyes were awful solemn.

Going all soft and squirmy inside, my throat tightening on me, I hurried over to her. She stood and I took her in my arms. She held onto me tight. 'What's wrong?' I asked. 'What is it?'

'Oh . . . everything.'

'*Everything?*'

'Can't we . . . stay here? I don't wanta . . .' She shook her head.

I held her and patted her. 'We'll stay here. Maybe not *here*. We'll find ourselves a good spot to camp. We won't go into Tombstone. Not tonight. All right?'

She nodded.

'We don't need to go into Tombstone at all,' I said. 'We'll just ride on by, tomorrow, if that's what you want.'

She kept holding onto me for a spell, then eased herself out of my arms. She put her hands on both sides of my face. She gave my lips a gentle kiss, then gazed into my eyes.

'We'll go in,' she whispered. 'Tomorrow. But I just ain't ready for it yet. Not yet.'

PART FIVE

The End of
the Trail

CHAPTER FORTY-SEVEN

Tombstone Shy

We made our camp in a dry wash on the north side of the rise so we couldn't see Tombstone. Jesse was uncommon quiet, maybe embarrassed by the way she'd backed out of going into town, or maybe it was just that she had too much on her mind in need of sorting out. Whatever, I didn't press her.

We sat by a small campfire, and ate our jerky in silence.

When we finished, we kept on sitting there. I opened my mouth time and time again, figuring to ask her what the trouble was. Each time, though, I thought better of it.

She was on the other side of the fire, and sometimes gave me strange looks through the smoke.

Finally, I said, 'I'm not actually eager, myself, to ride into Tombstone.'

'You're only just saying that.'

'It's the honest truth.'

'What about that-there fine meal in a restaurant?'

'Oh, I should like that. And I daresay you should enjoy having a bath and new clothes.'

'But not a dress.'

'Certainly not.'

'So how come you ain't eager?' she asked.

'I don't quite know, really. It would be different, I suppose. I reckon I've just gotten used to traveling with you. I hate for that to end. There'd be other people about. We wouldn't be alone together. It just wouldn't be at all the same. I like things the way they've been.'

Jesse stared at me for a bit, then got up and came around to my side of the fire. She sat on the ground beside me, leaned against me and put an arm around my back.

'You'd have yourself a real bed,' she said.

'In a hotel. Where the wind wouldn't freeze us up and

363

make you lie with me to keep warm.'

'Maybe I'd lie with you anyhow.'

'Would you do that?'

'Maybe. Long as you behaved.'

'Tombstone might be all right, then.'

Jesse went quiet again, but not for long. 'Maybe you'd rather have Sarah in the bed with you.'

'Jesse!'

'Well? You ain't thought about it, *I* sure have. She might just be in town there, waiting for you. What'll you do, then? Give me the boot?'

'No! Good grief! That's what you've been fretting about, is it?'

'I know you claimed I'm prettier, and all, and how you're done with her, but you might just see things different when you're face to face. Maybe you forgot how pretty she is. Maybe you'll remember, right quick, and remember a few other things, besides, like how it was to be *with* her. You been *with* her, Trevor. You ain't never been with *me*.'

I looked at Jesse.

'Don't you get no funny ideas, buster!'

'You're the one who brought it up, actually.'

'Well, put it right outa your head. I'm gonna stay pure for the man that marries me, or die trying.'

'Perhaps I'm that man,' I said, my heart all of a sudden bashing fit to explode.

'And perhaps not. Just perhaps you'll run into your fancy Sarah tomorrow and that'll be it for Jesse Sue Longley.'

'That won't happen,' I said.

'I reckon we'll find out, soon enough.'

'She's nowhere *near* Tombstone.'

'It's where you were heading with her.'

'That was before I got pitched off the train. For all she knows, I might be dead. You're daft if you think she made the rest of the trip and she's waiting around in town for me to pop in.'

'That's where I'd be,' Jesse said.

I pondered on that for a while, and judged Jesse was right. She *would* go on, hoping I'd finally make my way to Tombstone. *She* would. Jesse. But I had strong doubts about Sarah. Mostly because of how Sarah had taken on with Briggs.

'I'll be mighty surprised if she's there,' I said.

'Like I said, we'll find out tomorrow.'

'Even if she is, there's no call for you to fret.'

'So you say.'

'If it worries you so, why don't we put the town to our backs and head elsewhere?'

'How we gonna track down Whittle if we don't go in and ask around? It's where we gotta go if we're gonna pick up on his trail.'

'I doubt he *has* any trail to pick up, actually. It must be two months since he murdered those Clemons women. He likely dodged off long ago.'

'He didn't bolt straight outa London.'

Indeed, he'd continued his grisly work in the East End for more than two months, and might've kept at it longer if I hadn't mucked him up. 'That was quite a different situation,' I pointed out. 'London's a great metropolis with vast crowds of people and hundreds of streets and alleys. A bloke might duck around a corner and disappear forever. *Whittle* might've gone on forever there. But not in a town like Tombstone. Why, he was lucky he didn't get himself caught. Especially being a stranger there, and without a nose. I doubt he stayed in town long enough to see the sunrise.'

'Maybe,' Jesse said. 'Maybe not. He'd have no call to run off if nobody saw him kill them gals. He might just be in town this very minute.'

'*That's* why you wanted to stay out!' I blurted, having her on a bit.

'That ain't why, and you know it.'

'You've got Whittle and Sarah both down there, just itching to have a go at me!'

'Whittle don't worry me none.'

'Well, he ought to.'

'I hope he is down there in town. We can have us a race to see who's first to pump him full of lead. With any luck at all, maybe we'll catch your Sarah in the crossfire.'

That last was an ornery thing to say, but it plucked a laugh out of me. I locked my arm around Jesse's head and clamped it tight and gave her a few gentle punches in the belly. Then she slipped her head free, flung herself against me and bowled me over sideways. I didn't struggle much except to swing my boots clear of the fire. While I concerned myself with that, she got me onto my back and straddled me. With her knees, she pinned my arms to the ground. I was still

365

laughing, spite of her weight on my chest.

'I always knew I could take you,' Jesse gasped.

'You've got me.'

'Yup.' She gave a bounce that made the air grunt out of me. 'Gotcha right where I want you.'

'Delighted to be here,' I said.

At that, she backhanded my face. Not so much a slap as a pat. 'Don't get crude, Trevor.'

'I meant nothing crude. Not at all.'

She fetched my face another whap, a bit harder than the last. 'Did too.'

'You're the one that's put me between your legs!'

'Ah-ha!' She whacked me again.

So I kicked up my legs, swinging them up till I hooked her shoulders with my boots, and flung her backward. She let out a whuff when she slammed the ground. I scurried up right quick, knocked her knees out of my way, and dropped down flat atop her. She squirmed under me, laughing fit to bust.

Instead of pinning her arms, I used my hands to dig into her sides. She fairly squealed. She bucked and thrashed and grabbed at my hands, trying to hold them off.

'Quit!' she blurted between her squeals. 'You quit!'

'Gotcha right where I want you!'

'I mean it! Quit, now! 'Fore I bust a seam!'

'Have at it.'

'Trevor! I'm gonna wet!'

So I quit. Jesse spent a while giggling and gasping underneath me, but she finally settled down.

By and by, she said, 'It's downright mean, tickling a body.'

'Meaner than slapping?'

'I didn't hurt you.'

'I didn't hurt you, either.'

'You dang near split my gut.'

'Shall we call it even, then?'

'Give me a kiss.'

Well, that suited me. So I lowered my mouth to hers, fixing to kiss her real sweet, and she gave my lip a nip.

'Ow! Bloody hell!'

'Now, we're even.'

'Bloody hell! You *bit* me!'

'Ain't the first time.'

I licked my lower lip and tasted blood. 'You made me bleed!'

Smiling, she nodded. 'Don't fret about it none. I ain't got the rabies. Not as I know about, leastwise. Did I ever tell you about that feller down El Paso way that . . . ?'

'You told me.'

'Let me kiss your hurt and make it better.'

'And give you another go at chewing on me?'

'I *said* we're even. Don't you trust me?'

'You've got some mighty peculiar ways about you, Jesse.'

'That may be. But we're pardners, ain't we? You can't trust your pardner, who *can* you trust.'

'Do you promise not to bite?'

'Word of honor.'

So I eased my face down toward hers, not quite knowing what to expect. What she did, she slipped out her tongue and licked the blood off my lip. Then she raised her head off the ground and kissed me, just as soft and gentle as you please.

Pretty soon after that, I rolled off her. We lay on our sides, holding each other.

I felt ever so peaceful and contented. But it didn't last. Before long, I took to feeling all hollow and achy inside. This was to be our last night on the trail. Tomorrow, we'd be riding into Tombstone. No matter what else might happen, it would mean the end of our times together in the wilderness. Our times alone, just her and me.

It would all be over.

Things would be different, starting tomorrow, and I didn't want that at all.

I might never again find myself stretched out on the ground by a campfire, holding Jesse in my arms.

It gave me the fantods, thinking about such things.

And it didn't make a lick of sense, really. We'd still be together in Tombstone. But I couldn't shake it out of my head that our fine times together were just about over.

I squeezed Jesse tighter, and she did the same to me.

'It'll be all right,' I whispered.

'Glad you think so.'

'Still fretting about Sarah?'

'It ain't only just her.'

'Whittle?'

'I just don't want to lose you,' she said. 'I've got me some bad feelings about tomorrow.'

'We don't need to go in straight away,' I said, and suddenly felt like whooping with joy. '*We won't go in at all*! We'll head on somewhere else. Perhaps we'll have a go at Tucson.'

Jesse's fingers curled into my back. 'I don't know,' she murmured, but I could tell she liked the notion. 'What about Sarah? What about Whittle?'

'They aren't likely there, anyhow.' Even as I said that, I realized I didn't quite believe it. I was lying to myself, lying to Jesse. They *might* be in Tombstone. And I realized then that Sarah and Whittle were the two reasons I wanted no truck with that town. The *only* reasons, when it came smack to the truth. 'I want nothing to do with either of them,' I said. 'I want nothing to do with anyone except you, actually.'

'Oh, Trevor,' she murmured, and brushed her cheek against mine. 'You can't just let on they don't exist. I can't either. We've gotta face 'em. Might as well be tomorrow, if that's what's meant to be.'

'If it's meant to be, then there's no call to go rushing after them.'

'It don't seem right.'

'Do you *want* to go into Tombstone tomorrow?'

I felt her head shake.

'It's settled, then.'

Jesse didn't say anything for a while after that, and I thought she might be asleep. But then she raised her face off me and brushed her lips against my mouth and whispered, 'I sure do love you, Trevor Wellington Bentley.'

'Not as much as I love you, Jesse Sue Longley.'

'That so?'

'That's so.'

'Well, at least you didn't sell me to the German.'

Then she kissed me again and pretty soon I rolled so she was stretched out on top of me, the way we'd taken to sleeping every night since the flood. We lay still, not saying anything more. All my bad feelings had gone away, dragged off by my decision to stay shut of Tombstone. I heard the fire crackling and popping, heard a coyote howl off in the distance, heard Jesse's breathing close to my ear. Before you know it, I was asleep.

In the morning, we had us one more discussion about Tombstone. Jesse wondered if we ought to go on in just long enough to outfit ourselves with another horse, some equipment and supplies. I allowed as how such things would make our trip a sight easier. We'd only need to spend an hour or two in town, then we could be on the trail again.

We agreed to do it.

Jesse mounted on General, me walking, we made our way around the rise and headed for Tombstone. Going straight toward where we'd decided to avoid.

Even though neither of us wanted to go there.

We'll only be in town for a bit, I told myself. Even if Sarah *is* there, seemed likely we wouldn't run into her. And Whittle, he'd probably hightailed the night he killed the Clemons women.

In my head, though, it worked out otherwise.

In my head, we no sooner started down the main street of town than Sarah popped out of a doorway and her eyes lit on me. All surprised and joyful, she called out my name and ran to me and threw her arms around me. Wept and lavished kisses on my face as Jesse looked on. So then I had to shove her off me and say something like, 'Stop it, Sarah. Please. I'm afraid another woman has . . .' Just what *would* I say? If she was there, it meant she hadn't given up on me. It meant she still wanted me for herself. Whatever I might say or do, short of giving up Jesse (not a chance of that), was bound to give her loads of pain. I wanted no part of such a scene.

Nor did I want a showdown with Whittle. Not in the streets of Tombstone, not with Jesse nearby where he might get ahold of her. Much as I told myself he was long gone, I knew there was a chance he might be there. Maybe he'd found himself a job, or maybe he was living high and mighty off the loot he'd stolen from the *True D. Light*.

My common sense told me he wouldn't be there. For that matter, he might not even have been the bloke who murdered the Clemons women. Sarah wouldn't be there either.

That's what my common sense said.

But my stomach told me different.

We were on the trail leading into Tombstone for near a mile when I finally said, 'Hold up, there, Jesse.'

She halted General and turned her head toward me.

'This isn't at all where I want to go,' I said.

'I ain't looking forward to it much, myself.'

'So then, why are we doing it?'

She shrugged her shoulders. Then her face lit up with a

big smile. 'How many days to Tucson, you reckon?'

'Long as it takes.'

She turned General around.

We put our backs to Tombstone.

I quickened my pace to catch up, and felt like I was leaving all the grief of the world behind me. I felt so chipper that I actually ran for a while, and left Jesse behind until she put her boots to General and trotted up beside me.

'Don't go and wear yourself out,' she said.

'It's a grand morning! Smashing!'

It sure is peculiar how things work out. If we'd gone on into Tombstone that day, we would've missed Barney Dire. We might've avoided Whittle altogether.

Instead, by turning away from town, we started down a path that would lead us straight into Whittle's lair.

CHAPTER FORTY-EIGHT

Apache Sam

'Hello the fire!' came the voice out of the darkness.

I'd shot us a jackrabbit that afternoon, so we hadn't needed to gnaw on mule jerky for our supper. We'd just finished eating it when the man called out.

It startled us both considerable.

I snatched out my Colt. Jesse put a hand on my knee to settle me down.

'Tell him to come on in,' she whispered.

'Step along into the light where we can see you,' I called. 'Don't let me see any iron in your hands.'

'If you're fixing to plug me, I'll just go on my way and leave you be. I ain't looking for no trouble.'

Jesse called, 'You're welcome to come in and set.'

'Thank you kindly, miss.'

With that, Barney Dire led his horse into the glow of the firelight. He held his reins in one hand. He held the other hand up, open to show it was empty. That one was short two fingers, the ring finger and pinkie.

'I seen your light,' he said. 'Hope you don't mind me joining you.'

'Long as you behave,' Jesse told him.

'I most generally do,' he said. 'I ain't the violent sort, Lord knows – though I run up against it now and again, much as I hate such doings.' He tied his reins to a tall cactus over near General, then sauntered closer.

Though he had a voice that made him sound like quite a large fellow, he was so pint-sized that he appeared half-lost inside his duds. Everything he wore looked too big for him. The brim of his hat was as wide as his shoulders. The bandanna hanging around his neck looked the size of a table-cloth. His vest hung down so low it draped the butt of his sixgun. His chaps flapped about his legs like a couple of sails.

Even his thick, dark mustache looked like it belonged on the face of a man twice his size.

He was all creaking leather and jingling spurs as he stepped to the other side of the fire and sat down.

With a sigh, he said, 'Much obliged. Name's Dire. Barney Dire.' He touched the brim of his hat.

'I'm Trevor,' I said. 'This is Jesse.'

'Pleased to make your acquaintance, folks.'

He had a rather calm, friendly manner about him. His eyes, shiny in the firelight, had a bit of humor or mischief that put me in mind of Jesse. Though it seemed smart to remain cautious, I went on ahead and holstered my Colt.

'I'm afraid we haven't any food to offer you,' I said. 'We just now finished eating all we had.'

'Less you've got a hankering for some mule jerky,' Jesse told him.

Barney laughed and shook his head. 'Nope, reckon I'll pass on the offer. Much obliged, anyhow. Just figured to set awhile and jaw with you folks. My old horse, Joey, ain't much for conversation.'

'It can get lonely, traveling alone,' I said.

'Well, there's worse things than lonely. I'd a sight rather run on my own than get saddled with a sourpuss. Or with a gal, if you'll beg my pardon, Miss Jesse.'

I gave Jesse a glance, and saw she was smiling. 'What's your problem with gals?' she asked.

'Why, they're generally a sorry lot. All the time bossing and whining. Not as I'm saying *you're* any such nuisance.' He tipped a wink at me.

'Jesse's quite all right, actually,' I said.

She laughed.

'First thing you know, they're after you to settle down. Don't want you having no fun, seems as how they look at things. Why, they raise a fit if you have yourself a drink or a chaw, and they treat your friends ornery. If they could, I reckon they'd lock you up and never let you out, 'cept when it suited them, and that'd only just be to work chores.'

'I say,' said I, 'you do have a rather low opinion of them.'

'Been married to two of the critters. They was both fine gals till we got us hitched. First thing you know, they up and changed on me. Seems like they was both of 'em cut out to be penitentiary guards.'

Jesse laughed.

'Not as I'm saying *you're* any such,' Barney told her.

'Thanks kindly.'

'You gonna hitch up with Trevor here?' he asked.

'Why, I don't reckon he's likely to ask, now that you've filled his ear with such manure.'

That got Barney to chuckling softly. 'Well, you're both mighty young yet. Not more than children by much. There ain't no call to rush into such a tricky game as marriage. How'd you two throw in together, if you don't mind me asking?'

'Jesse had a go at stealing my horse.'

She blurted, 'Tell the whole world, why don't you!'

'Well, you didn't get it, did you?'

'Only just because I took it easy on you.'

'I got the drop on you!'

'I kept my knife to myself.'

'Settle down, folks,' Barney said. 'Lord alive, I didn't aim to start up a war between you. We don't want no bloodshed here.'

'He started it,' Jesse said.

'I did not.'

'Did too.'

'This is what comes,' Barney broke in, 'of poking my nose into matters that don't concern me. I'm right sorry I asked. Somebody oughta cut it off for me so's I'll stop sticking it where it don't belong. Already missing enough parts, though.' He held up his hand to show us which parts he meant. 'Got 'em shot clean off in Phoenix back in eighty-four. Minding my own business, too. Just having myself a beer when a couple of hotheads down the other end of the bar took to throwing lead and a stray slug found me. Took off both my fingers clean as a whistle.'

'I had it figured,' Jesse said, 'that one of your wives took a knife to you.'

'Ain't how it happened. Not that you're far off the track, though. My first wife, she took after me with a knife every time I came home with a snootful. Got me some scars to show for it, but she never got off a piece of me. Not for lack of trying. I'm small, but quick.' He held what was left of his hand close to the fire and studied it. 'Nope, it wasn't Aggie carried off my fingers. Just a dang bullet.'

'Does it cause you much trouble, being without them?' I asked.

'Oh, I get by. They don't amount to much. Knew a feller got his thumb shot off. Caused him a *sight* of bother, as he was in the midst of gunplay when it happened. Couldn't cock his sixgun, what with his thumb on the ground. He went to drag back the hammer with his teeth, but never got to finish. The same rascal that shot his thumb off plugged him full of holes while he still had the hammer in his chops.' Barney wiggled his own thumb. 'You're better off losing just about any old part than your thumb. I'd a sight rather lose a couple fingers. Comes right down to it, a feller can get by minus an ear or an eye better than a thumb.'

'I bit off a feller's ear, once,' Jesse said.

I looked at her, surprised.

'Well, I did.'

'You never told me.'

'There's a heap I've never told you.' Leaning forward, elbows on knees, she grinned across at Barney. 'It was a sidewinder name of Hank Dappy.' That name sounded vaguely familiar. I judged it might be one of those she'd reeled off the time she was telling me about all the rascals who'd had a go at her. 'He jumped me – fixing to have some high times on account of me being a girl, you know. Well, I bit his ear clean off. You should've just seen him, how he cried and carried on. Well, he chased after me. Went raving as how he'd take his ear back and stick it up my you-know-what.'

I didn't know what, exactly, but didn't speak out.

'I allowed as how that was likely to pain me some, so I didn't aim to let him get his ear back. He was just about to catch me, so I turned around and plonked that stinky old ear of his into my mouth and ate it whole.'

'Jesse!' I blurted.

'Well, I did.'

Barney gazed across the fire at her. He looked purely astonished. 'Ain't you the spitfire!' he said. 'My Lord!'

'And did you swallow it?' I asked.

'Why, sure. Dappy, he was so flummoxed he stopped dead in his tracks. Reckon he figured I was a crazy woman, so he took to his heels and that was the last I ever seen of his mangy hide.'

Barney, grinning under his mammoth mustache, shook a finger in my direction. 'You'd best watch yourself with this one, young feller. She'll be having pieces of you.'

Not to be outdone, I spoke up and said, 'I once cut off a bloke's nose, myself.'

'Why, you pair of rascals are *meant* for each other. Did you gobble it up?'

I shook my head.

'She's got you beat, then. Won by a nose.'

We all spent some time laughing over that. Barney rocked back and forth some, holding his knees. After we'd settled down, he said, 'Now how came you to cut off the nose of this feller?'

'He was trying to kill me, actually. And I him. I was rather hoping to give him a fatal wound, you see, but his nose intercepted my knife.'

'Took it clean off, did you?'

'Indeed. It fell to the street.'

'Should've eaten it,' Jesse said, and gave my ribs a knock with her elbow.

'I was rather too busy trying to save my skin.'

'I once saw me an Apache squaw that'd lost her nose,' Barney said. 'Sure didn't help her looks none. Which is why they done it to her. Any time as you see yourself a squaw that's had her nose sliced off, you know she got herself caught fooling with a feller that weren't her husband. Lets everybody see what brand of woman she is. It's plain as the nose off her face.' Barney chuckled softly and shook his head.

'It seems a trifle extreme,' I said.

'That's Apaches for you. They're the downright extremest sons a bitches that ever walked the dirt. And they ain't particular who they butcher. I've seen such things as give me the night sweats.'

'Sure glad we ain't gotta worry about 'em,' Jesse said.

'Who ever told you that?' Barney asked.

'Why, they're all either killed off or cooped up on reservations.'

'I understand that Geronimo and his band are prisoners in Florida,' I put in.

'That don't mean there ain't renegades skulking about. One's been raiding these parts fairly regular. They figure it's Apache Sam, a Chiricahua that run off from the San Carlos reservation a while back. He's killed a heap of white folks, past couple of months. Creeps up on 'em in the night, murders whatever feller might be about and carries off the

375

women. Does such manner of butchery on the women as would curl your hair.'

When I heard that, my heart commenced to pound like thunder. 'Are they quite sure it's an Apache?' I asked.

'Ain't no white man with the stomach for such doings.'

'He's been seen, though?'

'Not by any folks as lived to tell the tale. They found his hideout, though. Got himself a cave no more than a day's ride from here. Heard all about it from a feller this morning. Seems a week ago, maybe longer, a prospector tumbled onto the cave. Had himself a stroll inside, and what he found was dead women. Eight or ten of 'em, all carved to pieces and moldering. Some was fresher than others, and one appeared as how she'd only got killed just the day before. That prospector, he figured it had to be the work of Apache Sam. So he made tracks to Tucson. They got up a posse, and he showed 'em back to that-there cave. The feller I met, he'd been with the posse. Went in that cave with the rest, and what he saw near unhinged his mind. He couldn't take no more, and lit out. When I seen him, he was still a mite green.'

'And it was just this morning that you spoke with him?' I asked.

'A shade before noon, I reckon.'

'And when did he leave the posse behind?'

'Oh, not long after sunup. The way he told it, the posse got to the cave after dark last night. Didn't go in, though. Figured to keep an eye on it and wait till morning. See, they had no idea if the redskin was in there. Hoped he might show up so they could take a crack at him, and save themselves the bother of searching for him in the cave. Well, he didn't do them the favor. So they went sneaking in at first light. The feller I met, he took one look at them gals and vamoosed. He allowed as how they was the worst sight that ever met his eyes, and the stink would've choked a maggot.'

'And did they find the Indian?' I asked.

'If he was there, he was keeping outa sight. What I hear, though, it's a ripsnorter of a cave. The kind of place where a body might lose himself forever, pretty near. Now I just don't know if they aim to have a try at hunting him out.'

'Do you suppose the posse's still there?'

'Wouldn't surprise me none. I was them, I wouldn't go

and waste my time. They won't never find him if he's in there. Injuns are that way, you know. Slippery boogers. If he's got a mind to, he could likely pick 'em off one at a time, they go hunting him in a cave. Best thing'd be to hide around outside and see if he don't put in an appearance, sooner or later. That's how I'd work it. But then, I ain't the reckless sort. You put a bunch of fellers together like in a posse, they can get mighty brave. Start to figuring it's the other guy'll catch what-for, not their own selves. Sides, don't none of them wanta look yeller front of their pals. So they'll do the dangdest things. I reckon they'll hunt all over that cave till they either run short of supplies or get themselves whittled down to nothing.'

'You say the cave's only one day's ride from here?'

It wasn't me who asked that. It was Jesse.

I looked at her. She looked me back, and one of her eyebrows gave a little upward jump.

'A mite close for comfort, huh?' Barney said.

'Sure is,' she told him. 'Whereabouts is it, so we'll know to keep clear?'

'Up on the north slope of Dogtooth Mountain. That's what the feller told me. Where you folks heading off to?'

'Tucson,' I said.

'Well, I'll give you a steer so you stay clear of Dogtooth, then. Up yonder about a mile, you'll hit a fork in the trail. Either way you go at the fork, you'll get to Tucson by and by. You wanta take the branch that veers off to your right, though. Stick to that one, and you'll miss Dogtooth by more'n ten miles. Take the other – that's the one I rode in on – and it'll lead you through a pass at the very foot of that-there mountain.'

'So we go right at the fork,' Jesse said, nodding.

'That'd be the safe way. Not as you can count on a few miles of distance to keep you safe from that Apache. Ain't no saying where he might be. That cave's only just a place he's been at from time to time. And fairly recent. You ask me, though, he don't live there. Don't live nowhere particular. Just stays on the move. He could be a hundred miles off, right now. Or he might be near enough to hear us talk.'

'I sure hope not,' Jesse said.

'Well, I reckon he'd best watch himself, he's creeping up

on us. You'd likely bite his ear off.' Barney laughed.

'I've had my fill of ears,' Jesse told him, and he laughed harder.

After that, we stayed by the fire and talked about this and that for a spell. There was no more talk, though, of such matters as Apache Sam or the posse or cave. By and by, Barney asked if we'd mind him keeping us company till morning. 'Safer all around,' he said.

'You're welcome to stay,' Jesse told him. 'Long as you behave.'

I had no objections, either. He seemed a fine, trustworthy chap. Besides, my mind was too troubled by what we'd heard about Apache Sam to be bothered by Barney's presence.

He spread his bedroll on the other side of the fire. Jesse and I stretched out beside each other. What with him right there, neither of us was eager to snuggle up in our usual manner.

'You ain't got yourselves no blankets?' he asked.

'We lost them in a flood some time ago,' I explained.

'Well, you're welcome to make use of my saddle blanket if you can stand the aroma.'

So he fetched it. We thanked him and spread it over us.

Still, we didn't snuggle up. Not for a while. When we heard Barney snoring, though, we rolled toward each other and hugged.

'You reckon it's him?' Jesse whispered.

'Who?'

'Who you *think*? Whittle. You reckon he's Apache Sam?'

'It shouldn't surprise me at all, actually.'

'Same here. You wanta be in on it, don't you?'

'If he's there, I reckon the posse'll get him.'

'Not if they're looking for a redskin. We gotta go on up to Dogtooth and set 'em right. If we don't and he gets clear, it'll be our own faults.'

'I suppose that's so,' I whispered. Then I yawned and shut my eyes. 'We'll see about it in the morning,' I murmured.

CHAPTER FORTY-NINE

Off to Dogtooth

Much as I wanted to join up with the posse and be in on the kill (if Whittle was holed up in the cave), I sure didn't want Jesse to be anywhere near that place.

She would wind up carved and dead, I was just sure of it.

Yet no amount of talking was likely to persuade her against heading for Dogtooth Mountain, come daybreak.

While I laid there beside her under Barney's blanket, feigning sleep and working my head over the matter, I hit upon a plan.

What I'd do is keep still for a while. Wait for Jesse to be fast asleep. Then I'd sneak away, walk General off a distance, mount up and race off. Jesse wouldn't catch on till morning that I'd lit out. By then, I'd already be at the mountain or pretty near it.

A dirty trick to run off on her that way, but it'd keep her out of Whittle's range.

What might she do, however, once she figured out that I'd dodged off without her? She'd be spitting mad, of course. But would she take off after me on foot? Or would she talk Barney into giving her a ride? They might both come after me. I'd have a great headstart on them, but they might show up at the cave too soon, anyhow. Of course, Barney might want no part of pursuing me. If that happened, would Jesse have a go at stealing his horse? Just no telling what she might do.

It crossed my mind that I could take Barney's horse, Joey, along with me. Or just chase it off. That'd be too lowdown, though, and likely to start a whole new passel of troubles.

I would leave Barney's horse right where it was.

I no sooner settled that in my head than I took to worrying about Barney himself. How did I know that he could be trusted? With me gone, he might decide to have himself a

379

good time with Jesse. She would likely kill or maim him if he tried such a thing, but what if he took her by surprise? She was tough, but not invincible. The German had proven that.

Well, I finally came to the conclusion that leaving Jesse behind wouldn't be a clever move.

We'll just steer clear of Dogtooth Mountain tomorrow, I decided. No matter how Jesse argues, I'll stand firm. That posse can have its go at Whittle without us.

Might not be Whittle anyhow.

Now that I'd decided the proper way to handle the matter, my mind eased off and let me relax. By and by, I fell asleep.

I woke at sunup and Jesse was gone.

At first, I figured she'd wandered off to scare up some firewood or maybe answer a call of nature.

Sitting up, I had a look at Barney. He was still busy snoring. A horse gave a snort, and I swung my eyes over to where we'd left Joey and General tied to some cactus.

Joey was still there.

Alone.

Well, I jumped to my feet, all of a sudden scared. Looking about, I saw my Remington propped against the rock where it belonged. The Henry rifle wasn't there. And one of the water tubes had gone missing too. I scanned off into the distance, all around, but didn't spot Jesse or General.

I called out anyhow.

My yell startled Barney awake. He bolted up, gun in hand. 'What the tar!'

'Jesse lit out for the cave! Blast her!'

He scrunched his leathery face, looking as puzzled as if I'd spoken in a foreign tongue.

'She took my horse and snuck off in the night.'

'What's that you said about the cave?'

'It's where she's going! Bloody . . . !'

'Why in the notion'd she wanta go *there*?'

'Because she figured I'd keep her away from it.'

Still scowling, Barney used the muzzle of his Colt to scratch himself above the ear. 'What's she want at the cave?'

'It's just her way of making sure I wouldn't go there without her. Or not go there at all.'

'You gone and left me behind, Trevor.'

'I need to borrow your horse.'

'No you don't.' He spoke calmly. He eased the muzzle

away from his head and pointed it in my direction.

'I'll pay you for him. I've got quite a good deal of money.'

'Ain't got much use for your money. But I got a heapa use for Joey.'

'It's your fault, you know. All your talk of Apache Sam. Why, you even told her where to go!'

Barney still looked mighty perplexed. But he looked wary, too, and kept his revolver ready in case I should have a go at him or Joey. 'You trying to say she's rode off to join the hunt for that danged Apache?'

'Exactly!'

'What is she, touched?'

'We've got to stop her.'

Barney shook his head. Then he stood up, jammed the huge hat down atop his head, and holstered his sixgun. 'This is what comes,' he said, 'of taking up with women. If it ain't one brand of trouble, it's another.'

I rode along behind Barney and his bedroll, sitting astride his saddle bags and other gear. I carried my own saddle bags across my thighs. The Winchester was slung across my back by a rope. Barney kept his horse at a trot that bounced me about considerable.

'I sure am obliged to you,' I said after a spell.

'Don't go and thank me till I've gotten you to Jesse.'

'I'll be most happy to pay you for your troubles.'

'No call to part with your money.'

'I'd like to do *something* for you.'

'Well, now. I'm a feller that enjoys a good story. Suppose you tell me why she's so all-fired eager to go chasing after Apache Sam?'

'It's not Apache Sam she's after. When you told us last night about the bodies being found in the cave, we both realized the culprit was likely not this Apache at all, but Jack the Ripper. I came out west intending to hunt him down and kill him. He's the bloke whose nose I cut off.'

'Aim to finish the job, huh?'

'No woman's safe, so long as he's above ground. He murdered at least five in London. The last was a sorry wench named Mary. I was there in her digs, hiding beneath her bed, the night he butchered her.'

'Now how came you to be hiding under some gal's bed?'

'It was the fault of Rolfe Barnes, actually. Mother teaches

violin, you see. She'd been off giving a lesson to One-Legged Liz . . .' And so it began.

As we were likely to be on the trail all day and Barney appeared to relish the story, I didn't hurry it along. I recounted in great detail the whole course of my misadventures. I ran with the truth about all that had happened in London and aboard the *True D. Light*. It wasn't till Sarah Forrest entered the tale that I took to fudging some. The omissions there forced me to bend the truth in regard to Briggs. Then I felt disinclined to tell about running with the outlaw gang, as that would've shown me for a horse thief and a murderer.

Instead of meeting up with the gang after I was pitched off the train, I told Barney that I'd walked to the nearest town, found myself a job there washing dishes in a restaurant, and worked at that till I was able to buy a horse and supplies and set off for Tombstone.

By and by, I got back to the truth. I told him about Jesse ambushing me, and how we'd thrown in together. I told him about the flood. About the German capturing Jesse, and how we'd shot him. About the uses we made of the mule. And finally I got us to where we'd decided against going into Tombstone, after all.

'Jesse feared that Sarah might be there. You know women.'

'That's the plain truth.'

'As for me, I figured that I'd rather give up on my notion to chase after Whittle than to put Jesse at risk. I'd seen what he did to Mary and Trudy. Just couldn't allow that to happen to Jesse. Anyway, we allowed as how we might find him in Tombstone – or at least get ourselves an idea as to where we might start looking. But I didn't want Jesse to have a hand in it, and she was mighty determined to stick with me, no matter what. So I judged the best course was to stay clear of Tombstone and forget Whittle. It was a great relief, actually. But then you came into camp last night with your story about Apache Sam.'

'Makes me right sorry I opened my yap.'

'If you hadn't come along,' I said, 'we likely would've run into Whittle one way or another, anyhow. It's rather as if it was all meant to be that way.'

'One thing's sure. That Jesse of yours, *she* means you to finish the job. That girl's a caution.'

'She's got more sand than sense,' I said.

'Oh, I reckon she knows what she's doing.'

'What took y'all so long?' Jesse called from her perch on a boulder at the foot of Dogtooth Mountain.

It was late afternoon. I'd been walking, the past few hours, so as to give Joey a rest.

'Blast you, Jesse!' I shouted.

She smiled down at us. 'No call to get riled there, Trevor. Howdy, Barney.'

'Howdy yourself, Miss Jesse.'

'Hope you folks didn't wear yourselves out.' With that, she stood up and turned her back to us. She dropped out of sight for a spell, then came walking around from behind the boulder with General in tow. In spite of the cheery words she'd thrown at us from up above, she had a rather sheepish look about her. To Barney, she said, 'Mighty kind of you to show Trevor the way.'

'Saved his feet some, I reckon.' He smiled at me. 'You can thank me, now. Gotcha to her.'

'I'm very grateful. Thank you ever so much.'

'Well, I heard me a good story outa the deal. You two take care, now.' He touched the brim of his hat.

'You're not leaving?' I asked.

'Yep. Done what I aimed to do. Got no room in my plans to hunt after Apache Sam or Whittle or none of their ilk. I always figured it's a sight more healthy to shy away from trouble than to go looking for it. So it's *adios*, kids. Try and keep alive.'

He wheeled Joey around and trotted off.

'Thank you again!' I called after him.

He gave his hat a wave in the air. Then the trail curved around behind some rocks and he was out of sight.

I turned to face Jesse.

'Now don't you look at me that way,' she said. 'I only just did what I had to. Surprised you didn't think of it first and take off on *me* last night.'

'I thought of it,' I admitted. 'But I had more sense than to *do* it. That was mighty lowdown and ornery.'

'Well, it worked. You're here and so am I. How'd you get Barney to come along?'

'He was quite willing to help, soon as I explained what you'd done. He said you must be touched.'

'I just didn't aim to get left out, that's all.'

'I wasn't aiming to leave you out.'

'Was, too. I know you, Trevor Bentley. Ain't no way you would've struck out after Whittle without you got rid of me first.' She jammed her hands onto her hips and shoved her face at me. 'Am I wrong or am I right? You tell me, now.'

'I wouldn't have dodged off and left you alone.'

'Don't go saying I left you alone. You was with Barney.'

'I wouldn't have left you with Barney, either. I wouldn't have left you, at all. We're "pardners", remember? Partners stick together.'

She let her hands drop away from her hips. Her head lowered. Voice soft, she said, 'Well, I knew you'd come along.'

'I didn't want you anywhere near this place.'

'I know that.'

'It's only 'cause I care so much about you.'

'I know.'

Reaching down, I took hold of her hands and gave them a squeeze. She raised her head. Her eyes looked awfully solemn.

'I don't want Whittle getting you,' I said.

'Well, that goes both ways. I don't want him getting you, either, but you need to face him down. If you back out and call it quits, you won't never feel right about yourself. I don't want that for you. And I don't wanta be the cause of it. You turned away from Tombstone on account of me.'

'That had to do more with Sarah than . . .'

'It had mostly to do with Whittle, and you know it. You figured you'd rather give up on him than take a risk of me getting hurt. Well, I went along with it yesterday. But that was selfish. That was me wanting to keep you from Sarah, even if it meant you had to call it quits on your hunt for Whittle. It was wrong. For the both of us. I'm just almighty glad Barney came along so we'd get a chance to do the right thing.'

'What if it *is* Apache Sam up there?' I asked, tipping my head toward the mountain looming above us.

'Then we'll help the posse kill Apache Sam. After he's taken care of, we'll start after Whittle. We'll go back to Tombstone, if that's what it takes. But we'll pick up his trail, one way or another, and follow it till we've run him down. You and me. Together.'

'I don't know,' I murmured.

'What's not to know?'

'I don't want you getting killed, Jesse. I shouldn't be able to stand it.'

She gave my hands a squeeze. A corner of her mouth turned up, and a glimmer of her usual mischief came back into her eyes. 'I ain't easily killed,' she said. 'Nor are you, either. We'll be fine and dandy.'

'I do hope so.'

'You worry too much, Trevor Bentley.'

'McSween once told me that very thing. He's dead.'

Jesse leaned forward a bit and kissed my mouth. 'Come on,' she said. 'We've got us a cave to find.'

CHAPTER FIFTY

Troubles in Monster Valley

I tossed the saddle bags across General's back. I filled my hat with water from the mule-gut bag, and let him drink some. We strung both rifles together and draped them over his back so we wouldn't need to lug them ourselves. Then we led him along the trail.

By and by, we came upon a trail going up the mountain. It was steep, and hitched its way back and forth up the rocky slope. I'd had some experiences with such switching trails, and didn't look forward to it.

'Must be the way up,' Jesse said.

'Are you sure you want to do this?'

She didn't say a thing, but threw me a smirk. Then she commenced to slog her way up the trail.

I followed, leading General by the reins.

Soon, Jesse stopped and pointed down at a pile of manure. 'The posse came this way, all right,' she said.

'Was it headed up or down?' I asked.

'It's a heap of dung, Trev, not a Western Union telegram.'

'Then what makes you say it was dropped by the posse?'

'It was dropped by a horse. Posses ride horses, don't they?'

'So do Bible salesmen, don't they?'

'You watch yourself or I'll sling it at you.'

As we continued to plug our way up the trail, we came upon several more collections of manure. Obviously, they hadn't all been left behind by the same horse. So I judged that Jesse was right: the posse had come this way. More than likely, anyhow.

I sure hoped that the horses had made their deposits on the way down. I hoped that the posse had finished its business at the cave and departed. Taking the bodies of the women with them. Taking Whittle's body, too. Or Apache Sam's, if he was the culprit. I hoped that we would find nothing above us but an empty cave.

According to books I'd read, caves were supposed to be cool and pleasant, even where the weather outside is boiling hot. I hoped the books were right.

Even though the sun was low, it hadn't lost much of its heat. The sweat fairly poured off me. Jesse's shirt was wet and clinging to her back. We both huffed considerable, but we didn't stop. A cave sounded like just the trick for cooling us off.

Well, the trail went up and up, and so did we.

Every now and again, we stopped to rest and drink. We drank from the whiskey bottle in General's saddle bag. When it went empty on us, we filled it with more water from the tube of mule gut that was roped to his back. The tube was quite full. Jesse explained that she had filled it up that morning at a stream.

We rested often, but not for long. We had to add more water to the whiskey bottle twice.

At last, the trail took us over a summit of sorts. We ran into a good stiff wind that felt mighty good. Halting, we studied the area ahead.

We weren't at the top of the mountain. In front of us, the ground dropped off into a sunless, shallow valley, all rocky and bare, not a tree or bush growing anywhere. The valley was all aclutter with boulders and columns and high heaps of rock, chock full of narrow passes. An army might've been hiding down there out of sight.

Nobody *was* in sight. Not a man, not a horse.

There was no sign of a trail, either.

Beyond the gloom of the valley, the upper region of the mountain stretched itself into the sunlight. It didn't have just one peak, but seven or eight. A couple of them stuck up taller than the others, so they rather looked like fangs. I could see why the mountain had gotten itself called Dogtooth.

'Where's that cave at?' Jesse asked.

'Somewhere across there, I should think.' I nodded at the valley.

'Sure is a nasty piece of land,' she said.

'The valley of the shadow of death.'

'Don't go getting odd, Trevor.'

'Looks like a place where monsters might lurk.'

Jesse gave me a jab with her elbow. 'Quit that. Ain't no monsters down there. You're giving me the fantods.'

'Sorry,' I said, and took the bottle out of the saddle bag. We each drank some water.

As I tucked the bottle away, Jesse pulled out the revolver that she'd taken off the German. She thumbed open its port and turned the cylinder until it showed an empty chamber.

We'd both been keeping only five rounds in our guns, leaving a chamber bare under the hammer to avoid mishaps. While I watched, Jesse dug a cartridge out of her pocket. Her hand trembled some as she plugged it into the cylinder.

I added a sixth round to each of my Colts, then holstered them again.

Jesse kept hers in hand. She started down the slope toward that awful valley.

'Perhaps I ought to take the lead,' I suggested.

'Don't see as it matters,' she said. 'We're as likely to get jumped from behind as the front.'

Or from above, I thought.

I let Jesse stay ahead of me as we made our way down. I judged as how that was for the best, actually. If I took the front, I'd have General between me and Jesse. I wanted no obstacle in the middle to block my field of fire. If it should come to that.

We left the wind behind. And the sunlight. Even before we reached the floor of the valley, my back felt all aprickle. The nape of my neck crawled.

'I must say I don't care for this.'

'How'd Whittle ever find himself such a place?' Jesse asked.

'If it's only Apache Sam, shall we leave?'

She glanced over her shoulder and cast a smile at me. It was as nervous a smile as I'd ever seen on her.

All too soon, we found ourselves at the bottom of the valley. I stayed close to Jesse's back as we made our slow way in among the rocks. They walled us in. They loomed over us. They stood in front of us, blocking our path so we had to go around them.

Except for our footsteps and General clomping along behind me, all I could hear was the wind gusting about. Sometimes, it made a whishy noise like a rushing stream. Other times, it seemed to moan. The sounds of it surrounded us. But stayed high and far away. The wind never came down to where we were. There, the air was still and hot.

It seemed a bit unnatural, actually.

As I followed Jesse through the labyrinth, I couldn't help but think about Whittle bringing his victims through such a strange, forbidding place.

And no birds sing.

He'd likely kept them alive till he got them to the cave. It plain sickened me to imagine the terror they must've felt.

In front of me, Jesse froze.

'What?' I whispered.

'Shhh.' She pointed her gun at the ground a yard ahead of her.

I heard the snake before I saw it. A soft chh-chh-chh. Silence. Another chh-chh-chh. I spotted it. A rattler. So near the same speckled, dirty gray color as the rocks that it was the next thing to invisible. But there it was, as long as my arm, twisting its way across our path.

General must've noticed it then. He gave out a startled snort and backed up. I gave the reins a tug. He stopped, and groaned in a manner that near sounded human.

Jesse thumbed back her hammer. The cocking sound was so loud it seemed almost to echo.

'Don't shoot,' I whispered.

She held fire. A moment later, the snake vanished beneath a lip of rock.

We both kept our eyes on where it had gone, and hurried past it.

I said to Jesse's back. 'Let's not shoot unless we're attacked.'

'I don't aim to get snakebit to spare your ears.'

'It's not my own ears that concern me. I don't like the notion of announcing our whereabouts.'

'Then you best hope we don't meet up with no more rattlers.'

I watched for more as we continued along. And I couldn't help but listen, too. Now that I knew the sound they made, I heard it here and there – off to one side or the other, behind us, in front of us, sometimes even above. It played on my nerves, particularly the notion of a snake dropping down on us from the rocks as we walked by.

It got to be almost more than I could stand. I switched the reins to my left hand and filled my right with iron. Much as I was loath to unsettle the dead quiet with gunfire, the good

389

solid feel of the Colt was comforting. Jesse heard me cock it. She looked over her shoulder at me and smiled.

'Don't shoot unless you're attacked,' she said.

'They're *everywhere*,' I whispered.

'Pretty near.'

Everywhere, but out of sight. I heard them, but couldn't see them. That made it all seem worse, somehow.

Next thing you know, our way forward got blocked by a great boulder. The way to the left was shut off tight. Our only course was to make a turn to the right and pass through a gash in the rocks. It looked like a rough-walled corridor, twice our height and not much wider than our shoulders. It appeared to stretch on for about thirty feet before it opened up.

Jesse turned away from it and studied General. 'I reckon he'll fit,' she said.

'I doubt the posse came this way.'

'There's likely a passel of better routes through this dang mess, but nobody gave us a map. Do you want to turn around and go back the way we came?'

I recalled all those rattlesnakes we'd left behind, and didn't care to give them a second go at us. So I answered Jesse with a shake of my head.

'Look sharp, now,' she said. Raising her gun barrel as if she expected to be leapt on from above – by snake or by madman or by Lord knows what brand of creature – Jesse entered the narrow gap.

I went in after her, leading General and watching him over my shoulder. He seemed mighty reluctant to put himself into such tight quarters. He snorted and tossed his head. 'Easy boy,' I said. 'Easy.' He came on, but didn't appear at all happy about the matter.

The passage was wide enough for General, but not by much. Our tube of water, draped across his back, rubbed against a wall and tore. Water went splashing out of it.

'Damnation,' I muttered.

'What?' Jesse asked.

'There goes our water.'

She looked around at us and grimaced. The water was still pouring from the ruptured gut. But I had no way to get past General and stop the gusher, short of climbing over his head.

All me and Jesse could do was stand there. Pretty soon, the side of the tube that still held water dragged its way down between General and the rocks. It fell with a plop. I ducked and peered under General's legs. I could've crawled beneath him and fetched out the tube, but there wasn't any advantage to that. It was empty and flat.

'At least we've got some in the whiskey bottle,' Jesse said.

'It won't last long.'

'There'll be water at the cave.'

'Will there be?'

'I don't reckon the posse come here without a pretty good supply.'

I judged she was right about that.

'We'd better keep moving,' she said. Turning away, she continued through the gap.

'Come along, fellow,' I urged General, and gave a pull at the reins. He groaned at me. Sounded quite like a dog, as one might sound if you threatened to steal its bone. But he came along.

I kept my eyes on him, trusting Jesse to warn me of any trouble from the front. Our rifles still hung from General's sides by a rope across his back. And my saddle bags were up there. They seemed to be clear of the nearby walls, however, and in no great danger.

We were about halfway through the gash when General went daft. His eyes bugged out, his ears twitched forward, he squealed and reared. My arm near got wrenched off before I lost hold of the reins. I leaped forward to stay away from his kicking hooves. One knocked my hat off. I stumbled and fell. On his hind legs, General tried to twist himself around. For a while, he was stuck, his belly shoved against one rock wall while his rump was jammed into the other. He thrashed about awful. His front hooves clamored and threw off sparks. He screamed fierce. The rifles and saddle bags skidded down his back. As I got to my feet, hoping to help him somehow, he managed to tear himself loose. He fell, forelegs giving out, muzzle smacking the rocky ground. But he picked himself up right quick and scampered for freedom.

I gave chase, shouting. But General was in no mood to listen. He dashed out the way we'd come, and kept on running. Before you know it, he vanished around a bend. I quit racing after him. While I tried to catch my wind, the noise of his hoofbeats faded out.

'Bloody nag,' I muttered. I felt just about ready to cry. I kept it in, though, and headed on back into the gash.

391

At least General hadn't run off with our saddle bags and rifles. Jesse, crouching, opened one of the saddle bags. She pulled out our water bottle. It was half-empty, but unbroken.

'He's gone,' I said.

'Must've been the snakes,' she said. 'I figured he'd kill himself sure.' She returned the bottle to the saddle bag, and draped the leather pouches over one shoulder.

'We'd best go find him,' I said.

Jesse shook her head. 'Ain't much chance of catching him. Gonna be dark soon, and no telling where he's off to. He might not stop till he's off the mountain.'

'I shouldn't like to lose him altogether,' I said, my throat tight.

'I know.' She looked rather miserable, herself. 'He's a good old boy. We'll find him.' She squatted by the rifles and commenced to pick at a knot. 'What we'd best do right now, though, is try and hook up with that posse. We ain't got much water. We can go hunting for General come daylight.' She got the knot undone, slipped the rope off the stock of my Winchester, and lifted the rifle up to me.

I took it. She made a sling out of the rope and hung the Henry down her back. Then she stood up and drew her revolver.

'I wish we'd never come up here,' I said, picking up my hat. 'We've lost our horse and most of our water. We're surrounded by rattlesnakes. We're lost. Whittle's likely lurking nearby. Or Apache Sam. Things have gone all to smash.'

Jesse hoisted an eyebrow at me. 'You should've stayed home in London, I reckon.'

I saw her trap and dodged clear of it. 'Not at all. I'm quite glad we're together, you know. I only wish we were together elsewhere.'

'Well, Trev, you play the cards you're dealt. This ain't the best hand, but it's what we've got. Now, let's go and find us that posse.'

CHAPTER FIFTY-ONE

Ghastly Business

Night was near upon us when we came upon the posse. After losing General, we'd gone through the gash in the rocks, found ourselves in a clear area that gave us a view of the mountain peaks, headed that way, circled around some boulders and climbed a slope and squeezed through another tight gap.

We heard some rattlers along the way, but not many. Those we heard stayed out of sight.

As we came out the other side of the gap, we ran into the posse.

There were eight or nine men and about that many horses. They were spread about a clearing in front of the cave entrance.

Alive was one horse, tied to a stand of rocks off to one side.

Alive were also a fair number of buzzards, but they scattered when we showed up. Some perched themselves on rocks and others sailed around overhead, all of them likely hoping we'd leave so they could get back to their meals.

We stood motionless at the edge of the clearing.

'My God,' Jesse whispered.

Mostly, I felt numb. But part of me stayed alert, and I scanned the area to make sure whoever'd done the massacre wasn't in sight.

As one horse had been spared, I judged it likely belonged to the killer. So he was somewhere about. The horse, a pale palomino, was saddled. It glanced our way and took a few steps. When it moved, I heard its shoes on the rocky ground. So it was shod.

'Whittle,' I whispered. 'An Apache wouldn't have shoes on his horse.'

'Unless he stole it off a white man,' Jesse said.

I gazed at the carnage. The gloom of dusk wasn't dark enough to hide much of it.

'Whittle did this,' I said.

I knew for sure, and it had to do with a sight more than the shod horse. The killer had done more than slay the men and horses. He'd mucked about with them.

He'd dismembered a good many of them. The head of a horse had been placed between the legs of a naked man, its mouth on his private parts. All the men were naked. Some had been disemboweled, their entrails strewn about. (The buzzards had likely played a role in that.) Two fellows had been stacked up and arranged in such a way as to suggest they were busy at an unnatural act. The heads of four had been removed and set atop various rocks. The privates had been cut off some of the bodies. The severed arm of one chap had been thrust up the hindquarters of a dead horse.

The clothing and weapons of the dead men were nowhere to be seen. Except for four boots. Those were on the feet of a dead horse.

The atrocities were unspeakably savage, but showed a vile sense of humor.

Only Whittle, I judged, could've committed such acts.

Was he inside the cave? Was he skulking about, sneaking toward us?

'Let's take cover,' I whispered.

Backing off, we ducked behind a low boulder and leaned forward against it. Jesse slipped the saddle bags off her shoulder. She slung the Henry off her back.

We both cocked our rifles and rested them atop the rock, aiming toward the cave entrance.

'You were right about monsters,' Jesse whispered.

'The man's a fiend,' I said.

'But how'd he manage to kill them *all*?'

'He's quite clever, really,' I told her. 'And they were here looking for an Indian. He likely tricked them somehow.'

'Maybe he ain't alone.'

'I don't know.' I glanced behind us. Nothing back there except the maze of rocks. So I turned to Jesse and said, 'Whittle by himself is enough to worry about. There's only one horse, though.'

'If he don't know we're here, we can bushwhack him when he goes to ride off.'

I gave Jesse a nod. She bumped me gently with her shoulder.

Soon, night was upon us.

The dark was kind, actually, as it shrouded the scene of the massacre. We could still see the dim shapes out there, but not all the ghastly particulars. The buzzards were nowhere in sight. Whittle's horse was a light enough color so we could keep our eyes on it. The mouth of the cave looked like a patch of black in the gray wall of the mountain.

I couldn't figure any way for Whittle to get from the cave to his horse without us spotting him.

The trick was simply to wait him out.

Then shoot him down.

'Keep your eyes open,' Jesse whispered after a spell. She rested her rifle on the boulder, then crept backward. I glanced at her a couple of times to see what she was about. She pulled our bottle from the saddle bag and shook it. 'Thirsty?' she asked.

'We haven't much left.'

She popped the cork and took a few drinks. Holding the bottle out to me, she said, 'Water's no problem. Did you see all the canteens and water bags on them nags out there?'

'They might be empty,' I said, and took the bottle.

'They ain't empty, Trevor.' She sounded a bit annoyed. 'Landsakes, but you worry.'

'They may have quite a lot of water in them,' I admitted. 'But I shouldn't care to venture over and fetch any.'

'I will.'

'No, you won't.'

'You can keep me covered. Not as he's out there, anyhow.'

'We still *have* water,' I pointed out, and shook the bottle at her.

'Well, there ain't much. We oughta get more now, before the trouble starts.'

'What trouble? We'll simply ventilate him when he goes for his horse.'

'You never know. Anyhow, it's good and dark right now. Moon ain't even up, yet. This'd be the best time to go out there.'

'We needn't go out there at all.'

'You just stay here,' Jesse said. 'Make sure I don't get

395

jumped. Maybe I can find us some good food and smokes while I'm at it.'

'Jesse.'

She popped up. I reached, grabbed hold of her sleeve and tugged it hard. With a ripping sound, the sleeve tore off at her shoulder. It came sliding down empty, so I snatched her wrist and yanked her to the ground.

'You're *not* going out there!' I gasped.

'Look what you done to my shirt!'

'Stay here.'

She reached a hand toward me. I shoved the bottle into it, then leaped out of range. I rushed around to the front of the boulder, filled my right hand with a Colt, then halted and looked back. I waited till Jesse showed herself and hefted her Henry. She shook her head at me.

I turned away and walked into the massacre. Even though the moon wasn't up yet, there was enough starlight to see by. Not that I knew quite where to look. I wanted to keep my eyes on the cave, but feared what I might step on.

I walked toward the nearest horse. It had no head. Two of the posse men blocked my way – those that were sprawled one atop the other, feet at both ends, heads between each other's legs. I tried not to look at them, and gave them a wide berth. When I crouched over the horse, I found that it had fallen onto the canteen that hung from its saddle horn. But I pulled hard, and worked it free. I gave it a shake. Water sloshed about inside. There didn't sound like much, though.

Slinging that canteen over my shoulder, I set off for another horse. This was the horse wearing boots. Just behind it, one of the severed heads sat atop a stack of rocks. I couldn't see whether or not the eyes were open, but seemed to recall that *all* the heads had open eyes.

I glanced about at the other three heads. Every last one of them seemed to be staring at me.

I quit looking at them, and circled around to the far side of the horse. This one hadn't fallen onto its water bag. Crouching, I lifted the strap off the saddle horn. And heard a low grumble. Shivers raced up my back. I looked around quick. Another grumble. From the head just behind me. Well, it *couldn't* have made such a noise. It had no body attached, but simply rested atop a waist-high pile of rock.

As I gazed at the head, my skin all aprickle, it suddenly

rolled forward. It did an odd bit of a somersault, face first, the ragged stump of its neck swinging toward the sky. I let out a gasp and sprang up as it dropped off the edge. It clomped the ground. It rolled straight at me.

I was in such a state that I dang near shot it. But I held fire and danced out of the way. Just as the head was about to bump into the horse's saddle, a coyote dashed out from behind the rocks, snatched it up by the face and scampered off with it.

Well, I'd had enough, and raced for our hiding place. I dropped down behind the boulder, all breathless.

'Good job,' Jesse whispered.

'Bloody hell.'

She rubbed the back of my neck. After a while, she took the canteen and water bag from me and shook them. 'We're all set, now. All we gotta do is bide our time.'

She resumed her position, leaning forward against the boulder with her rifle at her shoulder. Once I was able to breathe right, I picked up my Winchester and joined her.

Nothing seemed to be moving, in among the dead. The coyote must've skedaddled.

Now that the sun had been down for a spell, the night was taking on a chill. There were likely a passel of bedrolls and blankets on the horses. I judged I'd rather freeze, though, than go out and fetch any such thing. So I kept still about them.

By and by, Jesse whispered, 'Maybe he ain't *in* that cave. He mighta rode off before we ever got here.'

'Why's the horse there, then?'

'Could be he just didn't kill it. No telling why.'

'It might not be his,' I admitted.

'What we oughta do is take a look in the cave.'

'Are you daft?'

'Beats waiting. If he's inside, that's where he's likely gonna stay. Least till morning. If he aimed to ride off tonight, he woulda done it by now.'

'No reason *we* can't wait till morning,' I said. 'Whenever he pops out's fine with me. In fact, it would be considerably easier to pick him off come daylight.'

'It'd be *easier* if he's asleep.'

'He might not *be* asleep,' I pointed out.

'Well, he might not be in there at all. But if he is, he ain't likely to stay awake all night. We oughta go and sneak in, see if we can't catch him snoozing. We can fill him with lead before he gets his eyes open.'

I gazed off at the cave's black opening. It was a narrow slot, not much wider than my shoulders, too low to walk through upright. We'd need to duck down and go in one at a time.

If we went in at all.

Spite of Jesse's logic, I wasn't at all eager to embark on such a venture.

'What do you say?' she asked.

'I say we wait him out. We go walking into that cave, we're likely to get ourselves killed. Whittle might have his eyes on us right now. He might just be hoping we'll try such a thing, so he can get his hands on us. And his knife.'

Jesse looked at me and shook her head. 'Well,' she finally said. 'All right.'

'I just don't see any call to rush into danger when we might simply wait here and shoot him from ambush.'

'Okay. If that's how we're gonna play it, though, we might as well get some shut-eye. You wanta go first? I'll keep watch.'

'And have you dodge off to the cave without me?'

Jesse's teeth showed, gray in the darkness. 'I don't aim to do that.'

'It's not at all funny.'

'I'm scared half witless, Trevor. I wanta get this done, and it won't be done till Whittle's dead. But I sure ain't so dim as to go after him by my lonesome. What do you take me for, an addlehead?'

I couldn't be sure whether or not she was having me on. But I saw no advantage to arguing. 'I'm not at all sleepy, anyhow,' I told her.

'You don't trust me, do you?'

'It's not that. How do you expect a person to sleep when . . .'

The words died halfway out as somebody heaved a scream.

CHAPTER FIFTY-TWO

Whittle's Lair

Jesse clutched my arm.

We gaped at each other through the darkness as the scream shivered through the night and died.

'My God,' Jesse murmured.

'It came from the cave, didn't it?' I asked.

'He's got a gal in there.'

'Where'd he get a *gal*?'

'Who knows? It don't matter.'

A cave was no place for a rifle, so I left it resting atop the boulder. I shoved myself away and got to my feet. Jesse did the same. 'Stay here,' I snapped at her. 'I mean it! You stay here!'

She pulled her sixgun. 'Let's go.'

'Jesse!'

'Go! That gal ain't gonna last forever.'

I took off running for the cave entrance, but Jesse was on my heels. So I made a sudden stop. As she bumped me from behind, I brought my arm forward, all set to drive my elbow into her. That was bound to let her wind out, and I figured to follow up my elbow with a blow to the face and put her out of action.

Couldn't do it, though.

Much as I wanted to stop Jesse from following me into the cave, the notion of causing hurt to her made me hold off.

She gave me a shove. 'Hurry!'

So I dashed toward the cave, Jesse at my back. And wondered if I was doing her any favor by *not* bashing her senseless. Then I judged that leaving her alone out here might be worse than letting her stick with me. This way, at least she'd be where I could watch over and protect her.

We reached the mouth of the cave. I went in first and

hunkered down. Much as I wanted Jesse to be shut of this business, it was mighty good to hear her breathing hard behind me.

I expected to see nothing. But away off in the distance was a fluttery glow such as might come from a small fire out of sight beyond a bend.

Only dark between us and that glow.

Needing the use of both hands, I holstered my Colt. When I commenced to make my way forward, Jesse grabbed hold of my shirt collar. I crouched low to spare my head, and walked slow and careful, keeping my arms stretched out in front of me.

I hadn't taken more than five steps when another scream came. It tore through the darkness. It seemed to make the air tremble as it passed over me. A scream of horrid pain.

'What's he *doing* to her?' Jesse whispered.

Well, my mind filled in plenty of pictures. 'God only knows,' I whispered. I judged he was likely skinning her alive.

But she's not dead yet, I told myself. We might be in time to save her.

It was slow going, though. Every few steps, the cave tricked me. It either put a barrier up to send me stumbling, or dropped its floor out from under me. Sometimes, Jesse's grip on my collar stopped me from falling. Other times, we both went down in a jumble. I banged myself up again and again, but neither of us let out a peep, and we kept moving.

The cool air of the cave now held a faint odor of corruption. I recalled what Barney Dire had told us about the stink, and judged we must be getting near to Whittle's collection of dead women. With each step I took, the odor grew worse.

The shimmery orange glow of light wasn't more than maybe twenty feet away when a third scream came along. Though it made my teeth ache, I was glad to hear it.

Hang on, lady!

The source of the light was still out of sight around a twist in the cave, but I could now see well enough to watch my step. I drew both my Colts. Jesse let go of my collar.

'Careful now,' she whispered.

'Keep behind me,' I warned, then stepped around the bend.

What greeted my eyes wasn't what I'd expected. I was ready to see the grisly array of bodies – and they were there, scattered about the large chamber, dismembered and spoiling, some propped up against the walls, some stacked together in unspeakable arrangements of carnal acts, some simply sprawled on the floor. They were all lighted up by a passel of torches standing here and there among the rocks.

Whittle hadn't cut off their heads, but he'd lifted their hair. Likely to make it look like the work of an Indian. Their scalps hung like banners from staves all about the chamber. Other staves held different trophies. Some had hearts stuck on top of them. Some had breasts. Some had parts I couldn't recognize.

But what I'd expected to see wasn't there – Whittle busy at work torturing a live woman.

Whittle wasn't in sight. Nor was any woman who wasn't already quite dead.

Had he somehow detected our approach and spirited her off? Perhaps the screams hadn't come from this chamber at all, but from the depths of the cave beyond it.

I stepped forward, entering the chamber, forgetting about Jesse until she came to my side. I looked her way as she groaned. Her wide eyes were taking in the scene of horrors. Her mouth was shut tight, lips pressed together in a hard line.

'I wish you'd stayed out,' I whispered. 'You shouldn't be seeing such things.'

'Where is he?'

'I don't know. Perhaps through there.' With one of my guns, I pointed out a dark cavity at the far end of the chamber.

We started toward it. To get there, we had no choice but to walk through the midst of the bodies, the staves with their hideous prizes, the torches.

We came upon a great heap of clothing. While I had noticed it before, I'd been too stunned and confused by the rest of the scene to give it much mind.

As we approached it, however, the notion struck me that Whittle might be buried within the pile. Hiding there, waiting for the proper moment to spring out and have at us. I halted and gave a nod to Jesse.

We trained three revolvers on the mound of garments. Then I commenced to scatter it, booting things this way and that. Near the top were men's duds – no doubt those taken from the posse. Mixed in among the shirts and vests and boots and trousers and longjohns were gunbelts, sixguns, rifles and knives. They all flew about as I kicked. Soon, the pile shrank down to dresses and petticoats and such.

'I don't reckon he's in there,' Jesse whispered.

She was likely right, but I waded in anyhow, stomping and kicking.

'By Jove, that *is* you!'

The merry voice, so familiar though I hadn't heard it for months, resounded through the chamber.

'Trevor Wellington Bentley! Is it possible? And in the company of a lovely young damsel! How utterly thoughtful of you to bring me such a gift!'

Whirling about, I tried to spot him.

Jesse did the same.

'Put down your weapons,' he called, sounding quite pleased with himself. 'I should hate to shoot either of you and ruin the sport.' A gun blasted, its explosion crashing through my ears.

The bullet struck neither of us. I didn't see what it hit, for my eyes were drawn to the muzzle flash.

'There!' Jesse gasped.

'Yes, here,' said Whittle. 'Now drop your firearms.'

He was forty paces away, his back to the rock wall, his front all but concealed behind the corpse of a woman. One arm was wrapped across its bare belly, hugging the body against him. I'd spotted this one before. The crown of its head was black and pulpy. The lips were cut away so its bared teeth seemed to grin most hideously. Nothing but holes remained where the eyes belonged. Both breasts were off. The torso was split open from throat to pelvis. I'd glimpsed this maimed horror before and averted my eyes fast, never suspecting that it might be shielding Whittle.

While one arm clamped it across the belly, the other jutted out straight from above the shoulder, pointing a revolver our way. Whittle's face showed beyond his gun arm. I couldn't see much of it, though.

'What've you done with her?' I asked.

'With whom do you mean?'

'The one who screamed.'

'Ah, *her*. Rushed to her rescue, did you?' With that, he let out a shriek. It sounded for all the world like a woman crying out in the throes of hellish agony.

'Quit it!' I yelled.

The scream trailed off into laughter.

'You knew we were out there?' Jesse asked.

'Oh, quite. Of course, I had no *idea* that one of the inter-lopers was my old mate, Trevor. And what would your name be, my dear?'

'None of your nevermind.'

Whittle chuckled. 'I'll get it out of you later. For the present, it will suffice for you both to drop your firearms.'

Jesse glanced at me, then turned her gaze toward Whittle.

'Shall I count to three?' he asked.

Jesse yelled, 'Three!' and let fly.

I followed her example.

Side by side, we blasted away. I used both Colts at once. Our sixguns roared, and Whittle's spat back. I reckon his aim wasn't up to snuff, for neither of us went down. Ours were nearer the mark. He would've been a dead man for sure if the woman hadn't caught most of our slugs. They smacked into her chest and shoulders. They punched holes through her arms. They gouged her sides. But they couldn't get past her and find Whittle.

Jesse's gun went silent. I gave her a glance. She was commencing to reload.

Whittle fired again, and the bullet zipped past my ear.

I turned all my attention back to him, determined to kill him before my Colts ran dry.

All that actually showed was a bit of his face, so I raised my aim and went for that. It ducked out of sight just as I fired. My bullet slammed through the gal's upper teeth. The next pounded her brow and knocked her head back. The one after that ripped out the side of her neck and Whittle cried out. I thumbed back my hammers and squeezed my triggers. Instead of blasts, there came only quiet clacks.

Whittle shoved the body away from him. As it pitched forward, we faced each other for just a moment. Through the drifting shrouds of gunsmoke, I saw that my last shot had gouged his cheek. Other than that, he seemed unharmed. He wore a black satin nosepatch.

He didn't raise his gun at me, so I judged it was out of ammo. He only had the one. An empty holster hung at his hip. His chest was crossed by twin black belts, each holding a sheathed knife. They looked to be mighty big knives.

Knowing Whittle, the knives came as no surprise. But the shiny star pinned to the front of his frilly white shirt surprised me considerable.

A badge!

I saw all this in just the blink of an eye, and then Whittle was dodging off to the side.

I whirled toward Jesse, shouted, 'Get him!' and then realized she was still busy thumbing rounds into her Colt.

When I spotted Whittle again, he was racing hellbent for the end of the chamber.

But not the end that would take him deeper into the cave.

The end that led out.

I holstered, dropped to my knees and scurried about the scattered clothes and such until I wrapped my hands around a revolver. I cleared its leather and swung it round.

I got off a shot that kicked sparks off the cave's wall near Whittle's shoulder. Before I could fire again, he vanished into the darkness. I emptied the gun after him, anyhow, hoping I might catch him with a ricochet. He didn't cry out, though. I judged they'd likely missed him.

I threw down the borrowed revolver. 'Bloody hell!'

'Don't fret,' Jesse said, sounding mighty calm. She, too, was gazing toward the place where he'd disappeared. 'We'll get him.' She snapped the loading port shut on her Colt. 'You might wanta reload, your own self, before he comes back shooting.'

It was when I went to stand up that I noticed Jesse'd been hit. The left leg of her dungarees was all ashine with blood and clinging to her. The hole was high on her thigh. My insides went all cold and shaky at the sight.

'He *got* you!' I gasped.

'Well, I reckon I'll live. I'll tend to it. You go on ahead and load up.'

My hands shook so frightfully that I had a rather difficult time of it. Also, I kept an eye out for Whittle and watched Jesse while I worked at emptying out the used shells and plugging fresh rounds into my cylinders.

What Jesse did was to sit down among the dead folks' clothes and pull the knife from her boot. Using that, she cut the leg off her dungarees. It put me in mind of the time she'd cut off the German's trouser leg to wear on her head. She'd gashed him some, but she didn't gash herself. Her hand was just as steady as you please.

Seeing the hole in her thigh, I dropped a couple of cartridges.

She turned her leg. It had a second hole on the outer side of the thigh, about three inches from the one in front. Blood was running out of both.

'It ain't still in me,' she said.

'That's good, isn't it?' I asked, feeling awful trembly and weak.

'Well, I'd a sight rather have one hole than two.' Looking up at me, she smiled.

I found the cartridges that I'd dropped, stuffed them into the cylinder, checked both guns to be sure they were fully loaded, then slipped them into my holsters and stepped over Jesse's legs. I crouched down beside the shot one.

'Does it hurt awfully?'

'Well, it don't feel good.'

'Watch for Whittle, and I'll bandage you.'

Nodding, she gave her knife to me. Then she leaned back. Braced up on one elbow, she lifted her revolver and rested it on her belly. She turned her head to keep a lookout.

'We near had him,' she said.

'I took a piece out of his face.'

'Too bad that's all.'

I snagged up a calico dress with faded flowers on it. After some cutting and ripping, I had it in pieces. I folded one into a thick patch and pressed it gently against her wounds. It was large enough to cover both of them. I held it there for a bit.

She'd taken off the leg of her dungarees quite high up. Our positions were such that I couldn't help but view a region, overhung by fabric but plainly visible, that took out my breath. A flood of heat rushed through me.

I looked away quick and lifted my hand off the pad. It had a pair of red dots, but wasn't soaked.

'You don't seem to be bleeding terribly,' I muttered.

'Reckon he'll ride off and leave us?'

'I doubt it.'

'Hope you're right. I'd hate to see him get away.'

'I just hope *we* get away.'

With a long strip from the dress, I commenced to wrap the pad into place. Jesse eased her other leg aside so it wouldn't be in my way. That pretty much bared her center entirely. I tried not to look, but couldn't help myself. I did

405

manage not to touch her there, though my hands got mighty close while I worked at winding the cloth around her.

She must've known what I could see, but she didn't complain or try to cover herself.

I felt lowdown for looking. But not so lowdown as to quit it. We were trapped inside a cave and surrounded by women in the most awful states of dismemberment and rot, Whittle was likely fixing to kill us, and Jesse was gunshot. Yet there I knelt, sneaking peeks and feeling like I might just explode with the thrill and wonder of it all.

After giving the strip of dress several turns around her thigh, I tied it secure with another piece.

'All set,' I said, and found Jesse staring at me.

The torches gave off plenty of light for me to see she had the old gleam in her eyes. 'You'd best take your mind off my southern parts and put it on Whittle.'

I blushed so fierce my skin near caught fire.

I stammered something, trying for a denial.

Jesse sat up. 'No call to fret about it. Give me back my knife.'

I handed it to her. She leaned forward, hitched up the cuff of her remaining pantsleg, and slipped the blade into her boot.

'Perhaps you should carry it in the other boot,' I suggested.

'The other boot ain't got a sheath sewed inside.'

'Still, it would be easier to retrieve.'

'That leg's ruined enough without getting knifed.'

'Will you be able to walk?'

'Reckon we'll find out soon enough.'

I got to my feet and held out a hand to her. When she took it, I hoisted her upright. She gasped and cringed. But she didn't go down.

'You can let go of me,' she said.

I did so, and stepped back. After a quick check to be sure that Whittle wasn't lurking at the front of the chamber, I turned my eyes to Jesse. She took a couple of steps. Though she winced with each of them, she stayed up.

I stared at her. She was sure a sight. Standing there with a sixgun in her hand. Her hair all a mess but golden in the torchlight. Her left arm and leg both bare (except for the bandage around her thigh). Her skin moist and shiny. Her shirt tails hanging out. The one leg of her dungarees hitched up over the top of her boot with the handle of the knife sticking out.

'Whatcha staring at now?' she asked.

'You look glorious.'

She reached down and touched the bandage. 'Well, you got me into a dress. Reckon now I'm a regular Becky Thatcher.'

'Becky Thatcher?' I asked, surprised and pleased.

'Ain't you never read about her and Tom Sawyer? They ended up in a cave, same as us.'

'I know them well,' I said.

Jesse fingered the opening in her dungarees, apparently to check that she was properly covered. 'Whittle, he makes their Injun Joe look like a piker.'

'We're quite better armed than Tom and Becky.'

She nodded. 'Let's go and kill him.'

CHAPTER FIFTY-THREE

The Final Showdown

'Let's do some figuring first,' I said. 'He's bound to be waiting for us, you know.' I went to Jesse's side. She leaned against me, and I wrapped an arm across her back.

'That's a sight better,' she said. 'Now what've we got that needs figuring? Only just one way out. He likely *is* laying for us, but he ain't much of a shot.'

'He got you, didn't he?'

'We was pretty sizable targets, and he still missed four outa five.'

'He likely only hit *you* by accident, anyhow.'

'We was *both* shooting at him.'

'He wants you alive, Jesse. You know . . . so he can . . . muck about with you.' I hated to tell her that, what with the remains of Whittle's handiwork all around us. But she needed to know the way of things.

Instead of looking troubled by the revelation, she smirked. 'Well, if he only hit me with a stray meant for you, he's a worse shot than I reckoned. We oughta just charge on ahead and blast him down.'

'That's a terrible idea.'

'I'll go first.'

'Are you daft?'

'You said your own self that he don't wanta shoot me. Not sure as you're right about that, but . . .'

'Anyway, there's no telling where he might be. We won't be able to see anything at all in the dark part.'

'We could take us a torch.'

'And light ourselves up for him?'

'Well, you got a better idea? Maybe we oughta just stay here and wait for him to die of old age. Course, my blood might all leak out while we're at it.'

We both looked down at her leg. Thick as the bandage

was, some blood had already seeped through it.

I didn't know much about bullet wounds, but it seemed to me that Jesse ought to be lying down and keeping still. Give her blood a chance to quit running out. She wasn't about to do any such thing, though. Not while Whittle still needed killing.

'What we need,' I said, 'is a good trick.'

'One that'll get us through him?'

'Or lure him to *us*. Like the way McSween and I led that posse into the ambush, something along those lines.'

'He ain't likely to fall for any brand of tricks. He's a tricker, himself. Look how he got us in here with his screaming.'

That reminded me. 'Did you see that he was wearing a badge? Letting on to be a lawman?'

'Maybe he *is* a lawman.'

Whittle a lawman? Odd as the notion seemed, I judged it was possible. Perhaps he'd actually led the posse up here to hunt down Apache Sam. That would go a long way toward explaining how he'd managed to kill the whole bunch. It's easy to kill folks that trust you.

'Perhaps he is above being tricked,' I admitted.

'We oughta just go. We'll play the hand that's dealt.'

'This isn't a card game, Jesse.'

'Well, I'm gonna fold if we don't do something quick. And I ain't bluffing.'

'Whittle!' I shouted toward the black opening. 'Whittle!'

He didn't answer.

'Jesse's hit! You shot her in the leg.'

'Trying to trick him with the truth?' she whispered.

'You can have her!' I called. 'What'll you give me for her?'

Still, no answer came. But I figured he could hear me, figured I'd caught his interest. Not as he was likely to believe a word that came out of me.

'Give me your gun,' I told Jesse.

She looked at me odd, but handed it over.

'I've taken her gun!' I called out. 'I'm throwing it away.' I tossed it some distance. It struck the rock floor with a clatter, and skidded.

'Trevor!' she whispered, scowling.

'That was her sixgun, Whittle! She's unarmed, now. You can have her. For a hundred dollars. Whittle? Do you hear me?'

'It ain't gonna work,' she whispered.

'You've seen how beautiful she is! I only want a hundred dollars for her. She's worth a good deal more than that. Imagine the fine times you'll have with her.'

'Trevor!'

'Stripping her down to the skin. Having your first looks. Before you start cutting her.'

'Quit it.'

I suddenly lurched behind her. She staggered, but I caught her up and hugged her to me, my left arm across her chest. My right hand shoved a Colt in her ear.

'Damn it!' she blurted.

'Come and get her, Whittle! She won't be much good if I kill her. You'll want those honors for yourself, won't you? You'll want to carve her up slow, a little bit at a time. That's why your brought all *these* gals here, isn't it? So you could work on them at your leisure? So you could savor their torment? So you could enjoy the sight of them thrashing about, bleeding and sweating? So you could hear their screams?'

To Jesse, I whispered, 'Scream.'

'I don't know how.'

'*Do* it. *You're* my hand. You're all the cards I've got.'

'Just stop all this.'

'*Scream.*'

She did it. And a mighty fine scream it was. Whittle himself couldn't have done any better. Her shriek hurt my ears and made me cringe. Even after she stopped, it echoed on through the cave.

'Did you like it, Whittle?' I called. 'Did it heat you up? There's more where it came from. With all your talents for torture, you might have her screaming like that for hours. But you won't have the opportunity. Not unless you come out and pay me. Dead gals don't scream. Dead gals don't squirm and plead. You're about to miss out on the time of your life, 'cause I'll be putting a bullet through her head if you don't come out and buy her off me.'

'Such an amusing lad,' Whittle said from the darkness ahead.

At the sound of his voice, my heart gave a jump. I'd intended him to hear. I'd hoped he would answer. But it came as a shock when he actually spoke out. Maybe I'd hoped, deep down, that he'd considered himself lucky to

410

escape from us, fled the cave and hightailed aboard his horse.

'Are you ready to pay?' I asked. 'Or shall I put a bullet through her head?'

He laughed. 'Come now, Trevor. I know you far too well. You would sooner die yourself than shoot that sweet morsel.'

'She's little more than a stranger I met on the trail,' I told him. 'I've no use for her.'

'Do you take me for a fool? Shoot her? You, who attacked me for the sake of an East End slut? You, who froze through half a night aboard the yacht to prevent Trudy from hanging? You, who leaped into the sea to save her from drowning? Though it was quite apparent that you disliked her from the start? Please. This is so obviously a primitive ruse to lure me into the light.'

'Believe what you will,' I called, and thumbed back the hammer of my Colt. 'Show yourself, or I'll blow her head off.'

'Proceed,' he said.

'Take that outa my ear,' Jesse muttered. 'He ain't falling for it.'

'Listen to her,' Whittle said. Mimicking Jesse, he added, 'I ain't falling for it.'

I kept the gun to her ear. 'I'll count to three,' I told Whittle. 'It's your play.'

'Take care you don't shoot her by accident. Poor lad, you've already put several bullets into one darling tonight. She wasn't alive to notice, of course. But it *was* such a shame. She was quite fond of you, really.'

He made little sense. Still my stomach went cold.

'I rode into Tombstone recently to deliver a prisoner. I've become a Deputy U.S. Marshal, did you know that? Deputy John Carver. John Carver, Jack the Ripper. Clever, what? And fancy, *me* a lawman.' He laughed. 'A marvelous job, actually. It allows me splendid opportunities for travel. I've quite the knack for pursuing felons, you know. However, the job also gives me the liberty to pursue a fairer game.'

'What happened in Tombstone?'

I didn't ask that. I was too full of shock and dread for words. It was Jesse who put the question to him.

'Why, a sweet thing recognized my horse. Seems I'd stolen it from her grandfather's stable.'

Sarah!

'Quite the spirited wench, she was. She had a go at shooting

411

me down in the very streets of Tombstone. Naturally, I prevailed.'

'You killed her?' Jesse asked.

'Oh, not at the time. My bullet merely knocked her senseless. Fortunate, that, as it prevented her from speaking out against me.' He chuckled. 'I simply explained that she was wanted for harboring a fugitive bank robber, and bustled her out of town. Being an officer of the law does have its privileges, you know.'

As I heard all this, I took to trembling fitfully. Fearing an accidental discharge, I turned my gun away from Jesse's head.

'You can't imagine my surprise, Trevor, when she spoke of you. I was rather certain that you'd drowned in Gravesend Bay. You'd not only survived, but captured the fair creature's heart. It's there on a pike to your left, by the way.'

Though my mind reeled, I kept my eyes on the dark where Whittle lurked. One of Jesse's hands gently pressed my leg.

'Oh, she told me so much about you. She was just full of fascinating news. In fact, I've a bit of news for you. She confessed that she interfered rather heartlessly with your mail. She loved you dearly. Not wisely, as they say, but too well. It seems that she chose not to post several of the letters which you intended for your mother. And she intercepted those that your mother sent to you. In the end, she rather regretted that she'd done so. In the end, I daresay, she regretted quite a lot. Most particularly, that my bullet hadn't killed her outright on Toughnut Street.'

I struggled not to believe Whittle. But his words gave me no choice.

'She was quite the most entertaining of my ladies. Indeed, she also proved the most useful. Ironic, that. I do relish life's amusing little ironies. That she who died under my knife should save me from the bullets of the chap she loved most.'

That hideous thing – that scalped and mutilated carcass – was Sarah?

'You bloody fiend!' I yelled.

He laughed. A merry cackle that echoed through the chamber.

'You'll not get your knife on *this* one!' I yelled, and threw

412

Jesse to the floor of the cave. As she fell asprawl on the scattered clothing, I swept my revolver down at her and fired twice. With each shot, she flinched and cried out.

Whittle shouted, 'No!' through the roar of the blasts.

He rushed out of the dark, raising his sixgun.

'She's better dead than in your hands!'

'Damn you!' He took aim at my head.

I got off my shot first. It took him in the left shoulder, turning him so his bullet missed me clean. He was staggering sideways when my next struck his chest. It ripped the leather of a knife scabbard, and sang off the blade. But the blow knocked him off his feet. As he fell, I put a round into his stomach. He grunted. He landed on his bum.

I stepped over Jesse's motionless body, halted, and leveled my Colt at his face. At the satin patch covering the remains of his nose, actually. Then I thumbed back the hammer. 'This is for all of them,' I said.

He flung himself sideways as I fired. My slug splashed his right eye. His head was turned at the moment, though, so it didn't drill through to his brain but only took out a corner of his socket.

He hit the ground screaming. And firing.

Already, I was slapping leather with my left hand. I pulled my second Colt. Before I could bring it into play, my arm was struck. Felt like a club had pounded it just below my shoulder. The gun dropped from my hand. I ducked quick, trying to catch it with my right as bullets sizzled past me. And catch it I did.

As I swung it up, a bullet smacked my *right* shoulder.

I lurched backward, tripped over Jesse's legs, and fell. My head thumped the rock floor.

Next thing I know, Whittle was looming above me, pointing his revolver at my face. He looked frightful. His right eye was a runny gorge. Half his face was masked with blood. He'd lost his nosepatch, so I saw the pulpy scar tissue in the cavity between the nubs of his nostrils. He was sobbing. Blood and drool dribbled off his trembling chin. His left hand was clutched to the hole in his belly.

'See what you've done to me!' he whined.

'Less than you deserved,' I said.

'I'm not finished yet, you scurvy bastard.' He threw his gun away. Whimpering and moaning, he hunched down over me, grabbed the front of my shirt, and hoisted me up

413

till I was sitting. 'I'm not *finished*! Not quite *yet*! Watch! Watch the Ripper at work! He loves his games!'

Stumbling backward, he swept one of the huge knives from its sheath. He stood up straight. A belch came out of him and sent a gout of red flopping out his mouth.

With more energy than I gave him credit for, he jammed a boot under Jesse's hip and sent her rolling onto her back.

I looked this way and that, hoping to spy either of my revolvers – *any* revolver. None was in reach, so I tried to shove myself up to my feet as Whittle dropped across Jesse's hips.

Grunting, wheezing, blood flowing down his chin, he glared at me with his single eye. 'You've never . . . seen the . . . Ripper at play!'

'She's dead!' I yelled. 'Leave her be!'

He ran the blade beneath her shirt. With an upward jerk, he sent the buttons flying. He used the tip of his knife to fling each side of her shirt away, laying her bare to the waist.

I got my feet beneath me. I leaned forward, hoping to stand.

'Splendid set,' he gasped, spraying blood on her face. 'Which . . . which shall I . . . have off . . . first?'

'I'm right partial to them both,' Jesse said.

She grabbed his wrist, pinning the knife down flat between her breasts. Her other arm swung up and chopped the gleaming blade of her Bowie knife across the Ripper's throat.

CHAPTER FIFTY-FOUR

Wounds and Dressings

The blood just leaped out of Whittle, slopping onto Jesse while he sat atop her and made gaggy sounds. Then she jabbed his side to tumble him off.

I crawled toward her.

Whittle's knife still lay on her chest. She tossed it away, then blinked blood out of her eyes and looked at me.

I keeled over.

I woke up once while Jesse was tending to my wounds. My shirt was off. She had me propped up some, a pile of clothes under my back. My left arm was already wrapped tight. She was straddling me, her knife clamped between her teeth as she used both hands to rip apart somebody's shirt that she held up in front of her.

With a popping sound, the fabric split. She hadn't taken time yet to clean herself. Her face and chest gleamed with Whittle's blood.

I passed out again.

By and by, I came around. I was still sitting up against the piled clothes. Now, both my wounds were bandaged. The cave seemed darker than before. I judged that some of the torches had likely burnt themselves out.

Jesse was gone.

I called for her, but she didn't answer.

Worried, thinking that perhaps she had passed out, herself, I looked about as much as I could without trying to twist my body around. Whittle was sprawled nearby, dead as all the folks he'd murdered. I glanced at several of his victims. Had no choice in the matter, as I was hoping to find Jesse. While I did that, my eyes lit on Sarah.

She was facedown where he'd flung her.

The pain from my wounds was nothing next to the agony I felt, looking at her. My poor Sarah. A scalped and gutted carcass. Not only butchered by Whittle, but gunshot many times by me and Jesse. Ruined beyond recognizing long before we ever battered her with our slugs.

My beautiful Sarah, come to this.

She hadn't run off with Briggs, after all. She'd traveled on to Tombstone in hopes that I had survived my fall from the train and would come to her. She'd tried to take on Whittle by herself. And ended here – spending her final hours, or days, suffering the most unspeakable of tortures.

All on account of me.

She had loved me, and died for it.

It didn't matter a bit that she'd cut me off from Mother in regard to our letters. No doubt, she'd feared losing me. A small betrayal, really.

I'd betrayed her in a far more grievous manner when I gave my heart to Jesse.

At least Sarah had been spared the knowledge of that. She'd died believing that I loved her still.

I suddenly let out a sour laugh that sent pains flashing through my body.

Indeed! It must've been a great consolation to her, believing in my love while Whittle was at her with his knives. What a trifling thing, the affections of a boy. When one is in the lair of a madman. When the body is afire with torment and death is certain.

With every cut of the knife, she should've wished that I'd never roamed into her house, that I'd been cast out into the blizzard the night of my arrival, that she'd never taken me into her arms or into her bed – certainly that she hadn't ventured west with me to search for Whittle.

She should've died cursing my very existence.

All of them should have done so. All of those who crossed my path or Whittle's, and died because of it, ever since that bitter night in London so long ago when I led him to the *True D. Light*.

At least *he'll* kill no one else, I told myself.

We finished him. Jesse and I.

My eyes lit upon a revolver some distance beyond my feet. I wondered if I had the strength to fetch it. A single bullet through my head, and nobody else would ever die on my account.

The last time I'd considered such a move, I'd held off because Whittle still needed killing.

416

I hadn't any such excuse, now.

Do it, I thought. Do it now, before you drag Jesse into some brand of trouble and get her killed. You near got her killed already. She'll never be safe till she's shut of you for good.

I stared at the Colt, but didn't go for it.

Shooting myself seemed the proper thing to do, and I felt rather lowdown and selfish for wanting to stay alive. Folks were likely to die because of it, and Jesse might be one of them. The thing was, spite of everything, I found that I had a keen desire to keep breathing, no matter what may lie ahead.

There were bound to be rough patches and narrow calls. There were bound to be tragedies. Heartaches and such. But I judged all that was just part of the game. It was the game that counted. Playing the hand that's dealt, as Jesse would say. But dealing a few yourself, too. And savoring the surprises and joys that come along the way.

I judged I would likely have use for both my Colts in the days and years to come – if I survived my wounds. But I knew all the way to my core that I would never again be tempted to use one on myself. They were meant for protecting me and Jesse. They were meant for sending varmints on the downward road.

With such thoughts working through my mind, I forgot to worry about where Jesse'd gone off to. But by and by, along came a sound of bootfalls on the rocky floor. I looked toward the opening at the front of the chamber. A yellowish glow shimmered in the darkness.

Then Jesse limped her way into sight.

She held a torch in one hand. Her golden hair sparkled in its light. Her face gleamed. She was huffing considerable. Saddle bags hung over one shoulder and a canteen swung by her side.

She was all decked out in a yellow calico dress. It was buttoned to her throat, had a frilly lace collar, long sleeves, and a skirt that draped her to the ankles. The gunbelt strapped around her hips, sixgun jammed in at one side, looked quite out of place and strange.

When she saw me looking, she halted and stood up straight.

'Well,' she said, 'don't wear out your eyes.'

'Jesse Sue Longley.'

417

'That's me.'

'In a *dress*?'

She started moving again, limping closer and grimacing. 'My other duds was in tatters, anyhow. 'Sides, you been hankering to get me into such a getup.'

'You look . . . just bully!'

'It's a mighty confining garment. Makes me feel like a ninny, too. I only just put it on cause of you being shot. You ain't bound to see me in another such rig till the next time you catch lead.'

She stood the torch upright in a nook, then hobbled over to me and sat down. 'How you feeling?' she asked.

'Reckon I'll live. For a while, at least.'

'Gotcha something here to ease the suffering.' She slipped the saddle bags off her shoulder and pulled out a flask. As she popped its cork, she said, 'Found us some food and smokes, too, but nothing'll beat whiskey when you've got holes in you.'

She passed me the flask and I took a few swallows. As the whiskey went down, a pleasant heat seemed to spread through me.

'I'm right sorry about your Sarah,' she said.

My throat tightened so I couldn't drink any more. I gave the flask back to Jesse. She went shimmery as I watched her head tip back. I blinked, and a couple of tears ran down my face.

'At least Whittle'll never get you,' I said, my voice shaking.

She lowered the flask and looked at me. 'He'll get no one ever again, Trevor. You and me saw to that.' Reaching out with one hand, she brushed the tears off my cheeks. 'You drilled him good, pardner.'

'You didn't do at all badly yourself,' I told her. 'For a dead gal.'

A smile lifted one corner of her mouth. 'You hit me, you know.'

'I did not.'

'You sure did.' She handed the flask to me, then commenced to unfasten the buttons of her dress. When they were open down to her waist, she slipped the garment off her shoulders and pulled her arms from its sleeves. She scooted herself around to face me. Her chest was bound, just below her breasts, by a narrow strip of cloth. It held a small

418

patch of cloth to the side of her ribcage. She untied it, peeled away the pad, and pointed at a raw nick. The wound was at just about the same place on her as where the posse bullet had creased me, so long ago. It wasn't near as bad as mine, though. Not really more than a deep scratch. 'Told you so,' she said.

'I did that?'

'Your second shot.'

'I'm awfully sorry,' I said, pained to see that I'd hurt her.

'Well, I reckon you had to make it look good.'

'I never meant to *hit* you.'

She raised her arm high and craned her head down to look at the injury. 'It ain't much, is it?'

I forgot to answer. With her eyes turned away, it gave me a chance to study something other than her wound. She'd found the time to clean the blood off her skin. Her breasts looked as smooth as velvet except for their tips, which were dark and puckered and pointing at me.

I didn't look away fast enough. She caught me. 'Trevor Bentley.'

'They're only *you*,' I said, pleased with my quick thinking. 'No different, actually, from your shoulders or face.'

'Liar.'

But she didn't turn away or cover herself, so I had lots of time to appreciate the view while she placed the pad atop her little wound and tied it in place with the cloth strip. After finishing with the bandage, she struggled into the sleeves and pulled the dress up.

'We'd best leave pretty soon,' she said. 'We got us a good, bright moon for our trip down.'

'Is the horse still there?' I asked.

'Yep. I gave him some water. He's a mite skittish, what with the stink and the dang coyotes sneaking around, but he ain't run off yet. Let's rest a bit and put some chow into us before we head out there.'

We had a few more sips of whiskey, then ate hard rolls and beef jerky that we washed down with water. When she finished with the food, Jesse rolled cigarettes and we had us a smoke and more drinks.

The whole time, she never bothered to fasten the buttons of her dress. As it was rather chilly in the cave, I judged she'd left them undone to keep my spirits up. Mighty thoughtful of her. The strip of bare skin down her front helped take my mind off my wounds and other bad things. Every so often, when she leaned certain ways, I caught glimpses inside that warmed me up better than the whiskey.

'We'd best get moving now,' she finally said. She swung the saddle bags over one shoulder, hooked the canteen strap over the other, then struggled to her knees. 'You gonna be able to walk?'

'You're the one with a shot leg.'

'It'll hold out if you will.'

I found that neither arm worked as it should, and moving them sent awful pains through me. I couldn't use them to push myself up, so Jesse had to lend a hand. She stooped in front of me, clutched both my sides just under the armpits, and hoisted me up.

As I came off the floor, I went dizzy, staggered, and would've fallen except that she held me steady.

By and by, I was able to stay on my feet without her.

'I need my Colts,' I told her.

'Aim to do some shooting tonight?' she asked. But already, she was hobbling along to fetch them. There were several revolvers scattered about, but she knew which belonged to me. She grimaced both times she crouched to pick them up, and I felt badly about making her do it. Needed my guns, though, and couldn't get them myself.

She came back to me, her face all sweaty from the pain.

'Sure these are the two you want? All this weaponry, there's likely better to be found.'

'They suit me fine,' I said.

She tucked one down the front of her belt, then emptied the shells out of the other. Stepping in close, she put her arms around me. I felt the heat of her body, the push of her breasts, the tickle of her hair against my cheek as she worked with one hand to take fresh rounds from the loops at the back of my gunbelt. Then she stepped back and plugged them into the cylinder.

She dropped that Colt into my holster, pulled the other and sent its shells falling. Once again, she snuggled in while she removed ammo from my belt loops. She was still at it when I kissed the side of her face.

Figured that would fetch me a remark. I was wrong, though. Instead of making a smart quip, she went and kissed me full on the mouth, ever so gentle and sweet. She didn't quit very soon, either, but kept her mouth to mine for the longest time. Her breathing filled me. I let my eyes drift shut, and felt as if Jesse was melting into me.

When she eased away, I near fell over. She braced me up with a Colt and a fistful of ammunition.

'Steady, pardner,' she said.

Pretty soon, she let go of me and finished loading my weapon. She holstered it for me. 'Reckon you'll need a shirt. The ones we wore in ain't much good.'

She commenced to wade through the clothes and weapons and such, searching.

It struck me that one of the dresses scattered about on the chamber floor had likely belonged to Sarah. None looked familiar, though. I hoped that the dress Jesse wore wasn't Sarah's, but judged that it wasn't. Jesse was shorter and slimmer than Sarah, so the dress wouldn't have been such a good fit. Perhaps Sarah's was the dress that Jesse'd used for bandages, and parts of it were even now wrapped tight around the thigh of the woman who'd taken me from her.

'Here you go,' Jesse said, and I was mighty glad to have my mind turned away from the track it'd been following.

She held up a shirt that was dark with dried blood.

'Nope,' she said, and dropped it. 'Ripped too bad.'

Continuing with her search, she picked up quite a few more shirts, one at a time, groaning some with the pain and effort. They all looked quite bloody. A couple had rents in the back. None had any bullet holes at all. One didn't even have a tear in the fabric.

The shirts showed how Whittle must've murdered the posse. He'd killed the men with his knives. Likely dispatched them one at a time in the cave's darkness, and hauled them outside afterwards.

While I pondered over that, it came to me that few of the dresses or petticoats or other female garments were soiled with blood. Whittle must've stripped the gals naked before laying into them. That came as no great surprise, actually.

I could wear a dress and stay shut of strangers' blood if I didn't mind looking like a girl. But the notion didn't thrill me much.

'That'll be fine,' I said when Jesse picked up still another shirt.

'It's awful bloody.'

'They all are.'

She held it up toward the light of a torch. 'Well, least this one ain't torn.'

'He must've slit that poor bloke's throat.'

A corner of her mouth turned up. 'Same as I done him.'

She helped me into that shirt. While it was still open, she ran her hands all over my chest and belly and sides. The caresses felt just splendid. Too soon, she quit and pulled the shirt together and buttoned it all the way up.

'We'd best get moving,' she said.

She took a few steps backward, watching me as I had a go at walking. Then she fetched the torch that she'd used during her earlier venture outside. With the torch raised high, she led us to the front of the chamber.

There, I took a quick look back at the array or horrors. At the carved bodies. At the scalps and such on pikes. At Whittle, sprawled out dead. Finally, at what was left of Sarah. I hated to leave her in such a place. There was no way to take her with us, though.

One thing I've learned, the dead don't need help. They call for some grieving and often need vengeance, but not much else. It's those still alive who matter.

And so I turned away and followed Jesse toward the outside.

CHAPTER FIFTY-FIVE

The Downward Trail

The coyotes scampered off, silent and eerie, when we came out into the moonlight. Jesse tossed the torch aside. It fell near a headless body, casting light on the ghastly work done by Whittle and the other beasts.

We staggered on, and reached the tethered horse. Jesse patted his neck and spoke gently to him.

Was this Matthew Forrest's horse, Saber? Quite likely.

I recalled the morning, so quiet, so lovely with fallen snow, when Sarah and I had entered the stable and discovered that Saber had gone missing. And how we had plotted together to deceive her grandfather. It seemed so long ago. It seemed almost as though a different fellow, not myself at all, had been the one to conspire with her.

Yet this must be Saber. Here, standing before me.

Quite suddenly, the many miles and months between that morning near Coney Island and this night somewhere in the Arizona Territory shrank down to nothing. It *had* been me, not a different fellow at all. It might've been yesterday when Sarah and I gazed into the empty stable stall.

Everything felt like yesterday. Standing there among the carnage while Jesse swung the saddle bags onto Saber's back, I quite fell apart. I bawled like a child. For Sarah. For McSween. For all of those who'd crossed my path and died. Even for strangers butchered by Whittle, as every victim this side of the Atlantic had died on my account. Maybe I cried for some I'd killed my own self, though certainly not for him.

Jesse took me into her arms. 'It's all right,' she whispered. 'It's all right.'

'It's awful,' I blubbered. 'So many. So many dead.'

'I know.'

She held me for a long while. At last, her embrace and

caresses soothed me down. She brushed the tears from my cheeks. She kissed me. 'You ready to go?'

I nodded.

She led Saber through the savaged remains of man and horse. At the boulder where we'd set our ambush, she tied our rifles together. She slung them over Saber, just in front of the saddle, then looped the straps of two canteens and the water bag over the saddle horn.

Holding the reins with one hand, she climbed atop the boulder. She lifted her long skirt, bunching it up so high I glimpsed the bandage around her thigh, then stepped into a stirrup and swung her wounded leg over the saddle.

I climbed the boulder. As Jesse snuggled the horse in close, I heaved a leg over his back and rather leaped with my other. Risky work, having no use of my arms. But Jesse stopped me when I started to fall off the other side. Her arm struck where I was gunshot on the left, and I yelped. But at least she saved me from a nasty tumble. I squirmed about until Saber was square between my legs.

'You okay?' Jesse asked.

'I've been better, actually.'

'Same goes here. You ain't gonna fall off, now, are you?'

'Hope not.'

'You can't hold on at all?'

'Not with my arms.'

She started Saber walking. Instead of heading away, though, she turned him around. Steered him into the midst of the bodies. There, she dismounted. She limped over to a dead horse, fetched a coil of rope off its saddle, and came back. She made a loop at one end of the rope, swung it about a few times, and lassoed me. Stepping up close, she raised the loop beneath my arms, then slipped it tight around my chest.

At the boulder again, she hoisted her skirt and climbed aboard the saddle. She wrapped the rope around herself. When she finished, we were bound together, only enough slack between us so I wasn't quite mashed against her back.

'That oughta hold you,' she said.

'It'll be a spot awkward if we need to climb down.'

'I don't aim to take us nowhere the horse can't carry us,' Jesse said. 'We just gotta find where the posse came in.'

She set Saber to moving at a slow walk. By and by, we found a gap that was wide enough for us. In we went, leaving behind the cave, the ghastly clearing, Sarah and Whittle and all the other dead.

It was mighty good to be going away from such things.

I figured we were lucky to get out alive.

And lucky to have a horse. Not that the bouncing about felt good. It shook me up considerable, and never gave me a rest from the pain. But this sure beat walking. No telling how we might've faired afoot. Not well, likely. But if we rode on steady and didn't get ourselves lost in the maze, we ought to be down off the mountain before sunup. From the trail at the base of Dogtooth, we'd be less than two days from Tombstone. We'd likely get there sometime tomorrow night.

I judged we could both last that long. Then we'd find ourselves a doctor and get patched up proper, and have no more business but to rest and recover.

The trick was to stay aboard Saber.

On a level trail, that wouldn't have been much of a problem. But our course through the rocks was rough. We not only had to wind this way and that and sometimes back out of dead ends, but every so often Saber had to charge up a steep place.

The first time that happened, it took me and Jesse by surprise. I yelped and pitched backward. I tried to reach for her, but my dang arms wouldn't move fast enough. The rope jerked taut, pretty near tearing Jesse out of the saddle. She cried out with pain, but clutched the pommel in time to stop us both from smashing to the ground.

At the top of the grade, she reined in Saber. Then she hunched over. I put my face against her back, and felt how she was twitching.

'This won't do,' I told her.

She didn't answer.

'You'd best let me down. I'm fit enough to walk.'

She sniffed. 'You stay where you're at,' she said, her voice tight and shaky. 'We'll get by.'

'That must've hurt you terribly.'

'I ain't gonna have you walking.' Slowly, she unhunched herself and sat up straight. 'Next time, I'll give you a warning. Just lean up against me tight as you can.'

So that's how we played it. Enough moonlight made its way down through the narrow walls of rock for her to see ahead of us. Usually. And usually, she gasped out 'Lean!'

425

just before Saber lunged up a slope or leapt across a gully. We'd both duck forward and come through it fine. Sometimes, though, he surprised us.

No less than eight more times, on our way across that damn valley, Saber took unexpected jumps or clambered up night-shrouded slants in such a way that I was thrown backward against the rope. Each time, my fall was stopped by Jesse. It's a pure wonder that she was able to hold on, again and again, as the rope tugged so savagely at her chest. But hold on she did.

She rarely cried out, though the pain must've been terrible.

By the time we finally came out of the valley and halted before starting our descent down the mountain, my back was so abraded by the rope that it burned near as bad as my bullet holes. I felt blood sliding down beneath my shirt. Jesse's chest, I knew, could be in no better shape than my back.

I leaned forward against her. She was bent over the pommel, shuddering and sobbing.

'I'm so sorry,' I gasped, weeping myself for her torment and bravery.

I longed to wrap my arms around her.

And did so, though the pain almost drove me senseless.

My hands met warm, slick blood.

'Oh, Jesse,' I murmured.

She sat up a bit. Her trembling hands found mine and pressed them to her. She sniffled. After a while, she lifted my hands. She crossed them at the wrists, then eased them inside the open front of her dress and held them to her breasts. I pushed my face against the side of her neck. Later, I kissed her there.

We stayed that way for a long while, Saber shuffling beneath us but going nowhere. Off in the east, the horizon was going pale with the approach of daylight.

Jesse finally sat up straight and took a deep breath. 'Reckon your hands ain't useless, after all.'

I realized that I was caressing her with them. 'They're all right for this, anyhow,' I said.

'Lord, that was a hellish ride.'

'You were bully.'

426

'I sorta kept a lookout for General. Maybe we'll find him down below.'

'Maybe.' I couldn't bring myself to care a whole lot, one way or the other.

'Least we didn't run into no rattlers,' she said.

'Matters were dicey enough without them.'

'Well, we're likely past the worst of it. Downhill won't be a problem.'

'Before tomorrow morning, we ought to be in Tombstone.'

'Not if we sit up here all day.' She let go of my hands. They fell. I gasped and flinched. She caught them by the wrists. 'I'm sorry. Lord.'

I hissed through my teeth for a spell. Then said, 'Quite all right.'

Jesse gently lifted them, reached around, and eased them down on my lap.

'Ready?' she asked.

'Take it slow and easy.'

She clucked her tongue and Saber started down the steep, narrow trail. It was easy going. All we had to do was lean back some and keep our balance, and Saber took care of the rest.

As we descended the mountainside, the sun came up, spreading its rosy glow across the desert. A glorious thing to see. And wonderful to feel its warmth after the rather chilly night.

The morning was lovely, and ever so quiet and peaceful. There seemed to be no other sounds than Saber's hoofs thudding on the trail, some birds calling out, bugs buzzing and chittering. Every so often, I heard the quiet chh-chh, chh-chh-chh of rattlers. Though they unsettled me some, they sounded far off, and I didn't let them ruin how good I felt to be riding down that trail with Jesse in front of me, her hair all agleam in the sunlight.

Sore and stiff as I was, I did feel good. It was the fresh, new morning. It was being with Jesse. It was knowing that my hunt for Whittle was over.

Jack the Ripper would never harm another poor soul.

Jesse and I had the world before us, all splendid and bright. After Tombstone, after recovering, we would be free to go on about our lives together. Of course, I would ask for her hand in marriage. More than likely, she'd accept. Maybe she'd even stoop to wearing a gown for the wedding, and I wouldn't need to get shot again before seeing her in another dress.

We weren't a great distance from the foot of the mountain, and I was busy entertaining myself with thoughts of having Jesse for my wife, when Saber bellowed out a frightful scream and reared up. I flew back till the rope stopped me. Jesse cried out. Though jerked so roughly I feared her spine might snap, she stayed in the saddle. I hung from her as Saber scurried backward on his hind legs, staggered and stepped off the trail. Squealing, forelegs kicking at the sky, he dropped into space.

'No!' Jesse yelled.

She leaped sideways, hurling us both off Saber's back, no doubt hoping we might land on the trail.

But we fell short. The slope struck us. Down it we tumbled. It was frightfully steep. It flipped us this way and that, all the while drubbing us with its rocky wall. Tethered together, we crashed against each other as we rolled. My weight pounded Jesse against the mountain. The back of her head clubbed my brow and cheeks and nose. Over and over we went.

As we plummeted, I somehow hugged her to me and clung to her with what little strength I possessed in my feeble arms.

On we tumbled, skidding and rolling, battered by rocks, torn now and again by brambles as we crashed through them, only to be gouged and hammered by more rocks.

Then we went off a ledge.

I was on top of Jesse as we plunged straight down. I twisted myself about in hopes of turning us over so that I might be first to crash against whatever might wait for us below. But I failed. All too soon, we slammed the earth, Jesse's body saving me from the brunt of the impact. My face hit the back of her head. Darkness swallowed me.

When I regained my senses, I found myself sprawled on Jesse's back. I raised my throbbing head. A mat of her hair lifted with it, glued by blood to my face. It peeled away as I looked about.

We had come to rest at the foot of the mountain. Saber lay nearby, dead, a buzzard plunging its beak into his vitals.

Was Jesse also dead?

I spoke her name, my voice dry and rough. She didn't respond.

My arms were trapped beneath her, one hand flat against her belly, the other higher. With it, I felt the rope that bound us together. And her skin. Her skin was sticky with blood. I lay very still, all my thoughts on that hand, hoping to detect the throb of Jesse's heartbeat.

I felt nothing.

Perhaps my hand was too low, too far from her heart. Or perhaps it was so ruined by my many injuries as to be rendered incapable of finding so small a throb.

I tried to move my hand higher. All I gained for the effort was a burst of pain from my gunshot and battered shoulder.

'Jesse!' I gasped. 'Jesse, wake up! Please!'

She didn't answer. She didn't stir at all.

'You're not dead!' I blurted. 'You're not!'

At that, I quite lost my wits. I bucked and thrashed until my arms came out from under her, and kept at it. Finally, I managed to turn myself over. I lay there, gasping and whimpering, the sunlight blazing in my eyes, my back to Jesse's back.

I sat up, straining against the rope. Jesse came up with me. Lunging forward, I got to my knees. Then to my feet, quickly ducking low and bouncing till I jarred Jesse higher on my back.

I commenced to walk. Stagger, actually.

A few steps towards Saber. I needed a canteen. The buzzard flapped off. But I turned away. How could I fetch a canteen? How, with arms all but useless? How, with Jesse hung on my back?

So I stumbled past Saber, and found the trail.

The trail would lead us . . . where? Somewhere. Away. Where we could rest and get better.

On and on, I trudged.

Jesse's head wobbled against the side of my neck. Her arms hung behind mine, and all four swayed like the limbs of a lifeless beast. Her legs swayed, too. I couldn't see them, but often felt the heels of her boots bump against the backs of my legs.

I liked the feel of that.

The bump of her boots. As if she was alive and giving me playful kicks.

On and on, we made our way together down the trail.

Now and then, I fell to my knees. But I always made it back onto my feet again, and struggled onward.

Near sundown, we came upon a covered wagon stopped by the side of the trail.

I couldn't make it that far.

My face met the dust.

Sprawled out under Jesse, my mind half gone with weariness and agony and grief, I tried to call out for help.

When I opened my eyes, I was seated, propped up against a wagon wheel. Jesse was stretched out on the ground, just beyond my feet.

Her face was bloody, her dress a tattered ruin. It was primly spread over her legs and its front was buttoned shut, but her poor skin showed through a score of rents. Her hands were folded together atop her chest.

The wagon wheel shook against my back as someone jumped down out of the rear.

A big old man, white-bearded, his head crowned by a bowler hat with white feathers rising from both sides like jackrabbit ears. Fringe trembled all around his shirt and knee-high moccasins as he bustled toward Jesse, a bottle of red fluid in his right hand.

I knew him.

'Dr Jethro Lazarus, at your service. We meet again, Trevor my lad!'

Crouching by Jesse's head, he clamped his teeth around the bottle's cork, popped it, and spat it toward a nearby cactus.

'We'll have her fit as a fiddle!' he called, and winked at me.

'Is she . . . alive?'

'Dead as a doornail, sorry to say. But don't fret.' He hoisted the bottle toward me and gave it a shake. 'Glory Elixir. Good for what ails ya.'

'Howdy there,' Ely greeted me, coming into sight from somewhere near the wagon's front, all gawky and grinning. He flapped a hand in my direction.

He looked so . . . chipper.

Dead. Jesse was dead. *Dead as a doornail.*

Of course, I'd feared as much.

I stared at her. My 'pardner'. My love.

430

I'd known it would come to this, if she rode with me.

Lazarus pried open Jesse's mouth.

'All set to watch the miracle of the Glory Elixir?' he asked me.

All the Glory Elixir under heaven wouldn't be enough to bring Jesse back to me. And I hated the old fraud for playing out his game.

'Just leave her be,' I muttered.

'Leave her dead? When I, Dr Jethro Lazarus, am possessed of the mighty revivification powers of the Glory Elixir? Prepare yourself for the miracle of miracles!'

'Hallelujah!' Ely shouted, and clapped his hands.

Lazarus poured Glory Elixir toward Jesse's mouth. Some splashed off her bloody lips and chin, trickled down her cheeks. But not all of it. Plenty found its target.

And Jesse coughed.

EPILOGUE

Wherein I Wind Things Up

Jesse and I talked it over considerable, later on, and judged she'd likely never been dead at all. That's our opinion, and even Lazarus confessed he hadn't been sure, one way or the other, when he gave her that dose of his Glory Elixir.

Though a flim-flam artist down to the soles of his moccasins, Lazarus claimed to be an actual doctor. He had surgeon's tools to prove it, and did a fine job with them when he went into me for the bullets.

He and Ely spent most of the evening patching us up. Ely stank considerable, but we didn't complain.

Jesse was in awfully poor shape. Among her many injuries, she had a split on her forehead, and underneath it a lump the size of an egg. It had likely come from the last part of the fall, when she crashed to the ground face-down. She stayed out cold after choking on the Elixir, and didn't wake up till late the next day. Then she was too dizzy and weak to move under her own power.

Lazarus and Ely seemed in no great rush to press on. For a week, we all stayed put at their wagon by the trail. They took the casket out of the wagon, and we slept in there at night.

They tended to us like a pair of nervous mothers. They cleaned us, fed us, saw to all our other needs, and poured Glory Elixir into us every chance they got.

By the end of the week, Jesse and I were both on our feet. We were still banged up and hadn't a lick of strength between us, but we were eager to move on.

We moved on with Lazarus and Ely, riding in their wagon.

And got to Tombstone.

Jesse entered the town inside the casket. I didn't like the notion, but she'd insisted. She'd also insisted that she lay in that casket by herself, saying to Ely, 'You just keep that dang stinky varmint outa here, pal!'

After a crowd gathered, Lazarus and Ely dragged the casket out and set it onto the ground. Lazarus was in fine form, expounding on the miraculous healing powers of the Glory Elixir. Soon, he threw the lid off. Jesse, stretched out in the pine box, her face still cut and scabbed and bruised and swollen (with some fake blood added to improve her appearance), her dress soiled and torn, looked so ruined and dead that the sight of her made my heart sore.

Then Lazarus dumped some Elixir into her mouth.

She slurped it down, groaned, and came to life so spry it was purely astonishing. I was dumbfounded, watching her. She cried out 'Glory hallelujah!' as she sprang from the casket, then acted like a nitwit and hobbled out and hugged just about everyone. She hugged me, too. I was the only chap she kissed. She had a grand, merry sparkle in her eye.

Afterward, Lazarus allowed as how he'd never sold so much Glory Elixir at one show.

Well, Jesse had put Ely out of his job. He didn't seem to mind, though.

We joined up with that pair of flim-flam artists and traveled south with them.

Down in Bisbee, we got married. It was Lazarus's idea to make it part of the show. Jesse figured it was a bully notion. So she no sooner got herself revivified than her eyes lit on me and she limped over and threw her arms around me.

'Marry me!' she cried out.

'But we don't actually know each other,' I claimed.

'Don't matter! I been dead and now I'm alive, thanks be to the Glory Elixir! You're a handsome feller! I've gotta have you!'

The crowd went plumb wild, and likely would've carted me out of town on a rail if I'd denied her wish.

So I agreed to have her.

So they sent someone off to fetch a preacher.

Jesse climbed inside our wagon. A while later, out she came. The fake blood was gone from her face. And the nasty old tattered dress was gone, too. In its place, she wore a splendid white wedding gown that she'd bought after our Tombstone show. The crowd just oohed and ahhed like they'd never seen anything so glorious.

I'd never seen anything so glorious, myself. She was still banged up some, but looked ever so beautiful.

Pretty soon, along came the preacher.

And marry us he did.

The whole situation was a sight peculiar. But we had us a grand time, and Lazarus sold enough Elixir to keep the Bisbee folks fit as fiddles for at least a century.

We all of us partied and whooped it up till late into the night. Then Lazarus and Ely showed us to a hotel room, and left us there by ourselves.

We had a passel of aches and scars and the like, but didn't let them hold us back.

On the bed with Jesse, kissing her, feeling her skin against mine, and finally at last joining up with her – it was all so much finer than I'd ever imagined.

We spent the rest of the night in the room. And all the next day. And all the next night. Food and drink were brought to us. We slept part of the time. Mostly, we didn't.

But it came time to move on.

We found Lazarus and Ely in a saloon, surrounded by other folks who'd been present at the revivification and the wedding. Another party ensued.

Finally, around dusk, the four of us made our rather drunken way to the wagon, boarded it, and set off for parts unknown.

We figured to make the wedding a regular part of the show. But that's getting past the rightful end of our story. *Adios*, folks. Carry on.